STELLA
CAMERON

now you see him

MIRA

MIRA

ISBN 0-7783-2219-X

NOW YOU SEE HIM

Copyright © 2004 by Stella Cameron.

All rights reserved. Except for use in any review, the reproduction or
utilization of this work in whole or in part in any form by any electronic,
mechanical or other means, now known or hereafter invented, including
xerography, photocopying and recording, or in any information storage or
retrieval system, is forbidden without the written permission of the publisher,
MIRA Books, 225 Duncan Mill Road, Don Mills, Ontario, Canada M3B 3K9.

All characters in this book have no existence outside the imagination of the
author and have no relation whatsoever to anyone bearing the same name
or names. They are not even distantly inspired by any individual known or
unknown to the author, and all incidents are pure invention.

MIRA and the Star Colophon are trademarks used under license and registered
in Australia, New Zealand, Philippines, United States Patent and Trademark
Office and in other countries.

www.MIRABooks.com

Printed in U.S.A.

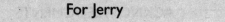

For Jerry

ACKNOWLEDGMENTS

Gerry and Julian Savoy, my Louisiana consultants, gave invaluable assistance during and after the writing of *Now You See Him*. I thank them for being my safety net.

There is a beat in this city, like the throbbing of arteries when the heart contracts.

New Orleans has its own pulse. I hear it now, getting faster. Steam vents through grills in the street. If they pumped blood from those grates the air would turn red, but the pressure would ease.

It's early, early enough the breeze through jasmine doesn't take the edge off last night's scent of booze, sweat and urine.

This waterproof bike suit makes me sweat and the helmet doesn't help anything.

Concentrate.

My timing must be as perfect as it was the first time. I've already seen her several times. The one. Rich, spoiled, dissatisfied and looking for more treasures to buy, to stuff in the bottomless cavity she thinks is her desire. Boredom is the name of that cavity, and fear. The boredom of a woman who has everything but purpose. She would never confess to fear but it's there, fear of being alone with herself. I loathe such women. One of them has ruined my life by using my talent and ignoring my existence.

Concentrate.

Antiques, Diamond and Gold Jewelry by Xavier Tilton.

Whooee, that is some name to fill up an awning over a shop door. Shops like this one cram Royal Street, but I picked out Xavier Tilton's place for the diamonds—and the long-legged woman who comes at the same time on the same morning each week. Tilton carries more diamonds than any other place I've checked. They shimmer and flash inside glass-fronted display cases lining the walls. No fingerprints on that glass; Xavier carries a half-mitt in his pocket and moves behind customers discreetly wiping away any evidence of their presence.

He's doing it now, sliding behind her, talking and wiping.

It's time. They're alone in there and the street is almost empty. Nothing but a few stinking, sleeping no-names covered with piles of rags. Once I'm in the shop I'll close the door to keep the sound down.

Wait, there's a delivery truck. If it stops here I'll have to change plans.

Come on, come on. Jeez, a friggin' turtle. Move. Good, it's parking over there, the driver's leaving the engine running. Any distraction is good.

Call Xavier to the courtyard behind the shop, to the deliveries gate. Now! Move your feet. Walk into the alley beside the shop and press the button beside the pretty iron gate.

"Xavier Tilton here."

"Mornin', Mr. Tilton. Gift delivery from Blossoms."

"Bring it into the shop."

Shit. "It's a fern of some sort. A tree. 'Bout seven foot."

"I'll meet you at the delivery gate. Give me a couple of minutes to get through the courtyard."

Do that, Xavier. Take your time getting to your gate. I'm the one who has to get inside the shop and keep moving until this is finished.

It's raining again. Quick, inside, close the door quietly. Smells of ammonia and stinkin' candles.

Bless you, Xavier, for the classy music. Nothing like a little opera early in the morning.

The seconds are ticking away now. How long before Tilton comes back?

The woman has heard me coming into the shop. "Mornin', ma'am." Don't I sound friendly?

"Good mornin' to you," she says. "He'll be right back." Pretty face. Smooth blond hair. Much younger than I thought. Too bad. She wants something in the case, can't look away from it for more than a second.

Her purse is small—no straps. Fate is smiling.

Take out the pick and palm it against my thigh. Cram the dark visor down.

Stay cool. Two steps…and strike. Ouch, it goes in easy enough until she falls and her weight hangs on the pick. Damn blood everywhere, running down the visor and blurring everything. Wipe it on your sleeve. She's doing it right. With a little guidance from me she falls forward and through the glass and she doesn't say a word, doesn't scream. That's because she's already dead—or close to it.

How many more seconds? If he catches me it's over.

I can see her in the mirrored back of the case, sliding down, breaking shelves, tipping all the pretty things. She's not pretty anymore.

Pull the pick out. NOW. Grab the purse and stuff inside the suit. Move my feet, back away, put the pick in its thigh pocket, open the door, close it behind me and walk away. Walk fast but not too fast—to the corner, turn, and there's the bike.

I'm away and heading for that coulee and the ruined shack. It wasn't the woman's fault, not really, she was in the wrong place at the wrong time—for her.

This suit doesn't keep the wind out, or am I cold? How can I be cold? Warm rain hits my neck and should turn this oil-skin stuff into a sauna. I'm going where I went before, out past the zoo.

Soon the scenery gets lonely, the undergrowth is burned, and rotting trees lean this way and that. The deeper I go, the more deserted it feels.

The coulee isn't deep enough but it'll have to do.

The rented bike goes into the barn. My own wheels never looked so good. Off with the suit and wrap the helmet and purse inside, and the gloves, the black tennis shoes, underwear, too. Now I stuff the lot into a double garbage sack but I can't load it until I wash.

The soap is still where I hid it. Colder, the water should be colder and chafe my skin red and clean. My feet cling to slimy gravel and tree roots. Why do I shiver when I'm not cold any-more? Soap coats me and I rub it in hard, dig my fingernails into the soft surface of the bar.

Not enough. I want to bleed, I want to hurt. A pebble, large and porous like pumice—yes, it will clean me. It tears into my upper arms, into the skin on my belly and buttocks, the backs of my thighs and my elbows. Long red stripes that pop bubbles of blood, then begin to seep in ragged rivulets quickly mixed to a bloody wash by the water. I want to lay the flesh on my face raw but everyone would see it.

Sometimes a sacrifice must be made—as an example. I didn't want to do it the first time or this time, but I had to, Sonja made sure of that. Sonja owes me.

God help me, one more to go.

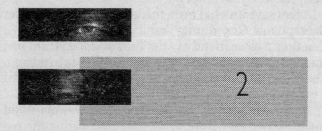

2

The Times *Online*
New Orleans
Tuesday, October 23

Yesterday morning an as yet unidentified woman died when she fell into a jewelry display case at a Royal Street antique shop.

Owner Xavier Tilton, alone with the woman at the time, received a call to go to the outside service entrance and left the woman in the shop. By the time he returned she appeared close to death and did, in fact, expire before the police and aid units reached the scene.

Although Mr. Tilton is sure the victim carried a purse, no purse was located at the Royal Street shop. Mr. Tilton reported that the deceased had been interested in an antique diamond ring in the case. After the incident, no merchandise appeared to be missing. The ring the victim was considering remained on her finger.

No official comment has yet been made, but information from a credible source revealed that the crime has been classified as murder.

A tentative link has been made to the bizarre murder of Stephanie Gray during Mardi Gras two years ago. At that time a close friend of Miss Gray said the victim had traveled to New Orleans to try out for a place in a band. The friend did not hear from Miss Gray after she boarded a bus in Bismarck, ND.

At the autopsy it was discovered the woman had most likely died before being trampled during the parade. A weapon later described as probably an ice pick had been stabbed beneath the base of her skull, then removed. No purse or other personal possessions were ever found. Our sources tell us yesterday's Royal Street victim also sustained a mortal wound to the brain, most likely inflicted with an ice pick, and used in part to drive her through a heavy glass door in the display cabinet.

Last Friday, Charles Penn, convicted murderer of Stephanie Gray, escaped while being transported between maximum security facilities. He remains at large.

"Think it's going to rain?" Father Cyrus Payne, pastor of St. Cécile's parish church in Toussaint, Louisiana, pounded along the path beside Bayou Teche with his friend Joe Gable at his heels.

"Nope." Joe Gable didn't say a lot when they took these early morning runs together.

Cyrus figured Joe only stayed behind him because he was too polite to leave the narrow track and pass. Cyrus turned his face up to the hazy sky and said, "It'll rain."

"What evidence do you have to back up that claim?" Joe sounded like the lawyer he was.

"Purely circumstantial stuff," Cyrus said. "It's almost eight and there's no sign of the sun."

"Pretty thin," Joe said. The church and rectory came into view and he made sure, politely, that he was the first on the faint path from the bayou to Cyrus's garden gate. "When the haze shifts the sun will be out."

"I *feel* rain coming."

Joe laughed. "Well, now, that changes everything. You've got me convinced."

Cyrus thumped his friend's shoulder. Once inside the white fence that surrounded the garden, they slowed and walked side by side on crunchy, sunburned grass. There wouldn't be much time to get cleaned up and have a think before mass at eight-thirty.

"Madge is here again," Joe said, pointing to Madge Pollard's car, parked beside Cyrus's red Impala station wagon in front of the house.

"Madge works here, she's here every day." He'd almost said she was always here.

"This early, Cyrus?"

"Not all the time." This line of questioning didn't come up often, but when it did Cyrus felt awkward, almost cornered. His own fault for being so dependent on Madge as his assistant—and his friend.

"She's a special woman," Joe commented. "And she's lovely."

"Yes, she is."

Joe slanted him a look and said, "I'll carry on back to the office and shower there. Wills, wills and more wills today, not that I'm complaining."

"Cyrus!"

They both stood still and looked across Bonanza Alley, the little street between the church and the rectory. There was Madge, just as if talking about her had conjured her up. She ran between graves in the churchyard, waving a piece of paper above her head. "Wait!" she cried, even though they hadn't moved since her first shout.

Alarmed, Cyrus hurried to meet her. Today she wore red, his favorite because it showed off her dark curly hair and even darker eyes—and it went with her bright spirit. "Mornin', Madge. You're awful early."

She didn't smile or greet him in return. "Where have you been? I looked for you everywhere."

Joe caught up with him and they said "jogging," in unison.

"I'm glad you're here," Madge told Joe. "You probably know Ellie Byron better than any of us."

Cyrus felt Joe stiffen. "What about Ellie?" he said.

"Maybe we should get out of the street," Madge said, although there wasn't a moving vehicle in sight. She looked hard at Cyrus and said, "There's coffee ready in the kitchen. Let's get some and you can both read this." She waggled the sheet of paper again and led the way around the house to the back kitchen door and inside.

"I don't need coffee, thanks," Joe said. He'd turned pale under his tan. "Let me see that, please. I've got to get back."

Back to the town square where his offices were only two doors away from Ellie's bookshop, Cyrus thought.

Joe scanned the computer printout he'd taken from Madge, read it again—more slowly—and gave it to Cyrus.

When Cyrus finished it, his hand fell to his side. He watched Joe's reaction. The man crossed his arms tightly and looked into the distance, as if he'd forgotten where he was and who he was with.

"Well, *say* something," Madge demanded. "*Do* something."

"We probably won't need to do anything," Cyrus said. "Ellie happened to be on a hotel balcony—staring straight down—when Stephanie Gray died. Other people were there and they didn't see a thing. For some reason Ellie did. In all that crush she noticed a woman fall like a log, not get accidentally pushed the way it was supposed to look. But she didn't see the killer—or she's not sure if she did. Ellie couldn't identify him."

"What if Charles Penn doesn't really believe that?" Madge said tightly. "What if he decides to come after her?"

"He may blame her," Joe said. "I've thought about this plenty. She couldn't identify him, but she wouldn't rule him out."

Suddenly Madge's eyes shone with angry tears. "He got caught because he was there, exactly there, and he ran. He got in the way of people trying to help Stephanie, he was in such a hurry."

Joe scrubbed at his face and said, "I can't get it out of my head that maybe if Ellie had been down there, she'd have been the one who died."

"God rest the soul who did," Cyrus murmured.

"Not everyone believed Ellie had never seen Charles Penn before," Madge cut in. "And some said she must have seen him but she was afraid to admit it in case he ever came after her."

"Poor girl," Cyrus said. "She'd barely come through the nightmare at Rosebank and managed to pull herself together for Spike and Vivian's wedding and this happened." Rosebank belonged to Vivian and her mother. They ran it as a hotel with a few long-stay apartments. Sheriff Spike Devol and Vivian Patin had been married at St. Cécile's a few weeks after the Patins' lawyer was found dead on the grounds of Rosebank and Ellie got singled out for some unpleasant attention. Cyrus glanced at the headline again. "Ellie's been through too much and I don't think we know all of it."

"I'll tell you this much," Joe said, his dark blue eyes flat and hostile. "If Ellie said she'd never seen Penn before the lineup, she'd never seen him. Ellie doesn't lie."

Madge said, "We all love Ellie. I'd do anything for her."

"It'll take me about fifteen to run back there," Joe said, the defensive expression still on his face.

"Take my car," Madge said.

"Or mine," Cyrus offered.

"I'd rather run," Joe said as he opened the door.

When they were alone Madge poured coffee for Cyrus and herself. She put the cups on the table before the kitchen windows and they sat down.

"We mustn't frighten Ellie," Madge said. "But we're all going to have to keep watch on her."

"And pray Penn gets picked up quickly," Cyrus said. The first drops of rain hit the windows but he didn't feel any triumph. "We're going to have to watch both of them, Ellie and Joe. He could put them both in danger if he rushes in without knowing what he's getting into."

"The police will come poking around," Madge said. "It's the Sheriff's Department's jurisdiction out here, but the New Orleans people will want to talk to Ellie."

"NOPD probably has a detective on the way as we speak," Cyrus said. "But Spike will have a cruiser in the square all the time and he'll camp on Ellie's doorstep to keep her safe if necessary—with Joe. I'm glad she has the dog now."

Madge topped up their coffee. "Did you see Joe's face when he went out of here?"

"Uh-huh—and before. First he looked sick and scared, then mad."

"Did you have any thoughts about that?" Madge stirred her coffee and kept her eyes lowered.

"Maybe. Tell me yours first." Cyrus didn't like to start gossip.

"I think Joe's in love with Ellie."

So did Cyrus and he wasn't sure the idea gave him a warm and cozy feeling.

Ellie Byron reached to turn off the computer but couldn't make herself do it. Even when she pushed her chair away from the desk she could read the words on the screen, or maybe she'd memorized them in one reading.

Charles Penn on the loose.

And within hours another ice-pick killing had occurred, like the one at Mardi Gras two years ago.

Hungry Eyes, Ellie's bookshop and café, occupied the entire floor beneath her apartment and a second, vacant one she tried to keep rented. She had gone down to get ready for the day and popped back up to check the news online, as she did every morning.

Ellie forced herself to move and ran down to lock the shop doors again. She hurried to switch off all appliances in the small café. She kept a wary eye open for her regular early customers and printed on an index card: Sorry. Late Opening Today. This she attached to a window with a suction cup and hook.

Trailing a battered cell phone by its antenna, Daisy, her German Shepherd, loped into the shop and flopped on her bed, followed by Zipper, the moody cat Ellie had bought for Daisy. Zipper didn't lope, she sprang, all four feet leaving the ground at the same time, and landed on top of Daisy. The dog inherited the phone after she began stealing and hiding it at every opportunity. She had played up like a kid when a call came in for Ellie.

Outside in the square two early-morning delivery trucks, parked half on and half off the sidewalk, were the only signs that a new business day had begun. Boxes piled outside Cerise's Boutique, a dress shop that had opened a few months ago, meant Cerise was late getting started again. Ellie worried about Cerise's merchandise being left on the sidewalk.

The driver of the second truck carried supplies into Lucien's Hair Affair and Spa, where the first clients would already be lounging and tucking into fresh beignets and café au lait, unless they preferred champagne. Lucien had come from an upscale salon in New Orleans.

The only other vehicle in sight belonged to her friend Joe Gable, a lawyer with offices almost next door. His army-green Jeep hung out in its usual spot beneath a gnarled old sycamore. Ellie gave the vehicle a long look. The thought that Joe was so close by gave her courage.

From the way things looked outside, this was just another day in this old Bayou Teche town, only for Ellie it was anything but just another day. She switched off the little radio balanced between jars of loose candies on a shelf in the café.

Keep busy. Think about what you should do next, but don't think about ice picks. She stopped breathing and looked behind her, into the square, again. No one brandishing an ice pick out there.

The nightmare began again and she squished the urge to call Joe. That wouldn't be wise.

"C'mon gals," she said to the animals. She didn't attempt to soothe their injured feelings at being disturbed from a little morning nap for the second time. "Now! Heel, Daisy. Upstairs we go."

Keeping up with the news online became a habit after the death of poor Stephanie Gray almost two years previously, when Ellie was the only eyewitness in the case.

When the last tenant left the second apartment above the shop, Ellie hadn't hurried to replace her. She still toyed with the idea of making the two apartments into one large one but couldn't afford a renovation yet.

Ellie closed herself in but heard the insistent ring of the bell at the shop door. She knelt on the floor beside Daisy and held her muzzle. "You're a good girl but you mustn't bark." Some hope. Daisy thought barking at possible intruders was her reason to live.

The bell rang again and she shuffled on her knees with an arm around Daisy until she reached the front windows. She looked down at the top of a man's dark blond head. Behind him at the curb stood a gray Dodge sedan in need of a paint job.

Ellie couldn't think for the hammering of her heart and the pounding in her ears.

Calm down. Sure, Charles Penn had similar coloring, but he wouldn't come to her door in broad daylight and ring the bell.

She should call for help now. Joe would come, and Spike. The phone rang and Ellie jumped so badly her chest hurt. She picked up and said, "Joe?" Sometimes he called her around this time.

"You are there, Miz Byron. My name is Guy Gautreaux, Detective Guy Gautreaux, NOPD. I just want to ask you a few questions."

3

Ellie shut Zipper in the apartment, muzzled Daisy and put on her choke chain. No point having a well-trained dog, then leaving her where she couldn't be of any help.

Daisy's alert button had been pressed. Nose straight ahead, she didn't as much as whine while she walked beside Ellie. They arrived at the shop door and Ellie peered through at a rangy man dressed in jeans and a denim jacket. Detective Gautreaux gave a big white grin and looked back at her with liquid, almost black eyes.

The detective had an open face and his eyes were sincere.

Ellie stared at him, waiting. Just because he looked like someone's handsome, harmless big brother returned from a camp-counselor stint didn't mean he'd get inside Hungry Eyes so easily.

He mouthed something and indicated the door handle.

Ellie put her hands on her hips and raised her eyebrows. Daisy gave a single deep bark and strained toward the door.

He slapped his forehead in one of those "What was I thinking?" motions and produced his badge, which he pressed against the glass so she could read it clearly. Looked real, darn it. Now she had no excuse not to let him in. She took off Daisy's muzzle and opened the door.

Gautreaux stepped inside and locked the door behind him.

Ellie wasn't sure that made her feel comfortable. She could feel Daisy vibrating under her skin, see the way the dog's eyes went from her to Gautreaux.

The detective gave her a disarming grin and walked forward to take a look at the shop and café. "Nice place," he said, and she noted that he wasn't grinning anymore, although, even in repose, there were plenty of lines to prove he smiled a lot. "Some dog, too. What's his name?"

"She's Daisy." Ellie held on to Daisy as if she barely had control of the animal. "It's not a good idea to make nice with her."

Gautreaux nodded gravely. "Ex police dog?"

"No, but she's just as well trained. Friend of mine had a friend who trained her. And Daisy's in therapy regularly so she's fairly predictable." The devil made her say the last bit.

"Therapy?" Gautreaux looked blank.

"Both Daisy and Zipper. We've got one of the best animal therapists around, right here in Toussaint. L'Oiseau de Nuit. We call her Wazoo."

"Uh-huh. How interestin'. Is Zipper another shepherd?"

"Mean cat. She belongs to Daisy. Daisy gets lonely if she doesn't have someone to play with."

"Well," Gautreaux said, "I sure understand how she feels about that." The expression on his face didn't flicker, and he didn't give Ellie even a suggestion of an invitation with his eyes.

"I have a lot to do," Ellie said. This guy thought he was smooth and that she was a small-town girl waiting for a nod from an urban cowboy. If she had her way, he'd never find out how wrong he was about her.

"Look, these are informal questions but you're expected to take them seriously."

Ellie's sweating hand slipped on Daisy's cinch. She didn't comment.

"Where were you first thing yesterday mornin'?" He turned on the smile again. "Remember, this doesn't mean anythin'. Just a few routine questions to fill up the necessary spaces." His pen hovered over a notebook and he hummed while he waited. "Between the moonshine, and the shinin' of the moon..." He sang barely above a whisper. A pleasant sound—too pleasant.

"Yesterday mornin'?" he prompted.

"I was here."

"And you'd been here all the night before?"

"Yes."

"Alone?"

She blushed, darn it. "Yes, alone. I live alone."

"What time did you open up?"

"Around twelve."

Gautreaux looked at her sharply. "Why so late?"

She began to feel angry, and hot. "I take an occasional Monday morning off. I clean up the stacks, work on my books, pay bills."

"You can't do that without closin' the shop?"

"I'm the only one here. I'd be interrupted all the time."

"So there wasn't anyone here with you yesterday morning? Who saw—"

Joe, in a mesh tank top and running shorts, used his key and opened the shop door. With his jaw jutting, he advanced on Gautreaux. "What the hell's goin' on here?" He hooked a thumb over his shoulder. "I see NOPD's unmarked cars haven't gotten any better-looking."

At the very least, Ellie would like to stand beside him but she thought better than to move.

"You heard me," Joe said. He had a film of sweat on his tanned face and body and his navy blue eyes narrowed to slits. "Why are you here?"

"Who are you?" Gautreaux asked, flashing his badge. "This is a friendly conversation between Miz Byron and me."

"I'm her lawyer," Joe said promptly, although he wasn't. "Joe Gable."

"A lawyer with a key to the castle."

When Gautreaux showed his white teeth again, Ellie feared Joe might land a fist right there. Every muscle and sinew in his fit body flexed. His black curly hair clung to his forehead and neck.

Since it was obvious Joe didn't intend to answer the detective's question, Ellie said, "Joe is my neighbor, too, and we keep spare keys for each other."

"Cozy," Gautreaux said, apparently unaware that Joe's stance had changed. Ellie swallowed several times. Leaning forward slightly, Joe curled his hands into fists.

Without moving her feet, Daisy stretched her neck, sniffed Gautreaux's jeans and rested her big wet nose at the side of his knee.

Ellie didn't move her away and Gautreaux behaved as if he hadn't noticed.

"Why are you here?" Joe said to Gautreaux.

"I thought I told you. To ask the lady some questions."

Joe turned his attention on Ellie. "Did he tell you what the interview was about?" She'd never seen him like this. He seethed.

"No," she said. "But I figured—"

"It doesn't matter," Joe said, quickly enough to let Ellie know he didn't want her to finish what she'd been about to say.

"Hey." Gautreaux gave Joe a man-to-man look. "Why don't the three of us sit down somewhere. I don't have a lot to ask, but we could get through faster."

Joe appeared about to refuse, but he took a deep breath through his nose instead and nodded shortly. "How about the table at the back of the stacks?" he asked Ellie, putting a hand at her waist.

"Fine," she told him, very aware that for all the times they'd shared together, she never remembered him touching her except for one time when they danced at Pappy's Dancehall.

Gautreaux stood aside to let them pass between lines of books, and Ellie smiled when Daisy looked up at him and raised one side of her top lip. They took chairs around a table where customers sat to look over possible purchases. The circle of easy chairs for book-club meetings would be more comfortable but Ellie didn't want to get comfortable.

This time Daisy put her chin on Joe's thigh and proceeded to sniff him. He laughed and said, "I really do need a shower." But he kissed Daisy's head and, with a great sigh, she leaned against him.

"Let's pick up where we left off," Gautreaux said. "Did anyone see you here in the shop yesterday mornin', Miz Byron?"

Ellie thought about it and said, "I don't think so."

"Not even your lawyer?"

"Not even her lawyer," Joe said, showing his teeth in a vaguely Daisy-way. "Loads of people must have, though, Ellie. The early café customers at the very least."

"Miz. Byron didn't open the shop until twelve yesterday," Guy Gautreaux said without looking at Joe. "She says she was doin' paperwork and tidyin' up."

"Then that's what she was doing," Joe said in as close-to-a-deadly voice as Ellie had heard him use.

Gautreaux wrote and said, "Subject doesn't have an alibi for night of the twenty-first or mornin' of the twenty-second. I'll need to speak to anyone who did see you in the afternoon, but you can leave that to me."

"You're going all over Toussaint asking questions about me?" Ellie said.

"I'm a discreet man," he said, and stood up. Daisy squeezed past Ellie and planted that moist nose in exactly the same spot at the side of the man's knee. "As Miz Byron was about to say before you stopped her, Joe, she figured quite correctly that I'm here because of her connection to the Stephanie Gray killin'. By now I'm sure you both know there was a murder in New Orleans yesterday. Royal Street. Same MO as the Gray case. Charles Penn escaped from custody a few days back and hasn't been picked up, so I'll ask you to be careful, ma'am, and call me at this number if you encounter anything unusual." He passed her a card. "No one you couldn't identify has tried to contact you? Or even someone you did identify but wished you hadn't?"

Ellie stiffened and took short breaths through her mouth. She knew what the last, not very subtle question meant. Daisy moved her head ever so slightly and gently closed her big, white teeth on a smidgeon of Gautreaux's jeans.

"No," Ellie said. She might be scared but she wouldn't let it show. She hardly dared look at Joe, but she could feel him, feel his anger, although she couldn't figure out why he was getting so mad at her, or Gautreaux.

"This was just an initial contact," Gautreaux said. "I'm sure we'll have to come to you again—or have you come to us. We're there for you, and I mean that sincerely. I'll make sure the local Sheriff's Department is informed. Is there anyone you could ask to be with you until this is cleared up?"

"Yes," Ellie said. "Daisy."

"Not quite what I had in mind," Gautreaux said, his gaze flicking toward Joe. "I'll get some help from the local law. They'll do some drive-bys to check up on you." He glanced at Daisy's teeth and Ellie gave a little tug to disengage her buddy.

She wouldn't help Gautreaux with a thing. He could find Spike Devol himself, and later she'd let Spike know she was just fine.

The detective gathered up his pad and pen and, as an afterthought, put one of his cards in front of Joe, who left it on the table.

One last grin, a move to stroke Daisy—sensibly aborted—and he scuffed his dusty boots out of the shop.

Silence followed and Ellie's jumpy nerves sickened her. Joe was her friend. He'd always been there if she'd needed something. Their response to each other had been slow at first, but the liking had grown steadily and she enjoyed his offbeat sense of humor and spontaneity.

Joe stood up. He looked into Ellie's face. "I'm goin' to take a shower. Lock the door after me."

He walked out.

4

The shower didn't cool Joe down.

He didn't have an appointment for a couple of hours, so he pulled on a tracksuit and stuffed his feet into thongs. If the thought of leaving Ellie to her own devices didn't scare him out of his mind, he'd keep his distance. He felt angry with her, so angry he'd rushed out of her shop rather than risk giving into an urge to shake her.

Something was wrong with Ellie. Not with her health or stability, but with a whole area of her life she kept secret. He didn't feel great about it, but he'd tried to find out something about her before she came to Toussaint, only to discover that Ellie Byron had a short history. As far as he could figure out, Ellie had shown up in New Orleans five years earlier. She went to work in a bookstore, and had funds. A year later when the former owners of Hungry Eyes had been looking for a manager, Ellie had been given the post, and eventually bought the store.

There was one prior address in California, where she lived with a Mrs. Clark, and that was it, the whole story of Ellie Byron, only it couldn't be and he wanted to hear the rest—from Ellie's lips.

Damn it all. He hadn't combed his hair. His tracksuit clung to wet skin and his mood wasn't fit for public display, but he had to point out a few basic elements of survival to his neighbor.

He didn't stop to think through what he would say but shot through his receptionist's office and into the rain. He slammed the door and locked it behind him. Joan should be in at any moment, but she could use her own key.

Outside the air smelled dusty—or muddy. It would take a lot more of the wet stuff to wash the caked-on grime away. Even the windows needed cleaning again and the giant bougainvillea overhanging his porch should be hosed down so it was brilliant purple again, rather than gray.

Damn, Cyrus would be crowing about his bloody rain. Let him. Joe *felt* things sometimes, too, and what he felt now was trouble. He marched to Ellie's shop door and rang the bell. *Don't keep me waiting out here.*

Not a sound from inside. Not a move. He backed up to look at her apartment windows. No sign of her.

Joe got close to the door, cupped his eyes against a clear glass pane between the border of stained-glass books. He tried to peer inside but the lights were off.

"Damn, damn, damn," he said, not caring who heard him.

Staring hard, he made out something on the floor at the far end of the stacks. Something black and shaped like…it was Daisy's foot. Right where the dog had been when Joe left. Which could mean Ellie remained where she had been sitting.

He'd taken a bad situation and made it worse for Ellie. Joe rested his forehead against the glass. But he had to make her wake up, darn it all. It was time Ellie learned to recognize danger when it stared at her.

Once again he rang the shop doorbell.

He saw Ellie's forearm and the way Daisy scratched the floor. Ellie was keeping Daisy quiet.

Joe took out the door key and looked at it. He had never meant to use it unless Ellie needed him to. Well, she needed him right now.

He opened the door as quietly as possible and slipped inside, grimacing at the squelch of his soaked thongs.

"Who's there?" Ellie's voice rose too high. "Get out, now."

"It's Joe. Stop behavin' like a scared kid, Ellie. We need to talk."

He heard a chair turn over as she got up, then realized she was making a dash to leave the shop and run upstairs. He was faster and stood in front of the door leading to a square hallway at the bottom of her stairs.

Daisy led Ellie in what the dog thought was a joyful charge. Panting and tossing her head, she saw Joe and skidded to a stop in front of him, grinning her pleasure.

"I want us to talk," Joe said to Ellie, stroking Daisy and holding the paw she offered. "Here or upstairs?"

"Nowhere. And I want you to stop encouraging Daisy. She shouldn't trust other people."

Looking steadily back into Ellie's shocked bright blue eyes wasn't easy. He took a step toward her and she threw up a forearm to cover her face.

"Oh, my God." Joe retreated to the door again. "What's happened to you? Do you think I would hurt you?"

She lowered her arm and said, "No." Ellie didn't spend

time sitting around in the sun and her skin was pale, but never as pale as it looked now. "I'm sorry you walked into the middle of what happened but it's over now."

"Is it? Do you really want to deal with this alone? Cyrus and I saw the piece about the Royal Street killin' online. So did Madge. You can bet Spike will be on the case shortly, and he won't be the last to come to your aid. If you want to hide—" He stopped himself. "Let us help you through this."

"If I want to hide what?" she said.

He ran a hand into his hair. "I don't know. I'm about as muddled up as you. But I'm not too muddled up to know you need help. I haven't had breakfast. I haven't even had coffee. Okay if I make us somethin'?"

"Whatever." She made a listless gesture.

As soon as he moved, she opened the door and said, "Come on up. If someone sees us in here they'll want in, too. Bring whatever you want to eat. I've got coffee already made upstairs."

He took a couple of plates and put two sweet rolls from the bakery case on top before going through and taking the stairs two at a time.

Daisy wasn't in evidence, which meant Ellie had shut her away. A gust of relief hit Joe. She wasn't afraid of him after all.

He put the rolls on a brass-topped table, where an ivy plant in a red lacquer pot trailed its vines in all directions. Ellie had looped lengths of tapestry, in a mostly light burgundy color, at the upper corners of her windows and allowed them to puddle on the floor. She had two good Chinese rugs, one under the table and chairs in the dining area near the windows, the other covering most of the living room floor.

"Sit down," Ellie said. "I'll just pour the coffee." She darted glances at him, never for long enough to let him smile at her.

The open kitchen stood to the left of the living and dining areas. Joe sat on a rust-colored corduroy couch where he had a good view of Ellie. She had puzzled him—and intrigued him—from the day they met. She kept her brown curls short and wore mostly loose clothes, as if she didn't want to draw attention to a voluptuous figure. Beautiful Ellie, who could not be more than twenty-eight or so. He didn't think anyone in town knew her age.

She approached, watching the mugs which she had overfilled. Joe rose and accepted his before sitting again. Ellie chose a seat at the far end of the couch and sipped her coffee in silence.

"Charles Penn doesn't know where you live," Joe said.

"You can find anyone. Try it. See how long it takes you to find someone on the computer."

"It's not always that simple," he said, thinking of the way Ellie's trail had narrowed and disappeared as it went into the past. "What makes you think he'd hang around just because you're here? You couldn't identify him during the trial."

Ellie set her mug down, laced her fingers tightly in her lap and gave him one of her disconcertingly brilliant stares. "He hung around long enough to murder another woman in New Orleans. I think he was partly letting me know he's out there. And I *don't* believe he's convinced I told the truth when I said I couldn't recognize him."

"Did you tell the truth?" He hadn't intended to ask her. "Forget I said that, I was thinkin' out loud."

"Which amounts to the same thing," she said. "You think I lied because I was afraid to tell the truth."

Joe flexed his shoulders and rolled his head from side to side. Maybe that was what he did think. He looked down at his muddy feet. Now, what would make him come to a conclusion like that? Even halfway to it?

"You're not saying anything, Joe."

"Okay. Ellie, did you see Charles Penn at Mardi Gras that day?"

"*No*, I said I didn't and I meant it." She paused and looked distant, as if she were watching the scene in her head. "The whole horrible thing was over in minutes and my mind was on Stephanie Gray. I didn't see him…I don't think I did…." Her voice faltered. "Only the woman falling with her arms and legs limp. The bottoms of her feet as the weight of the crowd stopped her from falling to the ground. There were faces turned up. They heard me scream, even with all the other noise going on." She stopped and Joe felt what he'd felt before; Ellie had something otherworldly about her, something distant and intriguing.

She did have a point, it made sense that she'd be watching what happened to the Gray woman, not sightseeing in the crowd.

"Look, I don't want to upset you again—" this said, he could hardly swallow, he was so tense "—but you let that detective into the shop. Why?"

"He showed his badge."

"You didn't think you should call Spike to see about verifyin' the man was who he said he was?"

She raised her chin. "No."

"When I got here the door was locked. Did he ask you to do that?"

Red washed over her cheeks. "He did it himself."

Joe sat on his hands. He had to calm down. Racing to

find Gautreaux and punching him out sure as hell wouldn't help Ellie. Gautreaux's indolence didn't hide a tall, strong body Joe was certain the man knew how to use when he had to. Any fight between Gautreaux and Joe wouldn't be pretty. "So you opened the door, he explained he was there because of a second murder they thought was linked to Stephanie Gray's and then locked the door behind him."

"Stop it!" Ellie shot to her feet, hitting the brass table with her leg and sending coffee everywhere. "What does it matter *exactly* what he said and when he said it? No, if you must know. No, that's not how it went. You heard him talk about the Royal Street murder. Why would he say it twice?"

She got a cloth from the kitchen and mopped the table.

"What did he say when he got here?" Joe said, feeling his control gradually slide away.

"He asked me where I was yesterday morning and the night before. That's all he asked, questions about that and who might have seen me."

"Goddammit." He pushed forcefully to his feet. "How could you be so stupid? You don't trust me enough to let me more than a fingernail's width into your life, but I trust you nevertheless. I trust and care about you the way…friends should, the way they do. I try to look out for you, Ellie."

She scrambled up. Only inches separated them, and he realized as he had before that she wasn't a big woman, just well built and with a face that melted his resolve every time. Well, that wasn't going to happen now.

Her lips parted and he waited. "I got shocked," she said. "Scared, I suppose. I'd just read the online news about the case and I'd gone down and locked the shop again and come up here. I didn't know what to do. Then this man came to the door and I couldn't think anymore. I couldn't call you when you have a practice to run. Anyway, I wouldn't want to drag you into my problems."

"You should have called me. I would have *wanted* you to. And what do you mean, drag me into your problems? I already know about them and I want to be here helping you solve them."

She looked at the floor, then turned her head away.

"The first thing Gautreaux will do is track Spike down and start givin' orders. Cyrus mentioned Spike was goin' over there after mass because they're puttin' their heads together over somethin'. That means before you know it Spike and Cyrus will be on your doorstep. Probably Madge, too."

"But why?" Ellie looked trapped.

"You have to ask that after we've all come through some narrow spaces together? They'll want to be here to do what they can. Whether you like it or not, we're goin' to watch out for you until you can feel safe again. You are never goin' to be alone until that happens."

5

Reb Girard, Toussaint's only doctor, arrived at Pappy's Dancehall a few minutes after Ellie. Holding twenty-month-old William in one arm, she slid onto a seat in the booth where Ellie waited. Their table stood beneath a skylight vista of a purple evening. The room grew crowded with couples, groups and folks with children; laughter and shouting from the tables around Pappy's dance floor swelled in anticipation of good food and music to come.

Three miles or so north of Toussaint, Pappy's was an institution. Everyone came here—friends, neighbors, relatives—laughing and talking.

"Heartbreak Hotel" blared from the jukebox, turning conversation into code.

"Smells as great as usual," Reb said. Sniffing the scents of spicy gumbo from another table, she eyed bowls of grillades in the hands of a passing waitress. Steam rose from the beef in tomato gravy and Ellie's mouth watered.

Reb continued, "I'm sorry I'm late. I meant to be here

first to greet you. Young Wally Hibbs managed to lay a finger open with a fishhook so I had a little job to deal with before I came."

Thirteen-year-old Wally, son of Doll and Gator Hibbs, who ran the Majestic Hotel close to the center of town, found his refuge and often his home with Cyrus, who had accepted the boy as his shadow some years earlier. Cyrus and Madge even helped Wally with his homework and employed him around the rectory in the summer and on Saturdays during school.

"Poor Wally, he's still accident prone," Ellie said. "But I was early. I had to get away before someone tried to stop me."

Reb sighed. She shook her head at Ellie and looked around for a waitress. "I need a booster chair for William. He thinks he's too grown-up for high chairs."

William, dark-haired and dark-eyed like his father, squirmed on his mother's lap and gave Ellie a dimpled, slightly drooly grin. She scooted closer and nuzzled his face. Babies were so soft. That was about as much as she knew about them, not that holding a baby in her arms didn't appeal. She just didn't feel confident enough to ask.

Reb asked for the booster seat and said, "Marc's on his way in. He ran into Ozaire Dupre outside. Ozaire's got some flea in his ear about Cyrus not appreciating his cus-todial efforts at St. Cécile's—and he was saying somethin' about how Lil isn't feelin' Cyrus values her as his house-keeper."

"Nothing changes in this town," Ellie said. "Always a new drama. I wonder what set them off this time?"

"Ozaire's gym," Reb said, rocking William, who puffed up his cheeks and practiced spitting skills.

Ellie didn't know about any gym and shook her head. She picked up a corner of the red-and-white-checked tablecloth and tried not to draw attention to the way she peered at Daisy. The dog had scooched behind Ellie's legs so she had to sit on the edge of her seat. She didn't go anywhere without Daisy anymore. She had persuaded Carmen, the bouncer at Pappy's, to leave his favorite spot beside the flashing neon jukebox and bring Daisy in by a side door. Devoted to Elvis, Carmen had been known to show up in a fringed white jacket and black wig. He chose most of what played on the box.

"You didn't know about the gym?" Reb asked, pretending she had no idea a large German shepherd lay inches from her feet.

"No. First I heard of it."

The booster arrived and Reb plopped William into it. The baby said something that sounded like "help," and Reb made short work of unwrapping crackers and spreading them before him on the paper tablecloth.

Pappy's regular band, Swamp Doggies, moved into place at one end of the dance floor and children soon left their parents and held hands to go through their two-step paces while the Doggies warmed up. Colored lights flashed from the facets of a revolving silver ball and the children shrieked.

"Ozaire's been sulking because he thinks Spike's dad has stolen all his boiling-and-barbecuing business. What he really doesn't like is competition. So his new idea is to open a gym—in the church hall."

Ellie wrinkled her nose and laughed. She couldn't stop laughing. She loved Toussaint and all—make that most—of its citizens. "Surely Cyrus didn't say no?" She giggled some more.

"What do you think?" Reb's red eyebrows rose. "Imagine the bingo folks trying to play around Exercycles and treadmills—and sweatin' guys bench-pressing. Or the quilting group yackin' away and tryin' to get their lunch together."

"I can't," Ellie said. "Didn't there used to be a gym in Toussaint?"

"Uh-huh. Went out of business for lack of customers."

"But Ozaire thinks he can do better." Ellie sat back while the waitress placed glasses of Pappy's red house wine—the only wine in the house—in front of them. An overflowing basket of hush puppies followed, with sweet butter and honey. "Reb, it was nice of you and Marc to invite me here tonight, but…" She couldn't quite bring herself to say she didn't know why they had asked her.

"But why did we?" Reb said. "I should wait for Marc but I'll tell you now, anyway. It's been four days since you found out Charles Penn's on the loose, and you've already made a good job of letting most of your friends know you don't want them around. You're worrying all of us."

"I love my friends." She did, but she didn't want them feeling responsible, or sorry for her.

"You love them, so you open late and close early and won't let any of them stay in that spare flat of yours at night? All they want, all any of us wants, is to be there for you."

"I know. It's not necessary. I'm fine."

Reb watched while William's small, plump fists beat crackers to powdery heaps on the table. "No, you're not. Look at you—everyone's noticed. You haven't slept since it happened."

The lights lowered and the Swamp Doggies swung

into their signature number, "Toussaint Nights"; yells went up from the crowd. Dancers made a dash for the floor.

"You don't know if I've slept or not," Ellie said. "I appreciate your concern, but I have to do this my own way. I'm sorry I'm worrying people, but they should trust me to do what's right."

"Did you know Joe's had a crew in to clean and paint the rooms over his offices and he's using a sleeping bag on the floor until some furniture gets delivered?"

Ellie couldn't look away from Reb's green eyes. "Why would he do that? What about his sister? Jilly will be alone." Her heart beat faster. No man in her life had ever been reliable, except her brother, and he probably thought she was dead, or married with children and uninterested in revisiting the life she'd been in such a hurry to escape. Joe Gable could be one more of those men who meant what he said and really did want to help her. The risk of disappointment was too great to allow herself to give in to what she really wanted and give him a chance—and herself a chance.

She came out of her struggling thoughts to find Reb studying her speculatively. "Ellie, try to focus. I can almost see you arguing yourself out of letting your friends be in this with you. Don't worry about Jilly. She's got a lot going on in her love life and she isn't being threatened by anyone. And they've both been talking about Joe moving out."

"Who says I'm being threatened?" Ellie said, surprised by her own anger. "You're all making assumptions. There was a terrible, horrible crime in New Orleans. That man Penn got away not long before and they haven't found him. That doesn't have to mean he's the killer this time and it doesn't mean he's interested in me."

"You had a visitor from NOPD who told you to be careful." Reb's very red hair glimmered in the light of a candle on a shelf behind her. "He wanted Spike to make sure the square was patrolled regularly."

"I know, I've seen the cars. Thanks for making me feel better." Ellie put her face in her hands and shook her head. "Forget I said that. It was childish."

"Here comes Marc," Reb said. "Try not to get mad when he starts telling you what you're going to do. William, here comes Daddy."

Carrying a blanket over his arm, Marc Girard—an architect who also happened to own a good deal of the property in town—wound his way between tables, smiling toward Reb and Ellie, pausing to talk to people who stopped him along the way. One day William's black hair would be as thick and curly as his father's, but it was too soon to know if his eyes might become as dark.

"Hello again, *cher*," Marc said to Reb, kissing her long enough to make Ellie smile. He leaned over Reb to accept a soggy-cracker offering from William, then sat down with the blanket on his lap. "Good to see you, Ellie. There are rumors you've left town. I'm glad they're wrong."

For Reb's sake she wouldn't snap at him. "Thank you for inviting me to dinner."

The blankets wiggled and Marc glanced around. Reb leaned to whisper in his ear and he looked down.

"Gaston?" Ellie said. She should have remembered Marc and Reb took the precocious apricot poodle everywhere. "This isn't going to work. I'd better put Daisy in the van."

"Isn't she muzzled?" Joe said in her ear, startling Ellie. With his chin resting on his folded arms and his face only inches from her head, he knelt in a booth behind her. Ellie hadn't seen him arrive. "She's good with other dogs." He smiled at her.

"She's good with Zipper," Ellie said, looking up at him. She shouldn't be so glad to see him, if that was the right way to describe what she felt just having him so close.

"Join us," Marc said. "Shift closer to William, Ellie. There's plenty of room."

Enough room without her squishing around. Ellie moved a few inches, anyway. "Did you tell Joe we would be here?" she asked Marc. She couldn't get mad when he gave a sunny nod.

Joe sat beside her and touched her arm. "Marc's tryin' to help me out. I asked him to do this."

"Really?" Heat flooded Ellie's face. She wondered how she could get out of the place without making a scene.

"If we hadn't wanted to be here with you we wouldn't have asked you," Reb said. "So relax, soften up and quit seeing conspiracies against you wherever you look. Joe needs our help to make you listen. And we need to do it for ourselves. You'd be the first in line to do what you could for someone else."

Hunched forward, his elbows propped on the table, Joe looked at Ellie over his shoulder. "For a tired woman, you look wonderful."

She opened her mouth but not a single comment came to mind.

"We're friends, all of us," Joe said. "It's possible this whole thing is being blown out of proportion, but if we keep an eye on you we can make you invulnerable."

"Is that why you're sleeping on the floor over your office? What is that helping? You wouldn't know any more about what's happening to me from there than you would from yours and Jilly's place."

"Ellie!"

Joe interrupted Reb, "It's okay. This is a hard time for Ellie."

She was afraid, dammit. "Thanks for defending me." Every time she opened her mouth she embarrassed herself afresh. "I'm sorry, Joe. I'm horrible. Speaking of tired—" she looked more closely into his face "—how about you? You've got…oh, no, please tell me you aren't sitting up at night watching my place."

"I'm not sitting up at night watching your place," he said promptly.

"Yes, he is," Reb said. "Ruining his health."

"How else am I supposed to try to keep her safe?" Joe said to Reb.

Marc set his disguised poodle on the seat beside him. "Cyrus is here." He raised a hand in the direction of the entrance, where Cyrus edged past an eight-foot stuffed and lacquered alligator on a plinth festooned with artificial flowers. "And Madge," Ellie said. "And Spike and Paul Nelson bringing up the rear?" Nelson, a writer who lived at Rosebank, the hotel owned by Spike Devol's wife, Vivian, and her mother, Charlotte, wrote guidebooks. He and Jilly spent a lot of time together. "How many more people are coming?"

"That's everyone," Marc said with no sign of shame. "Jilly wanted to come, and Vivian and a few others, but we didn't want to turn things into a carnival."

"No," Ellie said. "I'm not real fond of carnivals anymore, either."

Joe rubbed her shoulders and she liked it too much to tell him to stop. "Trust all of us, okay?" he said, low enough that she was probably the only one who heard. Ellie looked into his deep blue eyes, then glanced away from him, at Cyrus, Spike and all the others making slow progress toward the table. Whether Marc thought he had things under control or not, that carnival would soon be an entertainment for anyone who wanted to make an effort to watch and listen.

"Excuse me," she said to Joe. "I need to take Daisy out."

Without missing a beat Joe responded, "Let me do that for you. Just take it easy."

"No, but thank you, anyway." She adjusted Daisy's chain. "She only likes me to take her. But she's the best watchdog around, so if anyone gets fresh they'll be looking for their fingers and toes."

With his nostrils flared and annoyance written all over him, Joe stood up to let her get out of the booth. She saw him working hard to keep his mouth shut. Ellie smiled at him when she passed, but he barely twitched the corners of his mouth.

6

Hopping into her van and taking off seemed like a great idea. Ellie turned and walked a few backward steps, away from the dance hall, making certain she hadn't been followed.

Maybe running away—and that's what it would be—wasn't such a good idea. She'd run away once before when she should have stayed. Life hadn't been easy but it only got harder after she left. Too many horrible years had followed before she'd gotten one more chance, right here in Toussaint, and she liked it.

It was a good thing she loved this place because there really wasn't anywhere else to go.

She would put Daisy in the van with the windows down, go back to the others, and say she could stay only a short while.

Daisy whined and pulled on her chain. Ellie walked her toward a grove of old oaks. She and Wazoo had once gone deep into them to a clearing with a fungus-sprouting picnic table. Wazoo said there was a connection to the "other side" there and dogs felt it because their senses were so highly tuned. Wazoo had told Ellie that in the presence of spirits, dogs forgot their disguises so it was easier to delve into their complexes, their fears, their deepest insecurities.

At least Wazoo had eased up on exorcisms, and the townsfolk were good-natured about paying a little for her time with the dogs just to help her out. She also did a steady trade in palm and tarot readings. Unfortunately, that paid poorly, too.

Ellie reached the oaks and Daisy wandered happily back and forth between trunks and through crackling brush. A vine of spider orchids hung from a branch. Ellie picked two blossoms, stuck one behind her own ear and the second into Daisy's collar.

"Hurry up, girl. C'mon, c'mon, c'mon, it's getting darker."

Daisy, who had a gender dilemma, raised her leg on the nearest tree, then set about marking one after the other.

"You've got to quit tanking up at fire hydrants along the way," Ellie said. "You *can't* have anymore left in you."

Daisy faced her, ears perked and the whites of her eyes showing too much.

"If you don't scream, I won't hurt you," a man whispered from Ellie's left. He was not far away.

Ellie's head spun and she stumbled. The great leap of her heart winded her. Looking around, she backed up, breathing through her mouth as she went. Pain stabbed at the bottom of her throat.

"Stand still. Let the dog pull you into the trees." He coughed. "If you let it go, it won't reach me alive."

She couldn't move. Then Daisy looked up at her and

Ellie realized she was still muzzled. A scream swelled in her head. With shaking fingers she reached to free the dog's mouth.

"*Leave it.* And keep that thing calm. Come on. Come into the trees. I only want to talk to you."

Keeping an eye on Ellie without her seeing him wasn't so easy to pull off. Joe stood inside the door and watched her through a small, steamed-up window not intended for sightseeing.

He could almost hear what went on in her head. Bringing so many people together for the sole purpose of insisting she allow them to guide her had made her embarrassed and angry. A lousy idea and his fault. She wanted to hightail it out of here, but so far she hadn't convinced herself she could do it. Ellie was gentle and didn't have all the confidence she deserved to have, but she was no coward and he might have known what she'd think about a committee formed to keep her in line.

How long did she intend to stand in the oaks, one arm wrapped tightly across her middle while the other stretched way out, as if she wanted Daisy to take her time in the trees but preferred to stay where she was herself?

He had watched her lean over Daisy as if she intended to take off the dog's muzzle, then change her mind. He would have liked to be the one who put a flower in Ellie's hair. He'd like to walk and laugh with her and know she wasn't hiding anything from him. He'd like to hold her.

Joe the romantic. That was something new.

She still hadn't moved. Ellie would be in soon enough. He'd better at least let everyone know where she was.

* * *

"You left me to rot."

Ellie's jaw locked. Charles Penn, killer, didn't have to raise his voice above a whisper for her to hear him clearly.

"Make noise and I'll have to stop you. Your friends couldn't get here in time to help."

A puff of air slid across her back. She managed not to scream. No, she only imagined she felt his breath on her neck. She didn't want to look at him—he'd be even more real then.

Daisy strained at her chain. She paced back and forth, growling low and steady in her throat, looking from Ellie to the man behind her.

"Handle that animal," the man said. "Yank the chain. I don't like dogs. One less is always a good thing. I don't want the attention, but I'll shoot it if I have to. Shorten the leash and go forward, around the big trunk to your left."

"It wasn't my fault—"

"*Move.*"

She did as she was told, cranked on the chain until Daisy came to heel, and all but hauled the dog forward and behind the old tree he referred to.

"Stand still."

He had cut her off from Pappy's now. "Someone will come looking for me," she told him. "It's getting dark." *Keep quiet, fool.* Her long, loose dress stuck to her back. She couldn't control her shaking legs.

"You don't have to be afraid of me, you. See the three little trees close together there?"

She wiped sweat from her eyes. "Yes." But only barely because gloom crept in, and mist.

"Tie the dog to those. Don't try anything. I've got nothing to lose, remember."

"Why are you doing this?" Her voice sounded steadier than it should. She wanted to scream. She wanted to run.

"Tie that up! You're in no danger if you do what I say."

Slowly, praying she'd hear the others calling her name, she went to the clump of slender trees, crouched and looped Daisy's chain around them. Snarling, leaping against confinement, the dog crushed links into Ellie's hands. "Down," she told Daisy, who dropped to the ground, quivering.

"I'm watchin' you. Tie it. Over and under. Over and under."

She did it, willing her clumsy effort to work free.

"Good. Go on, now. Straight on. I'm takin' you with me for a little chat."

Blood thundered in Ellie's head. He intended to murder her, too, just like the others.

"Go *on*."

He killed with an ice pick.

Ellie took a step, and another, and she stiffened her neck, expecting the thrust of steel. Then she took off, she couldn't help it. She ran, threw out her arms for balance and went as fast as sandals in tangled undergrowth would allow.

He ran, too. She heard him.

Branches slapped into Ellie's face, scratched her neck, snagged her dress. Sound thundered. Her breath hissed in and out, turned her throat raw.

I have nothing to lose now, either. She screamed, sobbed, screamed again, and slammed her left foot into a mesh of woody vines.

The vines brought her down.

She couldn't see past tears and sweat and stumbled to her feet again, blind.

He was almost on her. Ellie blinked and her vision cleared a little. She cast about, zigzagged, tried to rush in the direction of the parking lot and Pappy's.

"Help!"

Down she went again and a hand closed on her ankle. "Shut up," he hissed at her, dragged her deeper into the trees. She couldn't stop her skirt from rolling up to her hips. Pin-sharp twigs, thorns and rough ground clawed at her bare legs.

Ellie grabbed a root and held on long enough to twist onto her back, yelling again and again.

The man had already dropped her foot. She made out his shape, running away, crashing downhill through the trees.

Joe couldn't see enough through the window now. He went outside and stood, running his fingers through his hair and frowning into the darkness. The old building didn't muffle raucous voices, and laughter seemed as loud out here as it was inside.

Where was Ellie?

He'd only been away a few minutes, just long enough to explain how she was taking her time walking Daisy.

Night had come on fast.

Her van stood exactly where it had when he got there and he ran to check it out. Locked doors, empty, and no sign of a scuffle.

His gut jumped and clenched but he stood quiet to listen, or listen as well as he could over the din from Pappy's. He'd like to go back for the rest of them, but if something had happened to Ellie every second counted.

A car drove into the parking lot, spraying gravel. Joe

reached the trees but took an instant to watch the vehicle. A giggling couple tipped out and made for Pappy's.

This was the spot where he'd last seen Ellie. He scanned to his left and his right, hoping to see her walking toward him.

Nothing.

She had stepped forward a few paces so Daisy could explore. Joe walked between the first oaks. A big one loomed ahead and he approached that. A low growl sounded, and the tight clank of a chain at full extension. Daisy, leaping against her leash, foamed at the mouth and growled. The whites of her eyes glared in the darkness.

He heard crashing among bushes and undergrowth, somewhere downhill from where he stood, and went after it. He couldn't do a damn thing about the noise he made. Unleashing Daisy could be a good thing, but he didn't know all her commands and she might complicate rather than help.

Someone sobbed, or dragged in one painful breath after another. Joe sidestepped, peering ahead, cursing birds arguing in the treetops. It had to be Ellie and she had to be coming uphill. If he was real lucky, she didn't have a maniac in tow.

Then he saw movement swaying in the saplings, and finally a shape he knew was Ellie. He rushed to her, and the moment he said "Ellie. Cher."

She said his name and a second later fell into his arms.

"Charles Penn," she said, and even in the questionable light he saw how her eyes stretched wide open. "He was here. He wanted me to go with him."

"Oh, my God." Joe pulled her into a bear hug. He caught her neck in the crook of one elbow and rocked her, pushed her damp hair away from her face, rubbed her shoulders and kissed her brow. "Did he hurt you?"

"Just hold me for a little while," she said. "I'm strong. I'm really strong, but he was going to take me away and kill me. I thought he'd kill me here. He's got to be caught before he murders again."

He's also got to be caught before he can get his hands on you again.

Her body grew heavy. "Sit down," he told her. "Here. On my sweater." He worked it off and spread it on the ground. She sat on it immediately and reached for his hand.

He mustn't read anything into her reactions. Shock made people behave out of character.

But he sat beside her, surrounded by shrubs and dry underbrush, and drifts of mist curling in beards of Spanish moss that trailed from the trees. Now he dared to take a wafer-thin flashlight the size of a credit card from his pocket and shine it on her. She covered her face with crossed wrists.

"Your arms are bleeding," he told her. "Really bleeding. Let me, please." He eased her arms down and more scrapes and scratches confronted him. Welts with raised specks of blood crisscrossed her neck. "You need to be seen. Reb will take care of this."

"Not yet, Joe," she said very quietly. "I've got to get Daisy."

"I will," he said. "Don't move."

"I'd better do it."

"Please don't move. If I need you, I'll ask."

The dog's strength didn't flag. She threw herself into the air and twisted her body and her black coat shone with moisture. "Daisy," Joe said, moving in slowly. "Down, girl. Let me help you."

Daisy heard his voice. She panted and strained, but gradually subsided until Joe could release the knot in her chain and stop her from rushing away. When she reached Ellie, Daisy behaved like a lapdog, crawling against her boss, rubbing her head on her face. Ellie unbuckled the muzzle, ordering silence at the same time.

Using his light again, Joe stood over them. Ribbons of fabric hung from Ellie's dress and the skirt was hiked above bloody knees. He crouched down to examine her leg. "How did all this happen?"

Her voice shook. "He grabbed my ankle and tried to drag me away with him. It hurts." She showed him her thigh and the sight of red streamers and places where gravel and stones had taken the skin off destroyed any shred of control he'd clung to. The contusions were filled with ground-in dirt. *He'd kill the bastard.*

He had to seem calm for Ellie. "Let me help you up."

"Just a minute or two more, please. I can't bear a fuss, Joe. And I've got to think a bit." Seeing the plea in her eyes he sat beside her again. Daisy decided to share her affections and licked him from chin to forehead.

"Spike will do things by the book this time," Ellie said. "He'll be kind, but this is too serious for him to play around. I wouldn't want him to. There will be some sort of arrangement for cooperation with NOPD. Detective Gautreaux will walk the straight and narrow and even if he doesn't want to hurt me, he will if that's what it takes to get his job done. They'll do more digging this time. I can't face that. Not yet."

She didn't sound as if dealings with the law were new to her. *They'll do more digging this time.* What the hell did that mean? He hugged the woman and the dog. The dog was sweet, but he would have liked to give all his attention to Ellie. She still trembled, but her body was soft and pressed against his without resistance. This was absolutely the most unsuitable time to react to this woman sexually, but this was absolutely the time his body and mind had chosen. He had to control the urge to pass his hands over her, to raise her chin and kiss her.

"I want twenty-four hours, Joe." She looked up into his face. "Can you help me get that? Can we just say I fell over in the woods and got scraped up? That's what I did."

"With a lot of help from a murderer." He needed to talk with Spike but Ellie's desperation stopped him, at least for the moment.

Her eyes glittered and he figured she could cry at any moment. He didn't go to pieces when a woman cried, but neither did he look forward to feeling useless. "Can you tell me why you want to hide out?" *Now she'd close up again.*

Ellie leaned across Daisy to rest against Joe's shoulder. Timing could be everything. Where Ellie was concerned his had been lousy and it was getting worse.

"You're askin' me to do the wrong thing," he said. "Whatever happens, I'm going to call this in to Spike and it needs to be done now. That doesn't mean I won't get you out of the way for a few hours until you're ready to talk. But if I have to put the rest of them off the track, I've got to be convincin'. They are going to be madder than wet hens when they find out."

She looked up at him again.

Her mouth was a breath away from his. Whoa, the kind of fear they'd come through made it easier to give in to desire. Joe surely did desire Ellie, and not only to kiss.

"What can I say to them?" Their faces almost touched.

Ellie slipped her arm around his waist and her hand landed where his shirt had pulled free of his jeans. She spread her fingers on his naked back. Joe grew more uncomfortable and he liked it.

"Just a day, Joe," she said. "You could help me figure out what I'll have to say to Spike—and to Gautreaux—and what isn't necessary. If you want to. I've taken too much from you already."

His chest expanded, but he had trouble letting the air flow out again. "Anything you want." Yep, he would just spread himself out in front of her like a cloak over a puddle. Might as well tell her to walk on him because he might like that, too.

"There's a lot you don't know about me."

That was for sure, and he felt heady at the prospect of her telling him about it. He wanted to feel connected to her.

"I can't just say it all. Just like that. I've taken years to put it behind me, but I'll tell you enough so you understand why I can't afford to get too involved with the law."

He had not expected that. He leaned away from her. "You're a convict on the run?"

Her smile was faint. "That's Charles Penn."

"Sorry." Dumb comment to make. "I didn't think."

"I can clean myself up and stay out of the way. I'll talk to Spike tomorrow—late tomorrow."

"Cher," he said, gently. "Right now I've got to report what's happened."

"They'll be all over me."

Joe stood and helped her up. He stuck his hands in his pockets and brooded over the rash next step he'd just decided to make. "I'm probably going to hate myself for this, but let's go. Don't waste time asking questions. Daisy mustn't bark."

Ellie didn't ask him to explain. Her fingers wouldn't work properly so he helped her put the muzzle back on. He grabbed her hand and they ran under cover of the trees until he figured they had the best chance to reach her van without being seen.

He stopped and pulled her well out of sight again. "Your keys? Where are they?"

"In my purse. I left it on the seat inside. There's a spare under the right rear bumper."

"That's something. *Run.* Damn it, the lights in this parking lot feel like strobes."

Ellie found the little magnetic box and gave Joe her spare key. Daisy leaped into the back and Ellie barely made it into the passenger seat before Joe squealed away. Her door didn't click all the way shut until he careened around the building, swaying hard to the left.

The employees parked on the far side of the back lot and Joe slipped the van between two trucks. "I'm grasping at straws here," he said. "Hide things in plain sight, isn't that what they say?"

"I guess so." Ellie stared over her shoulder. "If someone heard that reckless driving, we'll get company."

"You wouldn't hear a train wreck inside there," Joe said. "Let's get Daisy and go."

"Go where?" Ellie said, stepping out of Daisy's way when she jumped from the vehicle. "Joe?"

"We're leavin' in my Jeep. Save your breath till we're away."

Back to the front of Pappy's they ran. Joe figured Ellie had already suffered enough. She needed to rest and have her wounds dealt with, but it would have to wait.

"Still in the clear," Joe said, peering around the front of the building. "Walk normally."

He hardly believed their luck when they drove away from Pappy's and headed back toward the center of Toussaint.

Ellie clung to the dashboard in front of her and watched him.

"I'm making a call. Don't say anything."

"Who are—"

"Just listen." The phone only rang once before Spike's familiar drawl said, "Yeah?"

"Spike, don't let anyone else there know it's me. We've got a big problem on our hands."

Silence.

"Spike, it's Joe."

"Uh-huh."

Joe set it all out neatly and dragged in a breath after he'd said, "So I'm givin' Ellie a chance to gather her wits. You understand?"

"Nope. I'm movin', you dumb shit, I'm already outside. Where are you? Get back here or I'll get a warrant."

Joe smiled at Ellie, but her expression suggested she could hear the tone of Spike's voice. "Thanks, Spike," Joe said. "She's had such a rough time, maybe rougher than we know."

He heard Spike turn on his car radio.

"Just a few hours and we'll contact you," Joe said.

"*We*, huh?" Spike said. "I'm gonna set a search in motion for Penn. I'll try to stay off your back till mornin', then I come lookin for you. If my boss finds out what I've done, I'll be the new cook at Rosebank. If I don't see the whites of your eyes by eight, I'll put out an APB. That's a promise. And if NOPD gets wind Ellie's gone bye-bye before that, there won't be a thing I can do about it."

"Thank you," Joe said. "I owe you."

Ellie took the phone from him and said, "I owe you, too—" She cleared her throat. "He hung up."

"He's got a lot to do," he told her, feeling lame. "He's a good guy. The best. About now all he's thinkin' about is catchin' a killer."

"I can't go home, Joe," she said.

"I know."

7

Cyrus stood in the middle of Bonanza Alley and looked at the church. Even without a moon, the white stone walls shone. He considered going there to pray but turned away instead.

From the bayou came the rattle and clack of critters, the rustle of movement in dry reeds. And the frogs set up their nightly ruckus. He wouldn't change a thing about this place.

He had one refuge where he was never interrupted, except by the occasional phone call. Whenever he entered his own room a mantle of quiet descended. Up under the eaves in what used to be the attic, he'd made his own simple space. Initially he had told himself he did it to free up another bedroom for emergency use. But he knew he had needed a place where only he went—he still did. Not even Lil Dupre ventured up there and he did his own cleaning.

Reluctant to leave the outdoors before he had to, Cyrus walked toward the house at a leisurely pace. When Spike called him at Pappy's with the story about Charles Penn and Ellie, he'd offered to help search for the man, so had Marc and Paul Nelson, and they could have found plenty of other volunteers. Spike said this was too big a deal and deputies were being called in from all over.

When Cyrus walked across damp grass toward the kitchen door, frogs leaped and crickets let him know they were taking up noisy arms to fight him off.

The coffeepot was always on in Lil's kitchen. Cyrus poured a mug and sat at the big table in the windows. By day a clear view of land that sloped to the bayou never failed to delight him. The flowers he grew himself, the shrubs and trees, pleased him. Even the Fuglies, a primitive, two-dimensional sculpture given as a gift to the parish seemed to belong at last—ugly though it was.

By night, the only view at the windows was a reflection of the scene inside the kitchen.

Cyrus sat at the table and cupped the hot mug in both hands. Sitting there like that, still and quiet in the empty old house, felt familiar, but he wished, as he too frequently did, that he weren't alone. That was his battle and his burden.

He drank from the mug, set it down and rubbed at his face. This had been another long day. At least he wasn't worried about Ellie, or not too worried since she and Joe were together. He smiled into his hands. Joe Gable had been looking for a way to get closer to Ellie for a couple of years, and now, Cyrus guessed, Joe wasn't letting any grass grow under his feet.

He liked Joe—Ellie, too, even if she did puzzle him sometimes.

Why couldn't it be that when a man took the cloth certain human parts of him turned off for good? All the personal stuff, the feelings he wasn't allowed to have. God knew his vocation needed everything he had to give. Most times it got all of him, but in some ways one ache got worse. Little by little, the longing that closed his throat with forbidden love, and the awakening that came, unbidden, to make him hate his weakness, had become regular companions.

Before Madge had moved into rooms at Rosebank with the Devols, she'd lived farther away, in Rayne, but she had been on her own there and no one took notice of how many nights she worked late at the rectory.

He brought his fists down on the table, then spread his fingers. Madge still spent most of her time there. He was selfish. He was using up a young woman's life and he had no claim on it. But when she worked in her office, or joined him here for coffee, he felt complete peace. She'd become his best friend. But there were the other feelings.

Paul Nelson looked at her in that certain way, like he wanted to know her a whole lot better. People liked Paul and so did Cyrus. He liked the other man's wit and intelligence, and his quiet kindness. And he was successful. Ellie carried his travel books and she said you could find them in almost any store.

If he, Cyrus, encouraged Madge to take notice of the man… He pinched the bridge of his nose. That's what he should do, help Madge find a husband.

He'd go up to his room and pray for the strength to overcome his weakness.

Tapping at the kitchen door only startled him for a moment. Wally Hibbs often showed up late looking for a friendly ear. It would mean Cyrus must drive him home but he could handle it.

He got up and opened the door.

Joe Gable stood there with an arm around Ellie's shoulders. Her dog, Daisy, leaned against her legs. "Lost sheep?" Joe said. "Will that do? We need a place to hide till mornin'."

Cyrus clicked into gear at once. "Get in here. Go straight through to the hall, out of the light. We'll use the upstairs sitting room. Were you followed?"

"Don't think so," Joe said, hustling Ellie into the passageway with its perpetual smell of lavender wax. "We've been here awhile. I was already driving when I called Spike at Pappy's. We didn't want to give you a heart attack by coming at you outside—in the dark."

"Thanks for that." Cyrus led them from the ground floor, upstairs to the large, comfortable sitting room. He switched on lamps and closed brown velvet drapes over the windows. "Let me look at you, Ellie."

"I'm all right," she said, avoiding his eyes.

"My Jeep is in that old storage shed you don't use for much right now," Joe said. "The one with no roof."

Cyrus hoped he'd missed something and that the law would not come battering down the rectory doors anytime soon. Even if Spike wanted to, he couldn't stand in the way of a superior's order to find Ellie and take her in. "Does Spike know you're here?"

"No," Ellie said. Beads of dried blood decorated welts on her neck and arms and her face was all scraped up. "Spike's got to do things by the book this time. If he knew we were here, he'd pick us up."

Joe guided her to Cyrus's green leather couch and sat her down. He gave Cyrus a meaningful glance. They both figured that whenever Spike absolutely had to talk to Ellie, he'd know to come to the rectory.

"It's not as bad as that," Joe told Ellie. "The thing is, Spike said if he doesn't see Ellie by eight in the morning he'll put out an APB for her."

Cyrus wrinkled his brows. "That would be an All Points Bulletin? Don't they use that for criminals?"

Joe rolled his eyes at him. "It just means everyone—law types, that is—will be on the lookout for her. But she'll go in by then. She just needs time to think some things through first."

"I see." Cyrus didn't really see, but he was used to giving people space if they said they needed it. "I guess if Spike said she didn't have to show up till tomorrow, I don't understand why she wouldn't want to go home."

"I do want to go home." Ellie sprang to her feet with a look in her eyes he hadn't seen before. Anger, tiredness and frustration all bubbled together there. "I can't. That New Orleans detective will show up demanding answers. The first place he'll go is Hungry Eyes, so I can't be there. He's probably on his way there now. If Spike thought I was there, *he'd* be knocking on the door. All I need is some time to think and time isn't something I've got a lot of. Come on, Joe." She pulled his sleeve. "We're compromising Cyrus by being here."

Cyrus smiled and took hold of Ellie by her shoulders. "You're overwrought and puttin' words into my mouth. Sit down again, please. Let me get you something warm to drink. Does coffee keep you up? I want you to just spit everything out and tell me how I can help you. You, too, Joe."

Ellie looked chagrined. Joe's smile was even wider than Cyrus's.

"Coffee would be great," Joe said. "Would you let us spend the night here, please?"

"I could just sleep right here," Ellie added, patting well-worn leather. "I like sleeping on couches. But Joe's had a really bad night so he needs a bed."

Joe and Cyrus laughed together. "And you had a good night," Joe said. "We can see that. When she tried to get away, Penn grabbed her ankles and tried to haul her off. That's how she got cut up all over. Said he just wanted to talk to her. She needs a shower and cool sheets. And something to clean up all those cuts."

Thoughts of what could have happened, what was supposed to happen, turned Cyrus's stomach.

"No," Ellie said. "I don't put people out. I'll pop in the bathroom and use a washcloth, then come back here."

Cyrus saw a battle shaping up.

"I wish Madge was here to help with those cuts," he said. "I don't want you gettin' an infection."

The front door slammed below and footsteps hammered the stairs.

Ellie and Joe looked around as if they wanted to hide. "She's telepathic," Cyrus told them. "That's Madge." And there was that old leap of the heart again. "She's the only one with the front door key. I expect she forgot something. She goes round back to see if this light's on before she comes in. She'll help us out."

He opened the sitting room door and Madge tumbled in with Paul Nelson behind her. Paul couldn't see the comical face Madge made as if to say "It wasn't my idea for him to come."

"Paul writes half the night. He heard me moving around and insisted on driving me over," she said. "I wasn't sneaky enough gettin' out of Rosebank. If Spike ever finds out I figured Ellie would be here and didn't tell him, he'll croak. I hope Vivian doesn't get wind of it, either, because if it's a toss-up between her Spike and any-one else, you know who counts."

"I'd be happy if everyone got involved in what hap-pened to Ellie tonight." Paul's nostrils flared. "If it could happen once, it could happen again. This guy's got to be tracked down fast."

Joe said, "We're all on the same page here. But right now we're trying to get Ellie to take a shower and clean the wounds she has. We won't go into how she got them again now. Do you think you could do something with her, Madge? And maybe find a bed for her."

"Sure can. You stayin', too, Joe?" She paused long enough to make sure he didn't say he was leaving and added, "There's plenty of room here. I'll show you where to sleep. We've got anything you'll need. Then I'll get Ellie into bed."

Madge hustled Ellie and Joe out and Cyrus couldn't help seeing the way the two of them looked at each other.

"Thank you for bringing Madge over," Cyrus said to Paul Nelson. "Can I offer you something?"

"Please. Scotch if you've got it."

"I do," Cyrus said. He took out the bottle and two glasses. Scotch sounded good to him, too. "I'm glad you stopped Madge from coming out alone at this time of night."

"I saw her trying to be invisible on her way out of Rose-bank," Paul said in his pleasant New England accent. "With everything that's going on, I had to step in. Tous-saint is going to be an uptight place until this guy Penn is caught." He sat down and held his glass between his knees with the tips of his fingers.

Cyrus grunted. Paul shook his head. He was one of those solidly muscled men. He had honest blue eyes and thick, curly blond hair.

"How does Ellie seem?" Paul asked. "For what my opinion's worth, I agree she can't be left to her own devices, not until we know the killer's behind bars again."

Cyrus nodded. "We're going to have our work cut out for us convincing her of that, so I'm hoping this is all over real quick."

There didn't seem much else to say. They drank in silence. Cyrus heard the sounds of Madge and her charges moving around and he glanced at Paul Nelson. The other man stared into his Scotch, his forehead rucked. Good-looking, Cyrus decided, and decent. He wondered what Madge thought of Paul.

The writer took major trips for his work, but if he did what he'd promised, he'd be buying a place before long and making Toussaint his permanent home. Once they married, Madge would probably want to continue working...

"Cyrus," Paul said quietly. "Perhaps I should call you Father."

"Cyrus is fine. I don't like formality."

"Thank you. Cyrus, then. I have something big on my mind. I need help deciding what to do. Would you let me talk to you, then give any advice you can?"

Cyrus thought about it. This was the last thing he'd expected from the man. "Yes, of course," he said, and picked up the stole he kept on a table. "How long is it since your last—"

"No," Paul said. "I'm asking for advice, not reconciliation. I'm in a tight spot and I like you. I think you'll say what you think and help me make a decision."

He paused, but Cyrus could tell the man had more to say.

Paul took a deep breath. "It's been years since my last reconciliation, Cyrus. Why *not* do it now?"

Cyrus sat down on the couch. He made an open gesture and said, "I'm glad to be the one you came to."

Paul's discomfort showed in the edgy movements he made. "I'd like to have one special woman in my life."

Breath caught in Cyrus's throat. He nodded and said, "Yes, yes, of course you would. Take your time. Think your way through what you want to say." He wondered what Madge would think of Paul approaching her boss as if he were her father. Best not to dwell on any of that.

Paul put his glass on a table. "Sometimes you know you're wrong but you don't want to stop. I'm involved with two women. They don't know about each other. Anyway, I need to break it off with one of them without hurting her feelings but I don't know how to do it."

8

The door to the sitting room stood open. Madge listened and, when she didn't hear voices, tapped lightly.

She got no response and pushed the door open wider. Cyrus stretched out on the couch with his head resting on one arm. He looked asleep but she tiptoed closer to make sure.

Seeing him vulnerable, his features relaxed, held Madge exactly where she was. An intimate moment, warm, soft. She watched his face. Cyrus helpless—in a way—because he couldn't use that strong, controlled mind of his to make sure she only saw what he wanted her to see.

Her eyes stung. She was an intruder taking advantage of him. More than anything in the world, Madge wished she had a right to touch Cyrus. She flushed. Never, she would never know how it felt to touch his mouth with hers.

With her arms crossed tightly, Madge turned away.

Staying with him, working in this house with him,

gave her the deepest pleasure. They were friends, best friends who trusted each other, but she should go.

She blinked back tears.

"Madge?"

The sound of Cyrus's voice gave her a little jolt. "Yes. I'm sorry I disturbed you." Hoping her emotions didn't show, she turned around. "Ellie and Joe are in the two small rooms. Lily changed the sheets in both of them yesterday. The dog's got a big blanket on the floor. Cyrus, Ellie is covered with scratches and scrapes."

He swung his feet to the floor and leaned forward, head in hands. Two rakes at his hair with his fingers and he looked up at her. "They've got to catch this guy. Ellie won't have any peace till they do. None of us will."

Madge nodded. "It's good she has all of us."

"You know Spike must have figured out Joe would bring her here."

"He didn't have to figure it out, he knew. Where else would someone in trouble go but to you?"

He paused a moment too long before responding. "Thank you for saying that."

Madge remembered Paul. "Where did Paul go?"

To her amazement this was Cyrus's turn to show color in his tanned face. "I didn't know how long you'd be," he said, "so I told him not to wait. I'll drive you to Rosebank myself."

9

The whole point of buying time was to give her a chance, with Joe's help, to decide how much she needed to tell Gautreaux or Spike about her past. Or how little she could get away with telling them.

With Joe in the room facing this one, apparently having forgotten all about her request, Ellie couldn't think what to do next.

Make your own decisions. You always have.

Shock had made her talk to Joe about it in the first place. No way did she want him involved.

Yes, she did, and there was the rub. If Joe knew everything he would withdraw from her. *Don't tell him about that, the totally bizarre stuff, you can avoid it and pray the police don't dig it up.*

She lay in a single bed wearing panties and an oversize white shirt, and she hurt from the damage Charles Penn had inflicted.

A second car's engine turned over beneath the window. She slipped from bed and peeked out. The vehicle that had left about half an hour earlier must have been Paul's. This time Cyrus's landboat pulled out onto Bonanza Alley. He would be taking Madge home.

Daisy snored.

Ellie stepped around her and went into the hallway—and confronted Joe.

"We haven't had that talk," he said.

Panic took hold of Ellie. "I don't want to dump on you. I can deal with this myself."

"Uh-uh," he said. "We didn't go through hoops to get you away from Pappy's just to forget it. Don't try backin' out now, Ellie. Something's scarin' you and I'm not talkin' about Penn."

He spoke sharply enough to sting Ellie. "You're right," she said, feeling foolish. "I'll keep it short, though."

"Your room or mine, ma'am?" he said, and grinned in the shadowy light.

Ellie smiled back and closed her door softly. "Daisy's exhausted. She's asleep. So I guess it's your room."

Joe, looking too good in a tight white T-shirt and striped boxer shorts, pointed to his open door. "After you."

She went in and sat on the floor a little way distant from the bed.

Joe closed the door. "Up with you," he said. "Into the bed. I'll be the one to sit on the floor."

"Nope. You lie on the bed. I'm comfortable where I am." And she was sure she'd feel strange lying there. "No more bossing me around. You're really getting into that."

She hadn't intended to be amusing but let him grin, anyway.

"You're sure you won't take the bed?"

"Absolutely not."

He stripped off a blue chenille bedspread and draped it around her shoulders, then lay down on top of the remaining jumble of sheets.

Joe reclining on a bed, his chin supported by a hand, didn't do much for a woman's concentration.

"You'll have to start," he said.

"Madge will make sure someone gets over to take care of Zipper first thing in the morning."

"Uh-huh. That's a good thing."

"My poor little cat will be all mixed up."

"It'll probably be time for the services of Wazoo, animal shrink extraordinaire." Joe appeared serious but Ellie doubted he was.

"Right," she said, almost under her breath. She tugged the tails of the white shirt over her crossed feet. That left her knees flapping, but she'd look silly if she made a thing of covering up in the bedspread. The room was warm.

She glanced up to find Joe slowly studying her. He almost appeared to be thinking of nothing in particular, but not quite. The look in his eyes while he looked at her legs was too intent. His attention climbed, part by part, over her and came to rest on her breasts. Ellie wanted to cross her arms, but then he'd know she was embarrassed by his attention.

He drew in a slow breath through his nose. His face tensed and he looked into her eyes.

Ellie's stomach flipped. She knew a potent sexual response when she saw it. She would pretend she hadn't noticed a thing—or felt a thing. The open smile she gave Joe didn't ease the tightening between her legs, or deep inside. It didn't stop her nipples from hardening.

"I don't have a conventional past," she told him. Her

voice sounded breathy and strange to her. "I made a couple of really stupid moves. I didn't think they were stupid at the time because I was trying to make bad situations better."

Joe didn't take his eyes from hers. "What kind of mistakes?"

"Running away. I was ten the first time, then fifteen."

"Why did you run away?"

She bowed her head. "All I want is to figure out what will happen if the police get serious about poking around."

"They didn't do it after the Mardi Gras thing?"

"I was a witness on a balcony then. I gave one person's name and address as a personal contact. They checked it out and apparently didn't see any need to spend more time on me."

Joe sat up. "Excuse me, please. Madge picked out the sleepin' duds and this is so tight it's cutting off my circulation." He stripped the T-shirt over his head and threw it to the bottom of the bed before resuming his position. "What makes you think they'll do a more exhaustive background check this time?"

Not staring at Joe's wide, tanned, muscular chest took willpower. Ellie could be happy just looking at him for a long time. Slim hips, long, strong legs. A torso and arms where every muscle was defined and appeared permanently flexed. He had very white teeth and the kind of face she might see in her dreams even if she'd never met him.

"Ellie," he said gently. "Help me out here."

"This time Charles Penn attacked me. He intended to kill me and there's no reason to believe he won't try again. Since I couldn't identify him before, they don't have an obvious motive for him to come after me now. They're going to go looking for any motive they can find. I'm pretty scared about that idea and I have someone who doesn't deserve to be pulled into my mess. He only tried to do his best for me and this could hurt him."

Joe's dark blue eyes nailed her. "Who are you talking about?" He sounded tense.

She didn't want to tell him the truth. "Someone who was good to me when I was a kid. He tried to help me out. For years he was the only one who loved me. He would rock me and wipe away the tears and he wanted, more than anything else, to find a safe place and get us both out of there."

"Why would it hurt him if that came out?" Joe still sounded uptight.

She'd asked his help. Leaving out every single thing that was important would be pointless. "My brother made a good and useful life for himself. An impressive life. His reputation could take a hit if he got connected to me now. Especially if…I won't do that to him."

"You ran away when you were ten," Joe said. "From your parents' home?"

She shook her head. There had never been a reason to put all this into words before. "An uncle and aunt's place. They took us in when my dad left us and my mom got sick. We thought mom would get better and we'd be together again. It wouldn't have mattered where as long as we had each other. I prayed for that every night and in any quiet times I had."

Please God, bring my mom back to us. We'll be really good and take care of her. She's not strong, but we can manage. Please God, let us get out of here. Day after day that had been her mantra. And her brother, Byron, had tried to shield her from Uncle Cal and Aunt Dot, and the four cousins who treated them like servants.

After she ran away Ellie decided to change her name, to help save her from being tracked down. She took Byron's first name as her last name and become Ellie rather than Mellie. That had been a big mistake but, after all, ten-year-olds didn't tend to think far ahead when they were fighting to get a life.

"I'm going to ask you one or two questions you may find offensive," Joe said, shifting so that the meager light from his bedside lamp shone on his hair, and on the hair on his chest. Ellie followed that hair until it disappeared in a thin line beneath the waist of his shorts.

"Okay," he said. "I'll take it you don't mind. Have you ever been arrested?"

"No!"

"Have you ever kept company with people who were in trouble with the law?"

Her heart beat faster. She couldn't be dishonest with Joe. "I probably have. The son of the people in one foster home dealt drugs, I think. He was taken away one night. But I was moved to another place immediately so I don't know any more than that."

Joe's open expression closed down. He sat on the edge of the bed and leaned toward Ellie.

Coldness shuttered everything in his face.

"I was lucky to be taken into foster care," she said hurriedly. She swallowed and wished Joe would stop cracking his knuckles. "Really, I was. I had lots of luck. When I first ran away I was a ten-year-old from the sticks and I didn't stop to think why a man would pick me up at a truck stop in the first place. He was headed south and seemed nice, fatherly, so I thought. When we got to a weigh station, he pulled off and told me to get into the sleeping part, the cab or whatever it's called. I knew he was trying to hide me and I felt frightened because I couldn't figure out why."

"Oh, my God," Joe said. "Tell me what you can."

"Like I told you, I was lucky. He had to get out of the truck, so I got down and jumped out, too. I hid and saw the man go back to the truck. I don't know if he knew I was gone but he drove out of there."

Joe left the bed and knelt on the floor. He took hold of her hands. "None of that was your fault. You were the victim."

"Yes." She squeezed his fingers. Her stomach cinched tight. "I didn't know where I was going. But I remembered a small town back by the last entrance onto the freeway and started walking. Almost the first thing I saw when I got there was a bus station. I slipped on a bus with a family. No one noticed me. Then I got off in Burbank. It was night. I just walked till I found a street where there were people on the sidewalk. Mostly women and teenagers."

Joe held her fingers so tightly, they hurt, but she didn't want him to let go.

"I asked a girl if I could wait with her until I figured out what to do. She looked nicer than the rest—cleaner. She hit me, then a group of them beat me. There were sirens, but I couldn't think about much. The police took me to some sort of agency. It was foster homes after that."

"Ellie," Joe said quietly, and pulled her closer to rest her head on his shoulder. "Have you been more or less on your own since then?"

"Yes. Until I came to Toussaint and found people I want to stay around forever."

She held on to his wrist and turned her face into his neck.

"We all know kids fall out of the system. But the reality—or what you've experienced of it—sickens me. I'm glad you found your way to Toussaint."

He meant it, Ellie could hear that he did. "I ran away again when I was fifteen. The people I was with then were okay, but they didn't treat me like a member of the family and it was awful at school, so I took off. I thought I was smart enough to deal with it then."

"But you weren't." Joe's tone turned flat.

"I had a little bit of money I'd saved and I thought I'd go north. I ended up in San Francisco, living on the street. It was hopeless. My money went fast. I scrounged from garbage cans outside restaurants. Sometimes someone would give me a hot dog or a pretzel. Then a Dumpster diver asked if I wanted to be his partner. He had a bum leg and used crutches—said it was getting hard to work."

Joe gave up trying to restrain himself and took Ellie into his arms. He hugged her, smoothed her back, kissed her brow. And he felt her tighten up, then, slowly, relax against him.

"Ellie," he said. "This must be hard—talking about it all. Try to stay with me till we figure out what you do and don't say."

She put her arms around his body and dug her fingertips into his flesh. "That man seemed kind. He shared any food I got with me. Then he turned on me one night and hit me with a crutch. I'd found a coat and you know how cold San Francisco can get sometimes. When he saw me put it on he went mad. It wasn't mine to take, he said, not unless he said so."

Joe rested his chin on top of Ellie's head. She'd lived through it all, that's what he could hardly believe. His feelings for her had been growing for a long time, but they had taken a forward leap in recent weeks. He wanted Ellie.

"I met Mrs. Clark that night. We were out back of some warehouses and there wasn't a soul around. I never knew why she was driving in a place like that the way she was, but I heard her car stop and the door slam. She said if Willy hit me once more she'd shoot him. I passed out then."

"And woke up?"

"In a new green Mercedes. Mrs. Clark...Alice Clark drove me to her house and took me in."

Joe kept quiet, gave her some space to carry on when she was ready.

"It wasn't foster care. She just kept me."

What did he hear in her voice? Not the kind of gratitude he'd expect if everything had been rosy.

"Did she have a husband?" he asked.

"No."

He cleared his throat. The mention of a Mrs. Clark eased his mind. Ellie was not lying to him. "Did she have kids of her own?" He didn't want to sound as if he was prying, but what choice did he have?

Ellie took far too long to say, "One."

She wanted his help in making a decision. He hadn't figured out why, but he would lay odds that Alice Clark was a big part of the problem. "Ellie, what—"

"A son. He didn't live with her. Not exactly."

"Okay. So what makes you think there's an issue with being honest about all of it?"

Abruptly, Ellie shot to her feet and backed away. "Do

you think Gautreaux will accept how I lived with Mrs. Clark and then went away to school when I was eighteen? I didn't hear from her after that."

Joe stood up. Scratches looked livid against Ellie's too pale skin. He picked up the bedspread and wrapped it around her, then cupped her cheek and jaw.

"That was it," she said, and shuddered. "There isn't anything else to say."

She was too smart to think he'd agree and let it go. "College isn't free. Neither is moving to New Orleans, then here to take over a bookstore."

"How did you know I was in New Orleans?"

Recover from this one, you stupid bastard. "You mentioned it once."

Her expression flickered and she looked away. "I guess I probably did."

"What about the money?"

"Mrs. Clark was generous." Now the floor held her interest.

"There's more, Ellie. Isn't there?"

"I can't say anything else." Her voice rose. She crossed her arms and plucked at the edges of the bedspread. "Just leave it at that. It'll be okay, won't it?"

"You want me to say it will, but I can't. I don't know."

She cried without making a sound.

"Cher, I'm with you. I'll do whatever it takes to help you." He approached her with his arms opened wide and she stepped into them. She huddled close, trembling. "If you've finished all you want to say, I'll back up your story. If something else happened and it gets to be an issue, you'll remind anyone who wants to know that you were a kid who didn't get any luck."

"I did," she said. "I keep telling you. If I hadn't gotten

any luck I wouldn't be here. Thank you for wanting to help me."

"No problem. We've got to go see Spike pretty early. Get some sleep." The thought of sending her away made him one miserable man. She was lonely and he was lonely, too—among other things.

"You're right." Ellie summoned up a smile and ducked around him. She straightened the sheet and blanket on his bed and plumped up his pillow. First she flapped the bedspread in the air, then watched it settle over the bed before she went to work smoothing it out.

A gentleman would stop her, but even a gentleman could be forgiven for forgetting his manners while looking at a pair of pretty legs, and an equally pretty bottom clad in white lace. Lamplight through the shirt did dangerous stuff. When she bent over, it fell away from her body and Joe got a light show of full breasts—swaying softly with each move she made.

If she saw what looking at her had done to him, she might or might not be thrilled. He didn't recall jumping to attention with that much enthusiasm in a long time. He picked up his own shirt from the back of a chair and pulled it on.

He glanced down. Shit, when did a shirt become a skirt? When it hung in frills from the business end of a man's penis. He smiled through gritted teeth and laced his fingers together over the playful part. *It hurt, felt wonderful, but painful.*

"There," Ellie said, turning toward him. "All done."

Not even close, baby. "Thanks," he said. "Will you sleep okay now?" *He wouldn't.*

"You know I didn't tell you everything, don't you, Joe?"

"Yes."

"But you're not going to push for more information?"

"No. I can't do that to you."

She put a hand to her mouth. "If the police decide to go after everything and not quit till they find what they want, I could lose any credibility I have with them."

If he said anything at all, she could clam up. He might be selfish, but if there was something he needed to know about her, he'd better find out now.

Ellie closed her eyes and swayed. "They might find out about a dead man, and then figure out a way to get me mixed up in it."

Joe screwed up his eyes. He breathed slowly through his nose. "Were you mixed up in it?"

"No. Not the way you mean. But you've only got my word for it. There, I've told you. Now you have to decide what you'll do. Whatever you choose will be the right thing and I'll accept it even if…I'll accept it."

A light knock sounded at the door.

Ellie backed all the way to the wall, pulling the shirt as far down as she could.

Joe didn't answer the knock. Oh, no, Cyrus would not be invited in here tonight.

The door opened enough for Cyrus to extend his head until he saw Joe. "I took Madge home," he said.

"Oh, good." *Don't let him look to the right.*

"We talked about a few things. Do you know your sister is seeing Paul Nelson—a lot?"

"Everybody knows," Joe said. Cyrus's appearance had taken care of the skirt situation.

"Except me," Cyrus said loudly, his dark eyes glossy with anger. "You're careless, Joe. I can't say more than that."

10

"Hey, Jilly. Who's serving breakfast at All Tarted Up?"

Jilly and Wazoo had opened up at Hungry Eyes this morning. "Why you wanna know?" Jilly responded, knowing Paul Nelson was only making conversation. "Vivian Devol is filling in for me at my bakery. She loves it and she's certainly had lots of experience. She's got Missy Durand to do all the runnin'. And you're here. So why do you care about my shop?"

Wazoo had only been asked to feed Zipper, but the two of them, with Vivian Devol, had decided to help out in a bigger way. Wazoo worked at Rosebank to pay for her room, but she made her own timetable and loved being there for her friends. Jilly poured freshly made coffee into mugs and Wazoo carried them to early-morning drop-ins at Ellie's shop. Pleased as she was to do some trade for her friend while she was gone, she disliked the feeling that most people were there out of curiosity.

It wasn't that they didn't care about Ellie, but there could be no mistaking the excitement in the air, and on a hot, rain-soaked morning that threatened thunder, it didn't make sense for most folks to be there at all.

Paul got up from a table in the window and sauntered to the counter. He leaned far over and said, "Just talking for talking's sake, sweetheart. The reason I'm here and not at your place is because you're here." He smiled and she remembered why she was falling for this man.

"Thanks," she said, and popped toast out of the toaster. "Sit down where you were, hmm? I'll bring your toast over."

"As long as you're with the toast, that's just fine." He strolled away, glancing back to smile at her, and slid into his chair again. He smoothed the blue-and-white-checkered tablecloth out and Jilly felt his eyes on her all the time.

Wazoo worked with Ellie's sinuous, blue-eyed tabby cat draped over a shoulder. People might scoff at Wazoo's claims about her affinity for animals, but they held good for Zipper, whose eyes—always a little crossed—lost focus whenever Wazoo came near her.

Not one, but two customers browsed the books already. The taller of the two, a man with dark blond hair and almost black eyes, had settled a book on top of a stack and seemed intent on reading the entire thing. Jilly knew the color of his eyes because she'd caught him staring at her and he had not attempted to look away until he was ready.

Lucien, who ran the spa in the square, sat with Cerise, owner of the boutique, also in the square. This should be their busy time—opening and doing the early morning necessities, but they sat drinking coffee and, judging from the expressions on their faces, worrying.

They looked up when Wazoo put pieces of peach pie

in front of them and Lucien, a dark, dramatic man, cleared his throat and said, "When do you expect Ellie to get back?"

"Miz Ellie?" Wazoo said. "She sleepin'. She had a bad night, her."

Doll Hibbs from the Majestic, Toussaint's eight-room hotel, said, "Stuff on the radio 'bout it. That girl gotta be one scared puppy. I say we all gotta git in here and lend a hand. Let her know she's safe because we're keepin' her safe."

Wazoo moved Zipper from one shoulder to the other. "You right, Doll. We gonna keep that Ellie safe."

"You sure she's all right?" Cerise asked. Blue-eyed, blond, and with a perfect figure, Cerise wore clothes that invariably advertised the boutique. "How can we be sure someone can't get at her with all of us down here and her on her own?" Today Cerise wore a black-and-gray silk dress with an asymmetrical hemline, a point on one side almost hitting the ankle strap of one shoe while a similar point barely skimmed the opposite knee.

"She just fine," Wazoo said, and Jilly wished she had been able to stop the careless comment about Ellie being asleep.

The shop bell rang and a stranger walked in bringing the scent of rain and some muggy air with him. Lil Dupre from the rectory was next and Jilly closed her eyes an instant. Lil would only fuel the fire of curiosity. She joined Doll, her good old friend and partner in gossip-mongering, and the two of them put their heads together.

The stranger looked the crowded scene over and asked Paul if he could join him.

Jilly didn't remember the place being so crowded.

"Lil agrees with me," Doll announced, and the chatter went into a lull. "We need to make sure Ellie's never on her own."

Wazoo called out, "*Pain perdu*, Jilly? We got eggs to do that?"

At All Tarted Up, French toast was a specialty. "I brought the bread," Jilly said. "And Ellie's got eggs in the refrigerator."

"Anybody listenin' here?" Doll asked. "Ellie needs someone with her."

"She got that Daisy," Wazoo said without as much as a flicker of regret when she caught Jilly's eye.

"Ellie gets up early," Lil said, sounding petulant. "Never knew her to hole up like this."

"You never knew her to be in this kind of scrape," Cerise said. She put another small forkful of peach pie into her mouth. "She's got a killer after her. Wouldn't you shut yourself away if some crazy with an ice pick had it in mind to put a hole in your head?"

There was a general sucking in of breath. "Shame on you for sayin' a thing like that," Doll told Cerise. "Maybe where you come from, whatever sickly place that is, people appreciate your evil talk."

"Hey," Lucien cut in, smiling but with his arched black brows raised. "There's no need to speak to Cerise that way. What has she ever done to you?"

"Given ideas to a lot of girls in this town," Doll said, a spiteful glint in her eye. "Wrong ideas."

Wazoo began crooning. She held Zipper high in her arms and rocked the cat to and fro. "Don't you cry, little one. It's okay. Wazoo, she understand what you feel. Jest let it all go. Give it up to me."

Jilly, on her way to take Paul a second serving of the toast he favored, prayed Wazoo would cool it, at least until they got rid of the morning's rush of overexcited folks.

"So what is that cat's problem?" Paul asked. He looked up at Jilly and he wasn't smiling. He gave her that look that turned her weak.

"Zipper," Wazoo announced, pushing her wild and shiny black curls behind her shoulders, "has a common-enough condition. She needs all kinds of thoughtfulness from people who care about her. She's got low-member-of-the-pack syndrome. Always tries to work harder and make herself more noticeable because she feel inadequate. Bein' around a big dog like Daisy—and Zipper loves Daisy, mind you—but it make Zipper behave out of character. Notice how she springs up on her toes when she walk? And if things get quiet she flies around all over everythin'? Jest tryin' to make herself taller and git noticed."

When nobody laughed, Jilly was amazed, although she saw more than one mouth pressed firmly shut.

"What can you do about a thing like that?" Homer Devol, Spike's dad, had been eating breakfast, reading the paper and minding his own business—until now. Homer spent most of his spare time with Charlotte, Vivian's mom.

"Give her more responsibility," Wazoo said promptly. "And more praise, and be grateful she's not a male."

Homer, who continued to run the gas station and convenience store he'd operated with Spike until his marriage to Vivian Patin, swung onto the back two legs of his chair. "Feel like tellin' the rest of us why that is? And while you're at it, how do you give a cat more responsibility?"

In one of her long black lace dresses, this one caught at intervals around the hem with a pink flower, Little Bo

Peep style, Wazoo struck a pose with one finger raised in the air. "The male animal with the little-critter syndrome is a real pain in the ass. He can't git his mind off comparin' the size of his parts for long enough to even start dealin' with the other stuff."

"Hey, Wazoo," Cerise said. "Ellie's not here at all, is she?"

Jilly held her breath.

"Cerise," Wazoo said, her face screwed up as if even the question pained her. "Why would you make a suggestion like that? What you tryin' to do, frighten everone? I tol' you Ellie was sleepin' and I meant it."

"She call you and Jilly and ask for help?" Lil said.

"No," Jilly said, preempting Wazoo. "It was Madge who called because Cyrus let her know what happened at Pappy's last night—"

"When Charles Penn tried to kill Ellie in them trees?" Doll said.

"I wouldn't know anything about that," Jilly told her. Paul used the cover of the tablecloth to hide how he caressed the back of her leg. She clamped down inside, willing herself not to react.

"I guess it was on the radio," Homer said, and buried his nose in his paper again. "Let me know when you ready to git to the responsibility bit, Wazoo."

"Why, you leave her food in its bag so she has to figure out how to get at it." Wazoo had that "you shouldn't need to be told" look on her face. "If a cat don't get fed, she'll learn to feed herself soon enough. Teach her how to fetch. There's no reason the dog has to do all the work. Git the cat on a leash and teach her the same commands you teach a dog. Cats are smart. They like havin' a leash and learnin' to heel and sit and lie down when they're told."

A slightly hushed chuckle sounded.

Undeterred, Wazoo said, "You jest wait. No time a'tall you'll see sniffer cats at airports. What makes anyone think they approve of them drugs anymore'n a dog does?"

"Thanks for the explanation," Homer said. He balanced a straw Stetson on one knee and rocked on the back legs of his chair again.

"Another thing," Wazoo said. "Give this cat a cell phone like the big boss got—that's Daisy—and watch her ego puff up." Nobody pointed out that Daisy only got the phone because she played up when Ellie talked on one, and Zipper didn't care about small stuff like that.

"They was havin' some sort of shindig at Pappy's," Lil said as if sniffer cats hadn't interrupted her train of thought. "That whole hoity-toity bunch."

"Hold your horses, Lil," Paul said, laughing. "I was there and you can't call Marc and Reb, or Cyrus and Joe hoity-toity."

"Just a manner of sayin'," Lil said, her eyes expressionless. Year after year her bleached hair covered her head in long, thin, wiggly curls, edge to edge, a bit like an anemic brain on the outside of her skull rather than inside. "If Joe Gable thinks it's a secret that he's moved in over those offices of his to be near to Ellie, he thinks wrong. The furniture went in at night but we know about it. Ozaire knows the men Joe hired to paint the place, too."

"You got it all wrong," Wazoo said. "Joe, he gonna rent out them rooms."

Why is she finding things to lie about? They'll all come back to bite her—and me for not putting things straight. Jilly took two carafes from the hot plates and wove her way through the tables, refilling cups.

When she reached Paul, he said, "This is Jim Wade, Jilly. He's from Washington State only he hasn't told me why. We ought to make him take off his shoes and show us his webbed feet." He laughed.

Jilly did not see the humor in it.

Jim Wade was one of those average men with a pleasant but forgettable face and sandy hair, thinning on top. His neat, beige seersucker suit, cream shirt and brown tie suited him.

"You're right about Washington," he said. "We always say it's like living in a car wash. But we're the Emerald State, remember. Our grass is always green."

"I'm sure it's beautiful," Jilly agreed. "Are you just passing through?"

"More or less," Jim said. He hooked a finger over his shoulder. "I'm staying with the Hibbses at the Majestic. Very nice, too. I'm looking at properties for a client who might want to set up business here."

"What kind of business?" Paul asked promptly.

Jim wrinkled his nose. "I'm not at liberty to discuss my client's business. If he comes you'll know soon enough."

Jilly leaned over the table, supporting her weight on the edge. Without too much subtlety, Paul pressed a folded piece of paper into her palm. She put it into a pocket.

"Oh, that boy done up that place so he can watch over Ellie," Wazoo said. "There's no point keepin' on denyin' it. Joe's a gentleman but he's got the hots for Ellie Byron. Too bad he so damn slow gettin' to the point. Make things a whole lot easier if they slept in the same bed." She gave a magnificent shrug.

A chuckle and titter or two quickly died away. Jilly smiled. She wished Joe and Ellie would get together but hadn't seen much to suggest they would.

"My Ozaire was sayin' he don't think we know the half of what's goin' on around here." Lil pushed out of her chair and made her way to the counter, where she peered straight down into the pastry case, drumming her fingers on the glass at the same time. "Too much coincidence, that's what he say."

Jilly whipped out a plate and slammed open the case. "What can I get you?" She was furious with Lil.

"What kind of coincidence would that be?" Homer said, giving his newspaper a snap. When you looked at the man's rangy body and lean face you knew where Spike got his good looks from.

"Ozaire says we don't know much about Miz Ellie," Lil said. "She come here to work for Connie and Lorna, then she buy them out. But you ever see any family, anyone at all? You know somethin' about where she come from?"

"I don't know where you came from, Lil," Jilly said, seething now.

"Ever'body knows I come from Crowley, got my sisters in Crowley. What you tryin' to suggest, Jilly Gable? We know all about *you.*"

"You bringin' that pastry?" Doll asked. Her face was flushed and she mouthed "sorry" to Jilly. "You got anythin' with marzipan in it? Father Cyrus goes dotty for that stuff. Might as well see what all the fuss is about."

Jilly got a new insight into Doll. She could be a cantankerous soul but she wasn't as mean as billed.

There were several marzipan tarts and Jilly put one on a plate. "The fig turnovers are good," she said to Lil, keeping her voice pleasant. "Young Wally picked the fruit for me yesterday. Good boy, that."

Lil said, "Sounds good to me. They cheaper since you got the fruit free?"

"On the house if you're strapped for cash," Jilly responded. "The figs are from my garden but I've got plenty." She slapped a turnover on a second plate and pushed it across the counter.

Lightning cracked and rolled. The sky had turned purple, and within seconds, thunder bellowed. Rain fell in great splats on the steamed-up windows.

"This is one crazy October," Paul said, peering outside. "Drama, drama, but I like it. You should see Rosebank with the rose hedges dripping. Smells like a perfume factory. When are you going to give up that fabulous room of yours to me, Wazoo?"

"Miz Charlotte and Miz Vivian say those painted ceilings is mine forever if I want. I *do* want." She didn't look at Paul with particular approval. "You already got two rooms. How much more you want?"

"Joking," Paul said, holding up his hands. "Just joking."

He looked at Jilly and she felt giddy. Paul didn't know how to just *look* at a person. His every glance was loaded with sexy suggestion.

"About that coincidence you was talkin' about back there," Homer said. He draped his paper over a raised knee. "What you mean by that, Lil?"

"All right, I'll tell you. Why did she just happen to be in the right spot on the right balcony to see that poor Stephanie Gray murdered? Any of you think about that? Those parades are wild. It's not natural to notice something like that with all those people leapin' around."

"What's that got to do with coincidence?" Homer asked, undaunted.

"Then she reckoned she didn't see who did it."

"She didn't," Jilly said sharply. "That was established."

"What if she only said she didn't? To protect herself."

"That's an old saw people been playing on since it happened," Homer said.

Paul said, "They'd do well to leave it alone. If Ellie says she didn't see this killer, then she didn't see him."

Jim Wade made a food run. He leaned over the counter toward Jilly and said quietly, "Don't give this lot any mind. Sounds like they're fond of your Ellie but you know how people like to gossip. I do a lot of traveling around and I hear everything, I can tell you."

Jilly smiled at him with gratitude and gave him the largest of the egg turnovers he pointed to. He had a kind smile and she liked that.

"Well, I got another thought," Lil said.

I just bet you do. Jilly regretted coming here today. Lil had a reputation for rambling when she had too much on her mind—like she did now. She invariably searched for explanations to make trouble go away, and just as often got in an even worse muddle and made people mad at her.

"I been havin' a lot of thoughts, too," Wazoo said. She arranged a very relaxed Zipper on her cushion in the window. "Most interestin' subject I had recently is Vivian Devol's Boa. That little dog breaks all the rules. She ain't got no small-animal complex. She think—she really believe she one huge critter. Delusions of grander, that's what that one's called. Means she get in a whole heap o' trouble 'cause she don't know her boundaries."

"Would that be grandeur?" Lucien asked mildly. "I know plenty of cases of that."

"That's what I say. You see that pooch around Daisy? Well, if Daisy didn't have an inferiority complex she'd knock that pesky Boa out o' sight. But nope, she jest closes her eyes and lets that upstarty one sit on her head if that's what Boa wants to do. Daisy's one good watchdog but she don't feel deservin' of respect. Probably somethin' t'do with her mama cuttin' her down to size when she was a pup."

Homer made a grumpy noise. "Sounds like that Daisy's terminally mixed up. Must think she's Boa's husband."

Laughter took some time to calm down.

Lil stood with her plate in her hand. She looked at it as if she didn't know where it came from, then plopped it on the table. She didn't sit down. "You all think it's pretty funny to make a fool of me. Well, you'll see and you'll be apologizing for not taking me seriously. That man Penn escapes from jail and what does he do? Does he get the hell out of the area? Nope, goes right to New Orleans, scene of the last crime, and kills another poor soul."

She picked up her coffee and took a deep swallow.

"I heard Ellie wasn't nowhere around Toussaint when this one happened. Doesn't have to mean a thing, but it is a coincidence."

Cerise swiveled in her seat and scowled at Lil. "As in you think Ellie was up in New Orleans helping to murder a stranger."

"How'd you know that woman was a stranger? Maybe Ellie knew her. Maybe Ellie's had to help that criminal to save herself."

"*Lil,*" Homer bellowed. "Sit down and clam up. Now. You oughta be ashamed of yourself, and when Father Cyrus finds out what you been sayin' he's gonna have your hide. You'll be lookin' for work."

"No such thing," Lil said, "I'm independable at the

parish and Father believes in people speakin' their minds. Try this one. If Penn wants to get away, and he's got to unless he's mad, he don't have time to waste hangin' around here. You can say he is mad. We all know that, but he don't want to get caught.

"Anyway, why would he try to get at Ellie when she's said she couldn't identify him? Tryin' to drag her off in the woods when she's got that nasty dog with her."

"Daisy's the best," Lucien said. "You're in never-never land, Lil. Better quit before you make a bigger fool of yourself."

Lil turned red. "You a newcomer," she said. "A year at the most. What do you know? We only got Ellie's word for it that someone went after her in the woods. Either she's got something big to hide and she's lookin' for a way to shift any attention away from her, or she's in with this killer."

"*Lil!*" It was a chorus.

"Well, not a one of us really knows somethin' about her before she come here. I think she seen the killer's face and there's more things she don't say than she do."

"Lil," Jilly said, breathing through her nose and keeping as calm as she could. "My brother is a close friend of Ellie's."

"Noticed that," Lil said, sneering.

"That's all he is, a friend. They like each other and spend time together. If there was more, they wouldn't be devious about it. But if you've got questions, take them straight to Joe or Ellie, or better yet, to both of them. In the meantime, stop spreading rumors. Rumors can get bent into a kind of truth. Ellie doesn't deserve that."

"Rumors?" Lil puffed up her chest. "I don't know from rumors, but just days ago she was gazin' at nothin' and when she realized I was there, she said, "You can forget anythin' you want to forget." Just like that. Nothing else. But what do you think she was talkin' about if it wasn't Charles Penn's face. I'm tellin' you he figures she could identify him if she wanted to and he's goin' to make sure that don't happen."

In the following seconds, the place felt like a tinder box about to ignite.

"I don't agree with you," Paul said, his voice even. "What's to say the man who went after Ellie isn't a stranger? Happens all the time. He was hanging around and happened to see her. Seems much more likely to me. And since we're talking a lot about coincidence, it's very likely the timing of this guy showing up in Toussaint was a coincidence. I think the less we dwell on it all, the better."

"You and that tongue of yours can do a lot of harm, Lil Dupre," Homer said. He spoke softly and everyone kept quiet. "Listen to you. You don't know what you're talkin' about but you're makin' accusations. This isn't the first time you've mixed things up and made a mess because you're a busybody who wants to be important. You don't even know what you think about things yourself, but you keep on yackin'. Contradictin' yourself and yackin'."

He picked up his newspaper once more, but a pale line remained around his compressed lips.

"Excuse me." The tall man with black eyes emerged from the stacks and put a book on the counter. *Pressing Flowers.* "My mother enjoys flower pressing. Her birthday is coming up."

"Nice," Jilly said. She looked at the man's face, all angles put together in a way guaranteed to get attention. And his eyes. The eyes sent a shiver right down her back.

If he wasn't looking not just at her face, but inside her head, she'd eat her favorite straw hat.

He took a credit card from his wallet and tapped the corner of it on the counter. Jilly rang up the book, put it in a pretty bag and set it in front of him. The man signed his charge slip and tucked his package under his arm. He said, "Would you mind going up and letting Ellie Byron know I'm here?"

Jilly felt blank and she knew she looked blank.

"She sleepin'," Wazoo trilled.

"She'll want to talk to me," the man said. He had a long, loose-limbed frame and rested his weight on one leg, on one of his scuffed boots, to be precise. "Just pop up and give her my card." He took one of these from his pocket and handed it over.

Jilly read and wished she were anywhere but here. She also wished Wazoo hadn't told lies and that Lil Dupre had kept her analysis to herself.

"This is official business," the man said. "I'm sure it'll be all right if I go through and knock on her door."

Wazoo gave a little squeal.

Paul came to the rescue. "Can I help you, sir?"

"I never said she was sleepin' *here*," Wazoo said in a rush. "She wasn't feelin' so good after what happened last night so she went…"

"She went where?" The guy's irritation showed.

"Um—" Wazoo looked around, obviously searching for someone to bail her out.

"We just know she was too upset to come back here," Lucien said.

Cerise's eyes were wide. "That's it," she said.

Later, Jilly thought, she would thank them both for thinking quickly.

"Earlier you two were suggestin' she wasn't here," the man pointed out. "Lyin' to the police might not be smart."

Homer picked up his mug and said, "Is there somethin' real important you want to say to Ellie? I don't think I heard you introduce yourself."

"Guy Gautreaux. Homicide detective. NOPD."

Spike's official digs had supposedly been spiffed up the previous year. Joe rubbed the pads of his fingers over the scarred metal desk where he sat with Ellie. The latest coat of paint on the desk was a muddy beige, but sharp objects had achieved a pattern of initials, obscenities and general graffiti that was mostly green from the prior paint job and even dark brown from the one before that.

"I don't like it here," Ellie whispered. "Spike doesn't work in here, does he?"

"Nope," Joe said. "This is an interrogation room."

"Oh!" Ellie's fingers went to her mouth. "Can we just wait in the hall? Spike said eight and now it's after nine."

"This town needs a big-enough force to do the work—Spike gets a much bigger caseload than anyone would imagine. But the department's not going to get more money spent on it so Spike will keep on going without complaining. Obviously he's been called out on something. I know he'll be here as soon as he can."

Their foam cups of bad coffee were empty and they'd

each valiantly eaten one of the stale powdered doughnuts for which the Toussaint Sheriff's Department was famous.

Ellie stood up. She put her napkin inside her cup and gathered up Joe's. "I'll just wander out and get rid of these. Then I'll ask Lori when she thinks Spike will be back."

"Not a good idea," Joe said gently, and took the cups from her hands. "Best work on being calm and relaxed."

Drawing her shoulders up to her ears, Ellie frowned at him. He noticed that she took sharp breaths. Not much hope of getting her to calm down. "Cher," he said. "I hate what you're going through, but I'm not sorry for what time we had together last night. This is absolutely the wrong moment but I'm famous for that. I want us to be together again, Ellie. I want to make love to you next time—and soon."

Tears ran silently from the corners of her eyes. *Stunned* might describe the way she looked, but *shocked* might be just as good. *Hoo-mama*, when it came to women he managed to say the wrong thing at the wrong time. Little wonder he had never had a successful relationship for long. Hell, he'd never had what he expected of a successful relationship, and odds were that his communication skills matched his timing.

He got up but didn't attempt to touch her. "I'm sorry, Ellie. Don't cry. I shouldn't have blurted that out."

With no warning she all but fell against him and wrapped her arms around his waist. He felt her shudder.

"Hey, hey, pretty lady, what's goin' on? I guess I put my foot in it when I came on to you like that? Didn't I? Help me here, cher."

"I told you a lot of bad stuff but you don't hate me. Joe, I never knew anyone who didn't drop out of the picture if something got bad—not anyone but Byron, and now you."

He hesitated an instant then held her firmly against him. He used a thumb to raise her chin. Her lips parted. This was one beautiful woman, and anyone who was fooled by the loose clothing and simple makeup into thinking she was plain, dull or whatever, was every kind of a fool.

So what if Spike walked in on them kissing, Spike or anyone else? Joe looked into her eyes and bent gradually closer to her face. Her fingertips dug at him, but they only made him want her more. She drove him wild. The line had been crossed somewhere in the last days and he doubted he could go back to being good old Joe, good friend Joe.

Ellie's soft, warm breath met his lips and he couldn't stop them from parting. By the time he settled his mouth on hers, his eyes had closed. He didn't need his eyes to see Ellie; he'd had a lot of time to print the way she looked on his mind. Learning how she felt was a new skill, but he figured he could pick it up.

She made a little sound. Joe kissed her soft and long and without demanding anything but a chance to get close to her. Ellie left the moves to him. She did slip her arms up between them and hold his face in trembling hands.

A new sensation gripped him, as if his heart expanded and his gut fell. Goose bumps shot up his back and arousal, sudden and powerful, took his breath away.

Panting, Ellie took her lips from his and stepped back. She didn't release her hold on him. Her lips were pale and her cheeks flushed. She moved her fingertips over his face as if she were making sure she'd always remember the way he looked.

Joe knew better than to crowd her with questions—
or with moves.

"I like Deputy Lori," she said, rubbing her palms over
his chest. "I'm glad she decided to stay here."

"Uh-huh."

"It's cute she's having a baby. She says she is absolutely
coming back to work afterward. Folks respect Spike. They
want to stick around him and support him."

Joe looked at the high, grayish ceiling with its decora-
tive spattering of spit wads. He no longer cared if Spike was
late.

He didn't get to enjoy the sensation for long. The door
opened and Spike, with a large paper bag in each hand,
shouldered his way in. "Emergency rations," he said. The
shoulders of his starched khaki uniform were wet. He
took off his straw Stetson and water ran from the brim to
drip on worn green linoleum. "I hope I'm wrong, but I
feel somethin' really bad in the weather."

"Old joints achin'?" Joe asked him, with his most disarming smile.

"F… Your mouth needs fixin' and maybe I'm the one
to do it." Spike reached for Joe.

"Nah," Joe said. "Just pulling your leg." He ducked
Spike's playful swipe.

"Homer just dropped the food by when I was drivin'
in. Charlotte sent it from Rosebank."

"That's nice," Ellie said.

Still they didn't separate and Spike finally looked at
them. As quickly, he looked away.

Joe wrinkled his nose at Ellie and they moved reluc-
tantly to stand side by side. "Did you say *Charlotte* sent
those?" Joe asked. "You mean Charlotte Patin knows
we're here—and Homer, too? I thought we were going to

keep this as quiet as we could—just between the few of us involved last night."

"No one but Cyrus knows this is exactly where we are." Spike shrugged. "Which means Madge does, too. Homer had been to your place earlier, Ellie. The idea may have been to keep what's goin' on tight to our chests, but we all know what a hopeless deal that is in Toussaint."

"So he told you Hungry Eyes is closed and you told him where I—"

"You're not listening, Ellie," Spike said, tearing open the paper bags to show off an array of goodies. "I didn't tell anybody anything. A rundown of what went on at Pappy's was on the radio this morning. And in the papers. And what makes you think you could keep this all quiet, anyway? Do you know how many reporters have been sniffin' around this town all mornin'? A lot. But they don't know where you are. We'll keep it that way till somethin' bigger comes along to distract them."

He selected something that looked like a minimountain covered with coconut flakes. "Homer's getting some decent coffee. He'll be along."

Joe sensed black clouds gathering on the horizon. He'd never known Ellie to lose her temper or even to raise her voice much, but from the way she flattened her mouth he figured things were about to change.

And Spike, usually so tuned in to what people might have on their minds, didn't feel a thing. He charged straight ahead. "Hungry Eyes is open. Jilly and Wazoo opened it. Madge mentioned she was off to take care of Zipper, and Wazoo begged to go instead."

Ellie crossed her arms tightly. Her bright blue eyes weren't soft anymore.

"Anyhow, Jilly volunteered to go open up the café. They've sold some books as well, accordin' to Homer. Vivian's doin' the duty at All Tarted Up. She… Is there a problem, Ellie?"

"Meddling," she muttered.

The glaring overhead lights hit Spike square in the face and he screwed up his eyes to look at her. "Come again."

"Meddling," she said, a whole lot louder this time. Joe saw her start to shiver. "There's nothing to get uptight about. Not as long as I let you all do what you've wanted from the start. You want to be in charge. Not just you, Spike, but everybody."

Spike filled his lungs and let the air out real slow.

Joe felt how tight Ellie was strung and feared she could break down. It wasn't all about anger, there was fear in there and he was best able to know why. Too much talk was the last thing she wanted or needed.

"I shouldn't have said that." Ellie tipped up her face and blinked quickly.

Joe put an arm around her shoulders. He put his mouth to her ear and to hell with what Spike thought. "They can gab and interfere all they like but I want you to remember two things. First, they only want your happiness. Second, they don't know one thing you talked to me about last night."

She lowered her eyelashes and said, "No," almost under her breath. "Thank you, Joe."

"We do have a hummer of a problem coming our way," Spike said, running his fingers through straight, sun-streaked hair with a mind to stick up in front. "Gautreaux got to me on the mobile. He'd been to Hungry Eyes and found out Ellie was somewhere around but not there. He went to St. Cécile's. Cyrus said you'd slept there, Ellie, but you'd left."

"Amazin' how many ways Cyrus can find to skirt the truth without tellin' a real lie," Joe commented.

"Nobody better ever say something bad about Cyrus," Ellie said. "He's got the steadiest head in this town."

Joe and Spike looked at each other. "We know. Don't worry, Cyrus has a hand in most things around here," Joe said.

Spike raised his brows but said, "No use denyin' it. That isn't the only thing on Gautreaux's mind. He's got it fixed in his head that Ellie's keeping things to herself."

Ellie swiveled until her face was invisible to both of them. "How come he gets to come here and make demands? This isn't his turf."

"The murder was commited in New Orleans," Spike said. "That makes it their case. We'll do everything we can to help. What's happening here is obviously tied to what's happening there, so we have to cooperate."

"Cooperate?" Ellie looked back at him. "Does that mean you'll allow him to walk over me, and *you*, and everyone else around here? I wasn't in New Orleans when the murder happened on Royal Street, even if Gautreaux did try to suggest I might have been. He doesn't have a right to push me around, darn it!" She breathed harshly through parted lips.

"It's okay," Joe said to her. "You know how homicide detectives are."

Spike rolled his eyes, letting Joe know he wouldn't be collecting any subtlety prizes. "He's just doin' his job and he knows you didn't play any part in the crime," Spike said.

"Leave it," Ellie said, and without warning she stumbled, caught herself against the wall and stayed there with her forehead on her arm. "Just forget it."

"Has she seen Reb?" Spike said, and Joe could hear the concern in his voice. "She should have been checked over by now. You got scratches all over you, Ellie? Like the ones on your neck and face?"

She wasn't moving. Joe risked rejection and leaned a shoulder on the wall beside her. "We need to get you to Reb."

"I'm not going anywhere."

"Why?" Joe and Spike asked in chorus.

Ellie looked over her shoulder at them and Joe swallowed hard. He hadn't been prepared for the haunted face she showed. "Someone's trying to get me. He tried to get me last night. He knew I was out there at Pappy's. What's to say he doesn't know I'm here right now. And he's waiting, just waiting for a moment when he can get at me again—and make a better job of it this time."

"Charles Penn?" Spike said.

"Or whoever. How often do we know the whole story?" She connected with Joe's gaze and didn't try to look away this time. Her curly hair stuck to her forehead. "Things come along to shock your socks off all the time. People aren't what they seem to be. I never said I could identify Penn and I can't now."

This woman he cared for—maybe too much to be good for him—felt deep fear. Again and again she spoke in a way that made him think she was denying something. *Had* she seen Penn then chosen to say she hadn't?

"You didn't see him clearly last—"

"*No.*" She cut Spike off. "I didn't even try to see him because I didn't want to. And don't you glare at me just because I can't give you what you want. I was dealing with my life, not yours."

Spike sat on the old table. "I am not glarin' at you, Ellie Byron. Maybe there are times when someone else's expression doesn't have one thing to do with you." He pinched the bridge of his nose. "Well, it did have somethin' to do with you but not because I'm mad you tried to be careful. I'm just gettin' worked up over dealin' with faceless creeps. I need some idea what this man looks like."

"Getting Penn's glamour shot is easy enough," Joe said.

"Thank you for reminding me of that," Spike said, sarcasm dripping. "There's something about the way you talk about this, Ellie. Do you think…ah, forget it."

"Do I think what?" she said. "That we're definitely dealing with Charles Penn? I don't know, but then, I made it pretty clear I wasn't sure they had the right man when they arrested him. They wanted someone to put away and he drew the short straw."

"You believe that?" Joe said. He felt sick. If she was right, the wrong man could have been locked up and that happened too often. "Ellie, do you?"

She looked everywhere but at him. "I guess not."

"That's not good enough, dammit."

One loud knock announced Homer carrying a big carafe of coffee and some mugs. Spike's little girl, Wendy, followed her granddaddy. She had little containers of cream tucked the length of the arm she held against her body, and a fistful of sugar packets. It didn't take but a moment for the seven-year-old to feel the grown-up and irritable vibes in the room.

She waved shyly and backed to the door. "I'm going

out to help Lori," she said. "Where's Daisy?" Wendy was crazy over Daisy and spent a lot of time at Hungry Eyes with the dog.

"She's visiting with Father Cyrus," Ellie said. "I'll make sure you get to see her very soon."

As thin as she'd always been, Wendy had grown taller and her braids were lost to a silky, tow-colored bob. Joe thought she grew even prettier with passing time.

"Thank you," she said to Ellie with a little dip. Then she looked at her father, rushed to him and gave him a big hug. "See you later, Daddy. Vivian's cookin' a special supper."

Puzzled, Spike frowned.

Wendy kissed her granddaddy and ran from the room.

The beaten-up black phone on one corner of the desk rang and Spike picked it up. He heard Gautreaux's voice and the man was pissed. "Know where she is yet?"

Spike put a little distance between himself and the rest. "Here." Gautreaux was an odd bird. Too intense for a man who'd been in Homicide as long as he had.

"I'm on my way," he said.

"Hold it," Spike said, "Better give me—"

"I can't." Spike heard the cop's shallow breathing. "If she tries to get away, arrest her for something. Obstruction of justice would do."

Spike rolled his eyes.

"I've got to sit down." Ellie spoke clearly but didn't sound herself.

Women were wonderful, Spike thought, they were also crazy-making. "I've got your number, Guy. Everything's cool—no problems at all. Let me call you when the time's right. Okay?"

"It'll have to be, I guess." Gautreaux hung up without another word.

Ellie turned a blank face toward him. "He knows," she said faintly.

No one responded.

Spike exchanged looks with Joe. Yeah, to Joe this wasn't a simple case of helping a friend who was in a tight spot. He had a whole lot more invested here. Strange how it had taken this mess to make the situation between Joe and Ellie clear.

Joe put an arm around her waist. "What do you mean, he knows?"

"I'm going to be sick," she murmured with a hand over her mouth. Spike could see how she sweated.

"Let's get you to the bathroom and have Lori give you a place to lie down," Joe said. "We'll be back," he said, but didn't sound too sure. He half carried Ellie from the room.

"I'll go check on Wendy," Homer said, showing his old discomfort with emotional tension.

Spike nodded and turned away to stare at the wall. He heard the door close behind his father.

Who knew what?

"I'll be out here waiting," Joe said through the door of the only women's bathroom. He expected Ellie to tell him to go away but she didn't. "Would you rather have Lori here?"

Not a sound.

Fine. He didn't want to leave her, anyway.

"You okay, cher?"

Ellie didn't answer him.

Joe knocked on the door and said, "Ellie?" He looked down at the crack beneath the door. At least she'd put the light on. She wasn't up to the pressure.

A sliver of her long skirt had slid under the door.

"Ellie!" He dropped to his knees, trying to see more. "Open the door, Ellie." She had to be sitting—or lying—on the floor.

Heart pounding, Joe leaped to his feet and yanked at the handle. It gave and opened…and thudded against Ellie. She moaned. He saw how she half reclined against the wall with her head bowed.

He needed to push himself through the narrow opening and climb over her.

Deserted in both directions, the corridor ran behind the front offices. The only one likely to come back here was Lori.

"Ellie," he said. "Please say something, Ellie." Without waiting, Joe grasped the top of the door, slapped the bottom of a foot against the jamb so the door wouldn't swing shut and mangle his hands, and stretched his other leg over Ellie's head until his foot landed against the sink.

Either he got himself all the way over, or he'd do himself an injury.

Everything depended on the strength in his trailing leg. Working his foot higher up the jamb, he judged the moment when he had most leverage and threw himself sideways.

"*Shit.*" His second foot connected, but his balance wobbled on the edge of the sink. He would fall on her. "Ellie, move!" Just words.

His right shoe slipped along the edge and shot into the air.

He kept on going—until impact jarred his leg, pieces of fractured toilet seat shot up and he landed in the fetal position around the pedestal.

For a few seconds he held still, waiting to feel or see blood. His ankles moved just fine. "Get up, dammit." There would be plenty of bruises.

A sheen of sweat filmed Ellie's face and her hair clung, wet, all over her head. On his hands and knees, Joe scooted close to her and heard her shallow breathing. He grabbed a paper towel, soaked it under the faucet and sponged her face, her neck.

She looked at him.

"Good. That's right, cher. I've got to get you out of here." And get medical attention. "Can you help me? Put your arms around my neck."

Either she couldn't hear him, or she didn't understand. She continued to stare at him.

"Yeah," he said to himself. "Here we go, then." Hampered by the small space, he hauled her up and threw open the door.

Ellie planted her feet but clutched a handful of his shirt.

Relief weakened Joe's knees. "You feelin' better? Thank God. You fainted in there."

All he got was a silent stare. Tears coursed down her cheeks. She trembled, and when he put his hand over hers, she felt icy. "You're ill," he told her. "You need to lie down. C'mon, I'll carry you."

"I can't prove I didn't see a face and remember it."

Joe didn't move a muscle. He watched Ellie and he'd swear whatever she saw, it wasn't him.

"Sometimes it's an oval, no color, no features. Sometimes I see the mouth, or blood on the face. I've never seen eyes. But maybe his face was painted blue and gold and he wore feathers on his head."

He held her. "You mean you see the person who killed Stephanie Gray?"

"What are you talking about?" Ellie shook him off. "Of course I don't."

"You just said you did." He couldn't think what else she might have meant.

Her expression changed. She looked behind her then back at Joe. "No, you misunderstood. I was just mentioning a dream."

12

"Guy Gautreaux worked on the Stephanie Gray case, too," Spike said, talking to Joe while they came into the room. Ellie sat, cross-legged, on Joe's new couch.

Zipper looked at her from a distance, cross-eyed, bristling, and definitely bearing a grudge for being abandoned.

"That explains the man's crappy attitude," Joe said. "Poor bastard."

"It's business as usual for him, remember." Spike, still in uniform despite the late hour, approached Ellie. "How you feelin'? Joe said you slept all day."

She had showered, put on the clean pants and a shirt Joe went with her to get from her own place and didn't remember falling asleep on the couch. "I'm human again," she told Spike. "All I needed was a lot of sleep, but I'm sorry for making a nuisance of myself this morning. I feel such a fool."

"Do you want me to make a list of what's happened to you in the last couple of days?" Spike tapped the top of her head with a knuckle. "You've taken a beating in there, and just about everywhere else. What did Reb say?"

"I'll survive," Ellie told him. She didn't say how Reb had suggested some therapy to help deal with anxiety. No shrink would be poking about in things she'd rather keep private.

Joe eased down beside her on the couch. "Reb said Ellie's exhausted. She needs to keep her life as normal as possible."

"Which means I'll be back at work in the morning. I don't think anything's going to happen to me with people around."

The two men looked at each other in a way that irritated Ellie. A "we know something she doesn't know and now we've got to figure out a way to break it to her" look.

"Wazoo asked Vivian if she could come over and help you out for a bit," Spike said. "Vivian thinks that's just fine. The real busy time's over at Rosebank and Homer's always looking for excuses to leave Ozaire Dupre in charge for an hour or two and run around behind Charlotte. And be around Wendy as much as possible. He'll pop in to see if anything needs doin'."

Homer Devol and Charlotte Patin were the kind of unlikely friends who made you smile. Homer treated Charlotte with old-world deference while Charlotte pretended she didn't care if Homer was around or not. She cared very much. They enjoyed each other.

Ellie considered the idea of Wazoo being around every day. "Wazoo's got her psychiatric work to consider."

"*Get on*," Joe said. "You know folks only play along with that game to be kind to Wazoo."

"Darn you, Joe Gable," Ellie said, getting to her feet. "If you haven't seen Wazoo deal with an ornery critter you don't have any reason to have an opinion. She's the only one who can make that—that—" She pointed at Zipper. "Look at her. If she crosses her eyes much farther they'll turn backward. She's so mad she can taste it, and all because I wasn't there when I was supposed to be. Wazoo can soften Zipper up in no time. *I* can't."

Men were predictable. Spike tapped his nose with his hat, but Ellie wasn't fooled, he was hiding a great big grin.

"I haven't seen that," Joe said with a straight face that looked real. "I didn't intend to be mean."

Ellie marched toward Zipper, who got up, turned her back and sat down again. "That's enough from you. Who pays your bills? Huh? You'd better not forget it." She picked the cat up and held its rigid body against her while Zipper stretched her head and neck as far as possible from her boss.

Spike looked at his watch. "This has been a long day. I hope Gautreaux gets here soon."

"He's coming *here*?" Ellie felt like a nasty kid, but she didn't intend to talk with that man anytime soon. "I'm going home."

"No you're not," Spike said. "I've put the man off all day. He's been holed up in that interrogation room, working on the phone and with his laptop. You owe him for bein' reasonable, Ellie."

"He's going to ask me questions." Panic gripped her. "You said this was all just a courtesy so we don't have to do it if we don't want to."

"Believe it or not, he's doing his damnedest to deal with this in whatever way is easiest for you. My boss has already told me he'd agree if Gautreaux wanted to take you in."

"Take her in where?" Joe got closer to Spike than made Ellie comfortable. "Just what are you talkin' about?"

"It's not going to happen because Ellie's going to co-operate and be nice. You are, aren't you?"

This sterile room with its white walls and ceiling, brown leather couch, new rugs—in beige—and huge flat-screen TV, didn't give Ellie any warm, cozy feelings. But she did feel comforted, being there with Joe. If she'd been less tired she might have felt other things, too, but now she longed for her own familiar apartment.

Perhaps it wouldn't be such a bad idea if Joe slept in the spare apartment. It was really comfortable.

She must not give in or all the fighting would have been for nothing.

"You *are* going to cooperate?" Spike repeated and she jumped. She had never heard him speak like that before.

"Sorry," he said, waving a hand in front of his face. "Everything's going to be fine." To Joe he said, "I can't lie to you. I'm saying the obvious. We've got a killer on the loose, a very dangerous man. As much as Ellie hates it, she's connected to him."

"I am *not*, Spike."

Spike gave her a wry smile. "Okay, whatever makes you feel best. But if Gautreaux makes the request, you'll have to go in to New Orleans for questioning."

"That won't happen," Joe said. He took Zipper from her arms and set the cat down. With his wrists on her shoulders and his head bowed until their foreheads almost met, he rocked her a little. "You can do this and you can do it here. And remember, if the detective tries anything different I'll be right beside you."

"Yes," she whispered, and wished they were alone. "I'll do everything right."

"I know you will." He turned aside, listening. "Someone's driving down the lane. Engine's missing."

Spike cleared his throat. "That'll be Father Cyrus bringin' back Daisy."

At Daisy's name, Zipper virtually rose to stand on her claws and thrust her head forward.

A few minutes passed before Daisy galloped up the stairs from the back of the building. She slurped at Ellie's hands then went directly into a tight huddle with Zipper.

"Anybody home?" Cyrus called. "Can you receive visitors?"

"Surely," Joe said.

At the doorway, Cyrus stood back to let Madge walk in first. Raindrops clung to her hair and eyelashes, and the shoulders of her red jacket were wet.

"Hey," she said, smiling all around. "You're lucky I worked late. I reckon Cyrus was fixin' to keep Daisy another night. I made him do the right thing."

Cyrus laughed. He stood beside her, looking down into her upturned face, and Ellie caught her breath. They made a handsome couple, and for an instant before they turned from each other, only a fool would have missed how their smiles faded and the brief look that passed between them was more of a caress.

"Gautreaux worked on the Gray case, too," Joe told Cyrus, rushing the words out. "That's one tough job he's got."

"He told you that?"

"No," Spike replied. "I've still got a contact or two at NOPD. That's where I got it."

Ellie thought about what Spike and Cyrus said. "I didn't meet the detective until he came here," she said.

"He just wasn't one of the people who dealt with you the first time," Spike said.

"Why can't this be over?" Ellie said, not expecting any answers.

Cyrus took hold of her hand and patted it. "We all wish it was over, too. A lot of people care about you."

"I think that man Penn would be too scared to stay around here now," Madge said. "He's long gone. I still can't figure why he came after Ellie."

"Two reasons." Guy Gautreaux spoke as he climbed the last few steps in the darkened stairwell. "One, if Ellie really didn't see him on Bourbon Street that evening, he wanted her to help clear him. Two, if she looked at him and he saw recognition, he planned to kill her because he's a sicko and he can't stand the idea that somehow he messed up."

"I didn't hear your car," Joe said.

"I came from the station on foot. Walking helps me think."

"I'm sorry you've had to go through both of these murders," Ellie said, and meant every word—until she realized her mistake.

"How would you know about that?" He shifted his weight from one leg to the other. "We didn't meet before I came to Toussaint." His black eyes couldn't be more hostile.

"I told them," Spike said. "I want them to understand that if you seem tough and pushy it's because—"

"Thank you," Gautreaux said. He didn't sound grateful. "The woman who died on Royal Street was Billie Knight. She was twenty-nine and lived not far from Jackson Square. Troubleshooter for some computer outfit."

"Did she have a family?" Ellie asked quietly.

Gautreaux stared at her hard. "No family. No husband. She made fair money but not so much for someone who was going it alone. Tilton—Xavier Tilton, the guy who owns the jewelry shop—said she went in there regularly and looked around. Each time she asked if she could see the same ring and he said she was so soft-spoken and gentle, he'd just let her put it on her finger and look at it. He figured she'd never buy it, but he liked to see her smile. She was a very pretty woman."

Ellie cried quietly and heard Madge sniff and swallow.

"I'm not supposed to give a damn about any of it anymore, but it can hurt. I want this bastard. With a bullet in him or any other way I find to stop him."

Spike shifted. A significant glance passed between him and the detective.

Ellie looked at her watch. "Anyone mind if we watch the news? Just in case anything else has come up."

Everyone but Spike and Gautreaux sat on the carpet and Joe retrieved the remote from beneath the couch. He moved through channels and stopped when a red "alert" sign flashed on the screen.

"Let's get a New Orleans channel," Cyrus suggested.

"Just a sec." Joe protected his custody of the remote as any red-blooded man would.

"Late-breaking news in a New Orleans murder case," a national announcer said, and went on to give all the details Ellie wished she could forget. "Tonight a tip came in from someone who said he'd figured out a connection between the two deaths."

"Fuck it," Gautreaux said, the words explosive. "If I find the little bastard who couldn't wait to leak this to reporters…I will find him."

"Sonja Elliot, multi-bestselling author of the Garvey Jump thrillers, wrote *Death at Mardis Gras*, a book released almost two years ago about a woman who died during Mardi Gras. Another Garvey Jump title—Garvey Jump is the psychotic killer who is pursued in each book by Elliot's female sleuth—*Death in Diamonds,* went on sale early in the summer. In this story, a woman dies and falls into a display case of diamond jewelry. The New Orleans murders of Stephanie Gray and Billie Knight are carbon copies of the crimes in these two Sonja Elliot novels.

"Miss Elliot, famous for her extravagant lifestyle, lives mostly outside the United States, and has yet to be reached."

"You can turn it off," Gautreaux said. "They've covered it. I knew we wouldn't have long before that little gem blew up all over the country, but even a few more hours could have been useful."

He offered Ellie a hand up. "Let's talk."

"Is it okay if I sit where I am?" She didn't want him to touch her.

Madge and Cyrus said their goodbyes and left the apartment.

"You can call me Guy," Gautreaux said, surprising Ellie. "Are you comfortable talking to me here with Spike and Joe present, or is there someone else you think should be here?"

She shook her head.

"You don't think Charles Penn is guilty, do you?" He didn't waste time sashaying to the point.

"I don't know. I said that before. I don't have any way to be sure, that's all."

"You know Penn has a rap sheet that doesn't quit? He belongs in jail, anyway. For a long time."

She shook her head and felt dumb. Joe sat close beside her on the rug and he carefully took hold of her ankle in strong fingers.

"Assault. Theft. Rape times four. Attempted kidnapping. More theft. Disorderly conduct. Beating a prostitute he was pimping for—he did that a lot but the girls always said he didn't, they were that scared of him." He paused, rocking onto the toes of those well-worn boots, and made it too tough for Ellie to look away from his eyes. "I think he's our guy, and I want to be the one to bring him in."

In the strained silence that followed, Ellie wished she could wipe the slate clean, go back and never stay in that hotel on Bourbon Street, never go out on the balcony.

"I say we call it a night," Guy said shortly. "It's too late to start now." He strode away and his boots thudded on the floors. "Forget anythin' I said about you needin' an alibi. I was blowin' smoke. Don't try readin' yourself to sleep with scary stories, Ellie."

"He's a weird one," Joe said when the outer door banged. "I swear there's something over the top about him."

"Been in Homicide too long," Spike said. "Wears every one of 'em down in time."

Daisy chose that moment to get up and bound around the room in circles.

"Does she need to go out?" Joe asked, just as the dog flopped down on her side again and Zipper took a flying leap to land on her buddy's belly and curl up. "I guess I have my answer. I'd better see about some supper for all of us."

"Oh, my…stupid memory." Spike spat those words out. "Supper. A special supper. Vivian's making me—" he checked the time "—made me a special supper. We were all supposed to eat together."

He ran from the room and took so many stairs at a time it was a miracle he didn't kill himself.

13

"I'm glad you could come with me to take Daisy back."

"Me, too," Madge said.

She and Cyrus stood on the gravel parking strip near the rectory.

"I'll follow you to Rosebank," Cyrus said. "See you safely home." He'd have liked to ask her to have coffee but it was late.

Madge caught the shine in his eyes as he looked toward the sky. "I won't let you do any such thing, Cyrus Payne. I've got a good car and a good cell phone. And the rain's stopped so I'll see just fine. But thank you."

"I'm still going to see you home." He disliked thinking of her driving those deserted roads alone—more so with a killer unaccounted for.

"And then I'll have to see you home because that old beater of yours could die at any moment." Madge made it sound light, but she worried about him in the ancient Impala. "Please give in and get a new car."

He glanced down at her. The wind tossed her curly

hair. "One of these days, I believe I'll have to. It's fine for now."

Nothing was fine for now, Madge thought. There they stood on a wild night, using a conversation about her going home to keep them both right where they were.

"Well." *Well, what?* He should just see her into her car and follow her when she drove away.

Tree limbs scuffled together. The leaves rustled.

For once the frogs were quiet. Worn out from their earlier efforts, maybe.

"It's downright chilly," Madge said. "Spike keeps talkin' about expectin' wicked weather. Maybe he's right."

"What am I thinkin' of—lettin' you stand out here on a night like this?" Cyrus said, knowing too well what was on his mind. "You get on in that car of yours."

"Cyrus?"

"Yes."

"Nothin'. Just work stuff. It'll wait till tomorrow."

"You sure?"

"No," Madge said. "I'd like us to go in and talk awhile." Her skin felt too small for her body.

Cyrus hesitated. There was always a moment, an instant, when no harm had been done and it was best to make sure it stayed that way. But what did he say to her?

She had made him feel awkward, Madge thought. "You're right," she said. "It's too late. Another time will do. There's no hurry." She bent over her purse, searching out her keys. She found them and started walking, keeping her head down and watching the toes of her shoes. Her throat burned.

"Hey," Cyrus said, raising his voice a little. "You offered to visit with me. You can't offer a man a pleasin' hour then leave him standin' in his own parkin' lot." He couldn't let her go, not like that, not feeling bad and scuttling away with her head down as if she thought she'd done something wrong.

"You're tired," she said.

"Did I say I was tired?" He forced laughter into his voice. "When did you get to decide if I'm tired or not? I've got a guilty secret and I think I should share it with you."

She took in a full breath again. It was all right; she hadn't ruined everything. There were things that couldn't be changed so you accepted them, made the best of them...and you held them real tight.

Madge turned back toward him and walked through a slanting beam from one of the groundlights. She had narrow ankles, pretty legs. Everything about her was pretty—except for her tongue on occasion. He smiled and caught his bottom lip between his teeth.

"Guilty secret?" she said. "Oh, good. Mr. Clean has a zit. You're hard to live up to sometimes."

Madge caught up with him. She smelled of damp cotton and lemons. Nice. He was lucky to have someone like Madge working for him.

She worked with him more than for him.

"How the mighty are fallen," he murmured. "Come on. I'll show you."

A low light shone in the kitchen at the back of the house. Lil said a rectory ought to have a light on all the time, just in case someone needed to see it, to be guided there. Madge followed Cyrus along the side path toward the back door. It was amazing how even the most annoying of people could show caring and gentleness.

"Be careful you don't trip," Cyrus said, and patted his pockets until he found his keys.

"You, too." Walking behind him, watching his shoulders swing a little, his long legs cover the paving stones quickly, made Madge glad for even this much. What was she saying? There were more things than she could count to be grateful for.

"Here we go. At least it's always warm in this old house." Holding the screen open with one hand, he unlocked the door and pushed it wide with the other. "In you go. I hope you're feeling in a forgiving mood."

Madge grinned at him on her way past. "That's going to depend. I'll be fair. Even you expect that of me."

He touched her arm. "*Even* me?" He gave her a quizzical look. "Do you think that could possibly be—*most of all*, me?"

"Of course it could."

If she had thought herself ready to deal with Cyrus, to clear away some of the ambiguity, to arrive at an understanding, a way for them to live in less pain, she doubted she had been right. She wouldn't say anything after all.

"I'm going to get this over with right now." What did he intend to say tonight? Cyrus wondered. Nothing? Yes, that would be best.

Lil's old radio, the one she never turned off, played quietly on a white-tiled counter beside the stove. Like Madge, Lil's favorite music was zydeco. The two of them had been known to do a spirited two-step around the kitchen.

Waiting for whatever Cyrus reached for at the back of a cupboard, she tapped a toe and took a step or two to the beat. "Don't mess wi' my Toot Toot," she sang, barely audible.

Cyrus's silence stopped her. She looked at him over her shoulder. He leaned against the counter watching her, swaying to the music, but with a hard downturn to his mouth. He caught her looking at him and stirred.

"I'm goin' to give this to you," he said, pointing to a familiar, very pink box at his hip. "That'll make it okay, won't it? If I give it away?"

Her wicked grin made him smile right back. "Now, let me see," she said. "Is this stolen property?"

He laughed. "No. But I was sneaky about doin' the buyin'."

"Let's take a look." Flexing her fingers like a magician about to perform a trick, she whipped the string undone and pulled it from the box, threw back the lid and looked down on two of Jilly's famous marzipan tarts. "Get *on*, Cyrus Payne. I can't believe what I see. And hidden in a cupboard Lil never uses. Aha! This gets worse. Stealth. Sneakin' around so you won't have to share."

"I'd share anythin' with you."

Madge swallowed. He meant what he said but he was like that, always kind. "In that case—and as long as I get the biggest one—I think we can forget this little slip."

They were playing, Cyrus thought, playing with each other, trying to fool themselves. "Thank you. Will you join me now?"

"Yes." But she closed the cake box. "But we aren't really hungry, are we?"

He shook his head.

"I lied when I said I wanted to talk about work. You knew that, didn't you?"

"You didn't lie, you just tried to make things easier for me." *By filling in the silence while he was afraid to speak.* "It is time we faced up to some things, though." He indicated the table in the window. "Will this do?"

She shook her head no, then changed her mind. "Yes, of course. Just fine." This was as good a place as any.

Without thinking, Cyrus turned off the radio. Immediately he made a move to turn it on again.

"Leave it," she said. The possible outcome of whatever they were about to share meant too much. He must feel it as much as she did. When she left this house tonight there might be no coming back.

Holding a chair out for her, he asked, "Can I get you something? Iced tea, lemonade, coffee, a drink?"

"I'd like red wine, I think. I don't usually—"

"Drink?" he finished for her. "I know, but a glass of wine tastes good on a night like this."

Madge scooted her chair closer to the table and folded her hands on top. She listened to Cyrus uncorking the wine, watched his reflection in the windows while he poured two glasses, braced his hands on the countertop with his head turned away before he stood straight and came toward her.

"You've still got your coat on," he said, and put the glasses on the table. "Let me take it for you."

"Thank you." Every word sounded like a line from the wrong play. Quickly, she undid the buttons and shrugged out of the jacket. Cyrus hung it over the back of a chair. Smiling faintly, he unzipped his black windbreaker and took it off.

Should he sit beside her, or across the table? He decided on facing her and sat down. Madge slid his glass toward him. *Damn it all.* He opened his mouth to breathe. What was the answer, and he didn't mean the obvious answer?

"Cyrus?"

There he sat like a post, allowing her to swim in his silence. What kind of man did a thing like that?

"I'm sorry I'm quiet." He looked into her eyes. When he thought of her face, her eyes were always bright with laughter. She wasn't smiling tonight.

"We're both quiet," she told him. "We've never... This is a new place for us. It is, isn't it, Cyrus? You do know what I want to talk about?" If he didn't she would feel every kind of a fool.

He kept on staring at her. "I do know," he said finally. "But I don't know how you'll... How will we talk about this?"

She couldn't break eye contact with him. "I'm a coward so I want you to start." Beard shadow darkened his jaw and sharpened the angles of his face. "No. No, I shouldn't do this to you. Forget I started it. I'll have a few sips of this wine—it's good—and then I'll go."

"Love is the most precious gift we have," Cyrus said. *Please God, help me.*

The wine, dry and smooth, slipped rapidly down Madge's throat. Warmth rushed through her veins. Just like that, he said something she would never have been brave enough to put into words. Only he spoke of a very different kind of love and it wasn't romantic love. She couldn't speak.

Cyrus spread his long, blunt fingers on the tabletop. "I don't have any notion how to say what I need to, but it's my place to lay it out straight—for both of us."

"It's my job, too," she told him. "I have to wait for the words to come. I feel like I'm choking. Everythin's muddled up. No, it's not, it's clear, but I know I don't have the right to talk about it."

Trying to explain how he felt was almost beyond Cyrus. "I think we have the right to talk. I think that's what we're bein' led to do, and I don't say that to make excuses because I think I'm weak."

Hopelessness brought stinging tears to Madge's eyes. She had no right to give in to her need for him. Sure he was a man with a man's strengths and foibles, even a man's temper when he needed it, but he was taken. He already had a wife and lover and he would never betray her.

A song played in her head. *"What do you need a girl to do? Can't you see all she needs is you?"* Silly love songs written for immature dreamers.

If that's what she was, that's what she would always be.

"Trust," Cyrus murmured. This was one more test, not just for him but for her. Awkwardly, he reached across the table and rested his fingertips on the back of her hand. "We have to. You are my best friend. You are part of my heart and I mean that so much I shake inside. Just knowin' you're in this house feels right, Madge. I think it's okay for me to tell you my truly happy times come when I feel you here, goin' about your business, and here when I'm strugglin' with somethin'. You're a dreamer, but you've got common sense."

She was part of his heart? He was breaking hers, with a happiness she'd never felt, never expected to feel.

Her face glowed. Cyrus covered her hand and tried to smile at her. Not a great attempt on his part, but she smiled back. "Still no words?" he asked.

"Thank you," she said, and her eyes glistened, the corners of her mouth trembled.

"I've read so much lookin' for answers," Cyrus told her. "And I've talked to the special man who is my mentor. I find contradiction. But I also find reason. May I tell you what I believe, and what I think is meant for us?" He'd rehearsed this without ever intending to have the conversation.

"I will always listen to whatever you want to say," Madge told him. He felt at least a measure of what she felt. If he didn't, he wouldn't be struggling to make decisions. "Don't think this is flip, but are your eyes green or blue?"

"You say the darnedest things," he said. "I don't know what color they are. Blue, maybe."

"They are *not*, you silly. Green with a bit of blue, I think."

"Well, there you are then. They're pretty good eyes considerin' the hours I spend readin'."

He didn't care about things like that. "Make sure you always have good light," she told him.

"I do, Madge."

"I want you to tell me what you believe—about our situation," she said.

"Love isn't love unless it's selfless," he said. "I think my faith is based on God's passionate love for us, and human love is a passionate reflection of that."

She started to cry and didn't try to wipe the tears away.

Cyrus got up, all but knocking over his chair, and moved around the table to sit beside her. They didn't touch, they didn't need to.

"Can we—can I learn to understand what you mean?" Madge asked. "I don't know what you mean, Cyrus, not about the way it works for us."

She put the edge of her hand against his.

He frowned toward the blackness outside. "Love doesn't mean a desire to possess as much as it means a desire to *be* possessed."

"Yes," Madge said. She pushed her fingers gently beneath his palm and he took hold of her hand. "I understand that. I believe it."

"There are ways." A flush stole along his cheekbones. He stood and pulled her with him, held her elbows, seemed to look inside her. "I want to offer you…a pure but passionate affair."

Pure but passionate? "We could have passionate feelings, even speak of them, but never…touch?" An outlandish thought stunned her. For her, this was an agreement to love him forever. For him, he had offered her as much as he could. What he had to give, he would give, and he would never betray her. "Yes, Cyrus, I accept." She would take whatever he could offer.

"We can touch," he told her gently. "We are only human and we need to touch. We will find warmth and companionship—and passion, chaste pleasure."

"Yes," she said. "I feel…new." And she must be careful to tread slowly until he taught her all the rules of this chaste, passionate affair.

"We are new," Cyrus told her. He smoothed her cheek and gently put his arms around her. He eased her face against his shoulder, the shoulder of his black, short-sleeved shirt. She saw his white collar through misted eyes.

"From this night on," he told her, his thighs shaking, his whole body trembling deep inside. "From this night on I give you my heart. It's the heart of a faithful friend. Whatever you need or want, and whenever, I want to be the one you come to." The little deaths he would have to die. He had felt them too often already. "But, my friend, if someone else comes into your life, remember I would never try to bind you to me or stand in your way. I would welcome him because you wanted him."

Cyrus's mouth on her brow opened her up. His firm embrace spoke of what he'd said, a desire to be possessed, and a desire to give—chastely. For some it could never be enough. For Madge it was everything because it must be. And she would learn how to be there for him, without testing him or demanding more of him than he could give.

"From this night on, I give you my heart," Madge said, and she framed his roughened jaw with her hands. "It is the heart of a faithful friend. Whatever you need or want, and whenever, I want to be the one you come to. I only have one heart and I've given it to you, forever."

14

The wind almost took the outer door from Joe's hands. He grabbed the edge and held it, motioned Ellie outside.

With Zipper wrapped in a towel and complaining under one arm and holding Daisy's leash in the other hand, she hurried out. A blast of gritty air took her breath away.

Joe's closed expression showed he was an unhappy man. He didn't want her to go home and be alone. The idea didn't appeal to Ellie, either, but if they spent the night together, anywhere, they were likely to end up in the same bed. He had already said he wanted to make love to her.

She would feel she had invited him to have sex with her.

They walked down the lane to the gate into Ellie's big garden. Joe let them in and put an arm around her shoulders. "Are you ever going to rent the guest house out again?" he asked.

Ellie glanced at the little house in one corner of the property. "Eventually," she said. She'd had bad luck with renters in the past. On the other hand, she needed to put both the guest house and spare apartment to work.

Joe moved his hand to her waist. "I don't feel good about leaving you on your own," he said.

"I know you don't." She liked the warmth of his hand. "I'm not thrilled to be alone, either, but I have to carry on, Joe. I've got a business to run. It's a good business, but it won't be if I neglect it."

"I'm not suggestin' you neglect the shop," he said. "I'm glad Wazoo's goin' to be around to help you. You've needed someone for a long time."

Ellie disliked the idea. "That's a temporary arrangement. I don't see how she fits in at all."

"She'll take some of the load and give you more time to watch your surroundings carefully." His grip on her waist tightened. "Most of the day I'm in my office—unless I'm in court—but that's not the same as bein' with you. Wazoo plays a believable village idiot but she's got a good mind. She'll react if she has to."

Ellie didn't feel so hot. Every reminder of her predicament freshened the fear.

"You aren't responsible for me," she told him.

"I want to be."

Heat flashed through her blood. What she felt, what she wanted, her sexual response to him amazed Ellie. A long time ago she'd made up her mind that she would never risk rejection by a man she cared for.

Joe didn't know half of the baggage she carried. She didn't even know how she would react if they got really close.

He took her key and unlocked the door from the garden to the hallway at the foot of the stairs. Ellie let Zipper scramble free and shoot upstairs.

"I'll be fine now," she said. "I'll lock up behind you."

"Please stay right here while I check the place out."

"Joe, you don't need—"

"Yes, I do." He faced her. "Independence is a good thing, unless it ends up getting you killed."

"Shock tactics?" she said, determined to cover any signs that he'd succeeded. "You're a good man, Joe. I'd like it if you took a look around."

"You don't seem as edgy as you were earlier."

"I know," she said, very aware of the two of them close together in a small space. "I am scared. I won't pretend about that, but I've got a feeling Penn may have moved on. Look how much attention he's stirred up around here. Nobody in their right mind would stay."

Joe's raised brow and narrowed eyes said it all. They weren't dealing with someone who had a normal mind.

"Do you have any of the Garvey Jump mysteries in stock? I read a Sonja Elliot book some time back but I didn't pick up another one."

She gave him a guilty look. "We're running on the same track. I plan to check what I've got."

"When?"

Ellie wet her lips. "Once I'm on my own. You need to get some sleep, Joe." In truth she absolutely did not want him to leave, or rather she didn't want to be without him.

"Stand there while I check upstairs." His tone suggested he didn't expect an argument.

He jogged up the stairs, a lithe, physically fit man who showed no sign of hesitation. Ellie shifted her attention from his back to Daisy, who still behaved like a clingy kid when it suited her. She leaned against Ellie's legs and sighed from time to time.

Overhead, Joe trod, none too quietly, from room to room. First through the spare apartment, then through Ellie's. She liked listening to him. If she tried to hang on to the idea that their interest in each other was new, she'd be fibbing. The feelings had been there, not as strong but growing, for a long time.

She pulled off the jacket Joe had loaned her and put it on top of an oversize box of gift items for the shop.

Joe's feet, then his legs came into sight. Ellie watched the man until she saw all of him. She had never allowed herself to think of Joe as a potential lover—until the past few days. Now she didn't just think about the possibility, she visualized and felt them together and that shook her. In this light his dark blue eyes looked black. He didn't look away from her face.

A couple of steps from the bottom of the stairs, he stopped and held the banisters, stiffening his arms.

"No one hiding under the bed?" she said with a smile.

He shook his head.

"Thank you, anyway, Joe." She grimaced. "But you be careful going home, too."

"I will be. I'll take a look in the shop first."

He hopped down the last two steps and walked toward the shop, keeping her in sight. "Hey," he said, and offered her a hand. Ellie smiled a little. She slipped her fingers around his warm palm and the squeeze he gave comforted her even if it did feel foreign.

The dark shapes of the bookshelves loomed in the shop. One of the overhead fans whirred. Ellie put on a light at the back of the shop and started forward.

"There's no one here, but I'd rather go first," Joe said.

He released her hand and took a quick tour. As he had said, the place was empty.

"Do you want to look at the Sonja Elliot titles?" she asked, heading for the right section.

Joe met her there and ran his fingers along spines until he stopped at *Murder in the Market,* by Sonja Elliot.

"That's a different series." She ground her teeth together. "Here. *Death at Mardis Gras.* I did have *Death in Diamonds* but they sold through. I'm getting more of them."

The book cover showed Mardi Gras Krewe members doing what looked like a jungle-pole dance over the bleeding body of a woman. Feathered headdresses in violent shades tangled while the faces grinned, oblivious. That or they didn't give a damn.

"You look at it." Ellie stuffed the book into Joe's hands. The picture might seem bizarre, but it was too close to the scene she'd witnessed not to upset her.

Joe said, "Hoo mama, I wouldn't want to look at this if I were you."

She took it back from him and flipped through the pages. Never having read the story she didn't know just what she hoped to find.

There it was—in the first chapter. Bourbon Street. Confusion, loud music and screaming—the press of the crowd.

That's the one, the blond woman. She'll wish she hadn't come here today, only she'll die before she has time to think about it.

Shit, I've got to stay close. Right at her back. The pick gets slippery in my hand. Come on, come on, gimme the moment.

Oh, yeah. All the gleaming bodies. All the fabulous feathers. She's pushing forward. They're all pushing, bending me over her back. I can't fall with her.

The lovely noise. Mouths open wide but in a single scream of laughter. Huge laughter.

Now.

The pick punctures the skin at the base of her skull and I drive the blade in, deeper, harder. Down she goes. As good as dead already. Not even putting out her arms to break her fall.

Yank the pick back. Into the folds of my cloak it goes and I dance and grin with the rest.

Force myself backward.

Keep pressing myself away.

They haven't as much as noticed they hold a dead woman between their flailing legs.

Ellie slapped the book shut. "Take it with you if you like." She heard her own voice shake. "Come on, Daisy, upstairs with you." She removed the dog's leash and Daisy took off for a race around the shop.

With the book open again, Joe found the place and scanned lines rapidly. He looked up at Ellie. "Is this the way it was?"

"I think so." In her mind she saw the colors. Her heart pounded. "I don't know why I saw her go down, but I did. And she was sort of held off the ground by the crush for a bit. I saw her feet. One shoe was off." *And the man who held his arms at his sides and walked backward in the throng before he turned and…* A thunderous pulse beat at her ears.

"What else?" Joe said quietly.

"*Nothing.*" She shouldn't shout at him. She closed her eyes and shook her head. "Nothing else. I don't want there to be anything else. Every hour, every day—" Ellie rubbed her mouth, struggling against tears yet again. "Can't you see how it is? Questions, questions, and people always looking at me as if there could just be something horrible about me. I've got to deal with it. That means I'm alone with it. No one can really help me." She hurried to turn off the light and go through to the hall.

"Just go," he said when he arrived at her side. "Is that what you want to tell me, Ellie?"

No it wasn't, but she wouldn't tell him so. She raised her chin, praying the tears she felt would go away.

Joe crossed his arms and leaned on a wall. "I'm not leaving till you tell me to."

"That's not fair." But what did *fair* mean, anyway?

"The last thing I want is to be unfair to you," Joe said. "If you can't believe that, I can't make you."

Control had escaped Ellie. She covered her face.

"What we feel about each other needs some serious thought—together, alone," Joe said. "Wanting you didn't just happen. All this, all this madness may have given me the kick I needed to quit tiptoeing around for fear you'd reject me. But don't tell me you've never noticed... Haven't you ever looked at me and thought I might be thinking of more than your great conversation?"

She rubbed her hands together, tried to smile at him but failed. He thought he knew everything about her but he did not. The worst part she'd kept hidden. The rest of what she'd endured could well mean she'd freak if he touched her, really touched her.

"*Answer* me, Ellie. Tell me you've never thought I might be romantically interested in you."

She started to speak, only to stumble, several times.

"I'm embarrassed," she managed to say at last. "I have thought you might like being around me, but…I don't know what else to say, except I thought I was just dreaming."

Without warning, Joe shot an arm around her. He didn't leave his spot against the wall but pulled her against him and kissed her so hard he forced her head back. She heard him moan and saw how his face darkened and drew tight. Kissing him back, kissing him and feeling his equal, an equal part of his passion, sucked out all the energy she had. She strained against him, accommodated each position of his mouth, and accepted the almost violent way he took that kiss. Her heart tripped, ran away in frighteningly rapid rushes.

Violent?

Joe had no violence in him. What he felt and what he lavished on her was intense ardor.

He scared Ellie.

Forcing her hands beneath his wrists, she slid inside his collar to press her fingertips into unyielding muscles. She gentled her mouth, let it soften, and sensed that he felt the change in her immediately. He moved his mouth from her lips to her cheek. "Say I haven't waited too long to let you know how I feel?"

"Please, Joe," she said, "please give us time. Nothing's normal and you can't know exactly how you feel when your world's turned upside down."

He rested the side of his head against the wall and looked down at her through slitted eyes. "Is there any hope for us?"

If I make it through without being murdered, do you mean? "I have hope," she said, suddenly knowing what she really felt. "If we can hang together but still give each other enough room—and if what we feel turns out to be real rather than some reaction to my fear and your wanting to save me—we could have a chance."

Joe nodded, but rather than relaxing, his expression turned hard, and so intense she didn't want to analyze what was going on in his head.

"Don't laugh at me, please," she said to him. "Would you mind sleeping across the hall tonight?"

Shrugging away from the wall, he slid a forearm behind her neck and urged her face against his shoulder. He pushed her hair back and rested his cheek on her temple. "You'll never know how grateful I am for that suggestion. Beats the hell out of sittin' up in a dark room all night, lookin' out the front window and listenin' for any noise comin' from the back."

"I...I'm so grateful to you." Ellie held him and kept her eyes tightly shut. "Do you think they'll find him?"

"I do. I really do. Now, I've got to run back and make sure everything's locked up. I know the back door isn't."

"Go," Ellie said, and released him. "Are you hungry? I'll look around and see what I've got in my kitchen."

Joe slowly took his arm from around her neck. "Don't worry about it. Let me do what I have to and get back. I hate it when you're out of my sight." He locked the door from the inside and slammed it on the way out.

Sometimes Ellie forgot Joe had her keys.

He had let her know, more than once, that she was important to him. One of the reasons she'd hidden herself away in Toussaint was to avoid more than casual friendships. Joe had changed her mind, at least where he was concerned.

The man had to be hungry and she wanted to feed him. "C'mon, Daisy. Here, girl."

Daisy responded by taking another turn of the shop, snuffling and yipping as she went. Whenever Ellie mentioned Daisy's flashes of high spirits and unpredictability in front of Ozaire, he pointed out that she couldn't be considered full grown. Ozaire took exception to any negative comments about the dogs one of his good buddies raised.

"C'mon, girl," Ellie said, smiling at the sound of the mat inside the shop door flipping under Daisy's flying feet.

Death in Diamonds *was still only in hardback.* Ellie stood still. What was she thinking of to forget something that obvious? It should be out in paperback soon. Ellie headed back into the shop, this time using only a tiny lamp on the table in the reading area. Hardback fiction lined the back wall. She'd been right in saying she'd sold the three copies she got in originally, but maybe some reorders had arrived.

Thanks to Marc Girard, she now had sliding ladders along the three walls where the upper shelves were out of reach. He'd designed them, then turned up and put them in. Ellie smiled. She was so lucky in the friends she'd made.

She slid the ladder into place. As she inevitably did, Daisy showed up to sit at the bottom as if to keep Ellie safe.

An explosive cracking sound came from the windows behind her. Standing on the third step of the ladder, Ellie snapped around and almost fell. She stuck one arm through the ladder to balance herself and stood with her heels hooked over the rungs.

Daisy barked and Ellie cringed at the sound. The dog looked up at her, showing bared teeth.

"Stay." Ellie didn't want her dog in a position where she could be seriously hurt.

On the floor again, she grabbed Daisy's collar and got out of sight at the end of a long row of bookcases. The faintness she remembered from yesterday came seeping back. Not so strong this time, but still familiar.

A bright light bloomed outside but didn't wash into the shop.

Shaking, out of breath, Ellie peered out. The light came from a powerful flashlight held at about two feet from the ground and aimed upward. It illuminated a sign written in black on some sort of white surface.

The beam swiveled rapidly, picked her out before she could retreat. Ellie pulled back behind the bookshelf again. Daisy strained and made lunges until Ellie swung a leg over her back and clamped the animal between her knees.

"Joe." She whispered his name automatically. He'd come soon.

The light faded out of the shop. Ellie crouched, almost sat on Daisy's rippling back, and looked again. The sign read *Do You Know Me?*

Either she stood up, or she'd fall on Daisy. Ellie stood and squinted against the brilliance.

The flashlight moved again. This time straight up, straight up to blast over a man's face. He stared ahead, into the shop, and Ellie took a half step into the aisle between two bookshelves.

The flashlight distorted his features, sank his eyes deep in his head. She couldn't have identified him.

"Go away. I don't know you!"

The beam moved again. Ellie read, *Help Me. I Need You.* Ellie's legs crumpled and she fell to her knees. Singing,

singing, a whining song sawed at her ears and filled her head. She blinked to clear her vision. She didn't understand what was happening to her.

Daisy sniffed her. Ellie couldn't keep her grip on the collar and the dog rushed at the window.

The sign disappeared.

Once again the beam changed direction until it rested on the man's other hand, on the gun he pointed at Daisy.

"No." Ellie moaned. "No."

Again the man hit the window, this time with the butt of the gun.

The light went out and the bay window fell directly down in millions of glittering shards.

Ellie huddled over and rested her cheek on the floor. She waited, listening, not daring to show herself. He was out there, that man. And all he had to do was climb through the open window and get her. Daisy could well have been injured by the shattered glass.

What felt like endless, dead time went on and on.

How long had it been? Ellie rolled onto one side. She was the only resident at the end of the square—except for Joe.

"Daisy," she said. "Come."

Her dog wasn't in the shop, if she were she'd be at Ellie's side.

The back door slammed open. *"Ellie,"* Joe yelled.

15

"Let's go through this one more time," Detective Gautreaux said.

Joe dropped backward to lie flat on the carpet in Ellie's living room. "You sure you want to do that?" he asked.

"I don't," Ellie said. "I want to find my dog."

Joe rolled his head to one side and saw her look beseechingly at Spike. Now, there was a man who looked like death and definitely not warmed over.

Spike had dragged a chair from the little table in the window. "I've got an officer searching for her," he told Ellie. He sat astride the seat of his chair, his sun-streaked hair standing on end. His uniform was the same one he'd had on all day. And some sort of misery, something that had nothing to do with the present crisis, had settled in his eyes.

Joe pushed up onto his elbows. "Look at us. We're shredded. Can we carry on in the mornin'?" Ellie crowded a corner of the couch and he winked at her. She tried to wink back but succeeded in closing both eyes.

"What's so funny, Gable?" Gautreaux said. He sat in an easy chair and leaned forward to rest his forearms on his knees.

Joe waved airily. "Who knows? I think my brain's fried."

A fresh battering at the shop windows momentarily silenced them all. Cyrus was down there, and Marc Girard, Paul Nelson, Gator Hibbs—who had brought Jim Wade, the property prospector, along from the Majestic Hotel— and Ozaire Dupre. Ozaire and Gator had been drinking beer and watching baseball on TV.

"They're all so good," Ellie said. "And Spike made sure they didn't touch anything until things had been gone over."

"Hit and run," Spike said, his voice scratchy. "The fella was on his way when he hit that window. Must have used somethin' real hard. Like an ice pick."

"I told you it was a gun," Ellie said. "But I didn't hear him fire. If it had been an ice pick—"

"Don't think about that," Joe said. "Spike, why the hell would you say somethin' like that?"

"You want me to say I'm sorry?" Spike asked, and stood up. "You aren't the only one who's had a long day. Damn it all, *long day*? It's two in the mornin'."

Joe took a second to recover. "Never mind apologizing to me, buddy. Ellie's the one who doesn't—"

"Shut the *fuck* up," Gautreaux roared. "You, Ellie, I'm speakin' t'you and not these clowns. You never mentioned a gun."

No, Joe thought, she hadn't.

"I must have," she said, sitting straighter. "And don't you pick on Joe and Spike."

Gautreaux pointed his notebook at her. "You didn't say

anythin' about a gun. Y'all said the guy broke the window. Why wouldn't a gun be the first thing you said?"

Interfering at this moment wouldn't be a good idea, Joe decided.

"I thought I had. It happened fast. At the time everything seemed to go slowly, but it couldn't have been more than a couple of minutes at most."

"I heard the glass go," Joe said. Let Gautreaux take any tack he liked, but that wasn't going to include beating up on Ellie.

Gautreaux's black eyes pinned him. "Did you think it could have been shot out?"

"No gunshot," Joe said. "And like I said, I didn't hear a vehicle."

"This is how it's gonna be," Gautreaux said.

Joe got to his feet.

"Ellie here is a marked woman," the detective continued. Spike caught Joe's eye and neither of them said a word.

"She's had two attempts on her life. I'm thinking about the Witness Protection Program," Gautreaux said.

"You don't have a single lead on Charles Penn," Joe said. His head had been aching, now it felt as if his skull would break. "He's been out for ten days. A woman died in that time, but you don't have a thing on him, do you?"

"Take it easy," Spike said.

"It makes sense to get Ellie out of the picture," Gautreaux said. He shielded his eyes with one hand and didn't sound so good. "To keep her safe, and to see what kind of moves our man makes."

"Use her as *bait*, you mean," Joe said. "No, sorry, I know what you mean but I don't agree with you."

"Because all that matters to you is keeping your bed warm?"

Joe started forward but Spike stepped in front of him. "That won't help," Spike said. "Guy wants to be cautious. So do we all."

"And that excuses the mouth he's got on him?"

"*I've had it.*" Ellie pushed herself upright from the couch. "I've been doing a lot of thinking, too. Did he try to kill me twice?"

"Ellie," Joe said, reaching for her arm.

She moved out of his reach "Don't touch me. I want all of you to listen. You've had people combing the area for Penn. So far you haven't found him. He has to be somewhere here, so find him. Get enough officers out there to turn over every rock."

"We're doing that," Gautreaux said. He didn't show any chagrin and Joe figured that ticked Ellie off.

"Keep at it," she said. Joe could read her mind—almost. She had decided the only way to stop herself from being trampled under big, clumsy male feet was to quit behaving like carpet. She continued, "Next point. It would have been easy to kill me in the woods behind Pappy's. He didn't. Why?"

"The time wasn't right for him," Gautreaux said. "He wanted to ask you questions but you got away from him. Were we in doubt about any of this?"

"I'm just clarifying things, Detective Gautreaux. You said someone tried to kill me twice and then you started talking about the Witness Protection Program."

"I'd appreciate it if you'd call me Guy."

Joe smiled a little. Guy Gautreaux was a good-looking man. Joe figured the detective was used to females turning to jelly if he chose to switch on the charm.

All he'd managed this time was to make Ellie frown. She turned to Spike. "You don't look so good," she said.

"Please go home to your family. Guy will be on his way shortly. He's got a fair ride to New Orleans. We'll make a fresh start tomorrow."

Oh, but he loved the lady's way of cutting bigger fish down to convenient sizes.

"Maybe she's right," Spike said, reaching for his hat.

"The hell she is," Guy Gautreaux said. He pushed his notebook into a pocket and crossed his very muscular arms. "I don't know how you run things around here, Spike, but where I come from the witness doesn't decide procedure. I'm staying at the station house, Ellie. Lori's been kind enough to let me use the bed in her office. I take it Spike had it put in on account of her pregnancy. So she could rest if she had to."

"Spike is one of the best," Ellie said.

She smiled at Spike, who looked uncomfortable, then returned her unblinking attention to Guy. "Tonight that man out there could have shot me and gotten away, just as easily as breaking the window and getting away."

"What's your point?" Guy asked

"His second sign just read, 'Help me. I need you.'"

"Sure, then he broke your windows and ran like hell. Since you know everything and you say he doesn't intend to kill you, what does he want?"

"To kidnap me." She let that sink in. "The first time he went after me I didn't do a single thing he expected me to do, and I think he heard Joe coming, too. Last night Daisy ruined everything for him. He wanted to shoot her but that would have make me too difficult to handle."

Joe breathed in real slow. He believed the same thing but didn't understand why that would make Ellie feel any safer.

"Okay, and if he did manage to kidnap you, what then?" Guy asked.

Spike said "Hell" under his breath. He arched his neck. "Damned if we do and damned if we don't."

"Yes," Ellie said. "He wants me to be able to say I didn't see him do anything on Bourbon Street when Stephanie died."

"Doesn't make any sense," Joe said. "You already made a statement that you didn't recognize him."

"What I believe he wants," Ellie said, "is to find a way to make me say I did see who killed Stephanie Gray and it wasn't him. That's why all he's going to do is frighten me, not kill me."

"You scare the hell out of me," Guy Gautreaux said.

Joe came close to adding, *me, too.*

Spike put on his hat and dipped it forward over his eyes. "This is going to be hard, Ellie, but I think you should accept protection. Penn has a violent past."

"I already have accepted protection," Ellie said, smoothing nervously at her wrinkled shirt and slacks. "Joe has agreed to stay in the other apartment."

Women, Joe decided, were completely unpredictable. He nodded, making sure he showed only serious concern. Now wasn't the time to reveal he was doing cartwheels in his mind; low-life, infatuated man that he was. "That's correct," he said. "As long as she isn't all alone here at night, I don't think we've got as much to worry about. Wazoo will come on loan from Vivian and Spike during the day for as long as necessary. This guy's going to step right in it, we all know that. This town's too small to make a good hiding place."

Damn Guy Gautreaux's eyes. He couldn't resist giving Joe a boy-to-boy look.

"My father, Homer Devol, he's going to help keep Ellie

covered during the day," Spike said. "Homer's no push-over."

"No," Guy said. "Not good enough."

"It's going to have to be," Ellie told him, but gave Joe a long sideways glance. "I'm not going anywhere. Got it? My plans are made and I'll be safe with my friends. I'm also going to get a gun."

"No." Guy and Spike echoed Joe. Joe went on alone, "Don't do anything hasty, okay, Ellie? You don't know anything about weapons and this isn't the time to start with them, not when you're scared."

"I know about guns," she said, and shut her mouth tight.

"Whatever," Guy said. "Promise you won't get a gun unless one of us is there to check you out on it. If you don't promise, I'll find a way to bring you in."

"You threaten that a lot," Ellie said.

Guy smiled faintly.

"I won't get a gun unless one of you is with me," she said, biting her lip while humor warmed her eyes. "It's quiet. I'm going down to see what's happening and find out if there's any news about Daisy." She went into the kitchen and returned with a key, which she gave to Joe. "You'll find everything you need over there. Tomorrow we'll see about making it more like home for you."

This time Joe let himself enjoy Guy's raised eyebrows. He could think whatever he wanted to. All Joe hoped was that every hot thought Guy had came true.

Cyrus waited quietly in the shop. The glass had been cleared away. Most of the small leaded panes had clung in place.

"Marc worked those panes loose," Cyrus told her. He'd

insisted on waiting with Ellie until Joe got back with some of his things. "He reckons they're worth a lot but the rest of the glass is no big deal. The things in the window display got broken. I'm sorry about that."

Ellie threaded her arm through his. "You didn't break them. Thank you for coming, Cyrus."

"You helped me pass a difficult…" He shook his head and Ellie knew better than to press him. "Where's Daisy? I heard she was a hero."

"She went after him and she hasn't come back. I'm so scared for her."

"They'll find her." He smiled. "I'm glad you've got her."

He raised one very dark brow. "Come to that, I'm glad you've got Joe. He's one of the best."

"Why are you looking like that? Like you're giving me another message as well?"

Cyrus reddened a little. "Did I look like that? Hmm, well, if I remember what I was thinking about, I'll let you know. There's Joe. I'll go out the back. This door's already locked."

When they got to the hall, Joe held the door open with his heel while he plunked a suitcase and a couple of paper bags at the bottom of the stairs.

"Call if you need anything," Cyrus said in passing. "Anything at any time."

"Thank you," Ellie said, and pulled him back to kiss his cheek. "See you soon."

"You can bet on it," Cyrus said. He regarded Joe sternly. "I shall make a point of dropping by to see how everything is."

16

Some events, moments, feelings, were indescribable.

This was one of those, Joe thought. "Is everything locked up?" he said, and felt as if he'd asked Ellie an intimate question. Like a husband coming home after a day at the office. No, like a husband talking to his wife when they were getting ready to go to bed.

"They did miracles with that window," Ellie said. She looked up at him and smiled. "The place is tight."

"Time for bed, then," he said, and winced.

Ellie laughed. *Had he noticed before that her laugh squeezed his throat?*

"Yes, dear," she said, and chuckled, maybe too hard.

Joe picked up his suitcase and paper bags. "After y'all," he said, and followed her up the stairs. Ellie didn't usually wear pants. She should, much more often. The view he had was very nice.

Zipper's striped head poked from between two banisters on the landing. She focused entirely on Joe, and her blue eyes not only crossed, they narrowed to slits and a ridge of fur stood up along her back.

"Put that cat in the window at Halloween," Joe said. "You won't need witches or ghosts."

"Zipper doesn't like any change in her routine. She got yanked away from home for hours and now you're coming up to *her* place carrying her least-favorite thing—a suitcase. And Daisy's missing."

The cat curled her lips against her gums, backed away and disappeared.

"I'm sorry she's standoffish," Ellie said, reaching the landing herself.

Joe barely stopped himself from saying, *I'm not*. Then he felt mean. "She'll get used to me."

He stood behind Ellie, who looked back at him. "You are the best friend I've ever had," she said. "It isn't easy to play nursemaid to me and deal with your own work."

Her best friend? Okay, that was a start, although it didn't come close to the way he wanted her to think of him. "We've got a good setup with my place bein' so close," he told her. He couldn't just leave the other hanging. "I couldn't want a better friend than you, Ellie. Which is just as well because I'll never find one." And he meant every word. He felt good to have told her, even if the conversation felt unfamiliar and personal at the same time.

She pushed open the door to her apartment.

Joe swallowed. "I'll get acquainted with my new digs."

"No, no. I'm going to show you around and get you settled."

"Will you tuck me in?" *Damn your glib mouth, Gable.*

"If you'd like that," she said, and he noticed her eyes were wet.

He'd told her she was his friend and she'd gotten teary. A soft but definite *whump* hit somewhere about his midsection. One moment she stood her ground and told off a tough NOPD detective, the next she showed how vulnerable she was, how easy she would be to love.

All she feels for you is gratitude because she's alone and you've reached out a hand. For the past few years he'd tried to let her know she intrigued him, but she'd never been more than congenial, fun even on occasion. He'd realized that either his signals were too weak or she wasn't interested.

"You've got the key," she said, and when he fished it from a pocket, she took it and opened the door to the second apartment. "Samie Machin lived here while her husband was overseas in the service. Now he's out and they've got a cute little house not far from Homer and Spike's store."

"I know," Joe said. "Nice people."

A living room, smaller than Ellie's and furnished with a red sectional, pumpkin-colored chair, two sets of stacking tables and a TV, invited a visitor inside. In front of floor-length ivory linen drapes stood a Chinese screen in black, red, yellow and a spattering of lime-green bamboo leaves.

"This is just fine," Joe said. *Fine if you want to be across the hall from a woman you'd rather hold through the night.*

"Oh, good. When I did it I was trying for inexpensive but cheerful. I'll change things if it's all too overdone for you."

"It's not."

"The kitchen is separate." She hurried past him and flipped the light on in a squeaky-clean white kitchen. "Don't bother getting in any food. If it's okay with you, we can share. I'm up early and the coffee's on. As long as you don't want eggs Benedict for breakfast, we'll do fine. Never did like looking at that fancy stuff in the morning."

"No eggs Benedict," he said, unable to take his gaze from her face, from her bright blue eyes and the animated way she spoke. She'd been terrified of staying here alone. Now her relief at having him with her made her giddy and talkative.

"There are two bedrooms. Same as in my place. The girls get my second bedroom. It's a little animal palace and they don't even mind if I have to shut them in." Ellie looked faraway for an instant but raised her chin and focused on Joe.

She picked up the paper bags he'd dropped and wouldn't let him take them back. "I'm a tough one," she said. He could see a pulse racing in her throat, and the way her fingers shook. "You'll want the bigger bedroom. The bathroom's small but it's okay."

He wanted her bedroom.

Slow down, boy.

She led him into a softly lit room with pumpkin-colored walls and wall-to-wall carpet of a slightly deeper color. "I know," she said, touching his arm lightly. "What's with all the pumpkin? It makes everything seem warmer—not exactly what you need tonight. It's so muggy and the fans in here don't do much. Do you really hate it?"

"I really like it," he said honestly. "The next time I have somethin' decorated, I'll insist you pick everythin' out. My new place isn't finished yet. There's still plenty you can help me with."

They looked at each other. Joe didn't feel like making light of the familiar suggestion he had made and, apparently, neither did Ellie.

"I'll always help you if I can."

This was sad. Sweet, sad. Two grown-up people who

cared about each other but who couldn't seem to get past tippy-toeing around as if looking for hidden trip wires.

"How about the bedspread?" Ellie asked. "Samie insisted on leaving it behind because it didn't go with the new place."

"I've always thought fake fur was underrated. Looks comfortable."

Ellie hauled the bags on top of a fake mink affair. "You haven't had a thing to eat for hours," she said. "I've got homemade soup in the refrigerator. You get yourself sorted out and I'll heat some up."

Was he the only one who thought they were dancing slowly, several feet apart but maybe getting a little closer? He wanted to say it wasn't soup he wanted but nodded instead. "Sounds just the ticket. Be right there."

She hovered. "Do you have something cool and really comfortable to put on? Maybe whatever you're going to wear to bed? That way you'll be ready to get to sleep."

No smiling, Gable. You should be too tired for hot-and-heavy thinking. "Thanks for thinking about that. I'll take you up on it." Sometimes she seemed as tough as she reckoned she was, at other times and more often Ellie came across as purely naive.

The instant Ellie left he stood like a man who'd had a hard blow to the head. What was the matter with him? Grab the pajama pants he'd managed to resurrect from the bottom of an unpacked box, take a quick shower and quit behaving like a wolf in mating season.

A small bathroom opened off the bedroom. Again this was all white, so it didn't seem quite so claustrophobic. Joe stripped like a madman, throwing everything into a corner. He leaped into the glassed-in shower enclosure, scrubbed all over and washed his hair.

Out he got, gave himself a quick towel off, put on the annoying pajama bottoms and hightailed it from the bathroom. He only stopped long enough to grab an undershirt and drag it over his head. "Something cool to put on…" Ellie has said. "Maybe whatever you wear to bed." Most women would think there was a good chance he slept naked—which he normally did.

Fingering his hair to make it settle down, he crossed the hall, tapped on Ellie's open door and went in the instant she told him to.

His legs wouldn't take him farther, not just yet. She folded napkins and placed them beside two place mats at one end of the table. Ellie, too, had managed to pass through the shower. Her curls formed a mussed halo. He could smell the scent of lavender soap. Her cotton nightie and robe hit just above the knees. A belt, cinched at the waist, made the most of what was already a dream body.

She looked up at him and he saw her swallow. The breath she took expanded her chest, pushing her breasts against the fabric of her robe. He wanted, more than anything, to hold her in his arms, naked, and to make love to her until they were both exhausted.

"Soup won't take long," she said. "I felt filthy. I had to take a quick shower."

"Me, too," he said. "What can I do to help?"

"Keep me company," she said, so naturally that he knew she hadn't considered how it might sound. "Sit here. I'll give you the head of the table. Just don't get above yourself."

"I wouldn't dare." There wasn't a laugh or smile left in him. He'd better make sure she didn't guess how emotional he felt, how aroused he was. How much he wanted to take her right here and now. He slid into the chair she indicated.

"First, look in that bedroom over there. Mine's this end. The other one is…well, look at it."

Joe got up, ruefully aware of his condition. Ellie stood very close. He touched her shoulder and she moved back, but not before a glance down the front of her loose robe and nightie made his head light. Blood rushed to inconvenient places. Damn, damn, damn. This wasn't the time to indulge his hormones.

"Go on," Ellie said, and he took a long look into her almost too-blue eyes. She teetered, he could see it, she teetered between gratitude and relief at his being there, and awkwardness that he was.

He went into the second bedroom and smothered a laugh. Jungle motif gone mad. Great brown painted tree trunks curled up the walls and across the ceiling, and huge green leaves with the occasional outrageous flower peeking out. Oversize snakes in brilliant colors, monkeys, frogs, and in the middle of all this animal heaven stood a regular double bed. Toys scattered the floor. A cat perch built like a vertical maze took up a lot of room.

"Hey, Daisy," Joe said. The dog opened one eye, made grumpy, sleepy noises, and settled down again with a big paw on top of her battered cell phone.

Ellie put her hands on Joe's back and pushed forward. "Daisy?" she said in a squeaky voice. "You sneaked in through the back door when I wasn't looking. Oh, Daisy, you sweet thing. I thought you might be dead."

She leaned over the bed and hugged both pets, then kissed Daisy.

"Does the tabby fiend hide—" He never finished his

question. Jungle cat, Zipper, who had apparently lined herself up to make a dash into the room, flashed by like a mini gray-and-white-striped tiger. She moved so fast, her paws literally hit several inches up one wall. A second race around the room and she leaped onto the bed, on top of Daisy, scrunched and squiggled around until she fit into the dog's bumps and dips. Apparently it was Daisy's bath time and Zipper started with a good face scrub. The dog didn't stir.

"She's lethargic," Ellie said. "She could just be tired after all she's been through, but I'll get her checked out tomorrow."

"If I get another life," Joe said, "I'm comin' back as your dog."

Ellie's chest tightened. Now she'd given in and done what she'd wanted to do all along. Joe would be with her tonight, possibly for several nights until they caught Charles Penn, but she couldn't bear to think of how she'd cope when Joe left.

"The soup will be hot by now," she said, returning his steady appraisal even though she could hardly stop herself from turning away. He looked at her from head to toe and she tingled. "I'm going to find a candle or two. The overhead light seems harsh to me."

Conscious of every step she took, Ellie walked away from him and found two green candles in a kitchen drawer. She put them in holders before lighting them.

"Nice," Joe said.

He stood by the table and waited for her to ladle the soup and sit down. Moisture shone in his thick, dark hair. He took the chair next to hers. A glass of white wine stood beside each bowl. "I hope the wine's okay. It's the only kind I have. Homer brought over the crawfish so I threw in everything else I had and made soup. There are enough crawfish left to put into a scramble in the mornin'."

Joe put a hand over his heart and said, "Crawfish scramble. Mmm-mmm. I think I'm in love." He coughed and tore off a piece of bread—Jilly's bread from All Tarted Up—and took a bite.

The overhead fans weren't moving the air in this room, either. The wind had stopped blowing but the stillness, the heaviness, came as a warning of more bad weather to come.

"Are you hot, Joe?" she asked.

He looked at his soup and his dark lashes shifted. "Good soup," he said. "It is hot now. Seems like the big weather is hittin' all around us. They're talkin' about a hurricane, a long way off yet, but it's lookin' like it could come on shore in the Gulf."

"I hope it weakens before it gets there—or doesn't come at all," Ellie said. She popped up and opened both the blinds and the windows. She returned to her seat and looked at Joe. "Does that help?"

He shook his head. "This isn't polite behavior, but would you mind?" With crossed arms he made to remove his undershirt.

You're going to make this really easy on me, hmm, Joe? "Of course I don't mind." Too bad she couldn't take off her robe, but the nightie was a little thin. "Maybe the soup was a silly idea. Don't eat it."

"I'm going to eat every mouthful. It'll put hair on my chest."

Joe had pushed the undershirt onto the seat of the chair beside him. His tanned chest already had just the right amount of smooth hair. His body beckoned to her, his broad chest and smooth sides, his flat stomach and his navel behind the slightly loosened drawstring below his waist.

Ellie clasped her hands between her knees.

The last time she'd been alone with a man... She breathed through her mouth. Once she had got through those terrible times she had promised herself she would never think about them again, not in detail. Yet the memories had drawn a semitransparent curtain around her mind. Mostly she could keep her distance from the days, the years of the half life from which there had seemed no escape.

Joe kept his eyes lowered and did as he'd promised, ate his way steadily through the soup.

One night a week, she'd thought it happened on Fridays but couldn't be sure, that strange man, her captor, had come to the locked room where she slept. He entered quietly, locking them both in, and didn't say a word until he lay down on top of her, his weight crushing her into the bed.

Unlike hers, Jason's skin—what she could see of it— gleamed from the sun. His light hair shone. She hadn't been outside in many months. "Why do you take my clothes off and keep yours on?" she'd asked him, even though the thought of him naked brought her close to screaming.

"It isn't seemly for a woman to see a man's body," he'd told her, drawing her skirt above her hips. "Your place is to please me by doing what you're told."

His hands, big and scarred, passed up her thighs.

"You're not eatin'," Joe said.

Ellie jumped. Why would the scenes come back now when she had so much to cope with?

Smiling, focusing on Joe's face, she slowly stretched her arms above her head, bent them at the elbow and rubbed the back of her neck. It was wet and her fingers shook. "Too warm," she said, grateful even for the heated breeze that slipped beneath her loose sleeves.

Joe took up his wine and touched the rim of his glass to her lips. "Drink some. It may not cool you off, but it'll make you feel good."

She kept her arms where they were and took a long, slow swallow of Joe's wine.

Heavens. She caught Joe looking at her, looking at the place where the sleeve of her robe fell back on the arm closest to him. Quickly, blushing madly, she made to bring the arm down.

"Don't," Joe said. He moved before she could, held her upraised elbow in one hand and softly stroked his way downward and inside her clothing with the other. "Say the word and I'll stop."

Rigid but for her clamoring heart, Ellie didn't say anything.

He didn't handle her breast, but with the backs of his fingers, he rubbed the side gently. She leaned gradually forward until her elbow rested on his shoulder.

This wasn't Jason in the basement of his mother's house. Ellie had nothing to fear now.

With his mesmerizing attention, the millimeter-by-millimeter movement of his fingers beneath her breast, the way he feathered across her ribs, watching her all the time, he tensed her flesh even more, made it ache, burn. She knew nothing of being treated like this, touched like this.

The removal of his hand was sudden and left her mortified at her response to him. She placed her hands in her lap again and lowered her face.

"Forgive me," he said. "You have a beautiful body."

"Not as beautiful as yours," she said. *Did she have no control over her tongue?*

"Thank you." Once more he tipped the glass to her lips and she drank, then watched Joe take a swallow himself.

He put down the glass and kissed her. The thought came, unbidden and unwelcome, that she knew she was playing with fire and could unravel before Joe's eyes at any second. Joe, on the other hand, had no idea he could be provoking a disastrous encounter.

He framed her face with his hands. The next kiss, deep and not the kiss of a man who was kissing her good-night, tightened the skin all over her body. Her nipples hardened and she longed for him to touch them.

"You're hot, too," he said. "Take off the robe."

Deep between her legs, she stung. "I can't," she said.

With no warning, he dipped a napkin into his glass of wine and passed it over the tops of her breasts and the sides of her neck. A drizzle of wine ran between her breasts.

Ellie leaped up, holding the damp lace at the neck of her gown to her chest. She looked at him, amazed, and got a completely wicked, clenched-teeth grin in return.

"Cooler now?"

"Joe Gable, you're awful. I'm sticky. What possessed you to do that?"

"May I show you?" He advanced on her and Ellie backed away.

There was no place to go, unless she wanted to try running away. She made it behind the couch and pointed a shaking finger at him. "You just cool down. I'm surprised at you."

"Are you?"

"I, yes." Unless she wanted to set Daisy on this man

who happened to be the only man Ellie had ever cared for, where did she think she was going? Into her bedroom? Not a good idea.

"If you want me to trot across the hall and climb into my lonely bed, I'll do it. Just say the word."

"You're playing with me."

"What was the first indication?"

"You, well—" She let her arms fall to her sides. "You know what you did."

"And you didn't like it?"

She had liked it. She hadn't expected it, that was all. And things were going too fast.

"Ellie, answer the question."

"I did like it, a lot, but it wasn't anything I thought you would do."

He rubbed at his forehead. Ellie couldn't keep her attention from his chest, or the way his pajama pants sat low on his hipbones. He blew her a kiss and she giggled.

"C'mere," he said, advancing with measured but definite steps. "You have had me sweating through the night over you for a couple of years. You never showed much interest, so I didn't push it."

"I've always liked you."

"That's nice," he told her. "But you never considered me as a man you'd enjoy making love to?"

The heat in her body became unbearable. "I—I like looking at you."

"Touch me, then." He beckoned her. "Touch me wherever and however you want to. Maybe you'll like that, too."

"I couldn't."

Ellie still stood behind the couch and Joe closed the distance between them. She didn't want to run from him.

She just didn't know how to deal with a man like him who obviously intended to make love to her.

"So here we are," he told her, placing her against the wall and pressing her hands to his chest. Holding her wrists, he took her fingers over his shoulders, down his sides, across his chest, and behind him to his buttocks. He pressed her hands against the hard flesh there and released her.

"You feel so good," she whispered.

He dipped his head and licked a line along the straight neckline of her nightie. Spaghetti straps held it up and like most of her clothes, the thing was too big and loose. "Mmm," he whispered against her skin. "You like the way I feel and I like the way you taste. A bit like wine. Shall I stop?"

She shook her head. Mature people didn't fib when there was no need. Having him so close to her was going fine. He didn't just take, he gave. Joe gave more than she knew exactly how to give back, but she could try to learn from him.

"Take the lead, Ellie. It's your turn."

She shook her head again. With an economy of movement, Joe slipped her belt from around her and stripped off her robe. He sucked in a breath and stood as far from her as he could without removing his hands from her waist. "My God, you're fantastic. You can hide under those dresses when you're anywhere but with me. But when it's just the two of us, I want to see you."

"You frighten me," she said. "It's only sex."

Completely still, Joe studied her face, tipped his head to one side, narrowed his eyes and took a long look at every feature. "It's not only sex. But it is about sex, too. Go to bed. Would you mind if I sleep on the couch here rather than across the hall? I want to be close to you."

"I'm sorry, Joe. I led you on."

"You have nothin' to be sorry about, cher. And you didn't lead me on. I'm tryin' to go too fast. I ought t'know better. Go on and get some sleep. I'll be here, cher."

"You're so sweet," she told him, even though she felt such a fool. "You really do want to keep me safe."

He left her and shut the door to the landing. "I really want to keep you safe, but I'm not sweet. I'm hanging in here, Ellie. I've got to because I'll do whatever it takes to have you for myself. Now go."

There it was again. He didn't intend to give up on their becoming lovers. "You need blankets."

He gave a short bark of a laugh. "Blankets? I'm nicely warmed up, thanks. In more ways that one. I'll be fine."

"Okay."

"Good night," he told her.

"Maybe a sheet. The corduroy could get uncomfortable."

He looked at her through the room's subdued light. "Yeah, good idea. A sheet."

"Joe."

"What? What's wrong?"

"Just about everything. Most of all, I don't know what to do right now. What am I supposed to do? Leave you to be uncomfortable on the couch in a room that's too hot, or make you go to bed across the hall—where it's also too hot?"

If there was some perfect response, he did not appear to know what it was.

"A sheet," she said, and hurried into her bedroom. She half expected him to follow but should have known better. When she returned he hadn't moved from where he stood. Ellie put the folded sheet on the seat of the couch.

Then Joe moved. He picked up the sheet, shook it out and spread it.

"I wouldn't have expected you to wear pajamas," Ellie said, and shook her head. Why would she say a thing like that to him? At this moment?

"These are in your honor," he said. Watching him stretch to finish his task presented Ellie with an engrossing spectacle. His stomach drew tight and the muscles in his arms shone as they moved. "That's done," he said, looking up at her.

"Yes." Each breath fought to go in and out at the same time.

"Is it really hot in your room, too?"

"Not so bad. I put in a really good new fan right over the bed."

"That's good, then."

He'd be cooler in her bed than in either the other apartment or this living room.

"What's the matter?" he said. "Waiting to make sure I'm comfy?"

"I said I would." She sounded a whole lot more flip than she felt.

Joe put a knee on the couch, leaned to slip a hand behind her neck and pulled her close enough for a long, long kiss. "Nice," he murmured. "I want a lot more of those."

She fought for breath. "So do I." *Ellie, the pillar of resolve and reserve.*

He released her and went around to her side. "Dammit," he said so suddenly, she jumped and her mouth turned dry. Joe stood close behind her. "I'm doing my best to figure out the best way to approach you, but I've never met a woman like you before. You're as sexy as hell but you give out signals that tell me to stay away. What is that all about?"

Ellie leaned against him, turned and put her arms around him and felt the sharp pinch of longing and breathless need when her breasts flattened on his chest.

"I'm dyin' here," he said.

Lightly, she skimmed his body and this time she included his rigid belly and the powerful muscles in his thighs. Trembling, she slid her thumbs down his groin then, loosely, held his penis. It wasn't the way it should be done, but she was too afraid to grip him, to stroke him.

Joe dropped his head back and let out a strangled moan. He made fists at his sides.

Ellie's heart beat so fast and shallow she felt faint, but hot and intensely excited at the same time.

She held him, overwhelmed by the weight.

"Ellie, Ellie, Ellie," he said in a broken voice. "I can't— do this any longer."

She stumbled backward, held up her hands. A painful beat started in her temples. "Forgive me," she said. What did she think she knew about any of this? Nothing, she knew nothing but how to do as she was told when the alternative was punishment.

He caught the front of her nightie in one fist and drew her to her toes. Kissing her, her mouth, her face, her neck, her breasts, he excited and confused her. His left hand slid around her and the fierceness of his kiss drove her backward over his arm. Squeezing her buttocks, he panted and gave a muffled moan.

"Joe, I—" She didn't know what she wanted to say and he didn't respond at all.

He moved too quickly for her to react, grasped the neck of her gown and pulled it below her breasts.

Ellie cried out. She took a step backward but he swung her back against the couch and held her knees between his. Trapping her feet between his own, he cupped her breasts. Her control, if there was any left, drained away and she arched her back. Joe pulled at her nipples, shook them, rolled them between his fingers. He held her still while he licked a circle around one of her breasts. He repeated the action, moving closer to her nipple by a fraction of an inch.

She wanted him to suck at her. Deep in her limbs she quivered.

Jason had never bothered to try to excite her. He'd looked, squeezed, bruised her flesh with his pinching, but she'd known his aim and how quickly it would all be over, even if he did want her to walk around naked afterward. But was that really different than this in anything but the time the man took to get inside her?

Ellie almost retched. Boneless, her legs threatened to betray her.

Joe pressed the heel of a hand against her pelvis and flicked his fingers over moist flesh that ached.

"No," she said, pressing her legs together and dipping to evade his hand. "Not like this." The gown slid down her arms to restrict her elbows.

"Like what?" Joe kissed her neck and worked her nipples with his thumbs. He slid his hands up her thighs and held her hips tightly.

"No, no. Please. Not this time. I'll be good next time. Let me be tonight."

She heard her own sobbing, felt tears wash her fiery cheeks, and scrambled to pull her gown up. She saw herself, half naked with Jason on top of her. He kept pulling at her skirt and she did not have the strength to stop him. His jeans scratched her legs.

He would hurt her later but she punched him and screamed.

"Ellie!"

Now the beating would start because she'd angered him. Why not make him angry enough to kill her? At least it would be over then.

His hard fingers closed around her wrists, ground the bones together, and he shook her. "For God's sake, Ellie, take a breath. Hold on, just hold on. Everything's okay. No one's gonna make you do anythin' you don't want to do. Look at me." He shook her again. "Ellie, *look* at me."

It was too scary to see him.

Soft kisses, pressed lightly to her face, calmed her a little.

"Open your eyes," he said.

Stillness fell over her. Sweat ran on her body and down the sides of her face, but she was cold. *Dear God.* Joe's voice. Joe's voice pleading with her while he cradled her in his arms.

Ellie looked at him.

"I'm putting you to bed now," he said. "You've got something terrible eatin' at you. It's somethin' to do with a man, isn't it?"

When she swallowed her dry throat tickled and she coughed. She didn't have to look at herself to know her nightie was shredded and displayed more of her than it hid.

Joe carried her easily into her room. He reached up to start the fan and pulled a second string to turn on muted and frosted lights. Ellie tried to cover herself.

He sat her on the edge of the bed and went into her bathroom to return with a wet washcloth and a towel.

"Pretend I'm your mother," he said, sponging her down. Ellie looked straight ahead. She must make sure their paths crossed as little as possible after this.

"Where are your clean nighties?" he asked.

"On a shelf in that armoire."

He found a plain white shift, handed it to her and turned his back while Ellie discarded the destroyed gown and pulled on the deliciously cool, smooth cotton. "Thank you, Joe," she said quietly. "I'm not going to ask you to understand what happened just now. I blew it and I'm sorry. You should never have to put up with something like that."

"I want you to get into bed," he said. He pulled back her blue chenille spread and turned the sheet aside.

"Thank you," she told him, although climbing into bed felt beyond her.

"Here we go." With a hand beneath her knees and the other around her waist he lifted her onto a sheet that would stay cool only until her body heated it. "Stretch out, cher." He left her again and brought another washcloth, this time to stroke it repeatedly across her brow and dampen her hair.

The look hadn't left his eyes. Men have to have sex—how many times had she been told that to justify the way she had been taken, again and again?

"I'm going into the living room now," Joe said. "We'll both need to be rested in the morning. I've got to be in court. You've got to start getting your business back to normal."

"He's out there," Ellie told him, turning her face toward the windows. "I won't feel normal until I know he's gone. But I'll do my best to get my routine back."

"You'll do it. Now get to sleep." He walked toward the door.

"This is the coolest place up here," she said. "A man and a woman can sleep in the same bed, can't they? Without the other, I mean."

He looked back at her. "I need to turn those lights off for you."

"I can do it." Kneeling on the bed, she pulled the string. "Can a man and woman do that, Joe?"

"Of course they can." She heard him swallow. "It's all an attitude of mind and fortunately I haven't completely lost control of mine. I'd love to share your fan."

Ellie scooted to an edge of the bed to give him plenty of room, and the mattress sagged when Joe stretched out on top. "We'll need to talk," he said.

She didn't want to. "Don't worry about my problems. I'll work them through."

He was quiet for a while.

Ellie closed her eyes. She hurt all over and realized she had locked her joints.

Joe held her hand and brought it to his lips. He kissed it for a long time, just pressed his warm mouth into the base of her fingers as if it satisfied his needs.

"Do you sleep on your back or your side?" Joe asked. "Or your stomach?"

"My side."

"Which side?"

She rolled away from him, even though she'd have had to face him to be on her favorite side, and all but hung off the bed.

"You'll fall off, cher," he told her very quietly. "Come here. I promise you're safe, but you need comfort. We both do."

He eased her across the mattress and settled her into the cradle he made with his drawn-up knees.

Tension made her back hurt but she held still.

"Relax," Joe said, his mouth close to her ear. He used his fingers to draw her hair away from her face. "Some bastard took advantage of you. We'll talk about that, but not until you're ready. Let it all go, sweetheart. Let it float away."

His low voice vibrated against her shoulder. She squeezed her eyes shut. Over and over again Joe stroked her arm, ran the backs of his fingers across her cheek, caressed her neck.

"Joe..."

"Hush. You're here and I'm here. We're safe. I won't let anything happen to you, Ellie."

She began to let go. Her body softened. She sat in his lap with so little to shield the most vulnerable parts of her body from the intimate signs of his masculinity, yet she knew Joe would not do a thing she didn't want.

Tiredness swept over her. It didn't cut her awareness of him, but it demanded its share of her.

"Is it okay if I hold you, Ellie?"

"Uh-huh."

His arm was heavy around her waist but she liked it just that way.

"Sleep," he said into her hair. "Just let me hold you through the night."

17

"Quit playin' with those things," Cerise said from the back room over her dress shop. "If I'd known they'd get to botherin' me I'd never have bought them for you."

He muffled a laugh. She'd bought the night-vision glasses for herself and pretended they were a gift for him.

"Paul." Cerise could win a whining contest hands down. "Come on, I want to talk to you. And we've only got a few hours for us. The movie's ready to go."

He had squeezed himself between racks of hanging merchandise in the night-black front room so he could look out the window without being seen. "I'll be there, honey." For the moment, what he saw through the night-vision goggles interested him more than the woman waiting to fuck him. "You know you bought these for yourself, anyway." Paul laughed and kept his attention on Hungry Eyes.

"You were real late," Cerise said. "I thought you'd decided not to come. You think long and hard before doin' that to me. I could make your life real difficult."

He had learned to keep any anger to himself—not that he got angry often. Cerise pushed him too hard, but that was all part of the attraction, her demands, her imagination and her bone-crunching energy.

Joe and Ellie operated in the dark with the blinds pulled up. Paul figured it was as hot over there as it was here so they'd opened the windows. Joe had carried Ellie to the bedroom and Paul had seen when Mr. Squeaky Clean Attorney followed the woman into bed. So far they hadn't moved much but he figured that would change soon enough.

Mmm-mmm-mmm, who would have thought the mousy little book lady had all that under her ugly dresses. He had expected them to go right at it against the couch.

"Paul. That's it. I'm comin' to get you."

"Don't blow it, Cerise. Don't let any light show in here." God, he was sweating and he had a hard-on he'd have to get taken care of.

"Paul loves his nasty glasses." Cerise had crawled through the darkness and wrapped herself around his legs. She stuffed a hot little hand up one leg of his boxers, exposed the part of him she liked best, and put her eye to its tip. "What do I see in here? More to the point, what do I feel here?" She giggled and took him in her mouth. Paul pushed her away, ready for her to fight him. When she let go with her mouth, she said, "Who's a hard boy, a ready boy? C'mon. Come with Cerise." She smacked his rear hard and used her fingernails. Paul shoved her hard.

No action showed in the bedroom. Too bad. That was the most fun he'd had with the new toy.

He removed the glasses and tucked them under the lid of a trunk. He bent to pick Cerise up by her thighs. Facing him, with her calves gripping his head and her face exactly where it belonged, he walked carefully into the windowless box room with her big breasts bouncing against his belly at every step. She beat at the backs of his thighs. Cerise had turned the room into the perfect night spot—or any-time-of-day spot if the opportunity presented itself.

Once they were shut inside he let Cerise fall onto the pillow-strewn mattress on the floor, stripped off his shorts and climbed to sit behind her head. A plasma screen covered a large section of one wall and she'd paused a disk in the player.

Frozen in place and about life-size, the stud in the porn flick had just torn the crotch out of a woman's black panty hose. Paul noted her sweater was pulled up above huge, oiled breasts. She wore white shoes with her black hose.

"With the door open, the light from that thing could be enough to give us away," he pointed out.

She stretched out on her back with her arms above her head, rocked from side to side to make her boobs sway, and reached for him. "Fuss, fuss, fuss. C'mon down here."

He moved what she wanted away. He'd rather give it into her tender loving care, but tonight they'd work for whatever pleased them.

Cerise had a good body and it was naked, the way he liked his women to be at all times if possible, with the exception of Jilly. With Jilly it was something different from anything he'd felt with a woman before.

"Did you bring the stuff?" Cerise said. "You promised."

"Couldn't get it. Next time, though." He rolled Cerise onto her stomach, sat astride her back and slapped her behind until she squirmed and giggled—and finally shrieked. Cerise could be trusted to suck up the unexpected and she believed in payback. Fucking wonderful payback. He pushed his face between her thighs, lifted her hips and found her very hot button with his teeth and tongue.

"Oh, Paul," she cried. "No, you bastard, I'm not ready... Oh, shit, oh, yeah, yeah."

Seconds of squirming and sobbing and she fell limp. It never took long.

The remote had managed to remain on the mattress. He clicked the disk on again and scooted to sit on the pillows with a foot on either side of Cerise's head.

"Why were you so late, baby?" she asked, her voice muffled.

She never let a gripe drop. "I told you I showed up in the square right behind half the town, including Spike. I think some of them thought I came from Rosebank with him."

"How would they think that when you were on your scooter?"

"I parked it in your shed out back of this place like I always do."

Cerise raised her head and shoulders and crossed her arms on the mattress. "But you didn't hurry in to me." Her lips glistened and her pale breasts shone. "You just had to go see what was up at Ellie's shop. So her window got broken. Big deal. When did you turn into Spider-Man?"

Paul took a length of her blond hair and wound it in and out through his fingers. "Father Cyrus saw me. What would he have thought if I didn't help out?"

"Now you find religion. That's dandy."

He pulled her hair lightly. "I never lost it. And you're a bad girl to tell me what I should or shouldn't do." Remembering how he'd felt compelled to tell Cyrus about his love life made Paul squirm. Some things got ground into you when you were a kid and never completely went away.

"Paul," Cerise said in a little-girl voice. Her big blue eyes shone with amusement. "I've got an idea for you. A new guide- book. Nelson's Way to this, that and whatever is a big success. It has to be. I can tell you're rolling in it. How about Nelson's Way to the best fucking orgasm you ever had?" Her knees were bent, her ankles crossed in the air, and she scissored them absently. "I could be your research helper. Whenever you get stumped, I'll help you figure out the next move."

"Cute," he said. He'd produced twenty volumes of the Nelson's Way books and wished he never had to look at another one of them.

The games must begin. Time to woo his way back into the lady's graces. "A little waiting for the main event can be a good thing," he told her. "Makes a man a whole lot hungrier."

"Show me."

This time he tugged her hair until her head tipped backward. "See?" he said, pinching her nipples hard. "I'm hungry." Flinging her, yelling and kicking, to her back and holding her shoulders down with his knees, he rocked forward and flicked his tongue deep between her legs. When she jerked, he laughed. She writhed and moaned. Teasing her, bringing her close to the edge, then depriving her of his tongue for seconds at a time, he enjoyed the spectacle of her voluptuous body squirming and seeking release. Finally she finished what he'd started herself. She slammed her rear up and down on the mattress and the jiggling of her breasts mesmerized him.

He let her go.

Wild, throwing herself at him without warning, Cerise slapped his face and screamed with laughter when he yelped.

She didn't stop. Slapping and pinching, she attacked him, squirmed around and slid out of reach of his hands, and punished him.

"Hey," he said, striking at her and missing. "Look what you did." With her long, sharp fingernails she'd made his wrist bleed hard.

"Oh, come on, baby. You can handle it. I couldn't have caused that all on my own."

He threw up an arm, the arm with the wounded wrist and snapped, "Ellie's window got smashed in—I got cut on the glass. Watch the face, bitch!"

She kissed his mouth but kept on pinching him and laughing in her throat. Paul wrestled her arms behind her. Cerise liked pain.

Moving so fast that he flinched, she slithered to grip his waist and take him in deep enough for him to feel the back of her throat—before he stopped knowing just what he felt anymore.

Her head bobbed and his eyes closed. He let his knees fall wide apart. She teased, speeded up, slowed down, took her lips away then attacked all over again. He panted and felt the stinging work her nails had done.

The movie played patterns of dark and light over his eyelids. The sound had been muted. He squinted at the screen, at the stud's member playing hide-and-seek through torn black panty hose.

Paul turned the movie off. His skin prickled. Cerise

went after her task in a frenzy. She looked up at him, frowning, and used her hands on him.

Goddammit, he'd never had any trouble. He felt himself slacken in her fingers. *He was losing it.*

She was too demanding, that was it. He'd worked hard and ended up tired out, but she didn't have what it took to tune in to how he felt and what he needed.

"What's wrong?" Cerise said. "Put the movie back on."

"I don't want the movie back on. I've seen it before, several times, and so have you."

"When did that ever matter?"

"Give it a little rest," he told her. "You're too pushy and you're turning me off."

Cerise rose over him, her eyes narrowed and angry. She raised a hand to hit him again but he caught her wrist the moment before she would have slapped his face. "What's the only rule around here?" he asked, and heard the

menace in his own voice. Good. He felt menacing.

She looked away. "Never touch the face. We never mark each other's faces."

"That's right. So how come you were about to forget?"

Cerise settled herself on the mattress again, curled on her side this time with her cheek in his crotch. "You made me mad."

"We always get mad. Some of the best sex happens when we're mad. No excuse to go for the face."

"I won't do it again."

She cradled his balls, inclined her head so she could lick them. "Mmm-mmm, you taste good. Salty and sweet all mixed up together. Paul, I need to talk to you."

Shit. If there was one thing he detested it was women who thought conversation was part of a good fuck. He liked her ag-

gressive participation, but he didn't want to listen to her dumb ideas, or her declarations of love. He really hated that.

"Paul, baby?"

"Talk." He entertained himself watching her treat his balls like a breakable work of art—like the androgynous crease between a Chihuly cherub's glass legs. He was at full mast again.

"You've got money and I've got money. That's not a revelation."

He squinted down at her. "So?"

She stroked him. "We could do very well together."

Laughing wouldn't get him what he wanted and that was to make sure she didn't hang on to her fantasy for long. "A cottage with a white picket fence?" he said. "And babies?"

"You don't like babies?"

"Other people's children are just fine. I'm not the settling-down kind."

Cerise let him go and her fingers curled tightly.

"Come on," he said, stroking her shoulders. "Be honest with yourself. You're a playgirl. You were made for the good times, not to turn into a bored housewife." Or *his* wife, and he knew that's what she'd just asked for. Just one woman would fill that bill and she couldn't be more different from this one.

Jilly looked at him with love. He felt hot at the thought. But that's what she did and he wanted to be with her. She was good for him in ways he couldn't explain to anyone. A sweet, funny, gentle girl. Sweet to hold, and straightforward. She didn't have an agenda other than to see where the future took them. It couldn't lead to this, his need for a mixture of secrecy and sex that got wild. That's why, when he figured out how to get Jilly for good, he would have to be sure he had the kind of diversions he needed. If she ever found out…he'd lose her.

"Paul," Cerise whispered. "I'd love to know you belonged to me. We're a match. Couldn't that be enough for you?"

He patted her head. "We're a great match and we're wasting time talking."

She sat up. "Did you talk to Jilly yet? Did you tell her it's all over between you?"

"I never promised to do that," he said quietly while he felt his temper rise.

She dug her fingernails into his thigh. "Yes, you did. I told you I wouldn't take being the whore to the ice maiden anymore. What did you think that meant if it wasn't that I expect to be first and only with you?"

"I thought it meant you were jealous."

"Damn you." She hit his face. "Damn you, Paul Nelson. You're making me so pissed off. Get rid of her, I tell you, or I will." Once more she drew back her arm and slapped him as hard as she could.

"Stop it," he told her. "Now." He didn't dare lose his temper. She wanted him to fight back again, to mark her this time. Then they'd both turn bruised faces to the world and someone would put the pieces together soon enough.

"Deal with Jilly Gable or I'll tell her what you get up to with me."

His control shattered. Roughly, he caught her behind the neck and shoved her face into his lap. "Open your mouth. You need comfort." Again he ground her face against him. "Do it. I'll comfort you. Suck baby, suck. You've got your very own pacifier. Now, please me and learn a lesson. No woman gets the better of me."

Cerise did as she was told and he could tell the moment when excitement stopped her from being angry. He came in her mouth and she swallowed, raised her face to grin at him while she wiped her lips.

Just the sight of her infuriated him. Grabbing her by the shoulders, he forced her, facedown, on the mattress and stuffed a pillow under her belly.

"Paul," she said, her voice thin. That was all she said.

He took her from behind—his favorite angle because he could drive harder and faster with his thighs between Cerise's while he used his hands to move her in opposition to his body. She came but he didn't miss a beat. Speeding the rate he kept going at her until she cried out for him to stop.

All part of the game.

At last he paused and fell to his back. He had to rest his legs, and if he wasn't dry he ought to be.

Cerise crawled up beside him, then eased herself on top of his body. "You're the best," she told him. "Whatever happens, I can't bear to lose you."

He didn't feel like talking.

"We can keep on seeing each other. Having fun." She hugged him and kissed his face. Cerise didn't usually do much kissing and that suited him.

"I thought you were going to tell Jilly about us," he said.

She laughed—not a convincing sound. "I was pushing to see if I could get my way with you. Now I know I can't and I like that better. I'll always know where I am with you."

What the hell? "You're a good fuck, Cerise. The best. But you've got to be a good girl or it won't work anymore."

"I'll be good," she said, rubbing herself against him. "I'm already being good, so would you do what you just did—again?"

18

Tomorrow, Ellie thought, she'd be able to open the shop again. Two days without the diversion of work had been too long. Folks stopped by, one after the other, to bring food they'd prepared or to offer help. Ellie loved them for it, but each of them wanted news and even if she wanted to, she had nothing to share with them.

The people Marc Girard had found to replace the window had worked fast and well. It saddened her that several of the leaded panes hadn't made it through in one piece, but squares of glass in solid colors didn't look out of place.

"Spike told you to bring me and go straight to the church?" Joe said, ducking his head to look through the windshield of the Jeep toward St. Cécile's. "You're sure of that?" Darkness had fallen.

Ellie turned in the passenger seat and watched him put on the emergency brake. "The church," she said. "A thing like that kind of sticks in your mind."

"True," he said, making no attempt to get out of the

vehicle. They had parked on the strip by the rectory. "Just seems funny Gautreaux would want to meet us here."

It seemed more than funny to Ellie. "You've said that several times. Spike didn't say why." She thought a moment. "Does Spike seem okay to you?"

"I guess so," Joe said, screwing up his eyes. "He isn't lettin' up on this case. One good thing is he's gettin' funds to fill more posts. And they've sent him help from all over... He does look kinda rumpled some of the time. No, he doesn't seem okay. He's uptight, but that's probably on account of havin' NOPD breathin' down his neck."

"You could be right," she said. She hoped he was, but what she felt in Spike was something sad and worried and she didn't know how or if she should try to help him.

Joe pushed back her hair. He touched her naturally, and often. Last night he had arrived with a dinner Jilly had cooked. Ellie smelled the spices as soon as he started up the stairs. A quiet meal followed by several hours when he'd worked in the other apartment, then he'd returned and made up a bed on her living room couch. Their first night together hadn't been mentioned again.

Waking up beside him had startled her, but then she'd settled on her side, facing him, and pretended to sleep. From behind the hand curled loosely in front of her face, she had watched his eyes open, seen him turn his head on the pillow to look at her, and his smile when he lifted his head to study her. She would never forget that moment, or the care with which he'd left the bed because he tried not to disturb her. She wouldn't forget how he'd looked walking across her bedroom, either.

In the intimacy of the Jeep, they looked at each other and she wondered if he was thinking about what had happened between the two of them. Joe continued to slide her short curls through his fingers.

Daisy hadn't been herself since the glass-breaking episode. Ellie figured she'd pulled some muscles. Daisy had switched her allegiance to Joe and seemed content to lie close to him. The dog found comfort being with the man. Ellie smiled to herself. Smart dog: that's exactly how Ellie felt about Joe.

"What's making you smile?" Joe asked. "No, don't stop doing it. You've been a pretty serious woman lately—not that I'm surprised. I feel pretty serious myself."

"Smile?" she said, making large, surprised eyes. "Me? Never. Probably some kind of spasm."

He laughed at that. "I wish we didn't have to spend even part of this evening dealing with Gautreaux. I don't like him."

"I don't know what I think." Ellie shrugged. "He's like two different people. Angry and pushy or thoughtful and sad. I can't figure him out. He's got a room at Gator and Doll's. I'm told he's working on the case full time. Doll's suspicious of everyone but Gator likes him. Says young Wally likes him, too, and I think Wally's a good judge of character. Cyrus is the boy's best friend, that stands for something when it comes to his taste in people."

"Wazoo reckons Gautreaux's a man of many levels, whatever that means." He leaned toward her, kissed her cheek and nuzzled her neck. "Not that we would take any notice of Wazoo." His breath felt warm.

Ellie lowered her eyes. He'd decided he wanted to pursue her after all.

"I love the way you smell," he said. "Ellie, I want you and I'll wait as long as it takes, as long as there's a chance."

Hesitantly, she patted the side of his face, smoothed his sharp jawline. "I can't promise you anything, Joe."

He covered her hand on his face. "Okay. But can I hope?"

Ellie's throat tightened. "I want to hope."

"Cher?" He sat straighter but kept his face close to her. "That means you'd like things to work out for us?"

She heard him swallow and saw the hope in his eyes. "More than I'm capable of explaining."

"Let me help you deal with whatever happened to you," he said.

That wasn't a place she was prepared to visit, even if it did begin to seem inevitable that she'd have to. "I'm going to try to forget all about it," she told him. "Perhaps being…I have to let go of it. Not bury it anymore but allow it to lose its power over me. And if I can I will tell the whole story one day. I'll tell it to you."

He looked at her mouth. "If that's the way it has to be for now, Ellie, so be it." Then he kissed her lightly, as if he was reassuring her. She returned the kiss and felt his composure slip.

The tip of his tongue slid along her lower lip before he took her face between his hands and reminded her how it felt to be really kissed by Joe Gable.

Someone tapped the window and Joe put his forehead on Ellie's. "The joys of livin' in a small Southern town," he said. "One big, happy family sharin' just about everythin'."

Ellie managed to peek past him. "Spike," she said, her nose all but touching Joe's. "Someone needs to talk to him about the places he doesn't have jurisdiction over around here."

"Mmm." Joe kissed the tip of her nose. "Let's pretend he's not there."

She gave him a little push and opened her door. "Evening, Spike."

"Evenin', Ellie. Y'all comin'?"

The driver's door closed hard. "We gotta do somethin' about your timin', lawman. It stinks." Joe walked around to slap Spike on the back.

"Save it," Spike said, sounding like a stranger. "Your little romance takes a back seat to things like murdered women and attempted kidnapping. And terror tactics."

Ellie was stung. She blushed and blessed the evening gloom.

"That's enough," Joe said. The banter was over. "When it comes to our private lives, keep your opinions to yourself."

"Is that you, Joe?" Madge emerged from the side of the house and hurried to join them. "Cyrus is over there on his own with that angry man. I don't like it. Spike, how come you left him?"

"I came looking for these two."

Madge noticed Ellie and said, "Hi, you. How you doin'? Cyrus and I have been worried about you. I'm real sorry for your trouble."

"Thanks," Ellie said. "Are you coming with us?"

"No," Spike said. "This isn't a tea party."

"Then I'm definitely coming," Madge said. She turned away and walked across Bonanza Alley toward the church.

"What the hell does it take to keep control in this town?" Spike said. "You do what you decide to do, all of you. That woman behaves like Cyrus's mother."

Or like his wife. Ellie walked after Spike and Joe lengthened his stride to catch up with her and squeeze her arm. She was wrong to misinterpret the strong friendship Cyrus and Madge shared.

"Did he tell you how long Gautreaux's been here?" Madge called back. "Hours, that's how long. We kept thinkin' he'd leave whenever someone came to talk to Cyrus, but no, that man just hung around lookin' at his papers and makin' notes—and angry enough to frighten off a gator."

Spike broke into a run. "Will you hush up, Madge? You don't want him to hear you. Go back to the rectory and wait. Please. Or go home where you belong at this hour."

Joe glanced down at Ellie and raised his eyebrows. She wasn't the only one who felt buffeted by sharp currents.

Madge marched on, walked into the open vestibule but didn't enter the church. Refusing to look at Spike, she turned her face away when he passed her and kept it turned away as Joe and Ellie followed him.

Electric wall sconces cast weak light over wooden pews and embroidered kneelers. Every other bulb had been removed. St. Cécile's coffers tended to be a challenge. Brighter lights shone from a chapel to their left and Spike walked, boot heels clattering on flagstones, to stand before a gate in the wrought-iron screen that closed off the chapel.

"There you are, Spike," they heard Cyrus say. "How about we all walk over to the house. We'll be more comfortable there."

Spike opened the gate.

"This is quite fine, thank you," Guy Gautreaux said in his deep voice. "No distractions to speak of. Any sign of them, Spike?"

Ellie and Joe went quickly into the chapel. Ellie said, "We would be 'them,' Detective. We got here as quickly as we could."

Spike crossed his arms in a manner that reminded

her that she and Joe hadn't exactly come as quickly as they could have. Joe rubbed her back and she actually felt safe, even in this strange interrogation cell. Spike had made it clear that Gautreaux planned to ask them questions.

"The detective here wanted to know how many mornings we run," Cyrus said to Joe.

"Father," Gautreaux cut in, looking as if respect cost him something. "I do the talkin' here. Sit down. Are we still on our own, Spike?"

"Um." Spike rubbed tired eyes. He had a good growth of beard stubble but not enough to cover two old razor cuts. "As good as."

"What the hell does that mean?"

"I expect Madge walked over with you," Cyrus said. "She'll be watchin' to make sure we don't get any interruptions."

"Watchin' from where?" Gautreaux said, and went to the gate. He peered out. "Ma'am, you can't be sittin' there. Best you get along."

"Madge?" Cyrus spoke sharply, more sharply than Ellie had ever heard from him. He followed the detective, put a hand on his shoulder and said quietly, "You don't speak to the lady that way, you. She's knows a lot of what I know and she doesn't repeat anythin' she hears. Come right on in, Madge."

Ellie scarcely dared check any reactions, but she saw Spike's jaw slacken.

"Hoo-mama," Joe said under his breath.

"Come one, come all," Gautreaux said, waving Cyrus and Madge into the chapel.

"I'll stay out here and keep watch," Madge told him, and walked out of sight.

"Let's get on," Gautreaux said, his black eyes expressionless. He returned but didn't sit down again. Cyrus came, too, and they were all silent as long as they heard Madge's receding footsteps.

"Why here?" Joe asked. "Not exactly regular procedure, Detective."

"This ass-backwards town drove me to it. All I want is a secure place and I'm not convinced the station is safe. Too much classified information gets spread around here and it—"

"Hold it," Spike said. "Were you about to say my people are talkin' out of school? If you were, *don't*. You know how it works in a place like Toussaint. Good folks, but they come to their own conclusions and sometimes they're right. Throw in comments by people who've been questioned and everyone's even closer to knowin' what's goin' on."

"My name is Guy," Gautreaux said abruptly. "I'd be obliged if you'd use it—all of you. I'm around for the duration—or until the action moves elsewhere—and I'm thinkin' we ought to try to get along."

He achieved silence until Cyrus shot out a hand and said, "Thank you, Guy. We'll be doin' our best to help any way we can."

Joe and Spike weren't shaking any hands tonight, but they nodded and muttered the man's name.

"I am afraid for security," Gautreaux said. "I'd be lyin' if I didn't say so. Didn't occur to me to talk here until I came to find Father Cyrus. I'm glad I did. Know what I think? I think we've got some major desperate people on our hands and Ellie's the pebble in their shoes. Charles Penn for one, I can't be sure he's workin' alone."

"Don't say that," Ellie told him. "Why? What makes you think so?"

"I'd say he's gettin' help, that's why."

"Yeah," Spike agreed. "That's what I figure. He knows too much about folks' movements. How would he find out on his own?"

Joe held Ellie's hand and squeezed it. "I've wondered about that."

"Okay, I see that, but why didn't one of you say something to me?" Ellie concentrated on the pressure of Joe's hand. "Penn knows where I'm going to be and when. He knew I'd be at Pappy's that night."

"I kept puttin' it aside," Joe told her. "Why stir you up even more when all I've got is a hunch?"

Guy said, "On the mornin' of the murder in Royal Street—Ellie, who can vouch for you bein' at home?"

"Damn it," Joe said, squaring off to the other man. "I thought you said you'd dropped that. If Ellie had anything to do with the killin' why would someone be in town tryin' to kill her now?"

Guy leaned against a stone wall and lowered his eyelids almost shut. A small stained window behind him, depicting St. Francis and a scattering of birds, looked ludicrous. "All I'm doin' is askin' questions," Guy said. "Put your mind to it and you'll know why. I want you to account for your movements, too, Joe. Cyrus can't seem to remember if you ran that day."

"We didn't," Joe said at once. "We ran the day before and the day after. I was in court early on the day of the killing."

"And a whole mess of people can tell you so." Spike said.

"Did anyone see you that mornin', Ellie?" Guy said. "We got to get this out of the way." He pinned her with a stare, and when she didn't speak soon enough for him he raised his voice a notch, "Don't mess with me anymore. Just speak your piece. Yes or no?"

Joe went for Guy, fists at the ready, and landed a solid punch to his chin before Spike and Cyrus could leap forward and drag Joe off. He strained, trying to lash out again.

"Son of a bitch," he said. "All that cozy talk was to loosen us up, right? You think that's what it takes to get what you want out of someone. Well, Ellie was wherever she's told you she was. This woman doesn't lie. I'm gonna see to it you get reprimanded and taken off the case. There's nothin' usual about the way you're conductin' things."

Guy laughed and turned his back.

"Spike, do somethin'." Joe shrugged off Cyrus and Spike.

"What d'you say, Guy?" Spike asked.

"That I agree. There's nothin' usual about the way I'm dealin' with this and that's because there's nothin' usual about the crime. Remember I've been in on this from murder number one. I thought things got screwed up then and I think they're screwed up now. Where is Penn? There's nothin' wrong with the search teams. You're doin' fine work, Spike, and so is everyone else as far as I can tell. So where in hell is Penn when he's not scarin' up fake attacks?"

"Fake?" Ellie sat down hard on the cane seat of a chair.

"What about it, Ellie?" Guy said. "Who can back up your story?"

"I don't get it," Joe said. "This conversation belongs in an interrogation room. I don't want it to take place there but this is wacko...Guy."

"Humor me." Guy looked anything but humorous. "This is the best way."

Best for whom? Ellie bowed her head.

"You were present for the Mardi Gras killin'," Guy said in a monotone. "If you can't prove otherwise, who's to say you weren't there when Billie Knight died?"

Spike and Cyrus restrained Joe.

"I don't know what you mean," Ellie said. Guttering candles caught her eye. She smelled old incense and older dust warmed to an intense odor by hot wax. The men's faces looked gray but their eyes turned dark in the up-light.

"Neither do I," Guy said. "But if you were there it would be some coincidence, wouldn't it? That ring Billie Knight kept lookin' at, it wasn't worth much, Tilton told me. Or at least not what I expected. I saw it. Simple but a pretty thing. Someone should have bought her that little ring, then she wouldn't have been there when a killer came callin'."

His comments were met with silence.

"I don't think you were there," Guy said to Ellie. "But you're in the middle of this and I want you to think hard. Think how it looks that Penn killed Billie then showed up here, supposedly after you."

"Fu—" Joe snapped his mouth shut.

Cyrus took over. "I'm glad you decided to have this talk here where there are witnesses. Seems a strange choice, though. If you really think Ellie's involved I can't think why you'd throw your idea around without anything to back it up."

"The only way this is going to get solved is by comin' at it from the inside," Guy said. "I want your help. And Ellie's goin' to want help from all of us. Think about this. The reason Ellie's still alive is because Penn wants her that way. He could have killed her by now if that's what he'd decided to do."

"He could have," Spike said. "But you're thinkin' somebody else is tellin' him what to do and when."

"Could be true," Joe agreed. "Question is still why."

"Because," Cyrus murmured, "Ellie doesn't have witnesses to what she says happened to her, and Penn, or someone else, wants to make it look like she's makin' it up to cover for somethin'."

"You're even the book lady and you've got those Sonja Elliot stories in your shop," Spike said, and turned red. "Forget I said that."

"This is turning into a parlor game," Joe said. "I'm takin' Ellie home. By the way, I'm also stayin' at her place so you'll know where I am if you need me."

"Are you thinking—you are." Ellie moistened her mouth. "You definitely are thinking I'm either being framed for murder or that I committed murder and I've got some incredible scheme for making myself look like a victim instead."

"Do you know what you're suggestin'?" Cyrus asked Guy. "You're makin' a case for Charles Penn being innocent in both cases."

Guy shook his head. "I'm throwing out an idea I think is fairly solid. Now, let's get on with it. I'll want to be at the field teams' briefing in the mornin'. You goin' back to the station now, Spike?"

"I reckon I'll hang out here for a bit if it's okay with you, Cyrus."

Cyrus said, "Anytime," but didn't quite hide his concern.

"Stop." Ellie stood up, her whole body shaking inside. "What happens now? If you don't believe someone's after me. Or not to do me real harm, anyway, are you saying you don't take anything I've told you seriously?"

"I think we're all on the same page," Guy said. "Calm down, Ellie. There are too many people who know too much. We're going to have to weed 'em out until we're left with a credible suspect."

"But—"

Guy cut Ellie off. "Relax. You should be happy. You'll be watched, but there's a good chance you're bein' used as a red herring to throw us off. But that's not the whole story. We need to retrace our steps and look in other directions—without taking our eyes off you."

"We've had too much serious crime in this town," Ellie said. "How come? We're ordinary people."

"Must be somethin' in the water," Guy said. "That and Toussaint is an easy in-and-out for types who want a fast getaway."

"You don't know this town as well as some of us, Guy," Joe said. "We've had more than our share of homegrown crazies killin' one another off."

Guy looked slightly impressed. "Is that so? Well, every crime is different and this one surely is. This is nothin' homegrown and I'm about ready to bet our joker is here for one reason—Ellie. The way I see it we've got two big questions hangin' over us. Is her only connection that she saw what she saw at Mardis Gras? And—"

"And how many people are involved and why?" Joe said.

Guy nodded. "And do they or don't they really want her dead, now or later."

19

Candlelight, holy smells and deep quiet ought to give a man some peace. At least, that's what Spike had pinned his hopes on.

He didn't know much about the praying stuff but he'd give anything a try, anything that might help him out of the pit he'd stepped into.

Quiet and the rest of the stuff didn't stop his mind from dashing around or help him quit calling himself every kind of a fool.

Guy Gautreaux needed a mouth transplant for rubbing it into Ellie that she could be the target for murder, *"now or later."* Some people just never got it how just because nothing much scared them didn't mean everyone else was made the same.

There he went, thinking about work again. Sure, Ellie and the others were dear friends, but he wasn't here, feeling the night slip onward, because of them. He was a failure in the area of his life that mattered most—with his family.

Once too often he'd gotten so hung up on the work he'd forgotten a message brought by his Wendy. Vivian had planned a special supper for the three of them. By the time he remembered and got back to Rosebank, a note on the kitchen counter gave instructions for reheating a plate Vivian had left in the refrigerator. He had gone to their bedroom but it was dark and Vivian didn't answer him when he said her name. He felt unwelcome.

The next couple of nights he hadn't been too much earlier getting home, and each time he'd slid into bed beside Vivian, hoping she would break the silence. Why should she? She'd heard every excuse in the book for being left alone.

Last night he hadn't gone home at all. He slept at the office instead. There were clean uniforms there and he'd picked up the other things he needed.

Three times today he'd called her and three times Charlotte had picked up her daughter's cell phone. Charlotte was "So pissed with you, Spike. Not that it's any of my business if you choose to ruin your marriage."

His eyes stung. He took out the pack of Marlboros he'd bought, looked at them and threw them on the chair beside his. That would really be a smart move, to take up smokes because he didn't have what it took to figure out what the hell was happening to his life.

He'd go home and insist Vivian talk to him, dammit. She could be difficult in her own way. So he wasn't always a saint, well, neither was she.

Giving the praying stuff a shot first couldn't hurt—if he could figure out how to do it right.

Vivian prayed with Wendy every night before she went to sleep. He'd always avoided joining them because he felt out of place.

You dumb shit. All he would have had to do was sit beside them and listen. That would be good for Wendy and make Vivian so happy. Making her happy took so little.

He took off his Stetson and instantly realized he shouldn't be wearing it inside a church. Even he knew that much. He held the hat between his knees and scrubbed a hand through his short hair. This had to stop. He'd turned himself into a disaster. How could he give his job what it needed if he couldn't do right by his wife and find out what he'd done to screw up so bad? Not just the last straw over the supper, but what it was she needed from him and didn't get.

Wendy's mother had left him for a weight lifter who needed a woman to admire his body. Spike had tried with her but the fool woman just walked out the door one day, leaving Wendy with Homer, and never came back. And for this small mercy, he was grateful.

See, he remembered something about prayers.

No, no, no, he wasn't going there with the guilt over why Wendy's mother really left. She went because she was too young, too selfish and because she couldn't control what went on in her pants. This time was different. This time he'd neglected his way right out of Vivian's graces.

"Okay," he muttered, bowing his head. "I'm goin' to have to make the best of what I can manage for now. Maybe later I'll have a word with Cyrus." His blood ran cold at the thought.

Silence could be a prayer. He'd heard that. With an elbow on one thigh and his forehead propped on the heel of his hand, Spike listened to that silence. The candles sizzled just a little. The wind that kept flirting with the town had set up a dance with trees outside the building and branches swept the little window with the saintly type on it.

Night never could quite get the hang of quiet around here.

"I'm sorry for being a doggone fool," he muttered. "If you gimme a hand to clean up my own mess, I'll figure out how to do things right from now on."

Panic grasped his throat. "Now, that wasn't supposed to be some sort of deal. I should have said I'm going to do my best in future and it would be nice if you could help me out."

Holy... Crying wasn't in his bag of tricks, but the stinging in his eyes got worse. He squeezed his lids shut, bent farther forward and used his spare arm to wrap his middle tight.

Footsteps came along the side aisle toward the chapel. Spike shot to his feet and backed to the wall, his hand hovering over his gun.

"Spike. Are you here?"

Vivian had come. He turned hot, cold and hot again so fast his skin couldn't decide if it should sweat. He found his voice. "Careful out there, Vivian. The lighting's bad. I'll be right there."

"I'm already here," she said, pushing open the gate and entering the little chapel.

Dear Lord, when had she gotten so pale? And the gray smudges beneath her very blue eyes? When had they arrived?

She'd come to tell him it was over.

"Vivian. Don't say a word, darlin'. Please sit down. You don't look so good and it's all my fault. I'm so sorry."

She did sit down and bow her head. Her straight black hair slid forward.

"Look," he said. "I've been sittin' here thinkin' and fi-gurin' out just how I turned everything into such a dog-gone foul-up. I never meant to, Vivian, honest I didn't."

"Hush," she said finally. "Are those your cigarettes?"

Lying wouldn't get him anywhere. "Yes."

"You don't smoke."

"I know."

She looked up at him. "So why buy them?"

He drew up his shoulders. "Just one more bit of proof that I'm an ass. Other people seem to get some peace or somethin' from them. Thought I'd try."

"Did you?"

"Nope. Pack isn't open. Never could inhale, anyway. The stuff always choked me. Hard to be cool with the other kids when you're gagging your guts up."

"Spike Devol, you *are* an ass."

He opened his mouth but forgot if he'd planned to say something. Vivian never spoke to him like that—or not until now.

She let her head lean back and closed her eyes. Wind or not it was hot and air felt rationed. Her yellow sun-dress had a full skirt that settled around her pretty legs and distracted him. Vivian was the loveliest woman in the world and she'd settled for a small-town deputy sheriff who didn't have the smarts to take real good care of the best thing that ever happened to him—in addition to Wendy.

"You're tired, darlin'," he told her quietly. "You go ahead and say whatever you feel like sayin' to me. I deserve it."

"You're an ass because you make stuff up in your head and let it become true to you. Ever heard of opening up? Coming clean? Just plain laying out what's on your mind?"

He felt a little hope but buried it at once. He knew what happened to a man who got overconfident too easily.

"What in goodness' name made you tell Wendy you'd be home in time for the supper I told her to mention to you, then not come?"

Spike didn't feel so good himself. He pulled a chair close to hers and sat down facing her. "Time got away from me and when I did start for home I only had to come back into town because all hell's broken loose here. We've got trouble around the clock."

"I know you have. Have you forgotten Ellie's a friend of mine, too?"

He shook his head. "No."

"Why didn't you call?"

"It was so late by then. I figured you'd be asleep and I didn't want to wake you up."

"Asleep, hmm? My husband didn't come home so I just went to sleep. I couldn't have been wide awake and praying he'd call and tell me he was safe."

"Ah, Vivian, don't."

"Do you think I didn't hear you come to the bedroom door, open it, then go away again? What was that about?"

"I did everythin' wrong."

She sighed.

"Vivian!" He glanced at the black outside the window. "What are you thinkin' of, coming here at night on your own?"

"I was thinking of looking for my husband. I haven't really seen him for days."

"I have called, a lot of times." He had to put up some defense.

No, he didn't, he just had to navigate the storm and come out with his hull in one piece.

"And my mother answered. I told her to because I didn't want to talk to you."

"But you just told me off for not callin'."

"The first night."

"Oh. Vivian, you shouldn't have driven here on your own. You could have got me on my cell and I'd have been right there. Boy, would I have been there. Wendy must wonder what's up, too."

"Nope, she knows men can be asses, too. I love you, Spike. You're kind. You're the best family man a woman could hope for. And you're sexy as hell."

Spike stared at her through narrowed eyes.

"You don't like me telling you those things?"

"Hell, yes. I'm just a man. I love you sayin' those things. You couldn't love me as much as I love you. I thought you wanted to be finished with me."

"From a misunderstanding? Because you made a little mistake then set about making it bigger and bigger?"

He felt foolish, and so turned on he shamed himself. But she'd had that effect on him ever since they first met. "How would it be if I—"

"Just fine, Spike," she said. "If you made a habit of making sure whether or not I'm in a teensy snit before you start wondering if you should get a lawyer, I think that would be wonderful."

He put his hat on top of the Marlboros. "This is a bit sudden, but I'd like to kiss you, cher. If I don't get to touch you soon I'm goin' to dry up."

She gave him one of her stern looks that never quite held. "Just as long as you make it an appropriate kiss for the surroundings."

"It'll be so appropriate," he told her, and slipped from his chair to kneel beside her crossed legs. She smiled and no trace of the smart act remained.

He stroked her bare arms and shuddered at the feel of her. Vivian rubbed the back of a hand over his stubbly face and looked at him as if she was crazy about having her fingers scratched.

"We are never going to let this happen again," she said, and leaned forward to run her fingers back through his hair. She held the sides of his head and touched her lips to his.

The way she made him feel had only gotten more intense. He returned the rush of small, intense kisses and inclined his head to nip at her neck and her ear. "Do you think it would be a sin to make love here?" he asked.

She waited until he raised his head to look at her. "Are you too tired for a wild night in our room?"

"It would be a sin, huh?"

"I doubt it, but with what I have in mind we could get pretty bruised up around here, Spike."

He loved her wicked grins. "Good thinkin'. Let's go."

She stopped him from getting up and the wide smile disappeared. "Maybe this is better than some old special supper at Rosebank."

"Your choice," he said, making sure he didn't look too pleased with himself. "I'm not sure I can wait till we get back, either."

"Whoa, boy. See if you can get your mind off your favorite subject. How long have we been married?"

"Two years," he said at once. "Why?"

"Don't you think it's about time something stuck?"

There were times when they needed an interpreter. "I think everything has stuck, Vivian. And if I can keep control of my negative imagination it'll keep stickin' more and more."

"Spike, I meant isn't it time something of you and something of me got stuck? Now, that's a perfectly horrible way to put it. Forgive me, this is all new to me."

Goose bumps crawled up his spine and he let her decide what to say next.

"It's happened and I hope you'll be as happy as I am. You did tell me it was what you wanted, it just didn't happen right away."

"It?" He couldn't control his smile.

"Him or her. I'm about ten weeks pregnant."

He cried.

"Spike? Honey?" Vivian cried right with him. "What's the matter?"

"Nothin'. I'm happy is all, and blubberin' like a kid. Thank you, thank you, Vivian."

"Thank *you*. I'm so over the moon I can't even think straight. If I could have we wouldn't just have gone through a piece of silliness."

He got to his feet, slammed his hat down hard on his head and lifted his wife in his arms. "I'm takin' you home and there won't be any wild lovin', my girl. You've got to be looked after."

"I don't need to be carried." Vivian poked him hard. "Try that nonsense on me and I'll make you suffer. There's nothing wrong with me. I'm healthy as a horse, Reb says so. I asked all kinds of questions and she said—well, she told me there's no reason not to do whatever we like however we like it."

"You asked Reb about that?" He wouldn't know how to face the woman.

"She's a doctor."

"Mmm. Off we go."

He carried her from the chapel and along the side aisle.

A tall figure emerged from the vestibule. At least Homer knew enough to get the hat off his head. "You two through with this lovers' spat or whatever you call it when you're already married?"

"Homer? What are you doin' here? Interferin' as usual?"

"I brought your wife because I knew you wouldn't want her to come alone. Now I'm leavin'. Can you be trusted not to mess up again?"

"Guess we won't tell you the news, then," Spike said.

Homer stuck out his chin. "What news?" Creases from a lifetime of hard work in the elements crazed his face. But he was still a handsome son of a gun and tough as tacks—in most respects.

Spike pretended to consider whether or not to answer his father.

"You're going to be a grandfather again," Vivian said, and gave Spike a poke.

"Well," Homer said. "I'll be an alligator's bellyache. If that don't beat all."

20

Dancing in the shop might not be appropriate but Ellie couldn't make herself ask Wazoo to stop.

"If I could be anythin' in this world, what would I be?" Wazoo sang, gyrating between mostly empty tables in the café. "Why, I'd be a dog, that's what I'd be. A good man's dog and feel his hands on me."

Ellie caught Paul Nelson's eye and they shared a grin. He tapped the table to Wazoo's beat.

It was the first light moment since Joe left that morning, whistling, his briefcase in one hand and a scrambled egg sandwich in the other. He had relaxed. As the days passed since that creature broke her windows, they all had. They thought the threat was under control. She put a hand to her throat and had an urge to scream. Nothing was under control and that man was out there waiting for another chance at her. All any of them had, Joe, Cyrus, Spike and Guy, was a notion they liked the sound of: Charles Penn only wanted to terrify her.

They had no proof.

If there was someone feeding Penn information about her movements, who was it, and why?

"You okay?"

Ellie jumped. Paul had come to the counter without her noticing that he'd moved at all. She said, "Fine. Just wondering if we're in for a big storm. It's barely past lunchtime but it's getting dark already."

"It's the sky," he said. "Looks like it's trying to fall down on us."

He'd brought his coffee mug with him and Ellie topped it up before he returned to his table. He had come in for lunch each day since she had reopened. The laptop he brought with him didn't get much use and she had a feeling Paul might be doing his bit to keep an eye on her—otherwise he'd be working at Rosebank or at All Tarted Up. Jilly had confided to Ellie that Paul's deadline on one of his travel books was tight and he didn't have a lot of spare time.

His concern was welcome.

Jim Wade had been absent for a couple of days but he'd come in today talking about his client's growing interest in buying property in or around Toussaint. He, too, smiled while he watched Wazoo's dramatic performance. There was no denying that the woman could sing and dance.

She paused, arms outflung. "Anybody need anythin'? Nope? Well, if I could be anything in this world…" She'd piled her heavy black hair on top of her head and secured it with a comb decorated with pink rosebuds and crystals. A gray, floaty dress was a complete break with her habit of wearing black and mostly lace at all times.

"That's enough entertainment for one mornin'," she said, bowing gracefully in response to a small but enthusiastic show of applause. "With Ellie's blessin', I'm holdin' a clinic upstairs today. If you know anyone with animal problems, sad critters, mad critters, mean critters, psycho critters...suicidal dogs or snakes, gators with attitude, cats with complexes, well then you just get 'em right on in here to Wazoo, who sees everythin' and knows how to cure all them woes."

"You should get your hands on that Boa of Vivian Devol's," Paul said. "That's one mixed-up little piece of dog nuisance." He had pulled his chair awkwardly close to the table to accommodate a stranger who sat behind him, a man who had his own chair all the way into Paul's space.

One of the many things Ellie loved about people in Louisiana was the way they put themselves out to be agreeable, most of the time. Not that Paul was Louisianan.

"All Boa needs is respect," Wazoo said. "Little Chihuahua like that spends her life fightin' the bad mouthin'."

Ellie left the counter and went to the sitting area at the far end of the book stacks where four ladies quietly conducted their reading group. "Everyone happy?" she asked. "Can I bring more coffee or something to eat? Jilly sent over a plantain pie that smells to die for."

The ladies shifted in their chairs and cast long glances at one another. "How about we have ourselves a piece of that before we leave?" Min Boyer suggested to her friends, who muttered what a great idea that was.

Ellie caught some not-too-subtle motions and realized all of them held their books closed on their laps and mostly obscured by clasped hands. "What do you think of your book this month?" she said.

"Hah." Wazoo arrived. "They hidin' what they got

there. Min had me place the order when you were off. They're Sonja Elliot fans now."

A cool current encased Ellie. "Is she good?" she managed to ask. "She's been a megaseller for years." Creepy books unsettled Ellie, and although she'd intended to read Elliot since the macabre connection had been pointed out, she still couldn't bring herself to do it.

"I like her stuff," Esther from the dime store said. "We decided to do the one about Mardis Gras first since—" She blushed. "Well, on account of it being kind of like what happened to you."

"*Esther,*" Min said through pursed lips. "It didn't happen to Ellie, it happened to the victim and Ellie happened to see somethin' similar in N'Orleans."

"That's what I meant," Esther said in a small voice. "I'm sorry you're goin' through a bad time, Ellie. We thought just maybe if we read the books we could help figure things out and get that killer back behind bars."

Oh, great. Ellie could imagine what Guy and Spike— and Joe—would have to say about that. "You're very kind," she said, and backed away, drawing Wazoo with her.

"They don't mean no harm," Wazoo whispered.

"No. It's just that too many people know too much." She put a hand on the other woman's shoulder and looked directly into her eyes. "L'Oiseau de Nuit—"

"She uses the whole name," Wazoo interrupted. "That don't sound good."

"Be serious. Please, you are my friend and I trust you. I'd like to be able to keep on feeling I can tell you what's on my mind, but you can't repeat it to other folks."

"Ellie," Wazoo said, holding their steady gaze, "what you say to me stays with me. If I've let on too much in the past, I was wrong and I am reformed."

"Thank you."

She wondered if Joe was in his office. Looking in and saying hi would help her mood. Nope. He didn't need her popping in when he had work to do.

"You're wrong, Min," a voice behind her said. "Just because the murderer's face is painted in the book doesn't mean it was painted when that poor Stephanie Gray died."

Ellie shook her head. Maybe she should be grateful to have people around and talking all the time. It might make it more difficult for someone to get at her—if they really were trying to.

The murderer's face is painted. On that terrible day the crowd ebbed and flowed but Ellie had scarcely been aware of them. Masks, wigs, painted faces. An oval, a face turned up toward her. *Blue and gold.* She turned away, hurried to the far side of a bookcase and clung to the edge of a shelf.

A face, half blue, half gold—she hadn't remembered until now. Light eyes. The room moved around her. She must be in control.

Tonight she'd start reading Sonja Elliot.

Paul's cell phone rang and a cryptic conversation followed. "I need to run an errand," he called out. "I'll leave my laptop here." He strode out of the shop.

Ellie watched him hop on his maroon Vespa and ride away. Scooters might have come back into fashion but the wheels would always look too small to her.

She opened the door to the back vestibule. "Daisy? Zipper? Come on down here." With an ear cocked, she waited.

A sharp snicking sound had Ellie staring at the radio. If it had decided to go on the fritz it was so old she couldn't complain.

With her sad-looking cell phone in her teeth and her head down, Daisy plodded into the shop, passed Ellie and went straight to Wazoo.

"Nice," Ellie said. "Who buys the food around here?" She followed the shepherd and crouched to pet her.

Snick.

"That radio's giving up the ghost, I think," she told Wazoo. A woman with itchy nerve endings didn't need more irritation. Ellie turned off the music and went back to Daisy. "She doesn't seem herself, Wazoo. She's not running around like she usually does and she doesn't eat properly."

Wazoo nuzzled her cheek against the top of Daisy's head and Ellie sat back on her heels.

Snick.

Ellie looked up quickly. No radio on this time. Jim Wade worked over some papers. The man who needed lots of space continued to read his newspaper and eat what remained of his muffaletta without looking. Now and again he paused to stuff fallen pieces of salami or cheese back inside the olive-oil-soaked bread.

Darn it all, anyway, she'd swear the sound must be electrical. Since she'd taken over Hungry Eyes she'd been aware that the wiring would eventually have to be replaced, but she hadn't expected it this soon.

"Ellie," Wazoo said quietly. "Daisy's in trouble."

"How do you know?" Ellie's tummy squinched tight.

"She told me."

"Not now, Wazoo, please. This isn't a good time to play around."

"You smell her mouth, you."

Ellie wrinkled her nose but did as she was told. Immediately, she backed off. "She's too young to have tooth decay."

"I don't think that's what it is." Wazoo's big dark eyes were shadowed with worry. "She need one of them vets."

"I'll take her. She goes way out to Dr. Weston in Loreauville. He's the one I use. The breeder recommended him and he's the best." Ellie caught sight of Zipper creeping toward them with her belly on the floor. "Now what?"

The cat reached Daisy and instead of taking her usual flying leap on top of her buddy, Zipper licked Daisy's face.

Ellie's stomach took another turn.

Wazoo ran her hands over Daisy. "She hot. Big fever, I think."

"Something wrong with your dog?" Jim Wade asked. "Anything I can do to help?"

"I don't think so, thanks, anyway. Wazoo, it could take too long to get to Loreauville. I'm going to call Reb to see if she'll tell me what I should do. I'll take her over there. Folks," she cried, "I've got to step out but Wazoo's here to take care of you."

Joe ran all the way from the square to Conch Street and Reb Girard's consulting rooms. He arrived neck and neck with Paul Nelson, who looked as worried as Joe felt.

"Jim Wade told me about the shepherd," Paul said. "I'd been gone from Hungry Eyes half an hour so I don't know what happened in that time."

"Wazoo called me," Joe said, annoyed that Paul would take it upon himself to come to Ellie's aid. "I can take it from here."

Paul nodded slowly. "I'd like to know the dog's okay," he said. "I know how much she means to Ellie."

A to-the-point chat with cagey Cyrus was in order. Joe hadn't been satisfied with the vague and angry comments about his failure to find out what was going on in Jilly's love life. For a man who showed every sign of being infatuated with Jilly, Paul seemed a little too interested in Ellie. Could be that's what Cyrus had meant, that Paul Nelson had a roving eye.

"Is that okay?" Paul said, sounding sarcastic.

"That's not my call to make," Joe said stiffly, and led the way along the little pathway and up steps to the pretty old house where Reb had grown up with her doctor father and where she'd continued to live as well as work after he died. Then Marc Girard came sweeping back into town and carried her off to his home at Clouds End, but she wouldn't give up her practice.

Joe rang the bell and walked in, as everyone did.

The waiting room was empty except for Ellie, who stood there with Daisy lying at her feet. The dog looked fine to Joe. Ellie didn't and he barely stopped himself from hugging her. She wouldn't want to think he saw her as weak.

"How's this girl doing?" he asked, and patted Ellie's shoulder.

"I wish Reb was through with her patient," Ellie said. She held Daisy's cell phone and showed it to Joe. "She never lets me touch this. Now she can't keep it in her mouth and she doesn't care."

Paul knelt by the dog and stroked her. "She's burning up," he said.

"I know." Ellie didn't look grateful to be reminded. A sudden rush of tears filled her eyes. "I don't care what's wrong with her, I won't have her put down. I'll do anything to save her."

"She's just got a bug, Ellie," Joe said.

Paul shook his head slightly. "I hope you're right There's too much that isn't acceptable in this town and nothing gets satisfactorily dealt with. We'll be lucky if we don't lose more than a dog some day soon. The women aren't safe." His face turned red. "If the law can't look after our women, what good are they?"

Joe grabbed his sleeve and stood toe to toe. "If you've got criticism or complaints, lodge them in the right place. But you'd better have ideas to back 'em up with."

Paul tried to push him away.

"Sorry!" Reb hurried from her consulting room with Ozaire Dupre behind her. She glanced at him over her shoulder. "Make sure you fill that prescription. And take the pills with plenty of water. I'll be checking up, remember." Fortunately she didn't notice the strung-out atmosphere in the waiting room.

"Daylight robbery, that's what those pills are," Ozaire said. His shaved head glistened and pretty much sat directly on top of his thick shoulders. "I come in here so she can say I ain't got nothin' wrong and what happens? Out I go a poorer man just because…well, enough said about that."

"Daisy's sick, Ozaire," Ellie said. "I was afraid to drive to Dr. Weston in case something happened on the way."

Reb already knelt beside Daisy and began checking her over.

"Can't be nothin' wrong," Ozaire said. "Strong as a horse, that one."

"Up you get," Reb said gently. "See if she'll stand, Ellie. I need to get her where I can see better."

When Daisy wouldn't move, Joe lifted the big animal. "Where do you want her?" he asked. Paul slid his hands under her rear and shared the weight.

They followed instructions and placed her on top of the several large waterproof pads Reb took into a sitting room and spread over a table. She turned on the reading lamp and palpated every inch of Daisy who then refused to have her mouth opened. "Watch her," Reb said, and disappeared from the room.

Ozaire looked significantly at his bound left hand. "All part of it," he said, without going on to say what "it" was. "I been out searchin' with one of them teams, y'know. If that Penn is out there he's invisible." They heard Reb returning and Ozaire slipped away, passing her in the doorway.

"Take those pills," she called after him. She carried a phone pressed to an ear. In the other hand she held a kidney dish draped with a blue paper sheet. "Yes," she said abruptly. "Thank you. I just wanted to be sure of the dosages. Yes, I'll let you know."

"That was Dr. Weston," she said, turning the phone off. "First I'm giving Daisy a tranquilizer to help her relax."

Hardly had Reb prepared and given the shot than Daisy slumped and didn't attempt to resist when Reb opened her mouth wide. "Hold this," she told Ellie, who made sure Daisy's bottom jaw stayed where Reb needed it.

Reb shone a brilliant little steel flashlight inside the large mouth.

"Is it tooth decay?" Ellie asked. "An abscess, maybe?"

Joe moved closer. "Her teeth look great to me. I hope she never decides I'm a threat to you."

Their eyes met and Ellie blushed. He noticed she avoided looking at Paul.

"You've got the diagnosis at least partially right," Reb said. She took up an instrument and reached into the roof of Daisy's mouth. For far too long she worked, carefully pulling something free. She redirected the light and her efforts on the other side of the upper jaw. "Abscessed both sides," she said, working to pull out the instrument.

"Oh, my God," Ellie said. "Joe, look."

He did look and saw that Reb held a piece of wire bent like a small croquet hoop with about a quarter of an inch hooked upward on either side. "This was no accident," Reb said. "Someone managed to quiet her down—could have used a number of things to do that—and they rammed this up into her mouth with the hooks driven in between her teeth and into her gums. It's too bad she's so brave. If she'd let you know how much pain she was in we'd have been on it faster."

White-faced, with sweat along her hairline, Ellie shook her head again and again. "Why would anyone do such a thing?"

Reb prepared another shot. "Antibiotics," she said, and looked up sharply. "Is she up to date on all her shots?"

"Yes," Ellie told her.

Bending over Daisy again she said, "She'll have to be carefully handled. Start praying the infection hasn't gone too far. She's dehydrated. I suggest you keep her comfortable and get her to Loreauville. Dr. Weston can give her IV fluids and watch her till she's stabilized. I'll call and say you're coming."

"Penn did it to get at you," Paul told Ellie, and Joe would have liked to punch the man. "He's telling you he can get at you, even at your guard dog. You're vulnerable, that's what he's saying. That and he wants the dog to die so she never gets in his way again."

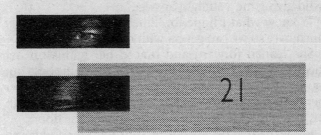

21

Joe drove straight past Hungry Eyes and in front of his own place, to the alley behind the buildings. Ellie saw him glance at the sheriff's vehicle parked outside the shop, narrow his eyes, then look ahead as if he hadn't noticed the car.

Ellie watched until she couldn't see it anymore.

Joe parked his Jeep and turned off the engine.

"This has been a helluva day for you," Joe said. "It's too late for Spike to be dropping in for coffee."

"I know. He's going to ask questions about what happened to Daisy." She turned to him. "There's nothing for me to say, is there? Nothing helpful. All I know is what he already knows."

Joe tipped his head against the rest.

"You think he's come about something else, don't you?" She thought so, too, but didn't want to be right.

"Possibly. I'm sorry the vet had to keep Daisy, but at least he seems optimistic."

"I'm grateful for that," she said. "But you're trying to avoid giving me a straight answer."

"Y'know what I hope for, Ellie? I hope this is pretty much over so we can get on with our lives."

She leaned forward and braced her hands on her knees, then gave his upper arm a pat. "You're the best, but you need a break from me, Joe. I'm sure Wazoo's over there bending Spike's ear. She keeps offering to stay with me. Tonight I'll let her do it." She opened the door.

Joe leaned across to pull it shut with a shuddering crash. "Listen to me." He took her by the shoulders and brought his face close to hers. "Do you think what I feel for you is nothin' more than some sort of duty?"

"You've spent hours helping with Daisy. You sleep on that couch every night—and it's too short for you—and what do I do for you? Nothing. I'm not a taker, Joe, never have been." She looked directly at him.

"Don't say that again, y'hear?" he said through his teeth. "You keep tellin' me how strong you are then—"

"No I don't. How stupid would that be when you've seen how nervous I've been. Joe—" she tipped her head defiantly "—you were with me when I passed out from fear. But that doesn't mean I can't be embarrassed by taking advantage of someone all the time."

Ellie knew her mistake before she'd closed her mouth. Faintly she heard rain start to hit the windows but she couldn't look away from Joe. Anger and hurt muddled his expression.

At last he said, "Am I *someone* you take advantage of all the time?"

She swallowed.

"Am I?"

"No," she whispered.

"Do you think that because you're not putting out for me you're not giving anything back for the time I spend with you?"

"No." She shuddered at his crudeness. He was angry enough to shock her with the kind of comment he never made.

He closed his eyes and his grip softened. "I'd be a liar if I said I don't think about making love to you—a lot— but I'm not an animal. I can wait until you're ready and you come to it yourself."

"Joe, I'm sorry I've made you mad."

"Don't say anythin' else right now. And don't try to send me away unless I give you a reason. One good reason would be that you plain don't want me around anymore."

He didn't try to stop her from kissing the corner of his mouth lightly. "Having you around is the best thing that ever happened to me," she said, and shifted out of range when he made a move to kiss her back. "I…we've got to get in there."

Even though they ran, they had still managed to get wet on the way from the Jeep, through the yard, to the back door.

A glance into the lighted shop had showed it was empty and Joe ran upstairs behind Ellie. She hardly reached the top when Zipper sprang from the shadows and clung on to her with extended claws.

"You okay?" he asked, but Ellie only nodded as she stroked the cat fiercely. He added, "I'm beginnin' to believe all this stuff about some animals havin' human feelings."

"Who told you that?" Ellie asked. "Don't answer. Wazoo did and she's right."

They went into the flat and found Wazoo sitting on the floor in front of Deputy Lori. Very pregnant, she sat in the armchair with her feet up on a little stool Joe would bet Wazoo found for her. She held a mug of what looked like warm milk. He wrinkled his nose at the thought.

Lori looked around for a place to set her mug. "'Evenin'," she said, shifting her feet to the floor. "Wazoo's been coddlin' me."

"Don't get up," Ellie told her. "Shouldn't you be at home by now?"

Lori shook her head and the tow-colored tail at her nape flipped back and forth. "I'm on duty and feelin' fine. I came to ask you a few questions, Ellie. If that's okay."

"Well." Wazoo slapped her knees and got up. "I'd better get back to Rosebank."

Joe had to ask, "Would you like me to drive you home?"

Wazoo shook her head. "I've got my van but you nice to ask. Y'all look after your woman. She the best and she not so safe."

"I'm fine." Ellie cast her eyes upward. "You'll see, this is all so much nonsense and someone's going to be in trouble for all the tricks they've pulled around here. Daisy's going to be all right, but I'm still not letting whoever did it to her get off free."

Wazoo unhooked Zipper from Ellie's shoulders and gave the cat a sound kiss on the nose. "It is upsettin', baby," she said in the animal's ear. "But your Daisy gonna be all right. Quit bein' mad, it'll make your head ache 'cause your blood pressure will get high." She put Zipper down. "Now, you go on in there and keep the bed warm for the invalid when she come home."

Joe covered his mouth. Nothing was ever dull around Wazoo.

"Off you go." Wazoo flapped her hands at Zipper.

The cat turned away and strolled off into the second bedroom.

Deputy Lori giggled.

"You laughin' cause you don't think Zipper really did what I said? You think it a coincidence? That's fine. You know if you have a boy or a girl yet?"

Lori said, "No. We decided we'll be tickled whatever we get."

"It's gonna be a boy," Wazoo told her. "A big boy and he gonna come early. Prob'ly in a week."

"I've still got three weeks to go," Lori said. "And Reb says first babies are usually late."

"One week," Wazoo said, wiggling her fingers all around then sweeping from the room, closing the door behind her.

"Where's Spike?" Joe asked. He didn't feel so good about Lori being sent. Didn't sit quite right.

Lori made to stand up.

"Please don't," Ellie said. "You...well, I was going to say you look comfortable, but you don't." She gave a bashful smile.

"You've got that right," Lori said. "But I'll sit if you're all right with that. Spike got called away late this afternoon. By the boss. He's still there but he called to ask if I could come see you. I guess the boss is on the warpath. Seems somethin' big's goin' down."

Joe kept his mouth shut, but he wanted to ask what the "something big" might be.

"It's okay with me," Ellie said, and sat on the edge of the couch.

Rain splotches hadn't quite dried on her blue shirt. She wore pants again, which made him a happy man. The trend toward clothes that didn't hide her figure meant something had changed the way she viewed herself and he was just pigheaded enough to hope it was him.

"I'm Ellie's attorney," Joe said. If Ellie said otherwise he'd look the fool.

Ellie didn't contradict him. "Joe's my rock," she said. "Ask away."

"I haven't been told why yet, but they want to know more about your background."

The worst thing he could do would be to react to the very line of questioning Ellie feared. He walked into the kitchen, poured two glasses of ice water and added a piece of lemon to each.

"My background was checked after Stephanie Gray died," he heard Ellie say. "I'm boring. No father, no mother, nobody."

She took the glass of water when he offered it to her and he admired her steady hand and relaxed expression. Then she ground her back teeth and blew her image as far as he was concerned.

With notebook in hand, Lori scribbled. "We pretty much know about the past few years, or from when you entered college and so forth. I can tell you've had some hardships and I don't like digging them up, but it seems we have to look farther back. Fill in the holes."

"I was born in California, but I don't know where and there isn't anyone left there to tell me. My daddy died, then my mother got sick and had to go into a hospital. She never got well enough to take us back. We were with an aunt and uncle—that was my mother's sister—and their four kids."

More scribbling.

Rather than watch her struggle, Joe turned away from Ellie and went to stand in the window.

"How long were you with them?"

"Until I was ten."

"Then what?"

"I ran away."

Lori said, "Lordy. Where did you go?"

"I told anyone who wanted to know that I'd been abandoned. I went into foster care."

A sniff made Joe look back. Lori fumbled for a handkerchief and wiped the corners of her eyes. "I guess you were okay there," she said. "They sent you to school and made sure you got some skills to work with."

"No. I was moved several times. I was lucky they sent me to school at all but that stopped when I was fifteen. That's when I ran away again."

Joe's back ached from holding it stiff. How much would Ellie tell Lori? He stared at the dark square but rain slanting past street lamps glazed before his eyes. Ellie at fifteen would already have been lovely. Lovely and alone on the streets.

"Tell me what happened after that?" Lori sounded as if she had a cold.

"If the transcripts from the first interrogation are checked you'll see the name, Alice Clark. Mrs. Clark saved me. She stopped someone from beating me to a pulp and took me home with her. I stayed with her until I was over eighteen then she made sure I had enough money and I left to go to school."

"Did she adopt you?"

"No."

"She was just your foster mother."

"No. She thought she was too old and too inexperienced for them to let her do that so she just kept me. She couldn't figure out how to send me to high school without someone getting suspicious. I learned at home. And I know she kept checking to see if someone was looking for me but they weren't."

"She sounds so kind," Lori said. "I expect you're still in close touch with her."

"We're not in touch at all. She was always afraid she'd get into trouble for having no right to let me live there so we agreed I shouldn't contact her again. She did speak to the police after Stephanie died and let them know I had been with her, though."

"So at eighteen you were on your own. That's terrible. How did you make the money last? Did you work?"

"I worked while I was in school because I wanted to help my future. Mrs. Clark was a rich woman, I wouldn't have had to work if I didn't want to."

"She gave you that much?" Lori said.

"Yes."

Joe returned to the two of them and took a seat on the couch. "You've done well," he told Ellie. "A lot of people wouldn't have survived all that."

"I was lucky," she said in a monotone.

The deputy slowly closed her notebook. "I'm sorry to bring all that up. It must be very hard for you."

"I was lucky," Ellie said again, staring at the floor.

Lori looked at her quickly, then at Joe. The look was hard and loaded with meaning. He nodded. She was trying to convey that she was worried about Ellie.

"Thank you," Lori said, and pushed her way out of the chair. Her oversize khaki shirt barely buttoned over her tummy. Joe decided he liked that tummy.

She took up her hat and put it on, tucked the notebook into a breast pocket and went to Ellie with outstretched hands. "You came to the right place," she said, holding

Ellie's fingers. "And you don't deserve what's been happenin' here. We'll get to the bottom of it. I've got a feelin' a lot's goin' down and soon."

22

"Let's watch the news."

Ellie snatched up the remote and turned on the TV. She had to have time to think, time before Joe began discussing what had just happened. Would the authorities be satisfied with her story? Or would they have more questions?

She found the news and turned up the volume.

The attacks had stopped. Why not let it alone? She had told Lori the truth—even if she had left out most of what happened in the last two years at Mrs. Clark's house.

The weather seemed the main news topic. After veering away, the hurricane had reversed its course and once more headed for the Gulf. There was talk of it coming inland. The radar didn't reassure her. They'd be on watch now, waiting for instructions to get ready if the time came.

The weather report finished and the anchor returned. "Let me introduce you to our next guest. Ms. Sonja Elliot, bestselling author, is experiencing a storm in her own life. Welcome, Ms. Elliot."

"Please call me Sonja."

Ellie started to turn off the TV but Joe put a hand out to stop her.

"I thought she was young," Joe said. "She writes edgy stuff."

"She doesn't look the part," Ellie said, swallowing and feeling sick.

Sonja Elliot, a tiny woman with gray hair that fell untidily around her shoulders, looked as though she had spent a lifetime in the sun. Her wrinkles reminded Ellie of an apple carving and her large dark glasses added a clownish impression.

"What do you think?" Joe said. "She could be sixty but she looks eighty."

"Sixty would be my guess. She's arrogant."

"I owe it to my readers to make sure the series continues," Elliot said, flipping back her hair as if practicing to be a Victoria's Secret model in a future life. "I don't like being in the public eye, but it's my duty to reassure my many fans that they shouldn't worry about what's happening. A writer becomes the property of her readers, she writes for them alone, and she has a responsibility to ensure their happiness. Let me tell you a little secret. The next book will be out sooner than expected. Any talk of a connection between my work and these crimes is completely bogus."

"Idiot," Joe muttered.

"Is she doing this because she's afraid her publisher will stop the series—because of all the fuss?" Ellie asked.

"Uh-huh, I'd say so."

"Is there any truth to the rumor that you have no respect for today's young women?" the interviewer asked. Elliot gave a short, high laugh. "Our young people are our future and I love them all." Her mouth came together in a straight line.

"Admirable," the interviewer said. "We're all—your fans, that is—grateful for the comeback you made some years ago. Ten or more, is it? What should we have done without you?"

Elliot sat straighter. "Hardly a comeback. I never went away. It was around then that I started a new series. Perhaps that's what you mean."

The interview finished but immediately afterward the interviewer looked into the camera and said, "So there you have it, folks. The show…or the books must go on. Evidently there's no truth to the rumors that Miss Elliot's sales have ever slipped." He leered conspiratorially.

Ellie turned the set off. "I could have done without hearing that," she said. "She didn't even say she regretted the murders."

Joe was quiet before he said, "I'm relieved Daisy is going to be fine. She's got courage."

"Yes, she does." *And you're just making noise to fill up space. You don't know what to say or do next, any more than I do.*

"I'd better go across the hall and shower," he said, smiling at her. He touched her cheek. "You're something else, cher, but if I could make it not have happened I would."

She believed him and she loved him for caring about her. He set a hand on her thigh, palm up, and she put hers on top. Taking his time, he brought the back of her hand to his mouth and let his lips rest there, warming her and making her tingle as if he touched her all over rather than just her hand.

"You'll probably be in bed by the time I get back, so sleep well."

Urgency shortened her breath. She felt hot. "Stay a bit," she said, taking his hand in both of hers and holding on tight. "This is the right time. If I'm wrong about that, there never will be a right time. I'm not picking apart the details but I want you to know what I'm afraid of. From before."

Joe looked uncertain.

"It'll be okay," she told him. "Unless you're too tired for this now."

"I'm not," he said. "But I'm worried for you."

She needed to put space between them and got up. Walking slowly back and forth in front of him, she ordered her thoughts, decided what to say and how to say it.

"My brother would know where I was born," she said. "One of these days—when things settle down for me—I'll try to get in touch with him."

"Might be a good idea."

In other words, Joe didn't think it a good idea. She wouldn't ask now but she wanted to know why. "What I said about being at Mrs. Clark's was true, only I left out a lot."

"I expected you to tell me this," Joe said.

Why would someone build their house so far off the beaten track? Ellie remembered her first thought when Mrs. Clark had driven directly into the four-car garage of a creamy stucco spread with dark wood trim and a tall iron fence surrounding the property. Ellie's benefactor had keyed in a code to open the gate.

"Her home was a long way south of San Francisco," Ellie said. "Really remote, and big. It had this complicated alarm system."

"Really rich people have to do that sometimes," Joe said.

"She wouldn't let strangers in the house so she never had anything delivered. The furniture was expensive but worn, as if she'd had it for years and years."

Now who was skirting the main issues?

Joe spread his arms along the back of the couch and looked up at her. Each time she glanced at him he smiled. He didn't really want to know all the sleazy horror she'd been through, not really. Like most smart men he knew it was important to women that the men in their lives listened to them, so he'd listen and hope she got through it fast.

"She kept a lot of the house closed off because she did her own cleaning and liked to keep the work down. Not a soul ever came there." How could she tell him the rest?

"What happened to you in that house, cher?" Joe asked. "Your Mrs. Clark didn't just give you a lot of money, did she? She paid you off and you decided you didn't want to push things further afterward."

"I was too scared," she blurted out. "An awful accident happened and she said I could take the money and run or get blamed. It was my money, really. It had been given to me."

"By whom?"

"I'm good to you, Ellie, just you remember that. You do as I tell you and I'll build you a nest egg to take care of you if you ever need it. Quit sniveling!"

"Jason," she told Joe. "Jason had put the money into an account for me, and when I left, his mother took me and closed it out. She had me take everything with me and I put it in the bank in New Orleans."

"You forgot to say who Jason is?"

Her heart took off and beat unnaturally fast. "Mrs. Clark's son."

"He lived with his mother, too?"

"In the basement."

Joe got up and pulled her down beside him. "Don't go on. You don't need to."

Yes she did. "Everything Mrs. Clark did was for Jason. I think he'd been in some sort of trouble and she was hiding him down there. He went outside to swim in the pool and do work around the place but she kept watch all the time until he went back inside."

"How old—"

"In his thirties."

"And he didn't work other than around his mother's house."

"He...he wasn't like most people. He didn't *trust* people. But he worked on things, invented them, I think. I heard them mention royalties. I know his mother brought letters from a post office box and when he opened them there would be lots of cash inside. He'd give me..." Honesty meant you told the whole story. "He gave me cash to keep for myself, for later, he said."

"But he had an account opened for you, too."

"Yes." She heard her voice start to rise. "I said he did. But he liked to look at money and touch it so he must have thought I'd like it, too. He had an account for me and he gave me cash. There was nothing to spend it on so I put it on a table in my room at first, then the dresser. In the end it was piled up everywhere."

Joe sat square on the couch but looked sideways at her. His eyes could be too blue, she thought, too all-seeing, as if they looked inside her head.

"Why did he give it to me? Isn't that what you want to ask?"

"You said it was because he liked having it around and thought you might, too."

"Yes. You keep me in line, Joe. Make sure I don't fib about anything. That night when Mrs. Clark found me, she was looking for a girl, for a girl in trouble who would be grateful for her help. She wanted me for Jason—to live in the basement with him so he…" Tears streamed and she could do nothing to stop them.

Joe bent forward and put his face in his hands. He was disgusted by it all just as she'd known he would be.

"Jason didn't know how to be around other people. It was a year before his mother took me into the basement to see everything down there. I never got to go up again after that, not till I—left."

"You lived in a basement for two years?"

"A bit longer. I had a room of my own and plenty to eat—and books. What I said about learning there was true. Jason told his mother what books I should have and she got them. He looked them up on the Internet but never ordered them from there in case they got traced to him. That's what he said, anyway."

Strangled noises squeezed from her throat. She breathed only into the tops of her lungs and gasped as if she'd been running a long time.

"Ellie, did you try to get away?"

Of course, he thought she should have escaped. "Every night I got locked in my room. I was locked in there during the day a lot, too. Jason let me out to eat the meals his mother brought. He made sure I couldn't get out."

Joe ground his thumb joints into his eyes.

"Once I was moved down there he didn't go outside as much, but there were no windows and he bolted the door from the outside." Why had she thought she'd feel better if she opened up to Joe? "They put me on the pill. He watched when I took them." Her voice assaulted her ears. "You know why he did that, don't you?"

"I know," Joe told her. He attempted to pull her into his arms but she pushed away. "Let me hold you," he said, and the pain she heard in him hurt her even more.

Her forearms, held tightly in his, burned when she fought to get away. Joe wouldn't let go.

Men used their strength to make women obey them.

"He came on Friday nights. Sometimes I'd forget what day it was and start to fall asleep, but he came and—he—did that to me. He kept on all his clothes and had sex with me. Then he'd make me undress in front of him and walk around like that." She swallowed a sob. "And when he was finished with me, he gave me money and told me I was wicked for selling myself."

"I thought you said—"

"I *did* say something different but it wasn't true. There, now you know my dirty little story."

"Why did his mother set you free?"

"You won't let me be, will you? You want to watch me, too. You want to watch me empty out to nothing, then you'll discover you have to turn me in."

"*No!*" He transferred his strong hands from her forearms to her shoulders and pulled her closer. "I will never do anything to hurt you. Somehow I'll make you believe that."

"Not once you know Jason Clark died because I hit him over the head with a wrench. I didn't mean to kill him but he fell into a bunch of loose wires. He got electrocuted."

"Stop it, Ellie. Stop fighting me."

"I'm a murderer. Just like Charles Penn."

23

Joe's eyes opened.

He brought his watch close to his face and peered at it. Couldn't read it but he didn't think he'd been asleep long.

His feet were asleep and they'd woken him up. Gingerly, lifting first one then the other, he put them back where they were supposed to be, crossed at the ankle with his knees slightly jackknifed and bent to one side.

With his hips flat, he torqued his upper body toward the back of the couch. The pillow squeezed out, leaving his neck bridged between the arm and the seat with no support.

"Fuck!" A complete revolution and he faced the room, jammed the pillow beneath his neck again and reversed the angle of his knees. Carefully, having felt the hard floor a time too many, Joe wriggled his hips around.

He had a reason for lying on his right side rather than his left, not that he could remember it.

Slowly, half inch by half inch, the weight of his legs

rotated his body. Much more of that and he'd be on the floor again.

"Shit!" Joe returned to his back and held absolutely still with his eyes squeezed shut.

He must not think about Jason Clark, the man who might well have ruined everything for Ellie and stolen Joe's chances for a great life with her.

The room felt different, as if shapes shifted in the humid air. Displaced matter.

A boom and rattle sounded, distant. Thunder. He slitted his eyes. He hadn't seen any lightning but it could have been what woke him up—together with the tingling in his feet. A thunderstorm would clear the air—if it rained hard enough. He thought about the hurricane warning but was damned if he would get up and check the radar on TV.

Violent crackling like a zillion firecrackers made sure his eyes were all the way open. Despite the closed blinds he saw the next flash rip across the sky followed by burst after burst of light and rolling, echoing funnels of thunder.

The night had gone to war.

Still the sense of displaced shapes assaulted him. Warily, he pushed a few inches up on one elbow. Rain hit the windows as if someone had thrown a giant bucket of water directly at them.

Joe took a breath through his nose and smiled. Would it be dereliction of duty if he stripped naked and ran outside?

Lavender. He smelled lavender but only faintly. Ellie had closed her bedroom door but the scent must remain.

Hair on the back of his neck prickled. A scent didn't remain that definitely, not when the wearer used it so sparingly. He peered into the shadows, then at the table where she could have sat in a chair, at the armchair, and toward her bedroom.

The door stood open.

Once more he revolved, this time onto his stomach. He ached from the effort of minimizing sound until he could push up on his hands and work close enough to see down from the top of the couch arm.

Hair, and he knew it was Ellie's, tickled his nose. She sat on the floor with her back to the side of the couch, and either she'd fallen asleep sitting up, or, like him, she'd tried to avoid shifting around.

The only reason for her to sit there would be because she was scared and needed to feel someone near her. "Ellie," he whispered. "Don't jump, it's only me, Joe." How dumb did that sound?

Ellie scrambled to her feet as if she'd been shot.

"Hush," he told her, sitting up. "Hey, hey." He could hear her throat clicking and her breath squeezing in and out through her tight throat.

"Don't move." Joe stood up. "Tell me you won't attack me if I touch you."

"I won't." And she landed against him before he had a chance to do a thing. "Sorry, Joe. I'm always saying that but I always need to."

"Afraid of the storm?" he asked.

"Storms are some of my favorite things," she murmured. "I needed to be close to you."

Optimistic thoughts about Ellie Byron were dangerous. "And it had nothing to do with the storm?"

She placed her hands flat on his chest, rested her cheek on top.

Joe lifted his arms and left them in the air, inches

from her back. "Damn it," he muttered, and rubbed her shoulders and neck.

"You've been doing a lot of swearing tonight."

Women said the darnedest things. "Beg your pardon, ma'am?"

"Forget it. I expect you were asleep at the time."

"Your skin's hot," he told her.

Lightning crackled on and the thunder answered.

"So is yours. I'd like to go outside in that rain."

He laughed. "Just thought the same thing myself. Want to go together?"

"Maybe," she said.

"The way I saw it, I'd be naked. Wouldn't be so much fun if you weren't naked, too."

"D'you know the word *improper?* Well, that's an improper suggestion, Joe Gable."

"I feel like I'm walkin' on pond scum."

Ellie snorted. "Oh, very nice."

"Meltin' ice then."

"In other words you don't feel too sure on your feet, is that what you're telling me?"

He breathed in. Her hair smelled of lavender, too. Smooth skin, so smooth and soft it reminded him of stroking a warm baby. "Ellie," he said, close to her ear, "I haven't felt sure on my feet for a long time, about as long as I've known you. The only thing that's changed is how bad I'm afflicted with this condition."

Her fingertips crept up his chest and around his neck. She clung to him, opened her mouth on his bare chest and made small circles with her tongue.

Whoa. He hoped time would heal her wounds and she would eventually loosen up enough to give them a chance. This had him scared. Not that he didn't like it, oh no, sir, no, he surely did like it, but hurrying things could mess them up for good.

He confined himself to her shoulders. Ellie played with his hair. She pressed tightly against him and took one of his nipples between her teeth. Her light sucking about took the top off his head. Points south had their own re-action and she would be feeling how pushy some things could be.

A man wasn't anything but a man—thank God. "Ellie," he said against the crook of her neck. "What d'you think you're doin, cher?"

"You know what I'm doing." She flattened herself against him.

Ellie wore a long cotton nightie and his penis wasn't the only thing saluting around here.

"I know what I want to do about this, but it's too soon for you."

"Pretty soon it's going to be too late for me, Joe. If I keep on suffering because of the past and being afraid be-cause of the past, I think I'll just turn to some of that ice you talked about and maybe melt away to nothing."

He wasn't convinced.

She broke away from him but took hold of his hands. "Try not to fall over anything in the dark," she told him. "Shall we find out if we work together?"

Holy… "I'm not one bit afraid things won't work. What I'm afraid of is that you'll forget—"

Ellie took his hands to her mouth and kissed his knuckles one after the other. "Forget that it's you making love to me rather than a sick man forcing himself on me? Is that what you were going to say?"

"You put it right out there, Ellie. You don't pull punches." But that was his fear.

She didn't pull punches, Ellie thought, because she couldn't afford to. What she wouldn't tell him, though, was that after she'd got into bed, after she'd heard him return from his shower and settle into silence on the couch, she'd seen her future too clearly to bear. Alone. Alone with nothing but bad memories and lost chances to keep her company.

And she wanted him.

She wanted what she'd never known except in those minutes when he'd driven her wild—before she fought him off—*you, Joe, only you.* "I can't read the future," she told him. "Not one of us can. But I'm not imagining that we've got a chance for some...hot nights." Her voice dropped away and she giggled. "Pretend I didn't say that. I'm getting carried away."

"No, Ellie, not carried away. You're sayin' it the way it is."

He slipped his arms around her waist and danced with her. Not a jig or a joke of some kind, but a slow waltz, turning and turning, aiming his fingers downward over her bottom. Then she rested, pelvis to pelvis with him, and he sped up the dance, pushed her legs with his. His body was rhythm from top to toe. In the shady, almost dark room she saw his smile and the flash of his eyes—and a glistening over his shoulders and naked chest.

He looked down at her. He crossed his arms around her back and touched the sides of her breasts fleetingly, repeatedly, and she squirmed but didn't stop the dance. She never wanted the dance to stop. Once more he slowed down until they hung together and only their hips moved, and their feet—barely.

Why should he be the one to make all the moves? Loving was instinct and the swell of a heart, two hearts, the raw response of the body just as it had always been, was always meant to be. She could do it. How else would he be convinced she wasn't pretending?

Ellie pressed a thigh between his legs and she kept on responding to the beat she felt in her head and in the deepest places of her body. Back and forth she rocked, gently, looking up into his face, at his closed eyes.

On tiptoe she kissed his neck, then his jaw and finally his mouth. He responded, his breath grating together with hers, his tongue pressing hers. Not a gentle kiss but a demanding kiss. Ellie couldn't stop, didn't want to stop.

He felt the beat of her heart, or was it his own?

She drove him beyond any point of turning back. Joe would go with her and if she was trying too hard and the whole thing blew up, he'd step back again and wait. He'd keep on stepping back if that's what it took—and he'd die another death every time.

He kissed her without finesse and couldn't do a thing about it. Her breasts rose and fell against him and she'd put her thigh between his again. Civilized behavior was pretty useless in these situations. He was cracking under her touch.

No, he would not say what he wanted to say to her. When he declared what he really felt for her it would be somewhere calm, in the open air, when he could say what he meant and she would know his words were not driven by his craving for sex.

Ellie slid down in front of him and pulled his shorts around his ankles. "Your legs turn me on," she murmured.

"I think I'm the one who's supposed to say that."

"I'm making new rules. I want to wrap my arms

around your legs and hold on. They're strong and beautiful."

He felt embarrassed. Then he didn't. Instead he felt as if he'd explode if he couldn't get inside her—right now.

"Oh, Ellie." She took him in her mouth and played, ran the tip of her tongue over the tip of his penis. "My beautiful legs are about to—Ellie!—they're about to collapse. Cher…"

She held his buttocks and worked over him. He looked down on her head, on her white shoulders. Ellie paused. "Tell me what you want. This time it's all yours. Next time it's mine."

A sound congealed in his throat.

"I read, you know. I read how it should be between a man and a woman when it's right. I've never done this before but I do like it, Joe." She paused and raised her face to look at him. "Do you like it?"

He gave a mock growl. "I need to read those books. Or maybe I don't." He lifted her to her feet and felt her gown between her legs. "You're wet, sweetheart. You do want this."

"How do you want it?"

"How?"

"Show me?"

He turned cold. "Okay, I can do that." The flimsy gown tore easily. From neck to hem he tore it apart. "Wild. That's the way I want it. Unforgettable. I want to be bruised when we're done."

"Yes," she said, but he heard how her voice dropped and shook.

They'd see what she really liked. He stretched her out on the carpet and lay beside her, rolled toward her. His voice wouldn't work if he wanted it to. With the tattered remains of her nightgown hanging from her elbows, she lay there, her body pale and voluptuous. The first time he kissed her breasts, she turned frantic, but whatever it cost he'd go slow, give her only a little at a time so the end of it all would just about knock the life from them.

With random kisses, random licks and nips on her full flesh, he covered every tiny area of skin without doing what he knew she wanted. The corner of his mouth came in contact with a nipple and her body arched from the floor.

Joe smiled and pressed his lips to her navel.

Ellie massaged his shoulders and he scooted down, kissing her as he went. A few more inches and his face hovered over the soft hair at the apex of her legs. He kissed just above and she trembled, dug her nails into his skin. With one hand he parted her legs and made way for his tongue to dart back and forth over her very center.

"Joe!"

He continued until her hips began bobbing from the floor and then stopped.

"Joe!" Desperation colored her cry.

"Soon," he told her, and he turned her to her stomach. The gown didn't remain long.

"Trust me." He winced. "Just know I won't hurt you or embarrass you."

"Hold my breasts."

She lifted her torso a few inches from the floor and he did as she asked. When he covered her with his weight, she went flat on the carpet again, her breasts filling his hands, and he spread her knees with his own. He covered her, rolled with her, rocked her, and put himself just inside the entrance to her body, just past the point that brought her wonderful bottom jerking against him.

Again he stopped, fell on her, kissed the back of her neck and her spine. He kissed her spine repeatedly all the way down and between her buttocks.

"Are you all right, Ellie?"

"I'm wonderful," she said. "Are you teasing me?"

"Maybe. Yes, I am. More fun that way."

"I want to tease you."

"You started it. You gave me the idea." He got up, lifted her to her feet again. "No more teasing," he said, whirling her toward him.

She took hold of him and tried to push him inside her. There was a point when ecstasy became agony. This was it. "Some things are physically impossible, cher," he told her. "You need to grow a foot to do that."

"I want to." Her voice, thin and high, only drove him wilder.

"Counter or table?"

"Huh?"

He lifted her by the waist. "Leverage is the name of the game, my love. Take your pick."

"Oh! I don't care."

Joe smiled and walked with her into the kitchen. Her lotion was where he remembered, in a pump bottle beside the sink. He grabbed it and went to the table as fast as he could. He stretched her out on the tablecloth.

A quick flip of the slatted blinds and only thin lines from the streetlight decorated her skin. He pulled her toward him until her bottom rested on the end of the table and her feet and legs dangled.

Streams of lotion pumped from the bottle and he squiggled them over her in deranged patterns.

Ellie shrieked. "It's cold."

"Be grateful. That won't last."

With his hands he slathered the lotion all over her and she jumped at each erogenous spot he touched and lingered over.

"Joe," she moaned. "Hold me."

"I'm going to hold you tighter than you've ever been held," he told her. "I want you to feel me inside you and think I can reach your brains. I want you to taste me in your mouth. I'll make sure you do."

No veil, not even a thin one, covered his aggression and his explosive arousal anymore. She hovered close to something, a sensation, and she wanted it.

He eased her up and slid their skin together, rubbed back and forth against her, and returned her to her back.

She reached for him.

Joe leaned over her, held her hips and pressed inside her.

She tossed her head from side to side. "Come on, Joe."

"I will, cher."

But instead of doing what she expected, he brought his thumbs together against his penis and her flesh and massaged that magical spot. He chafed softly, barely touching her skin. Butterfly kisses, she thought, and they drove her mad. Out from her center his thumbs moved, pressing, working in circles, subtle not harsh, and she could not keep her hips still.

Sounds climbed into her throat, sounds too high to be heard.

One long sweep and he filled her. He breathed heavier than she did and she felt his muscles constrict when the effort to measure his thrusts cost him almost too much.

The speed increased. His hips jerked against her, drove him into her, and he never took his thumbs away. A scream broke inside her head. Her breasts must be swollen and hard. Her belly contracted. She grabbed his head and made pathetic attempts to bring him even closer.

The tablecloth slid beneath her, and with each entry, he pushed her farther along the tabletop. The linen fabric burned her behind and her shoulders but she didn't care.

Joe's sob turned to a keening sound. He turned his face up and pounded into her harder and faster, all the while matching the speed with the touch of his hands.

A pain, an ache, an electrical current shot from beneath his thumbs, but a second jolt burst inside her and at that moment Joe cried out. He panted, fastened his mouth on a nipple and kept pumping. Heat and wetness filled her.

The inner burst faded. His thumbs were on her again and another wonderful and devastating response rippled through her. Joe broke into a rush of hard lunges, the dam of his fluids broke again, and in only seconds he reached for the far end of the table, behind her head, and hauled himself over her, slid her all the way onto the top of the table.

In the warm, clinging quiet that followed, their lives moved as one. He gathered her into his arms, one of his thighs raised over her belly, and kissed her ear gently, repeatedly. "That's it," he whispered.

She opened her eyes. "What's what?"

"You're mine. You will never look at me without seeing us making love on your dining table. And I will never look at you without wanting to do it again. You're stuck with me."

24

Through a warm, satisfied haze Ellie heard the phone. It didn't just ring, it roared.

Joe came to at once. His reaction was to hold Ellie tighter in her bed, where they'd staggered to fall among the sheets, who knew how long ago.

"Mmm. Go away," he muttered. "Let's make love."

The phone rattled and jangled again.

"*Go away*," Joe said. He used a palm to make circles over her nipples. "This time I'm completely in charge and you will never be the same."

"I'll never be the same, anyway. Joe, the phone. It could be something important." She sat up abruptly. "It *has* to be something important."

She leaned over him to reach the receiver and Joe took advantage of the opportunity to use his mouth on whatever took his fancy. Ellie tickled him but he didn't stop.

The bedside clock read 2:00 a.m. Seemed much later. "Hello." It could be a creep. She'd had more than her share of those.

"Ellie, you're there."

There could be no mistaking Spike's voice. "Yes." Where did he think she would be?

"Look, I know how late it is, but could we come over? This is really important."

"Spike?" she repeated. "You want to come over?"

Joe reached to take the phone from her but Ellie whipped out of his range and sat on the edge of the bed.

"Can't it wait till the morning?"

Joe already had one of his iron arms around her middle and started dragging her toward him. He reached up to whisper in her free ear. "No. No, no, no. Not tonight."

"What's that?" Spike asked.

"What?" she said, planning some evil punishment for Joe when she got off the phone.

"Never mind. You sound out of it."

"I am. Every day is so long."

Again Joe made a grab for the phone. Ellie covered the receiver and said, "Pull yourself together, Joe Gable. You're on the couch, remember. This is Spike."

He threw himself, facedown, on the bed and made fake sobbing sounds.

Ellie couldn't help grinning as she walked to the farthest corner of the room. "Okay," she said. "I'm finally coming to. Can't you just say whatever it is on the phone?"

"No. Be there in ten minutes." He hung up.

She switched on a lamp.

"Turn it off," Joe wailed.

"Spike will be here in ten minutes."

"We won't let him in. Come back to bed."

"Joe, will you wake up and put something on. Go lie on the couch if you like, but please be reasonable."

"Be reasonable?" He sat up, a big tousled, handsome man who didn't deserve to be turned out of her bed.

"Joe, dear, dear Joe, would you do it for me?" Now she sounded like his mother. "Do it for us, please."

Again the phone rang and she picked up once more. Cyrus said, "Spike said you and Joe are expecting him. Is it okay if I come, too? Vivian called and said she thinks I should."

"Cyrus, you should be in bed."

"I was."

Stark naked, Joe threw himself sideways across the bed and let his legs and arms hang over. Ellie flushed. Little wonder he wanted her back in bed with him.

"Of course I won't disturb you if it's too much," Cyrus said. "We can talk tomorrow if you want to."

"No such thing," Ellie said. "Please come. If Vivian thinks I need you then I do. I'll get Joe up and put some coffee on."

Once more she hung up.

"Spike and Cyrus are coming for coffee," Joe said, and crawled from the bed. "Later, cher, I shall show you how a man can be emotionally mangled by interruptions at times like this." He looked down at himself and shook his head. Then he moved fast and left the room.

Spike didn't arrive alone. Guy came with him and added to Ellie's discomfort at the general disarray in her flat. Joe's sheets trailed from the couch. She looked at the table and wished she could disappear. The bottle of lotion stood on the ruckled tablecloth and she could see oily marks from across the room.

"You aren't going to be ready for this," Spike said.

Joe, dressed only in jeans, shrugged and said, "We're ready for anything at almost any time, aren't we, Ellie?"

"I think we've learned to be," she said, chalking up another point to settle.

Ellie also wore jeans, and a yellow shirt. Fortunately her hair didn't take much to look normal—which was more than she could say for Joe, who hadn't attempted to use a comb.

"Cyrus is coming," Joe said, and reclined on the couch. "I wonder who he's bringing."

Ellie glowered at him.

The doorbell rang again and she ran down to let Cyrus in. He looked at her closely. "What's wrong with you? You look terrible."

She swallowed a smart retort. "Just tired." How come he could look great in a day's growth of beard, uncombed curly hair and a rumpled black shirt minus his collar? "Let's go up."

He waved her ahead of him. "Any idea what this is all about?"

"No. I'm surprised Vivian called you."

"She's a sensitive woman and I think she gets anxious about you dealing with the heat."

Ellie snickered. "The heat? You've been watching too many cop flicks."

"That's very likely," Cyrus said lightly.

The three men she'd left stood exactly where they'd been and she doubted if a word had passed between them.

"Hi, Cyrus," Spike said. "Did my wife contact you? She said she might."

"She's a good woman," Cyrus responded.

Spike's eyes took on a distant quality. "The very best. Sometimes I have nightmares about what would have happened if I'd never met her."

Guy cleared his throat. "If a man finds a special woman he's a fool if he doesn't hang on to her."

"Very true," Cyrus added.

"Oh, yeah." This was Joe.

Ellie looked from one to the other of them and felt as if she'd accidentally walked through the looking glass. "I'm glad you all understand that important fact," she said.

Guy was the first to reestablish contact with reality. He rolled items over and over in his palm—dice, maybe, Ellie thought. He said, "This isn't good news. We've got to rethink everything and our options aren't reassuring."

"Spit it out," Joe said. He got up and looped an arm around Ellie's shoulders. She was glad of it and leaned against him.

Cyrus went to her other side and patted her back.

Ellie felt she was about to be sentenced to death. "Tell me, Spike. You're scaring me."

"New cast," Guy said.

"Ellie," Spike said. "Charles Penn is in custody."

Her stomach leaped. "That's great news, isn't it?" She turned into Joe's arms and hugged him. She glanced at his face and his frown puzzled her.

"Don't drag this out," Cyrus said. "I can tell you two are skatin' around the edge of somethin'. You're only makin' it harder for all of us."

Guy deferred to Spike, who breathed out through pursed lips. "Okay. Charles Penn is in custody. In Canada. He was picked up drivin' a stolen car across the border and with false ID. That was late on the night before Billie Knight was murdered."

25

Gratitude, that's what Ellie felt for being inside the chalk-pink door of Jilly's All Tarted Up, Flakiest Pastry in Town.

She and Joe had spent the rest of the night locked together in Ellie's bed, and when the phone rang just before 7:00 a.m. Joe wouldn't let her touch it. He snatched it up himself, snapped out "Yes," "No," "No" and "Yes," and bundled her to stand on the floor without offering an explanation.

"Get ready," he'd said. "Don't ask questions. It's important and there isn't time to talk. I'm taking you to Jilly's. Now."

He hadn't stopped her from asking those questions, but neither had she managed to get an answer out of him. They would talk about his high-handed behavior later...

A warm, fragrant haze filled All Tarted Up. Ellie had been there more than an hour, arriving even before the shop opened and while trays of fresh-baked goodies were still sliding into the glass display cases.

"Don't look so worried," Vivian Devol said. She'd already been at the shop with Jilly when Ellie arrived. The green-and-gold Rosebank van hugged the curb outside.

Ellie tried a smile, then said, "I am worried, Vivian." She didn't know if Spike had told his wife about Charles Penn being caught in Canada. "I don't even know what's happening. Why would they roust me out of bed so early and tell me to come here?"

Vivian shook her head and her smooth black hair swished across the tops of her shoulders. "You mean you weren't told a thing?" She let out an exasperated puff. "Not about the big search this morning?"

"Nothing," Ellie said, and narrowed her eyes. Wait till she got Joe alone again. Her automatic smile surprised her and she pursed her lips.

"What's funny?" Vivian asked.

So much for control over her emotions and the way they presented themselves. "I think I'm getting hysterical," she fibbed. In truth she couldn't keep her mind off Joe, and Joe with her on the dining room table. She shivered and looked away.

"They've brought dozens of people in to search," Vivian said.

Jilly strolled to the table where Vivian and Ellie sat, wiping her hands on a cloth as she went. "Joe said you'll stay till he gets back," she said to Ellie. "Something about having to do everything all over again."

"Back to square one," Ellie said. "They don't have any idea who did those things to me."

Vivian and Jilly looked at each other.

"Exactly," Ellie said. "A fine army we three would make if we had to fight off the enemy."

A rap on the glass in the door and they all jumped.

Cyrus angled his head to peer inside and gave a little salute when they saw him.

"Now I feel better," Jilly said. "One day I'm going to tell Cyrus he isn't hiding a thing—certainly not his muscles—under his priestly disguise."

"It isn't a disguise," Vivian said quietly.

Jilly reached the door, and before she turned the bolt she said "I know that" over her shoulder. "Just a little joke."

"Good morning, ladies," Cyrus said, beaming. "I'm a lucky man. I drew the short straw. That means I'm here rather than digging around in the mud."

"What mud?" Ellie asked sharply.

He shrugged but colored slightly as he always did when he felt uncomfortable. "Just a figure of speech."

That earned him hostile stares all around and he ducked into a chair beside Vivian. "Could I get some black coffee and a marzipan tart?" he said, and picked up the paper.

"We're not open," Jilly said, although she couldn't keep a straight face. "And we won't be unless you agree to tell us exactly what's going on."

He turned his eyes balefully upon them. "Perhaps I don't know."

"Spike told you not to tell us," Vivian said at once.

Cyrus folded the paper and put it down again. "Not exactly. He said it would be better not to say too much."

"Why?" all three of them asked together.

"Is that Missy Durand I hear out there?" He craned around and looked toward the kitchens. "She would never keep me without coffee."

"Missy's busy with the ovens," Jilly said. "Tell the truth and shame the devil."

Cyrus leaned back in his chair and laughed. "That sounds like something Madge would say."

They waited.

"Very well, I'll go against my better instincts. Ellie, I'm not making fun of any of your problems, but if we don't keep our heads up it won't be a good thing. We may not have Penn to worry about—he's in jail in Canada and who knows when he'll be brought down here again—but what happened, happened. Now there isn't a single lead on Billie Knight's killer."

"But doesn't that mean it's unlikely he or she has anything to do with... There wouldn't be any reason for someone other than Penn to come looking for Ellie," Vivian said.

Jilly ran her fingers through thick blond-streaked brown hair and pushed a comb in each side to keep it back. "Someone did, though." She snapped her mouth shut.

"Jilly's right," Cyrus murmured. "And it won't make things better if we try to pretend otherwise. I hope they don't decide you need to go into the Witness Protection Program."

"I *won't*." They couldn't be thinking about such a thing. "Spike said...everyone said that if that man wanted me dead, I'd be dead. But I'm not, am I?"

"Who has proof of what he wants?" Cyrus asked. "What if they're all wrong and they get careless? If whoever's been hangin' around you is just settin' things up so we all decide he's a joke, well then, if we let our guards down we could...you might get hurt."

"Say what you mean," Ellie told him. "I might get killed."

"I agree with them," Cyrus said, fidgeting. "So does Joe."

"Agree about what?"

Cyrus took hold of her arm. He looked at Jilly. "Sit down with us." When she did, he gave his entire attention to Ellie again. "We agree with Guy and Spike that you may have to go somewhere much safer until the case is cleared up."

"Coffee, everyone?" Missy Durand asked, coming from the kitchens with her light brown hair twisted into tight curls by the moist heat. "Something to eat?"

"Coffee and pastries, please," Jilly said. "Father will want marzipan tarts."

"When did the search start?" Ellie asked when Missy returned to the kitchens.

"Spike called and said he and Guy had just left your place," Vivian said. "He didn't think he'd be home for hours so he wanted to make sure I wasn't worrying. They'd got the call on Penn and the manpower was already coming in."

"I'm not leaving," Ellie said. "If necessary Spike can lock me up, but I'm not leaving Toussaint."

The door handle rattled. This time Paul Nelson put his nose to the glass and Jilly hurried to let him in and left the door unlocked. "Hey," she said. "You're one early bird, Mr. Nelson."

"Maybe I've got a worm to catch," he said and kissed her lightly on the lips.

Ellie met Vivian's eyes. It was no secret that Paul and Jilly were getting close, but Ellie didn't recall any public displays of affection before. She glanced sideways at Cyrus and her skin prickled. His eyes were as cold as she'd never seen them and he stared at Paul.

"What's with the summit?" Paul said, smiling and holding Jilly with one arm. "I thought I'd find Jilly alone." His grin broadened and he aimed it only at her.

He didn't get a response to his question.

"Cyrus," he said, "I'm glad you're here. I want to tell you something if you've got a moment."

"Surely." Dread had filled Cyrus from the instant Guy called him. That had been around six-thirty. He'd joined Spike, Guy and a gaggle of various official types, and he had waited until they told him to go to Jilly's. Wasting time on a man whose intentions he couldn't read came low on his list of priorities.

Paul didn't come to his table so he waited, and took a long swallow of coffee from the mug Missy put in front of him.

"Cyrus." Jilly bent over beside him and whispered, "I don't know what's on Paul's mind but he really wants to talk to you alone. Over at the corner table, if that would be okay."

"Yes." Cyrus picked up his coffee in one hand and took a napkin and a warm marzipan tart in the other. He stood up, registered the anxiety in Jilly's face, and could have kicked himself. "D'you want coffee, Paul?" he asked.

"That would be great." Paul already sat at the little table between the far end of the longest counter and the windows.

Missy brought a mug and a coffeepot before Cyrus could slide safely into a chair without dropping anything.

The bell over the door jangled and Doll Hibbs from the Majestic pushed her way in. She made to sit at a table alone but Vivian called, "Join us, Doll. You work so hard we never see you."

Cyrus gave thanks that the women had removed Doll from a perfect eavesdropping spot. And it made him feel good to see a smile on Doll's usually worried face.

"Father," Paul said, leaning across the table. "I need to clear something with you. I want to. You've got the wrong impression of me and I'd like to change it."

"I thought I was Cyrus to you these days."

"Yes, Cyrus. I've unloaded on you without thinking things through first. I apologize for that. What I should have done was rely on myself to straighten my head out."

"Sometimes we just need someone to listen to us. I know I do." The least he could do, Cyrus thought, was to give the man a fresh start.

"I was a damn fool," Paul said. "Maybe the overload of attention flattered me. I know better now and I'm not sure I would have if I hadn't shot my mouth off to you."

Cyrus chewed a mouthful of marzipan tart and felt cheered all over again at how the small things in life could bring so much pleasure. He looked Paul in the eye all the time.

"I told you I'd sorted out the two-women thing," Paul said in a low voice. "I should have done that a long time ago. Not today, but soon, I want to give this to Jilly."

He slipped a small velvet box from an inside pocket in his gray linen jacket and kept it hidden inside his hand until Cyrus offered his palm.

Once he had the box he took it beneath the table and opened it carefully. "My, oh, my. This is very beautiful, Paul. Is it real?" He glanced up at the other man.

Paul chuckled. "Not many people would ask that question. Yes, it's real. I wouldn't give her anything but the best. I've never been married, never had anyone to take care of but myself. And I've done well. I can afford it."

"I see." What else was he supposed to say?

"So you approve?"

Cyrus returned the box and picked up his coffee mug. "What are you askin' me?"

"I'd like to go forward knowing you feel good about Jilly and me. She hasn't had all the luck in the world, what with her father putting her out once her mother died."

"That's true." Cyrus knew the story of Jilly and Joe's father marrying a quadroon, then turning his back on their girl when her mother died. Joe's mother had been the first wife.

"I want her to know how important she is," Paul continued. "But I need to shake the feeling that I turned into a man I didn't know anymore for a while. I made a mistake and now it's over."

Cyrus nodded. "I believe you and I'm glad you and Jilly have found each other."

"Will you marry us?"

Movin' right along. "When you two are ready we should get together. She'll want time to enjoy all the stuff that comes beforehand."

"Thank you, Cyrus," Paul said. "You don't know what this means to me. We'll do things however Jilly decides."

They both drank coffee.

"Here's Joe now," Ellie said. "He's got Cerise with him."

Cyrus had decided Ellie and Joe were getting close, real close.

Looking grim, Joe opened the shop door and let Cerise rush in ahead of him. Something had happened, something that upset both of them. Cerise went directly to stand close to Ellie.

Joe said, "Could I get some coffee, please?"

"What's going on?" Ellie asked him, getting to her feet. "Joe?"

Doll would broadcast whatever he said all over town, Joe thought. So what—if she didn't, someone else would. "They're sweeping areas spreading from the edge of town," he said. "Came up with a sort of hiding place in a dense spot out by the old Minere place. Nobody's lived there for years. Our man made a screen out of eucalyptus switches to pull over a hole through the roots of a big ol' tree."

Even though Ellie didn't respond, he could see her mind working. She couldn't figure out what any of this had to do with her right now.

"You think the person, whoever he is, is still hanging around and hiding out in some hole?"

"Nope," Joe said, matter-of-fact. "I think that place is one more example of a ruse. Another piece of window dressing. He had a picture of you pinned up."

Her hands went to her throat. "What picture?"

"From the newspaper. It's the same as we thought before. If he didn't—"

"Joe," Cerise interrupted.

He said, "I need to deal with this first. If the guy didn't want to be associated with the killings and with you, he wouldn't leave bad stage sets around."

Paul and Cyrus joined the group, as did Jilly. Joe didn't miss the possessive way Paul held Jilly's waist.

"He had *glass* in his mouth," Cerise blurted out, and she let loose sobs that shook her body.

"Hush," Joe said gently. "Try to hold on, Cerise. It's going to work out."

A circle of shocked faces stared at him. Doll Hibbs took hold of Cerise's hand and rubbed it. "Everyone's got trouble," she said, her light eyes filled with sympathy. "Things are goin' wrong all over."

"Don't say anythin' you shouldn't," Cyrus told Joe. "We can wait for word from Spike."

"It's okay," Joe said. "I was told to come and tell you as much as you need to know—as much as I know. Then it would be appreciated if everyone remained here until Spike gives the word. There's too much goin' on and extra bodies just get in the way."

Cerise cried louder and Vivian made her sit down.

"Lucien from the Spa got hurt—probably late last night," Joe said.

His audience drew in breaths but didn't press him to hurry.

"Like Cerise said, he had glass in his mouth and stuck in the palms of his hands. He fought with someone but it doesn't look as if there's anything to get from footprints. Other areas look more promising."

"Lucien's going to die," Cerise said, choking her words out.

"Not if we all get lucky," Joe told her. He pulled a chair close to hers and sat down, leaned over her. "He needs your strength now. He needs that from all of us. The next few hours are critical."

"Joe," Ellie said quietly. "What's happened to him?"

"He was taken to University Hospital in New Orleans," Cerise said. "I want to go there but Spike says I mustn't."

"He had crushed glass in his mouth," Joe said. "That probably happened when he was attacked. He's got a depressed skull fracture and he's in a coma."

"They don't expect him to live," Cerise said, and rested her forehead on the table.

"Ellie," Joe said. He hated telling her this. "Forensics are still at it and everything's taped off."

She frowned at him. "These things take time, I suppose."

"Lucien was found beside your guest house."

26

"On the weather channel this morning they said the storms we got were from the edges of the hurricane," Ellie said. "Looks like we're in the clear this time." The drive from Toussaint to New Orleans with Joe scowling at the road ahead hadn't been any fun.

He didn't answer her now.

"Loreauville's ten feet under water. They're using helicopters to get the citizens out. And I guess hail the size of footballs is killing people right and left."

Nothing. He hadn't even noticed her ridiculous comments.

She reclined in the seat as far as possible and shut her eyes. Since yesterday morning when Joe brought the bad news about Lucien to All Tarted Up, his mood had made a steady downward progress. Within an hour Ellie had been allowed back into her place. Between appointments Joe had rushed through the front door of Hungry Eyes to take a prowl upstairs, despite yellow tape across the alley and a pack of officers and science types in the backyard. The moment he could get away completely, he'd returned and hovered through the evening.

Joe told her he intended to return to the couch for the night to put himself between Ellie and anyone breaking in, and her temper finally broke. *You're scaring me to death.* She felt ashamed to think of getting angry with him but he had said he understood.

Then she had fumed through telephone conversations between Joe and Spike, and Joe and Cyrus, and Joe and Guy. Joe had not volunteered any information and she had refused to sink low enough to ask.

He did tell her he had business in New Orleans today and would be leaving early in the morning. No, he said, she would not be going with him. Someone would keep a close eye on her till he got back. No, someone wouldn't, she'd countered, because she intended to go to New Orleans, with or without him, and try to see Lucien.

A long, tense night followed.

"What?" he asked abruptly.

It was Ellie's turn to keep her lips sealed.

"What?" he just about shouted. "You said somethin' but I was watchin' the road."

"A person usually does watch the road when driving. Some people are talented though, they can talk at the same time."

He sighed. "If you sit up you can just see Lake Pontchartrain to the left."

"I've seen it many times."

"Look, Ellie, I'm havin' a bad day, okay?"

"We all have them," she told him, but she felt more unhappy by the second. "I guess I shouldn't have pushed you to let me come with you today. I thought it would be a good opportunity to see if they'll tell me anything about Lucien's condition. Face-to-face, I mean." She also wanted to know if Joe had something in mind other than a supposed visit to his accountant.

"They won't. For Lucien's own safety there's no information coming out of the hospital and he's under heavy guard. They definitely won't let you in to see him. Be grateful he's still alive."

The tears in her eyes annoyed her. "Maybe a familiar face would help him."

"If he could see a face, it might. Right now he isn't seeing anything. He's in a *coma*, Ellie."

"We were right there when Lucien was hurt and we didn't know a thing was going on." She rolled her face away and looked at the blue-gray shadows darkening moss-covered trees. "When I asked to come today you should have told me *no*. Come straight out with it. This is what happens when people aren't honest with each other."

"I did tell you not to come and I'm not up for a lecture."

No, he only wanted to be mean and put her down. "How long will your business take you?"

"You asked that once already and I said it's going to take as long as it takes."

Instead of coming up with a retort, she sat quietly and took some slow breaths. They passed through the outskirts of New Orleans and headed into the city.

Joe put his hand in front of her, palm up, and said, "Truce?"

"Truce," Ellie agreed, and smacked her right hand down on his.

"You didn't forget your cell phone?" Joe asked.

"Got it."

"I'm going to get out on the corner of Canal and St. Charles. All you have to do is go—"

"One block and turn right on Common to get to Tulane," Ellie finished for him. "The hospital's on the right. I'll keep my phone on and you'll call when you're ready."

"You've got it." He smiled at her.

As long as she was a good girl and followed orders he would smile at her.

In full swing, the city traffic clotted at every intersection. Horns blew and fists waved from vehicle windows. Pedestrians played their daily game of chicken whenever they crossed a road. More rain began to fall and folks in sleeveless cottons whipped up umbrellas, which would disappear quickly enough if the wind really picked up.

Joe stopped at his appointed spot, gave Ellie a quick kiss and got out. Too busy watching for an opportunity to run across Canal, he didn't see how quickly she threw herself behind the wheel and turned right on St. Charles Avenue.

She had decided on her next move and every second counted.

Right again on Common and she searched both sides of the street for somewhere to park the Jeep. A car pulled away from the curb in front of her and she took its space, thanking the parking karma she had been blessed with.

At least she knew Joe had crossed Canal Street going in the opposite direction. Everything depended on how far he'd gone.

Breathing hard even before she left the Jeep, Ellie broke into a run and dodged people on the sidewalk all the way to the last place she'd seen Joe.

Ellie looked in all directions for a glimpse of his short-sleeved blue shirt.

Her brain raced but she felt her adrenaline ebb. She had lost him. She made her way across Canal Street, continuing to glance back and forth and to hop from time to time in case she might catch sight of him over the crowd. On the other side of the road she paused. So much for her parking karma, it hadn't helped her much today.

On the opposite side of Canal, St. Charles became Royal Street. Ellie didn't want to go there, didn't want to look into a shop window and realize she was seeing Xavier Tilton's jewelry shop, where Billie Knight had died.

At the end of the block, about to join a stream of pedestrians crossing Iberville, Ellie saw a tall, dark-haired man in a blue shirt and she ran. She couldn't get close enough for him to take a casual look behind him and see her, but neither would it do to be too far back or he could disappear again too easily.

Joe walked on. He carried a lightweight navy-blue windbreaker slung over one shoulder.

Ellie stayed close to the shops and kept about a block between herself and Joe.

Without warning, he stopped on the next corner, where Bienville intersected Royal, and performed a slalom maneuver between vehicles to get to the other side. That was dangerous and if she could ever find a way, she'd tell him so.

Shop windows filled with paintings, lace, coin collections, antiques and fabulous estate jewelry went by in a blur, although she did notice an antique doll shop for the first time. Ellie stopped halfway down the next block where the reek of old beer did something to the sinuses that might not be helpful. No need to hurry anymore.

Drawing back into the doorway of a shop with wire mesh between the eye and the estate jewels inside, she had a good perspective on the building opposite. The police station there stood like a big, granite mausoleum, its steps rising straight up from the sidewalk. Joe climbed those steps and stood to one side of a doorway, scanning up and down the street and obviously waiting for someone.

Unlikely place to meet your accountant.

Ellie slipped inside the shop and began what she hoped would be mistaken for a careful examination of a large piece of Dresden tableware near the windows. Crystal prisms dripped beneath multiple candleholders. Presumably the prisms would twinkle when the candles were alight.

Keeping watch on Joe proved simple. In the hushed atmosphere of the shop customers were expected to take their time over an item.

A life without Joe Gable wouldn't be a life. Even from across a street and with glass between them, Ellie felt him. Looking at him made her happy, excited her…terrorized her. When you lost someone you loved it hurt so much.

She did love him.

"A beautiful piece, madam," a man said beside her. "One of a pair. Should you like me to show you other examples?"

Ellie realized she'd been holding her breath. "No, no thank you. I'd like to take my time with this one first."

"Of course." The dealer backed quietly away.

Standing on the front of his step now, Joe balanced on the very edge and bounced slightly.

He checked his watch several times.

Ellie looked so closely at the Dresden that her nose bumped a prism and set it swinging. She heard a throat clear behind her but pretended she didn't.

Joe jogged down a couple of steps and gave a short wave. Spike Devol, also casually dressed, strode briskly to meet Joe and they went inside the police station at once.

Curiosity ate at her. If their visit wasn't as much her business as theirs she'd be very surprised.

Now what did she do—other than get out of this shop?

On the sidewalk again she wandered on a short distance, weighing her chances of getting caught. Good thing she did move on because at the next corner she saw a second entrance to the station from the side street—Conti. Too bad her favorite antique shop was in Royal Street's six-hundred block rather that right where she needed it. Any excuse to ogle M.S.Rau's fabulous collections was welcome.

She'd come back on a happier day—she hoped.

A coffee shop looked like a more convenient answer to her prayers and she settled herself at a counter inside the window, where she could keep an eye on both entrances to the old building across the way. She called Dr. Weston to check on Daisy, who, he said, might be well enough to go home tomorrow. Next she dialed the number for the hospital and began bucking all the people who didn't want her asking questions about Lucien.

"That didn't take long," Spike said when they went back out to the street. Rain fell. "Pretty tight-lipped in there, not that I expected anythin' else."

"Yeah," Joe said. "Too bad we didn't catch Guy before he left the place."

"Maybe, maybe not. Thinkin' he might be plannin' to come here was only a hunch. He might not have been pleased to see us."

"Our hunch was right," Joe pointed out. "And in case you don't remember, we're agreed it didn't make sense for him to disappear yesterday—right when forensics arrived."

Spike pulled on a black waterproof jacket and turned up the collar. "Shouldn't be hard to find him."

Joe nodded. "Not unless he isn't where the sweet-tempered detective said he is."

Spike laughed. "All part of detective training," he said. "Cut the World Down to Size, lol. We might as well walk. Decatur isn't far and I could use the exercise."

"Isn't the bar on Peters?" Joe said.

"Decatur, Peters, they're steps apart."

"This is a helluva place but I'm glad I don't live here," Joe said.

Spike slapped his back. "Cheer up. We're gonna have to drink. Can't hang out in a bar and not drink. Could be we'll have to sit there and toss 'em back."

"Sure." Joe shook his head. "I've got a thing for throwing my guts up at lunchtime—particularly when I'll have to drive home."

"You've got a designated driver. I'm sure she won't mind if you pass out in the back."

Joe didn't want to imagine that picture.

They walked on through increasingly heavy rain. In the windows of a corner store metallic beads—blue, gold, purple—glinted between masks, voodoo dolls and white plastic skulls with flashing red eye sockets. From some angles the merchandise all but disappeared behind the dust-laden glass.

Decatur and Peters about converged at one end. At the third building along Peters, swinging double doors, cowboy-style, and impenetrable gloom on the other side, made an uninviting entrance to Double Ds.

"Why would Guy come to a place like this?" Joe asked. "He doesn't seem the type."

Spike leaned against a doorjamb and crossed one foot over the other. "What does the type seem like?"

"*Hell*. How should I know? I've never been here before but I've got a feelin' is all. Are we gonna loiter or get on with this?"

Spike straightened, threw open the bar doors and let them go once he'd passed through. Joe managed to make a catch before he got slammed.

"Eau de booze," he said to Spike. "The sawdust on the floors is a nice touch."

"Practical, I shouldn't wonder." Spike squinted around. "It's a dump but it's got atmosphere," he said. "I think the spirit of victims past just whispered, 'Watch your wallet, and your back.'"

Booths marched along the back walls and repeated thuds on wood came from table legs on the uneven floors.

Stools lined a long, carved wood bar and a mirror missing chunks of silvering tossed out distorted images of the patrons who slouched there. Lanky Guy Gautreaux sat all the way on the left side, talking earnestly to a barmaid with flowers in her long black hair. A telltale foot remained on the floor. It might be slowing Guy's personal Ferris wheel and it probably kept him from rubbing his face in the sawdust.

"He's gotta know the barmaid," Joe said. "He's holdin' her hand and yakkin' like she's his only friend."

"A barmaid is every drunk's friend," Spike pointed out. "Let's get us a booth where we can be pretty much invisible while we watch and wait. He's gonna need us before he's finished. See if I'm not right."

"I don't like doggin' him around like this," Joe said, but he followed Spike into a booth and sat against the wall.

"Neither do I, but he owes us an explanation. We've been straight with him. Know what I think? He's not much of a drinker and she knows it—like you said, she knows him. That isn't a fine, pale single malt he's having. She's watering his bourbon to cut down how pissed he gets."

For the middle of the day the place was fairly full. Two other bartenders moved smoothly and rapidly from one end of the counter to the other, dispensing drinks with both hands. Occasionally they glanced at the woman but with only faint annoyance. For her part she tried to disengage her hand and couldn't. Joe felt grateful that whatever Guy poured forth wasn't loud enough to be heard by the rest of the clientele.

"Shit," Spike said. "I think he's cryin'."

"What can I get you two handsome boys?" a waitress wearing laced-on red satin asked. "It's wet out there but it's hot. It's hot in here and it's time you got hot, too."

Joe managed not to remark on her originality. "I'll have a Coke—" A hard kick under the table stopped him. "A rum and Coke. Lots of ice."

"You've got it, heartthrob."

"I'll have vodka on the rocks." Spike smiled at the woman and said, "Nice outfit. You're probably the only woman in the world who should wear it."

She winked at him and left.

"Well, the lawman has a silver tongue," Joe said. "Wait till I tell Vivian."

"She knows." Spike smiled with one side of his mouth. "I learned on her. Easy lessons."

Joe nodded and grinned, and looked around the bar. His eyes had grown accustomed to the darkness, not that there was much to see but broken-down guys trying to stub out butts in ashtrays. Darn it if those things didn't seem to move every time a man took another stab at it.

"You got it in mind to keep the lady there all day?" a loud, slurred voice asked. A man leaned back from the bar to glower at Guy. "How's about sharin' so the rest of us don't have to wait so long?"

"Here we go," Spike said. "We should get him out of here."

"Too late." Joe pushed to the edge of the table and got up from the bench. "Will you look at that? Quick, before he kills someone."

In not more than a minute the loudmouth had left his stool to make a menacing approach on Guy. Drunk or not, Guy sprang up, caught the guy's head in one large hand and pushed it down. At the same time he gripped the back of his shirt, spun him around and used his belt to haul him high on his toes.

"Give it a second," Spike said. "It could pass real quick and that would help all of us."

Nothing passed quickly. Guy had his new friend dancing and clutching his crotch. What he yelled was blessedly incoherent.

Other stools emptied and those who didn't stagger into something closed in on Guy in the midst of his little entertainment.

"Move," Spike said.

They pushed their way to the bar and Joe said "Guy" really loud and grabbed the detective's chin until their eyes made contact.

On Guy's other side, Spike bent the hand on the belt

backward till Guy let go. The dancer spun around and swung at the same time. His punch landed on Spike's shoulder.

Guy stood there with his head hung forward and making noises Joe hated.

A bouncer appeared, taking his time, and looked at Spike and Joe awhile before sending several men out for fresh air.

"Come *on*," Spike said. "Help me get him back to the booth. We need to sober him up before we leave."

"I'm not drunk," Guy said, still looking at the sawdust-covered floor. Joe and Spike each took an arm and helped him to navigate the tables and fall into the booth. Joe sat beside him and shoved him along to the wall, where he'd have a tough time getting out.

Spike took their untouched drinks and put them on a vacant table.

"We just missed you at the station house," Spike said. "Good thing someone knew where you'd probably be. Looks like a good place to have a private talk."

Guy put his head down on the table.

"What's going on?" Joe said. The longer it took to sort the man out, the more opportunity their joker had to work on his next plan back in Toussaint. He shook Guy's shoulder. "Why did you drop out yesterday, then call Cyrus with an excuse about having to check in here this morning?"

"Go easy on my friend." The barmaid stood at the edge of the table, hanging on with short, unvarnished nails and whitened fingers. "You don't know him so well, do you? He never mentioned anyone like you."

"Like us?" Spike gave her his full attention. "Can you translate that?"

She reached past Joe and patted the back of Guy's hand. "It's okay," she said. "These are hard times, Guy. You got a right."

"I—"

She interrupted Joe. "He don't have many friends. If he'd talked about you I would have remembered. Are you friends?"

Joe thought about it. "Yes, I guess we are. We haven't known him long but he's likable."

"You some sort of law?"

"I am," Spike said promptly. "Sheriff's Department out in Toussaint."

She shook her head. "That explains it."

Guy lifted his head, rested his chin on a hand and looked sleepily at the woman. "Don't you worry your head, Sue. I can take care of myself."

"Do you think these men are your friends?"

"Yeah. They're okay."

She looked to be in her late thirties. Her hands had worked plenty, but despite dark marks under her eyes she was a pretty woman. "You know I'm here for you?" she said to Guy, who nodded and tried to smile.

Joe studied each of them and raised an eyebrow at Sue.

"Nothing like that," she said, shaking her head. "We're just buddies, not that I haven't tried to make more of it."

"Does he come in here like this a lot?" Spike asked.

Sue frowned at him. "Come in here and get drunk, you mean? Guy, they don't know you."

Guy shrugged and closed his eyes.

Spike looked around to see who might be listening. Apparently satisfied, he scooted in and patted the seat beside him. She didn't hesitate to sit down.

"Why are you here?" she asked before either Joe or Spike could get an advantage on her. "What does Guy matter to you?"

"I can handle this," Guy said.

"He matters," Joe said, and meant it.

"Don't," Guy mumbled. "Any way you cut it I prob'ly end up dead."

Sue made a little noise. "Don't you say that, Guy Gautreaux. I won't let some crazy kill you. Y'hear?"

Spike met Joe's eyes and they made an unspoken pact to let these two do the talking, at least for now.

"No reason to live," Guy said, taking a shuddering breath. "Don't care anymore. 'Cept about you, cher." His effort to smile at Sue fell flat.

"That's right. You need to stick around for me. Who's going to come when I need a strong man on my side?"

"You can have any strong man you want," he muttered. "But I've lost everythin', includin' my will. Can't see a way out."

"Okay, give up, then," Sue said, her voice low and mean. "But I think I owe it to myself to see if this pair can help me out with you."

She waited, and when Guy just held her in his unfocused stare she turned to Spike. "He lost his girl. Never saw two people love the way they did. Did you know that?"

Spike said, "No."

"Waste of time," Guy said. "Love gets in the way of life."

"He and Billie Knight would have died for each other."

"Holy shit," Spike murmured, and fell against the back of the booth.

Joe felt as if he'd been punched.

Guy sneered. "So she died for me. I'm a bastard. If she never met me she'd be alive right now." He poked at the scarred tabletop with an index finger. *"Bastard."*

"She wouldn't have let you say that," Sue told him. "You made her happy."

The waitress brought black coffee and put it in front of Guy. For an instant Joe thought the other man might sweep it off the table, but he picked it up and drank unsteadily.

"Are you hearing me?" Sue asked Guy. "Billie told me herself that without you she wouldn't have wanted to be alive."

Guy closed his eyes. "I know how she felt. I've got one thing left to do. I'll find whoever got to her and there won't be anyone left for a trial."

"Listen to yourself," Joe said. He couldn't keep his mouth shut any longer. "Why didn't you tell us Billie Knight was your girl? Listen, Guy, we all want the same thing. Let's work together."

"She didn't ask for much," Guy said. "It was me, I put the job first and that's how I killed her. She wanted a little ring to show how we were an item. And she hoped for marriage and babies, only I decided they didn't fit with my life. Tilton said she went there and tried on the ring all the time. It wasn't even expensive."

Tears glistened on Sue's cheeks. "I didn't know that. You told her she couldn't wear a ring?"

"I might as well have. But I never knew about it because I'd taught her what areas to stay away from. She was probably scared to mention it. I was a goddamn fool but I'd have got her the ring…I would now. I wish I could get it for her now."

Joe's throat hurt and a glance at Spike showed he was suffering, too.

"We're with you," Spike said. "We'll work as a team and we'll get this one—for Billie, okay?"

Guy didn't respond.

Joe ran his fingers through his hair. He wanted to see Ellie. She shouldn't have gone off alone in the city—she never should be alone. "Guy," he said. "Will you help us make sure Ellie doesn't die in the meantime?"

"She'll be fine." Guy sounded steadier and he downed the rest of his coffee.

Joe said, "When I try to go to sleep, I see her dead. It happens every night. Whoever attacked Billie is tied up with—"

"Probably," Guy cut in. "What can I do about it? I'll have my hands full doin' what I've got to do before they make it too difficult for me. You better hope I get him before he touches her, otherwise it'll be too late, anyway."

Spike rested his elbows on the table and looked into Guy's face. "Who are 'they?' The ones who could complicate things for you?"

"NOPD," Guy told him. "I was suspended the day Billie died, for insubordination and what they called dereliction of duty because I wouldn't work with a partner on the case and I took off on my own. Maybe I should have told them about Billie and me. They never met her so they didn't know."

When her cell phone rang, Ellie was still huddled in the darkness, in a corner of the booth behind the one where Joe and the others had sat. "Hello," she said, and listened to him telling her to meet him whenever she was ready.

"I'm ready now," she said.

She heard street noises over the phone and he cleared

his throat. "Give me ten minutes. Why don't you wait for me at Johnny's on St. Louis. It's only blocks from where you dropped me off."

Ellie felt cold. If she thought it would do any good, she'd run outside right now and go after him. He didn't intend to tell her anything about what he had learned today. "That'll be fine," she said. Only it wouldn't. She loved him for caring so much about her but not for behaving as if she couldn't deal with the truth; he didn't believe she'd been the victim of any diversions. He thought she was a murder victim in the making.

"You okay?" Joe asked.

"Fine. I almost didn't get past square one with the hospital. Or the police, I suppose I should say. I did get to a nurse who made a slip, though."

Joe actually seemed to listen to her. "What kind of slip?"

"They think Lucien could have been attacked by more than one person."

27

"I'm sober," Guy said. "Listen to me. I talk fine."

Spike stood beside the van he had used for the drive to New Orleans, looked at his feet and sighed. He talked to Guy through the open passenger window. "You look drunk and you trip over your feet. You can't go back to the Majestic like that and I don't think it's a good idea to take you to Rosebank. Vivian would be fine with it, Charlotte, too, but it wouldn't be so good if a guest saw me bringin' you in."

"Okay." Guy leaned back in the seat and closed his eyes. Just as quickly he opened them again, blinked and looked green. "So let me stay in the van. I'll sleep in back."

"That won't cut it. Wait here."

At least he'd remembered to take the keys out of the ignition. Spike ran from the parking strip to the rectory and sneaked rapidly toward the kitchens. Doubled over, he hurried beneath the windows to the corner, then along the back of the house to the far end of the big window overlooking the garden and the bayou. Knowing a place well could be helpful. Unless he had the rotten luck to discover folks sitting at the kitchen table and, therefore, staring right at him when he took a look inside, this was the perfect spot to see and not be seen.

Spike looked, grinned and retraced his steps. Lil worked over the stove. Engrossed in adding stuff to a pot, she'd be unlikely to leave the kitchen in the next few minutes.

He got to the van, opened the passenger door and groaned to find that Guy had fallen into a restless, moaning sleep.

"Out you come," Spike said.

Not a word from Guy—or not the words Spike needed to hear, or the reaction he needed to have.

Guy was big. He might be rangy but his height made moving him more difficult. Spike maneuvered the other man into a shoulder lift, managed to shut the door of the van and set off for the front door.

He didn't knock, just went in, immediately saw Cyrus and Madge through their open office doors, and carried on to climb the stairs with Guy.

When he got to the sitting room the other two were right beside him, and Madge rushed to the couch to arrange pillows for Guy's head. Spike let his load slide down, straightened the man up on his side and stepped back. He was short of breath, damn it.

Guy stirred and slitted his eyes.

"You're okay," Spike told him. "You're among friends."

Madge spread a light blanket over Guy and tried to move him to a more comfortable position. Cyrus stopped her, patted her back and smiled into her eyes. "I know you're superwoman but you're embarrassing Spike and me."

She returned his smile for longer than necessary, Spike thought. "Guy," she said, "would you like some coffee? Somethin' to eat, maybe."

His face twisted with revulsion and he shook his head. "No, thank you. Sorry. Really sorry. I—" He lost consciousness again without finishing.

"Let him sleep there," Cyrus said. "Later he can get into a decent bed and take the night to...to rest up."

He went to the door and indicated for Spike and Madge to follow him. Outside he whispered, "He's going to regret this even more later. Did Lil see him?"

"Nope," Spike said. "She's busy in the kitchen."

"God is good," Madge commented. She went first down the stairs but paused at the bottom to wait for Spike and Cyrus. "Will Lil get suspicious if we shut ourselves away?" she whispered.

Cyrus shook his head and went directly to the kitchen. "Lil?" he said, beaming at the housekeeper, whose blond corkscrew curls had started to unravel. "Why are you working so hard? This has been a long day. What are you doing?"

With one hand bracing a wooden spoon on the bottom of a big pot, and the other hand on her hip, Lil gave Cyrus one of her "He doesn't live in the same world as the rest of us" looks. "I'm making your dinner. A good gumbo if I do say so myself."

"Everything you cook is good," Cyrus said, with the same tooth-showcasing grin on his face. "And all that has to do is simmer. I can handle it."

"And be stirred now and then," Lil said, her face red from the heat of the stove.

"Yes, ma'am," Cyrus said. "I don't remember to thank you often enough for all you do. Please, I want you to track down Ozaire and head out to Pappy's for dinner. On me. I'll call up and arrange it."

Lil's reaction suggested she feared Cyrus had lost touch with reality.

"Run along," he said. "I insist."

"Ozaire's over at the church, mowing," Lil said, but she put her spoon on a rest. "He'll want to get finished."

Spike almost said he'd never known Ozaire to turn down a free anything.

"Tell him I said he's to take you out. You both need it." Spike picked up a phone and called Pappy's. He arranged for Ozaire and Lil's bill to be paid. Then he gave Lil a hug. "I've felt bad that I couldn't help him with his plans for a gym. Maybe a space will open up somewhere in town."

You're overdoing it, Spike thought.

Suddenly flustered, Lil took off her apron and picked up her purse. Faced with a gift, she managed to set her surliness aside and thank Cyrus. She actually gave him a girlish smile before she set off in the direction of St. Cécile's. Before long she and Ozaire returned and got into their truck.

"Off they go," said Cyrus, and caught Spike and Madge exchanging grins. "Lil may be difficult, but she does take good care of me. She's pleased with being told to take a break. That's a good thing."

"Yeah," Spike said. "Do you think it would be a good idea to go sit outside? I wouldn't want Guy hearing us talk about him."

Taking coffee and one of Lil's big molasses cookies each, the three of them walked downhill toward the bayou and sat in old wooden chairs with their legs sunk a couple of inches into the ground. A lot of rain had done its stuff.

"Today we got a new curve ball," Spike said. "Guy hasn't exactly been lyin' to us, but he's kept the truth too close to the vest." He continued on, telling them exactly what he and Joe had found out in New Orleans, paused then added, "He really loved her, see, but he didn't want anyone to know. He thought a wife and children would be a handicap to a cop. That's what he said. But I know what he wasn't saying. He worried about the safety of a cop's family. I understand that."

Cyrus and Madge fell silent, then they looked at each other. Spike stifled a sigh. They were empathizing with Guy because they understood how he must have feared losing the one he loved.

The two of them worried him sick. He hoped there were things in life he didn't understand and that this was one of them. "Off the subject, but we'll come back to it and decide what to do. Vivian and I are expectin' a baby. Vivian, Wendy and I, that is. Wendy thinks the baby's for her."

Madge gave a very un-Madgelike squeal. "Spike! Ya'll are havin' a baby? I know how much you've both wanted it. I am so excited."

"Congratulations," Cyrus said. "I'll expect to see the three of you in baptism classes. Has Wendy been baptized?"

Shit. Spike shook his head slightly.

"Well, that'll make it all the better. We'll do the two of them at the same service. The whole town will show up for mass—which will be a first."

Spike felt himself getting hot. "Vivian and I will talk to you, Cyrus."

"Y'know?" Madge said wistfully. "I've never been a godmother."

Panic wouldn't help him, Spike decided. He'd like to tell her they hoped she'd be the baby's godmother, but in truth he and Vivian hadn't even thought past being pregnant.

"You should be one," Cyrus told Madge. "Any baby would be lucky to have you. Don't you worry your head about it. I'll put an ad in the bulletin offerin' you for some lucky little tyke. I bet there're all kinds of people who would ask if they didn't think you've already got too much on your hands."

Spike felt worse and worse, so bad that when he saw Doll Hibbs trotting toward them, he was grateful. Madge's eyes were suspiciously moist.

"Ellie and Joe went to New Orleans, too?" Cyrus said with a question in his voice.

Spike nodded. "Yup. Probably still there. I think they had a lot of talkin' to do." He and Guy had been walking toward Royal Street with Joe when Ellie intercepted them. The truth was he and Joe were holding Guy up between them. For a quiet woman she surely could say a lot with her eyes. She was one angry female. "We should let them have their space until they say otherwise."

"Hi, y'all," Doll called out. "Can I have a word? Wouldn't want to interrupt anything."

Cyrus went to greet her. Spike unearthed the legs of another chair and settled it nearer to the others.

"Doll Hibbs, have you been to sleep lately?" Madge asked. "Get yourself over here and rest. Would you like coffee or somethin'?"

Doll sat down and Spike could swear she looked bashful, but then, he'd been known to misunderstand a woman's feelings before.

"Nothin', thank you, Madge," Doll said. "I'm such a fool. A silly fool who never got past pretendin' to be in charge when I'm not. I make believe I don't give a hoot about anybody's thoughts, but I'm scared silly to speak my mind when I should. Now I've really done it."

Spike tipped his hat back on his head and squinted at Doll. A valiant Louisiana sun hung low in the sky and turned moist haze into a dazzling sheet of yellow-tinted gray.

Cyrus leaned toward Doll and said, "Would you like to walk with me to the church?"

Embarrassment made way for misery in Doll's pale eyes. She shook her head no. "I just got to speak up. Y'all need to hear it. I come to Jilly's place to tell you some of it. That was yesterday. I couldn't make myself butt in on everythin'. It occurred to me y'all would think I was just makin' somethin' up so's I'd be important."

"It can't be that bad." Cyrus sat on the edge of his chair. "Just say whatever it is and get it over with."

"It's Ellie I'm worried about," Doll announced, looking around the circle. "Everythin' adds up now but who's gonna believe Doll Hibbs?"

This was a moment to let her ramble on until she came to the point, Spike decided.

"I thought Jim Wade was as nice a man as you could want to meet," Doll said. "Quiet. Polite. He didn't say much but he was decent when he did talk. Into his business and…"

Spike waited for her to gather her wits. Cyrus looked into her face and Madge at her own hands.

"The day before Lucien got hurt, that would be the day before yesterday, I was cleanin' up in Mr. Wade's room. That was in the afternoon. In one of his drawers…" She blushed but went on in a firm voice. "I looked in the drawer and saw photographs. They was mostly of Ellie and I don't think she knew they was bein' taken. There was some of the outside of Hungry Eyes, several pictures of Joe Gable and his offices—the whole building."

Spike took off his hat, scrubbed at his hair and plopped the hat on again. "That's interestin'." He avoided eye contact with Cyrus, who would know what Doll said was a lot more than *interesting*.

"He had some papers in there but I didn't look on account of… I didn't want him to catch me. But I did see a piece of newspaper. There was Ellie, again."

All Spike wanted was for her to get everything out before someone else turned up or she lost her nerve.

Doll held out a shaking hand. "I should've told you when I saw you, Spike. Or called you right then. But I didn't."

"You're tellin' me now," Spike said. He had to move on this. "Jim doesn't know you saw anythin'?"

"I don't know. He didn't have breakfast today. I just checked his room and he's up and gone. Not a thing left behind."

28

The bitch. This is her fault. The schedule wouldn't have changed if she had kept her nose out of things.

I don't make mistakes, wouldn't have made this one if I hadn't had too much going on. All she had to do was accept what came her way, stop fighting and poking around and mouthing off.

Between her, the deputy and the horny lawyer, my plans are about shot. The cop from New Orleans didn't help.

I've had some luck, though. Lucien got way too close and if I hadn't caught him he'd have blown everything. I thought I'd finished him, I should have, but even if he recovers he isn't likely to be much help to them.

So I'll be real calm and do what I've got to do—even if I'd rather wait for the date I had planned on.

When I think of it that way it makes me smile. It is almost over. The rush is back, the sexual thrill that comes with the promise of the kill.

29

If he could turn the clock back to last night and start over, he would, Joe thought. Right now he'd do about anything to get Ellie to smile.

Tape still stretched across the alley, and a deputy sat in his car at the entrance, so Joe had parked under the sycamore tree where he used to park before he'd moved in above the offices. He and Ellie had entered the building through the front door to Hungry Eyes and she continued to stand right there, leaning on the jamb, not saying a word.

And she looked whipped. He almost wished the anger hadn't gone out of her face. At least he could try to fight that, but this distance left him helpless.

"Ellie," he said tentatively. "Will you at least talk to me?"

"We couldn't talk in New Orleans or driving back. This definitely isn't a good time, either. It's too late."

"I tried to talk. I tried to talk at the restaurant. Don't do this to me. If I don't know, I can't do anything about it."

The cat sailed between them, looked from Ellie to Joe and chose his legs to wind herself around. Joe bent to scratch her.

"Our relationship isn't healthy," Ellie said.

You are so wrong. "That's crazy. Absolutely crazy. What we've had to deal with hasn't been healthy for anyone, but you and I are great together."

She gave him a measured stare and he didn't miss the way the corners of her mouth jerked down. He'd grasp at any hopeful sign and she didn't look happy about being cool with him.

"I never expected to say this to anyone, but I'm in love with you, Joe."

He took a step toward her but she held up a hand and shook her head.

Joe dropped into a chair at the closest café table. He felt elated and desperate and the mix tightened his scalp. He ran his fingers through his hair and closed his eyes. "Ellie, I love you. That isn't a knee-jerk reaction to what you just told me. I think I've loved you for a long time."

"It doesn't give us the right to think for each other," she said. "There's something in me—just being a woman, I guess—that makes me love your protectiveness. But there's a difference between being protective and suffocating someone."

Suffocating? "How have I ever suffocated you?" This was a twisted joke—for her to say what he wanted to hear, to know the two of them felt the same way, only to walk into whatever fight was going on in her head.

"When you left the police station with Spike, I followed you."

"You what?" His mind moved fast over the events in New Orleans. "You sneaked around after me? You shouldn't have done that. Now I'm sure I should have refused to take you with me."

"Because you want to manipulate what happens to me without letting me in on anything that's going on?"

"It was a bad idea." And he felt like a fool.

"I sat in the booth behind you in that bar. Poor Guy. He's lost so much and I wanted to get up and hug him. But I hated it that you talked between you, you and Spike, as if I don't have any right to be treated like an adult."

Joe got up. He couldn't sit and watch and listen to her anymore, not when there was nothing serious standing between them. "You are an adult," he told her. "So am I. You're not made to deal with people who play sick practical jokes."

"Stop it!" She pointed at him. "Just stop it right there. I *heard everything*, I told you. I heard how you think I'm a potential murder victim. You're just playing with me because you think I'm not strong enough to deal with what's going on."

He did think that, at least when it came to having a killer a few steps behind. "You're a strong woman. You've made it through a lot."

"We need a chance to be normal."

"Meaning?" His heart thudded.

"We've never even dated," she said. "We were thrown together because of something that happened to me."

"So what?" What was so unusual about that? "You're upset about something else and you're taking it out on me."

"No. But you help make me sure I'm doing the right thing," Ellie said.

"And what is it you're doin'? I'm not real clear here."

Finally she left the door, but only to pick up the cat. "If we're going to have any chance together, I've got to be allowed to stand on my own feet—just like I always have. I'm not afraid anymore and I thank you for that. You made it possible for me to adjust. As long as everything's locked up around here, I'm fine. It's time you spent your nights in your own place."

"Baloney."

"There's someone guarding the place and I promise you I'll come running if anything happens."

She was mangling his mind. "How will you come runnin' if someone bigger and stronger than you decides he won't let you?"

"Don't talk like that." Her voice sank low, and whether she knew it or not, she pleaded with her eyes. "I'll call your cell phone, just in case you step out."

"Please, Ellie, think. Damn it, will you see this clearly? If he wouldn't let you go, why would he let you make a phone call?"

"Once you leave, I'll lock up," she told him again. "There's no way for anyone to get in here without keys, and the locks have been changed so I know exactly who has a copy."

"I'm not leaving you here on your own."

"Yes, you are. That's the way I want it and I've got my reasons. I don't want us to ruin any chances we have. What we've been doing isn't normal…I don't mean I regret sleeping together. I loved it. You've given me the best memories I've ever had."

Joe crossed his arms. "You make it sound as if there aren't going to be more times like that for us."

"You're hearing what you want to hear. Leave it for now. Will you take a look around before you go?"

He swallowed and glanced back at the bookshelves. It was all so still and she was vulnerable here, damn it.

"Joe," she said softly. "The last time I called Dr. Weston was while you were at the counter in the sub shop. He said Daisy's getting stronger and he's almost sure she can come home tomorrow."

"So why not wait for tomorrow to send me packing?"

"Because it has to be now."

"You're stubborn." And he could be just as stubborn. "Daisy isn't going to be ready to take anyone on. Anyway, I haven't seen her do a great job protecting you in the past."

The fire returned to Ellie's eyes. She walked past him and picked up two stacks of neglected mail that had grown high in the past few days. Wazoo piled it up there. "You don't know everything Daisy's done for me. It wasn't her fault I had her muzzled out at Pappy's. The next time, she did go after him but he was ready for her. She's a big dog, but it wouldn't take much chloroform to make her collapse. It's no wonder she took so long to come back."

"*Chloroform?* You never mentioned chloroform to me."

"I forgot. I've had a lot on my mind."

If Daisy had been chloroformed, where did it happen? She couldn't have been lying in the street. "I haven't heard anything about what might have been in the glass Lucien had in his mouth. Does chloroform just disappear or would they know if it had been there?"

"I don't know," Ellie said. "The vet said people can get kidney damage from it—and other nasty things if they get too much. Daisy seems okay so I don't think she got more than a quick whiff."

"I'll sleep down here if you'd feel better about that." What he wanted to do was common sense. Why couldn't she see that?

"Please let it alone," Ellie said. "I think you should go.

I also think a call should be made to the hospital where Lucien is, and to Spike. They need to know about the chloroform. Why I didn't realize that before, I don't know."

She saw frustration tighten Joe's mouth. He turned away from her without another word and left the shop for the apartments. He would never know how heavy her heart felt about confusing him, and he was confused. Men seemed to see things as basically simple. He loved her, she loved him. He had explained his reasons for treating her like a child and now they should go to bed.

She heard him overhead and didn't have to see him to know he was putting his feet down hard. He thumped back and forth, opening and closing doors.

The phone rang and she hurried to pick it up. "Hungry Eyes."

"Spike here. I need to talk to Joe."

Everyone assumed Joe could be found with her at night. "You just caught him. He'll be going home any moment. Let me get him for you."

Spike started to say something about that but she held the phone away and called Joe. It sounded as if he only landed on about three steps on the way down. "Spike for you," she told him when he came into the shop again.

For a couple of minutes Joe listened while Spike did the talking. Then Joe grunted and launched into the chloroform possibilities. More listening followed before Joe hung up. With his hands in his pockets, he looked into the distance.

"What did Spike say?" Ellie asked when it seemed he wouldn't tell her anything.

"Lucien had surgery early this evening. They had to release the pressure from swelling inside his skull. He's got slivers under his fingernails, too, and the ends of his fingers are chewed up. That's from the forensics people. Apparently they've got some theory about what happened." Narrowing his eyes, Joe said, "I think they must have known about the possibility of chloroform, even though you rarely hear of it being used anymore. Spike says they're looking for the top of the bottle. He also said something to back up your two-attackers theory—maybe. Two blows to the head, two weapons."

"Nothing's going to happen before morning," she said. He had to know how hard it was for her to send him away. "You'd best get going."

"Okay."

She didn't have a chance to get out of his way when he took her by the shoulders and kissed her forehead. Not that she wanted to.

"'Night, Joe." She touched his jaw and the skin felt rough against her fingers.

He didn't answer her. Outside the door he waited for her to lock up before backing away and standing on the sidewalk, looking at her.

Walking away seemed too hard. She shivered, but not from being cold, and raised her hand in a wave.

Joe waved back. He didn't attempt to leave and Ellie returned the kiss he blew.

Torment her into submission, that's what he was up to. But he smiled and all the feelings, the sensations that he could cause so easily, rushed in. They'd work it through.

Carrying the mail, Ellie picked Zipper up again and tucked her under one arm. She walked through to the vestibule at the bottom of her stairs and shut the door to the shop without glancing in the direction where Joe probably still stood.

By the time she climbed into bed, Ellie could easily have called and begged him to come back after all. Or she could throw on some clothes and go to him. But she could hang on. At least he was nearby.

"Zipper, what are you doing on the bed?" she asked the cat, who usually preferred her own room. Zipper turned around and around, took time out to chew a few claws, then curled against Ellie's side.

And she was glad of it, so glad of it she ought to be embarrassed.

Bills, bills and more bills.

She riffled quickly through the mail, dividing it into piles. Book catalogs made up a hefty chunk of what she'd got. She started turning down pages. The shop did a good trade for a small place. Being the only bookshop in town helped. She smiled at that.

Zipper slithered onto Ellie's stomach and purred while she kneaded with spreading paws.

A fat letter had come from a sales rep who operated out of New Orleans. Ellie slit open the envelope. This was a guy she liked because he took the trouble to make the trip and visit her personally every few months. Most of those folks didn't have time to go out of their way for such small orders.

The letter sounded just like the man himself. Enthusiasm jumped off the page. *This is a chance to double your profits on our Sonja Elliot books.* She recalled putting in an order for the paperback version of *Death in Diamonds* about two months ago, and had more recently upped the quantity because of all the fuss about the series. The books should arrive soon. No doubt with all the publicity there would be an extra rush on buying this one.

The rep had written:

We have an exciting offer to make to you. You'll love it. In a surprise move we're rushing out Ms. Elliot's next hardback two months early and putting it on sale at the same time as *Death in Diamonds* in paperback. Not only that, but be sure not to miss our special discounts to clients who make an effort to take more copies.

Ellie checked the date on the letter and that on the envelope. This piece of mail must have circumnavigated the globe. The latest Sonja Elliot would be out in a few days. Ellie would have to call first thing in the morning to see if she could place a rush order. The publisher had played this one close to the vest and dropped it on the bookselling world. They had not even printed advance reading copies for the industry.

She read on:

Capitalize on this once-in-a-lifetime opportunity. See how close you can get to matching your mass-market buy with a like number of copies of the hardback *Death of a Witness: The Chosen Victim.*

30

Spike drew his cruiser in beside the deputy who had pulled guard duty on the property behind Ellie's place. He rolled down the passenger window and leaned across. "Evenin'," he said to a husky blond guy. "I'm Spike Devol." He hadn't seen this one before. The sheriff made extra officers available on an as-needed basis.

"Yes, sir. Tom Turner, sir. From Belleville."

"Glad to have you." Yeah, Spike remembered the name on tonight's detail. "How long ago did the Jeep arrive over there?"

"Around forty minutes, sir. Two people—one male, one female—went into the bookshop, then the male left and went in there." He pointed to Joe's offices where the bougainvillea over the porch whipped insanely in gusts of hot wind.

The only upstairs light Spike could see shone in Ellie's room and that went off a moment later. He'd feel a whole lot more secure if Joe was with her. What in hell was that all about? he wondered. Rotten timing for a spat.

Joe's windows were dark, too.

A white van slid along the right side of the square toward them. "Forensics," Spike told Turner. "If another officer comes, direct him out back."

"Will do, sir," Turner agreed.

Carrying two bags, a man with wispy white hair left the van and joined Spike. "Mike Wills," he introduced himself informally. "Let's take a look, shall we? Probably a good idea to take another close check now. If we do get the storm it's likely to take out any useful traces."

The other officer Spike had expected, Castille, arrived in time to accompany them along the alley and through Ellie's back gate. "Any need to inform these people?" Mike indicated where Joe lived, the empty house next door and Hungry Eyes.

Spike shook his head. "On either side, Ellie and Joe know there's activity out here. The middle place isn't lived in."

"Lucien came through the surgery," Mike said. "But his condition is guarded. You heard they think there could have been two assaults? Or at least two weapons?"

"Yeah. I hope Lucien makes it," Spike said, meaning it fervently for a number of reasons.

Castille carried a camera. "Where would you like me to start?" he asked Spike.

"That'll be up to the doctor," Spike told him. "He's in charge of this one. Doc, do you think Lucien tried to eat the glass because he's involved?"

"Nope," Mike said. With the other officer's help, he set up lights, and soon the area around the guest house glared under white beams. "It's much more likely he was forced to put the glass in his mouth. We're looking for a source of wood slivers under his fingernails."

Spike grunted. "Do you know if they've had any luck tracing the newspaper photo of Ellie Byron? The one they found in that supposed hideout?"

"Northern California," Mike said, crouching over the area of the struggle. "Some burg out of San Francisco."

"Jim Wade mentioned living up there," Spike said, and explained about the broker's disappearance.

"No luck bringing him in?" Mike asked.

"Not that I've heard." Spike braced his hands on his knees and peered around the area. "Lucien was supposed to die."

"Uh-huh."

"The siding on the guest house is wood," Spike said. "He could have thrown his hands out to break his fall and messed up his hands in the process."

"He could have," Mike agreed. "But I don't think so. The slivers are raw, not painted or stained like the siding."

Spike tilted his head. "See that?" he said. He touched Castille and pointed to the base of one side of the building. "All along there. The shadow's too wide, as if there's a gap under the siding."

Castille began shooting pictures. He moved around getting angle after angle.

Mike approached from one direction and Spike the other, crouched and moving one foot at a time, awkwardly.

"You got gloves?" Spike asked, and felt stupid. "Of course you do. Can you spare a pair?"

Mike took extra ones from his pocket and tossed them.

Once Spike had them on he dropped his knees to the dirt and bent almost to the ground. "There's a mark here. Several marks. Scratches on the foundation as if someone scraped it. With glass, maybe. Is it okay if I see if my fingers go under?"

"You got a bag?"

Spike shook his head and Mike handed him a plastic bag. He tipped his fingers under the siding and ran them back and forth, expecting to find nothing but a nail or two. What he got was a sharp jab and he eased out a small, jagged piece of brown glass. He dropped it into the bag and met Mike's eyes. Four more glass fragments followed. The other man had stopped to watch him.

"That's it," Spike said, feeling around. "No, hold it." He knew what he had, a bottle top. He got a nail under the rim and hooked it out and into a fresh evidence bag held open by Mike Wills.

"Bingo," Mike said, a smile narrowing his dark eyes behind thick glasses.

Voices, low but intense, sounded outside the gate. "See what that's about, please, Castille."

In minutes the other man came back. "The guy who's on guard duty is trying to persuade some woman to go home but she isn't budgin'. Says you need her help. Name of Wazoo or somethin'."

"Know her?" Mike asked.

Spike considered denying it. "Yes, I do. She turns up in the darnedest places."

He heard the gate open again and a small, dark figure flew in his direction with Deputy Turner hot on her tail.

Spike caught Wazoo as she launched herself at him. "Tom," he said to Turner over her head. "It's okay. Leave her."

The guy nodded and retreated.

"Now, what are you doin' here?" Spike asked, glaring down into Wazoo's ethereal face. Her hair was caught inside one of those old-fashioned black lace snoods. Her pale skin glowed. "You think you're untouchable, but you're just a little woman and you should be at Rosebank, not runnin' around in the dark on your own." Wazoo took dancing steps to combat the wind.

He heard her gulp. Then she said in a voice not like her own, "I'm sorry, Spike. All I got is the folks I love and I gotta help look after 'em. I heard about that chloroform what he slapped on poor Daisy. Wonder he didn't kill that angel. But you can bet your best skivvies he had other things in mind for that poisonous, wicked stuff."

Spike caught Castille's puzzled look. Mike chewed a thumbnail and amusement twinkled in his eyes.

"Do you know where this sex maniac got the bottle of persuasion?" Wazoo asked.

"Huh?" Castille said.

Spike knew what Wazoo was talking about but not why, or how she was so well informed. Pretty soon after they met he had summed her up as an insecure woman making a lot of noise to pretend otherwise.

Mike surprised him by saying, "Ever seen a cap like this before?" and holding the evidence bag out to Wazoo. "New Orleans address, I think."

She stepped away from Spike and took a cursory glance. "Tal's Toys," she said. Her eyesight had to be good to see the small script so easily. "Ain't there no more, but if you're lookin' to make sure your woman's easy you can still go to Fester's. Same shop, same owner, different name."

"You still lookin' puzzled, boy," Wazoo said to Castille. "You never did hear about folks usin' that chloroform for special effects?"

He shrugged his shoulders back. "Sure I did. But something tells me you know too much about too many things. Could be we need to ask you more questions." He gave her the evil eye.

Apparently Wazoo didn't see his mouth twitch. She sidled up to him and wound her hands under his arm. "I don't know nothin' more than any other worldly woman. How often do *you* use chloroform to juice up your sex?"

Spike and Mike laughed, then tried to smother the noise.

"All the time," Castille said.

Looking smug, Wazoo said, "Some men just can't go it alone, but I'm glad you make your own fun."

She turned to Spike. "I know that shop, and I'll go see if I can buy a bottle of this, if you like."

"No, you won't," Spike told her quickly. "All we need is you spreadin' our official business all over Louisiana."

"I surely will go," Wazoo told him, wagging a finger. "You can't stop me and I can get what you can't get. Trust me for once. I'll go first thing in the morning."

"Ma'am," Mike said, "be sure you don't end up in a cell—or worse."

She sighed and looked up into Castille's face. "All this talk's set my appetite to wigglin'. It's been too long since I sniffed that stuff in the company of a sexy man."

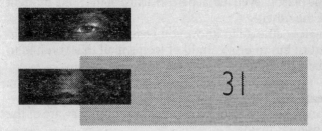

31

Ellie rolled over on Zipper, who hissed and shot from the room.

The clock showed two-thirty in the morning. She wasn't sure if she'd slept. The night dragged. All she longed for was morning, the sound of voices, life.

How was she supposed to keep her mind off the title of Sonja Elliot's unexpected new book? *Death of a Witness: The Chosen Victim.* In the previous two books the victims had been random. If her fears were well founded, the witness in question could be her and she would be chosen because someone feared what she might know.

Dim light from outside rolled a faint leaf pattern across the shades. She couldn't see the corners of the room and the open door showed an oblong more intensely black than the rest.

Usually she liked darkness. Most especially she liked it when Joe could be with her.

He could be with her now—would be if she had not sent him away. But her decision had been the right one.

Good relationships weren't built on the dependence of one person, even if that person ached at the mere thought of the other.

How strange to know you were in love and loved in return but to be so afraid of losing it all that you had to make the kind of choice she'd made tonight.

Yet again the air had been sucked out of the night. She heard wind in the big sycamore and the rattle of window-panes, but the sounds only made her more aware of the closeness inside.

She pushed a hand beneath her pillow until her fin-gertips touched a metal handle. Goose bumps shot over her skin. She pulled the old can opener, with a short open blade shaped like a hook, firmly into her palm. The tool had traveled with her since she first ran away from home. Back then she'd planned to open canned food with it. Since that time it had become her occasional weapon—even if only in her mind by giving her some small comfort. Tonight, without Joe's reassuring pres-ence, she'd taken the implement to bed again.

First thing in the morning she intended to call the vet and see if she could go over to Loreauville to get Daisy. Ellie missed the secure feeling the dog gave her, and the companionship.

She had already got rid of her light blanket; now Ellie threw back the sheet. Her short pink silk nightie barely covered matching panties. Bare legs felt good.

Joe would like the nightie. It was the sexiest thing she'd ever bought and she'd had it a week. What she needed was the courage to put it on for him.

When she lay like this, stretched out on her bed think-ing of Joe, of the feel of his smooth, hardened body, his weight, the way he touched her, arousal overwhelmed her.

Her panties felt damp. Excitement darted into places where she wanted him to be. Her nipples hardened and she touched them. The halter top on her nightie tied with a ribbon beneath her breasts. Slowly, she swept the silk away from her warm skin. She couldn't substitute for that man but she could intensify his memory.

A scraping noise, fabric on fabric, doused the sensual warmth, wiped away the arousal.

Ellie held her body still and stiff. She couldn't do anything about her runaway heart.

Ellie strained to listen. Maybe she had only imagined the sound.

There it came again, like new jeans, the legs brushing together as someone walked.

Her breath came in shallow gasps.

Propped on her elbows, she peered into the darkness. They told you not to turn on lights because it only made it easier for an intruder.

The form that rose from the floor beside the bed was no ghost. Ellie screamed. Solid, lunging at her, a man attacked.

One big hand covered her face and slammed the back of her head down on the pillows. The other hand kneaded and squeezed her breasts. She would have cried out in pain but he'd taken care of that possibility.

Ellie kicked at him with her bare feet, and she struggled, rocked her body from side to side. The inside of her head felt swollen and black, as if it would burst wide open. Terror closed her throat. Sweat burned in her eyes. He leaned so hard her face seemed crushed. His other hand ranged all over her.

She couldn't reach under the pillow.

Blood ran into her mouth, from her front teeth puncturing her bottom lip.

Forcing her mouth open, she bit down on him, kept on biting until he yanked the hand away.

His blow to her face snapped her head sideways and she screamed. Again he hit her.

For an instant she only heard the rasping of his breath. He concentrated on holding her down and her flesh burned beneath the pressure. *I will survive. God help me. I will survive.* She choked on her own breath, but he'd shifted just enough to allow her to force her right hand upward beneath his forearm.

She touched the pillow.

"Let me go," she managed to cry out. "I won't report this if you let me go."

He didn't speak and he pressed so close to her, his hot breath fanning her face and neck, that she couldn't make out anything except that he was big, heavy.

"Get away from me!" Arching her belly, she tried to throw him off. Again she screamed, the jagged sound ripping from her throat.

A pillow descended on her face.

Fighting for breath, Ellie worked her head sideways and found a little air.

She had the opener tightly clasped in her hand. While he had grabbed the pillow from one side, Ellie had gone for her prize from the other.

She felt every move he made over her, and she waited for her chance to strike. One shot would be all she got. If she missed, he'd turn the blade on her. She went from hot to cold.

He rubbed hard between her legs, as if he thought he could stimulate her into wanting his disgusting assault on her body. She couldn't get a knee into his crotch. When she tried, he punched her thigh and the leg turned numb.

With bile in her throat, Ellie battled, twisted, shoved herself sideways—and turned her fist, aimed the blade for his chest.

He dropped the pillow and rose up to undo his belt buckle. It made a snick-snick-slap sound as he undid it. And Ellie took advantage of the moment to strike at him.

Going for the place under his collarbone, she got both hands on the opener and drove upward. A single thrust, the only one she'd make before he retaliated, sank into him, squeaked as if it sawed through sinew, and the man howled.

He went mad. Another punch, this one to her belly, left her limp and gasping. She retched at the pains inside her. Agony clawed its way to her back. With both fists she pummeled him wherever she could make contact.

Wailing, coughing, he swished his belt free and whipped it through the air. She braced for the slash of leather, the tearing of her flesh. Sweat trickled across her face and body.

The belt hit some surface and he unsnapped his jeans.

She screamed and thrashed and he managed to get a pillow over her face again.

No, she would not die beneath this inflamed monster.

Say something. I want to know who you are.

Once more Ellie found enough air and scooted until her face was free. And she recognized his movements. He tried to work his pants down with one hand. Shrieking, tossing his head like a wounded animal, he reared back, and the can opener, buried in his chest, glinted.

A yowl, low, loud and furious, stilled him. The yowl punctuated hissing in a yell so eerie it amazed Ellie. *Zipper.* The cat had never made sounds like that.

With his body heaving and swaying over her, the at-

tacker rested his head on her neck and writhed. With
both hands, he batted behind him. The cat's claws must
be sunk into the man's back. He yelled, then screamed
and cursed. But Zipper didn't quit.

The weight left Ellie.

Instantly, crying as she went, she leaped from the bed,
taking the phone with her, and dialed Joe's number. He
picked up instantly and she cried, "Help me."

The intruder crashed about. She could make out his
body, his flailing arms, and still the cat used darkness to
cover her combat.

Ellie made it to the bathroom and locked herself in.
He'd get through the door soon enough, but she'd use
the phone until he stopped her. Joe had hung up at once.
Her teeth clattered together so hard her jaws hurt.

Quiet on the other side of the door stopped her. She
put her ear to the wood. Joe would already be on his way
and he'd have Spike on the phone himself.

Not a sound.

Shaking took over her limbs. She would not leave the
bathroom. Her bathrobe hung on a hook near the shower
and she pulled it on, tied it tightly about her.

A crash, and another, and another sent her stomach
into her throat, but it was Joe's voice she heard shouting,
"Ellie, I'm here. Hold on."

Thunderous footsteps on the stairs, sounds of running boots and Joe said, "Where are you? For God's sake,
Ellie—"

"In here," she cried out. Her fingers trembled so badly
she used both hands to unlock the door. "In the bathroom, Joe!" Now the tears streamed.

He stared at her for an instant then put his arms
around her. He sidestepped, walking her with him, and

turned on the lights. "Cher." Joe pressed his mouth shut, taking in her condition, and that of the room. "Who was it?"

"I don't know," she whispered. "He didn't make a sound until the end."

Joe's grimace bared his teeth. He hugged her so hard she couldn't draw a breath properly. "I'm going to find him and kill him," Joe said into her hair.

"Just hold me," she told him, and seized handfuls of his shirt. "Don't let me go."

"Spike's on his way."

Ellie said, "Don't leave me."

"Never," he said.

"Zipper stopped him."

He leaned back and brushed her hair from her eyes. "What did you say?"

She looked past him to where Zipper sat amid bloodied sheets, her eyes completely crossed and the occasional hiss still issuing. "She stopped him, Joe."

More boots hit the stairs and Spike bellowed, "Ellie? Joe?"

"In Ellie's bedroom," Joe yelled back, then muttered, "The cat?"

"Don't touch a thing," Spike shouted. "Nothing, got it?"

"Got it," Joe told him. "The cat," he said again, and felt Ellie's brow.

"No," Ellie said, shaking her head. Her teeth chattered together. "I'm not nuts. That man was going to rape me. Zipper attacked his bare rear and hung on. It had to be that. She took chunks out of his butt." Her own laughter came in uncontrolled bursts. "And...and I stabbed him with my can opener."

"Hush," Joe said. He took a bath sheet and wrapped it around her shoulders. "Try to hold on."

The bedroom door shut. "Keep still, you two," Spike said. "She's biting her nails."

Ellie wanted to sit on the floor. She couldn't stop laughing and shaking.

"Who?" Joe said.

"Ellie said the cat took chunks out of him. Good kitty. Kitty, kitty. We don't want her swallowing any DNA."

32

"I'm not dead yet," Ellie said. Bruises stained her already scratched face and her lower lip had swollen. "Why do I need a medical examiner?"

"You don't." Reb Girard smiled and put an arm across Ellie's back as if she could stop her spasms of trembling. "I just meant that folks forget I'm the medical examiner in Toussaint. And I get called in to help out after…after the kind of experience you've had."

"Do you want us in your consultin' room?" Joe asked, anxious to get out of the hallway. Reb's easy smiles were impressive. Nothing would amuse him in the near future, not until a single-minded pervert was where he couldn't keep on victimizing Ellie.

"Joe," Reb said, smiling as if he needed reassurance. "Marc's in the kitchen makin' coffee for the two of you. You'll be comfortable in the study. Keep it down, though. William and Gaston are asleep in my old bedroom."

"What is it with the women in this town and dogs?" Joe pretended to frown at her. "You just told me to get lost."

"I don't trust people who don't love dogs and Gaston's the best baby-sitter around." Reb looked at Ellie. "It'll be easier if Ellie and I work on our own." She looked at Ellie. "Don't you think so? If you really want Joe—"

"No," Ellie said quickly. Each time she spoke her jaw shook. "He'd be bored."

"No I wouldn't," he said before he could control his big mouth. "I mean—"

"We know what you mean, Joe," Reb told him. "Have you always had voyeuristic tendencies?"

"Darn it," he said, annoyed. "All I want to do is make sure Ellie's okay, Doc. I'll go in the sitting room."

Carrying a tray, Marc emerged from the back of the house where the kitchen was located. "You hungry?" he asked Joe. "Wake me up this early in the mornin' and I could eat a few fat nutrias—which I hate."

Joe grimaced. "If I was hungry, I'm surely not now."

Reb escorted Ellie away.

It was killing him to see her so bowed and he wanted just one thing, to get his hands on the creep who did this to her. He wanted something else, too—to be alone with her and start the rebuilding process between them. It scared him to think about how she might react to him as a man after being sexually attacked again.

The doorbell rang and Joe opened it. A female officer stood there, carrying a large, hard-sided bag and displaying her badge. "Officer Angelle. I'm here to see Dr. Reb Girard and an Ellie Byron."

"Take this, please," Marc said, giving Joe the tray. "Take it into the study. I'll be right there."

The study had changed since Joe saw it last, when he was a kid and the room belonged to Reb's doctor father. The old desk remained, but red suede had replaced studded leather on the couch, one chair and an oversize round ottoman. Dark blue quilted drapes covered the windows and two wing chairs were upholstered with the same fabric.

Joe put the tray on a painted Chinese chest used as a table in front of the couch. Fitted Persian carpet with a deep burgundy ground and a ceiling painted the same shade reminded him of Marc's involvement in architecture and design. For himself, Joe had long ago decided he was design-challenged, but he appreciated the room a lot.

"It's going to get busy around here," Marc said, closing the study door behind him. "That one records everything and takes photos."

"What kind of photos?" Joe asked, feeling irritable.

Marc shrugged. "I don't know about these things. Whiskey's available if you'd like a shot in your coffee."

"No—yes, please. Maybe I need whiskey with a shot of coffee."

"Here you go," Marc said, bending over to pour from a decanter, for Joe and for himself. He looked up at Joe. "It was bad, wasn't it?"

"Just about the worst." Joe averted his face. "But Ellie says he didn't actually rape her."

"Thank God."

"Saved by the cat."

"I heard about that," Marc said, and had the sense not to laugh. "Joe, I understand how you're feeling. You want to get your hands on him. I'd be the same."

"Spike said to leave her dressed like she was and put a coat over the top."

Marc nodded. "To protect any evidence," he said without emotion. "Makes sense."

Nothing made sense. She'd been through hell in her life and managed to come out of it. He still marveled at his luck that Ellie had put the prolonged sexual abuse behind her. Now he had to hope she wouldn't withdraw from him again, as she had in the beginning.

"Sit down," Marc said. "Beating yourself up won't help Ellie."

"I should have insisted on staying with her last night."

Marc sat on a the ottoman. "The way I heard it, she didn't want that."

"I think the damned pigeons gossip in this town." Joe drank coffee, grateful for the kick Marc had added. "What she thought she wanted shouldn't have put me off. She decided she had to be brave and stand on her own feet. She needs to be with me."

Marc drank his coffee but the corners of his mouth turned up.

"What's funny?" Joe asked.

"Sounds to me like you've made a big decision."

Joe understood him. "Maybe, but don't go mouthin' off because marriage takes two and I can't be sure where we stand. Some days I'm sure, other days I'm not."

"Sounds familiar. I remember courting Reb."

"Strong-minded women." Joe sighed. "You gotta love 'em."

"Yeah."

They sat quietly, drinking coffee. Marc poured refills from a carafe and added a larger measure of whiskey than the first time.

"Do you remember my sister, Amy?" Marc asked.

Joe hadn't really known her but he did remember her story. "Did you hear from her again?" She'd dropped out of sight several years back but kept in touch. Marc and

Reb kept trying to persuade her to return to Toussaint. Or that's what Joe understood.

"She calls most months. I still don't know where she is because she wants it that way, but she's starting to talk about visitin'. It's William, of course. She wants to meet her nephew."

"That's good news," Joe said.

"It will be if she ever comes," Marc said. "I thought of her because she's another hard-headed female. In her case it didn't always serve her so well. That's what brought Wazoo to Toussaint—Amy. They shared an apartment in New Orleans while Amy was going through some pretty awful stuff with a man who had used her since she was a teenager. Wazoo looked out for her in the way only Wazoo could. Reb and I have a special place in our hearts for that woman—even if she can make us all crazy."

A sharp, loud knock and they heard people come through the front door. Men talked over one another.

"Reb? Where are you?" Spike raised his voice.

Joe got up rapidly and went into the hall. "Keep it down," he said. "William's asleep upstairs. Reb and Ellie are in the consultin' room with a female officer. Come on in the study."

Cyrus, Madge and Guy Gautreaux were with Spike. "Now that Charles Penn's out of the picture, NOPD's off the case and the sheriff's on my neck for information. So is every other agency around. I need to see how things are goin'," Spike said.

"No you don't." Joe gritted his teeth. "I'll call through the door and let them know you're here."

Spike's face colored. "Sure. Why don't you do that?"

"I'll do it," Madge said, her expression too innocent.

Off she went and Joe led the others into the study. "We've been banished," he told them, taking a long look at Guy, who still didn't seem himself.

"Nothin' about tonight's events makes much sense," Spike said. "It's a forensics dream, though. The guy behaved like he wants to be caught."

Cyrus, who hovered, his expression badly troubled, said, "What does that mean? You'll catch him, then? The folks in this town have been through too much. The fear needs to be over."

"I can't go into all the details." Spike watched Cyrus. "You're jumpy. You're usually the cool one."

Cyrus went to the windows, pulled a drape aside and pretended to be looking at something in the blustery darkness outside. "We may be boarding up by some time tomorrow, after all," he said. "Looks like the hurricane's really comin' this time."

"So I heard," Guy said, meeting Joe's eyes. "We all heard it on the radio comin' over here."

Groans made the rounds.

"How long have they been in there?" Spike asked, angling his head in the direction of Reb's consulting room.

"Too goddamn long," Joe said. His control threatened to snap completely. "You know the state Ellie's in. Looks like Madge is helping out there."

"She's good at making people feel better," Cyrus remarked.

Marc said, "How did she know to come?"

"My fault," Guy said. He sounded grim. "Made a nuisance of myself yesterday. Drank too much. She and Cyrus ended up looking after me at the rectory."

Nobody commented.

"If you had to guess," Spike said to Joe, "what would

you say the perp wants? Is he only interested in scaring Ellie, and raping her, or does he intend to kill her?"

"I'd say keep your questions to yourself, moron." Joe breathed rapidly. Sweat popped out along his hairline. "You've got a wife you love. How would you like that question comin' your way?"

"Joe," Cyrus said. "Perhaps—"

"Perhaps nothin'. You'd be okay with someone askin' you if you thought Madge was supposed to die? Shit. You talk about Ellie like she's a thing, not a woman."

Spike's cell phone rang and he went into the hall to talk.

"*Shit,*" Joe said again and pushed his fingers through his hair. What was it with his mouth? "Sorry. Why is it taking so long? Do y'all think that jerk wanted Ellie dead? What kind of thing is that to think about?"

"No kind," Marc said. "I'll make fresh coffee."

"Deputy Lori checking in from Ellie's place," Spike said, strolling back into the study. "Says she never saw a crime scene like this one. We've got prints, hair, fibers, blood—two types. And the cat did have traces of tissue in her claws. And Einstein left his belt behind. Expensive, she said, and covered in prints."

Spike's phone blared again and this time he didn't bother to leave the room. "Devol," he said. "But… Yes, it was, thoroughly. I thought so." He listened, only adding an occasional word to the conversation. "Thank you. I want you to go home, right now."

He took the phone from his ear, looked at it and switched off. "Sheesh. She hung up. Wouldn't have happened when I was a kid on the force. Get this. The creep's been hangin' out in the attic of the empty house between Ellie's place and Joe's. There's a stash of canned food there. Water, and some stale baked stuff from Ben's Foods. Best of all, the guy left a receipt in a plastic bag. It's always the small mistakes that break a case. At least the folks at Ben's have got surveillance tapes we can look at. Something might show up. He made a hole through into Ellie's attic and sat there like a brown spider waitin' to strike."

"How the hell could that happen if your people searched up there?" Joe said.

Spike subsided with an expression that suggested he thought he'd been too free with the facts.

"C'mon," Joe said. "We're in this together."

"Anything I say won't be good enough for you. We did search but I'm thinking no one pulled down the attic steps."

"Spike?" Reb put her head around the door. "A word, please."

"What is it?" Joe beat Spike into the hall.

Reb glanced at Spike, who nodded.

"We're still bagging evidence and we'll probably get a few more shots. You'd better be thinking long and hard about who this might have been. He's an animal. We can all thank God he didn't finish what he started, and he got close. We've got semen."

Joe crossed his arms. His mouth was too dry for him to talk.

"Ellie will be fine. He beat her up. She mashed her lip pretty bad but it'll heal fast. She's got a couple of bad bruises on her face and scratches on her body—in addition to the ones that aren't quite healed from before. She said she bit his hand because it was over her mouth. In addition to Zipper's contribution, we've got more blood on Ellie. Blood that isn't hers, that is. There's pubic hair."

Guy had come to stand in the doorway to the study.

"Bastard," he said. "But if we can't find him with all we've got, we should try a different business. I just checked in with an old buddy who still talks to me. The clipping they found in that so-called hideout came from a San Francisco paper."

"Well, that's a big help," Joe said.

Spike turned on him. "You'd be surprised how much help it can be. It wasn't a local paper, or one for New Orleans. I wish we had the one Doll saw in Wade's drawer. He paid up before he left, by the way. Left the money with Wally and said he'd been called away unexpectedly. At least we can rule out Charles Penn."

"We can probably rule out Jim Wade, too," Guy said. "I don't know his deal with the photographs, but he's been traced to San Francisco. He's a P.I. And he's also left the country."

33

Time had about run out.

Paul looked at Cerise, sleeping facedown beside him, and then at his watch. He needed to get out of here, but he had not done what he came to do.

He sat up.

A line of pale light under the door came from the front windows of Cerise's upstairs stockroom. He heard gusts of wind rattle the sashes. Yesterday they'd talked about expecting a big one to hit, but if it already had there would be a lot more noise.

Cerise rolled to her back and pulled herself up beside him. Even in the dimness he could see that her eyes were wide open. She had not been sleeping after all. "You've got something on your mind," she said, running her fingers through the hair on his chest and down a still-healing mark she'd made on his arm. "I knew it when you got here."

"You didn't say anything," he pointed out.

She sighed hugely and shifted, worked herself higher

to prop her breasts on his naked torso. "I'm not stupid," she told him. "Why would I risk an argument *before* we had sex? Anyway, I thought what we did would put you in a good mood."

Paul slithered away from her. He put on the low-wattage lamp and searched out his clothes.

"Paul," Cerise said in a wheedling voice. "It's too early to get up."

"You don't have to. Go back to sleep." He dressed rapidly and went into the tiny bathroom, where he shut the door and turned on the light over the sink.

Cold water felt good even if it didn't improve his frame of mind. He cleaned his teeth, combed his hair, slapped on after-shave even though he didn't have time to shave. Next he retrieved the white plastic bag he'd stashed under the sink the night before and slipped his toiletries inside.

He opened the door to find Cerise waiting for him.

"What's going on?" she asked. "You're taking your things. Why?"

"Okay." He'd better manage this well. "Let's talk."

She didn't move and he couldn't get past her if she didn't, not without knocking her aside.

"Let's talk," she repeated. "So talk."

She had put on a white terry robe. Paul settled his hands on the rough material covering her shoulders and turned her away from him. He walked her forward. "Sit on the bed and be comfortable."

"I don't want to sit on the bed." Cerise shrugged him off and spun to face him again. "Do you think I don't know what the bag means? You don't want to come back."

"You're going to make this hard, but I knew you would."

"Make what hard, Paul? You haven't told me a thing yet."

He glanced at her breasts, mostly revealed in her gaping robe. She did have a body worth remembering. "I should have told you as soon as I got here but you made it impossible to concentrate. You were all over me and I'm only human."

"Yes, you are. That's what I like best about you." She looked up at him through her lashes.

"It's over between us." Playing this game had been dangerous and a mistake. All he wanted was Jilly and he intended to have her.

Cerise raised her chin slowly and brushed her blond hair back with one hand. She actually turned the corners of her mouth up.

"Well," Paul said, "evidently we've both come to the same conclusion. Thank God we're grown-ups."

Her hand, the palm open, landed so hard on the side of his face that his neck snapped to one side. The second blow came, to his ear, and this time he got her hard little knuckles.

"That's enough." He caught both of her wrists and she cried out. "Shut up. Now," he told her.

"You think you can treat me like a nobody. Just use me for fucking practice then walk away when there's something else you want. I've got news for you, Paul Nelson. If you insist on breaking off with me I'll make you wish you were dead."

He had asked her to meet him just outside of town to the south—on the overgrown track beside the bayou where a once-white wall marked the end of the Edwards property.

Jilly liked the early morning, the earlier the better,

even on a day like this one when a storm brewed. She couldn't have come later than five o'clock because pretty soon after that the work got crazy at All Tarted Up.

Paul had quite a trip to make from Rosebank, but he'd insisted they had to meet and sounded mysterious in a way that set Jilly's heart jumping. There had also been excitement in his voice.

A rain-laced wind buffeted her. Cypress trees bent and swayed over the slick green surface of the water, and a sky of a duller green packed down on the landscape. It looked like the major bad weather they'd been threatened with for days would come. By the time she got back it would be a good idea to haul out the shutters.

She studied the wall, mostly grayish from damp and pocked with places where bits of stucco had fallen away. Algae grew in the wavery cracks. The long-empty mansion was in the middle of the property. She'd never been inside.

Her tummy flipped. It had flipped a lot of times since Paul's call last night. Why pretend? She hoped, even expected him to ask her to marry him and she wanted to, more than she'd ever wanted anything. She loved him so. Her bloodlines seemed to please rather than concern him, which was a good thing since they pleased her, too. He told her how beautiful she was and that she wouldn't be who she was, or look the way she did, if her father hadn't had one piece of good judgment and married her mama.

She paced in the lee of the wall. He warned her he could be a little late.

His rooms at Rosebank were like Aladdin's cave to Jilly. The first thing a person saw on going in was a big Chinese desk Vivian and her mother had found for him among the wealth of beautiful old antiques available in the house. The motley bookshelves placed around the walls sagged under the weight of books Paul stacked there. He had written a whole shelf of guidebooks himself, and his laptop and printer always stood ready amid a littering of papers and reference books.

Paul's artistry, and it was artistry—just the way he explained what he did—bemused Jilly. She couldn't imagine writing a book about anything. Paul, sweet man that he was, said she was a kitchen artist and she had a personal flair that showed her own artistry.

She heard him a moment before she saw him, wheeling his scooter along the path. He looked ahead at her and waved. "Hey, you," he called out.

"Hey," she shouted back.

"I love you," he cried.

Tears welled in Jilly's eyes. She folded her arms tightly across her middle, afraid to respond until she could speak without breaking down.

"Ever been in there?" he said, nodding toward the estate.

Jilly shook her head. She hardly trusted her voice.

"We should take a look sometime. I hear it could be beautiful."

"Sure."

Paul's blond hair, thick and cut short, ruffled in the wind. He wore a green windbreaker that flattened to his strong, fit body, and muscular legs flexed inside his jeans when he leaned over and pushed the scooter. Jilly and Paul had taken the better part of two years to know each other well, but they had built a closeness that was worth every moment.

"Whew, this wind doesn't make things easier," he said, kicking out the stand for the scooter and leaning it close to the wall. Paul turned to her at once and caught her face between his hands. "Do you have any idea just how much I love you?"

Jilly pressed her trembling lips together and shook her head, because she wanted to hear him tell her.

He looked at her carefully. "Yellow is great on you, even if you should have a sweater or something on." The way he looked at her sleeveless dress showed his appreciation—and turned her legs to jelly.

With her arms wrapped around his body, Jilly nestled into his neck and kissed him there. Paul seized her chin and lifted it. His lips crushed hers, parted hers, and she held on to him. He stroked her back, squeezed her bottom and pressed his solid arousal against her pelvis. Heat flushed through Jilly and she wanted to be elsewhere with him, alone.

"We've waited long enough," Paul said. "I want us to be together."

She buried her face in his windbreaker. They said there was someone for everyone and at last her man had come along.

Tree limbs whined and cracked and Paul held the two of them steady.

"I can't stay long," Jilly said. "I need to get the storm shutters up, just in case."

"No, you don't," he told her. "I'll do it."

The feeling she had was like none other. She knew what he wanted to say and she was ready.

"Jilly?" Inclining his head, Paul looked at her closely, seriously. "The only way a relationship works is if there's honesty. I want you to expect honesty from me and I already know I have yours."

"You do."

"I haven't always been so smart, sweetheart, but I want to start fresh—from this day on. I've thought about this carefully and we could carry on without a word from me about something I'm not proud of, but we'll be even closer if I'm completely open."

Her stomach contracted and prickling climbed her spine. "You couldn't do anything bad," she said. "You don't have it in you."

"I have done something bad." His big hands settled on her shoulders. "I've been an irresponsible fool and for all the wrong reasons. I've been afraid, Jilly. You're a gentle woman and I decided you could be shocked if I let myself go with you."

Jilly looked into his clear eyes. She didn't know what he meant.

"You drive me wild," he muttered. "The way you turn me on makes me want to…I want to do things with you that you might find too much. That scares me so I've held back. And if you tell me it's what you want, I'll always hold back. As long as you're mine, I'll learn to be what you want me to be."

"I'm not a delicate flower," she told him. "I don't even know what you could do that I wouldn't like."

Holding her hands, he straightened and looked at her hard. Paul studied every inch of her until goose bumps rose on her skin.

"We're good together," he said quietly. "We'll learn how to please each other even more. God, I want to take you away now."

Jilly smiled up at him. "I can't believe this is happening. I've been afraid to want it too badly."

"You know I'm asking you to marry me?"

She knew, and if she were any happier she'd pop. "I want to," she told him.

Gusts on the surface of the bayou broke the opaque water into choppy eddies. The sky should be brightening by now, but a muggy pall slid over everything, holding back the light.

"I said I've been a fool," Paul said. He put an arm around her shoulders and held her close. "Let me get this off my chest so we can deal with it and move on."

He sounded more serious than when he'd first arrived. She could deal with anything he was likely to tell her, Jilly thought.

She stroked his jaw. "Out with it. Tell me your wicked secret."

"This isn't funny," he said, and his tone turned her cold. "I've been seeing Cerise."

Jilly gripped his sleeve. "Seeing Cerise?"

"It wasn't my idea. She chased me."

She might be naive on occasion, but that was a line she'd heard before. "So you've been seeing both of us? At the same time?"

He cleared his throat. "Don't say it like that. She never meant anything to me but… She threw herself at me. I was weak."

"You slept with her," Jilly said quietly. "That's what you mean."

"Yes. I wish I could take it back but I can't."

A deep sickness turned inside Jilly. She wanted to get away.

"Please believe me, sweets. It's all over and I didn't have to tell you but I had to. I owe you that. Jilly, I love you so much."

She looked at him sharply. He sounded close to tears. "How long have you been sleeping with her?"

His face twisted. "A while."

"How long?"

"Several months. There, now you know."

"When was the last time?"

"No," he said, almost moaning. "Leave it alone. Let us put it behind us. I don't care about her. I'm guilty, guilty of using her. But she used me, too, and there never could be anything more between us."

The weather grew wilder. Through blurred eyes, Jilly glanced at the gathering movement everywhere. "The last time?" she said.

Paul tried to hug her, but Jilly stood straight and as tall as she could. Her heart thundered.

"Last night," he said through his teeth. "I went to do the right thing. To break it off like a gentleman, but it wasn't that simple. She cried. She lashed out at me. I owed it to her to calm her down."

"By making love to her," she said flatly.

"This doesn't have to be a drama. Stuff like this happens every day."

"Not to me. You came to me from her, didn't you? You spent the night there."

He averted his face. "Yes. Do you think I feel good about that?"

"I've got to get back to the bakery."

"You can't leave me like this." He grasped her hands. "Jilly, I messed up. A lot of people mess up. I made it worse by taking too long to deal with the problem."

"She threatened you, didn't she? She said she'd tell me your dirty secret so you decided you'd rush to me and get your version in first. Not a bad idea, I guess."

"It isn't," he said, his expression clearing. "But it's never a bad idea to come clean. I promise you that as long as I live I'll never be unfaithful to you again. Jilly, will you marry me?"

Aghast, she closed her eyes.

"Open your eyes." He sounded panicky. "Don't treat me like a monster. I'm human, that's all, but now I've come to my senses and I know you're all I could ever want. Jilly, please."

"You and Cerise must have talked about me. She knew you were seeing me while she was sleeping with you."

"She knew, yes, but we didn't talk about you."

Her energy seeped away. "It doesn't matter."

"Of course it doesn't." He released one of her hands to lift his jacket and reach into a pocket in his pants. In his hand he held a blue velvet box. "I showed this to Cyrus. I had to show someone and it couldn't be you until the time was right. He thinks it's lovely."

He showed her a solitaire diamond that glittered white. Looking into her eyes, he took the ring and slid it onto her unresisting finger. "It's happening, Jilly," he said, his voice unsteady. "I've dreamed of this. I'll be so good to you. So good for you. I know how much you love it here and I like it, too. We'll buy a place we both like. I can work as well here as anywhere."

"You said you were at Rosebank," she said slowly.

"Last night? I was when I called you. Honestly. I left to deal with the other and it took longer than I expected."

She was afraid she'd throw up. "Do you even know there was another attack on Ellie last night?"

His frown pulled his brows together. "No. Tell me."

"A man tried to rape her." She told him as much of the story as she could. "You'd have known all that if you hadn't been with your lady friend. Maybe you'd even have been able to help."

"*Goddammit.*" His eyes screwed up and he clenched his teeth. "I want to get my hands on the bastard. He's a meddler, a menace. Hell, I made a big mistake and I'm sorry. But nobody else knows, and Cerise wouldn't have the guts to let everyone know what kind of woman she is."

"Too bad your finer feelings come and go," Jilly said. "If you could have kept your zipper closed, you'd have known what happened to Ellie at the time."

He hung his head. "My God. I didn't speak to anyone after you so I didn't know a thing."

"You spoke to Cerise."

"I've admitted that several times. Goddammit." He released her and paced. "What's the matter with the law? Between the cops and the sheriff's office and everyone else they've got swarming around this town they should have had the guy several times over by now. No woman is safe here. It's only a matter of time before he turns his sights elsewhere. I'm going to see the sheriff and have it out with him. I'll let him know I'll blow this thing wide open in the press if things don't get better—now."

Jilly couldn't look at him.

"Did they get anything on him this time?" Paul asked. "Did Ellie see his face? Where was that brother of yours?"

"My brother's name is Joe. He was at his own place last night. I don't know why because it's none of my business. You don't seem to care, but Ellie's doing okay. Really shaken up, but getting it together."

"Yes, yes. Thank goodness for that." He stopped in front of her and smiled. She could see that smile anytime she wanted to. All she had to do was think about his face. "Until this guy is caught, I don't want you out of my sight. Maybe I never want you out of my sight. Let's set a date."

All my dreams come true. No, not this time, probably

never. "I can't accept this." She took off the ring and held it out to him. "You can't expect me to deal with everything you've told me and start planning a marriage at the same time."

"I don't want that. I bought it for you and I've got the wedding bands. You'll love them."

"Will you listen to me? I'm not going to say never, but if we can be together at all it's going to take time. First I have to come to terms with what you've told me and think my way through it. Then I'll be ready to decide."

Still he ignored the ring and he grinned, his old, cocky grin. "Let's be blunt. I can't live without you and you can't live without me. I've been an ass and I'm paying for it, but you aren't the kind of woman who makes a man suffer on and on. Be honest with yourself. You want me and you're excited about getting married. We'll have a great life and I'm going to give you everything you've ever dreamed of. Let me put the ring back on you."

She saw her opportunity to return the diamond and dropped it into his open palm. Immediately she turned away and started walking.

"Damn it." He reached her before she'd covered a couple of yards and pulled her to face him. "You're behaving like this because you think you're supposed to. Well, you're not. You're mine and you want it that way. I want us to go back and tell the world we're engaged to be married."

Jilly yanked her arm away and took off again. "Don't come after me, Paul," she told him. "Leave me alone to think. I can't believe you were so sure of me. You don't know me at all."

34

Doll Hibbs and Wally sat at a corner table in All Tarted Up. "Jilly's late, ain't she?" Doll said to Missy Durand behind the counter. "Where is everyone, anyway?"

Wally had reached a stage when his mother's bluntness mortified him. He colored and looked beseechingly at Joe and Ellie, who stood close together and glanced frequently at the door. Joe had already put up the storm shutters and all the lights were on in the shop, giving it a warm yellow glow. Sandbags stood in heaps on the town's sidewalks, ready to be put in position.

Joe said, "There's a lot to be done this mornin'. Shorin' things up. We're lucky we invested in the shutters. For most people it's plywood." He felt edgy and very aware of how exhausted Ellie must be. She hadn't slept last night, and she couldn't go back to her place as long as the cops were still there.

"We're boarded up," Doll announced. "Least we don't have to go lookin' for supplies. Gator keeps everythin' ready. I was goin' to talk to Spike if he came in, but since you're here, Joe, I might as well tell you what's on my mind."

"That'd be fine. You want to sit down, Ellie?" He studied her closely. "You need some rest."

Ellie kept her face turned from him. "I know. But I don't know where or how to do that."

"Vivian and Spike want you out with them." He spoke low so Doll wouldn't hear.

"I can't take advantage of them. Anyway—" She looked sideways at him. "Nothing."

"Anyway, what?" He pressed her.

"I'm too embarrassed to say."

"Ellie."

"I only feel safe when you're around."

With that she made him feel ten feet tall and ready to take on the world. It was the first little hint that things were far from over between them. "I'll go out there with you."

"We said we'd be here if we're needed so we can't go anywhere."

"Yet," he said, and led her to Doll and Wally's table.

"Oh, my Lord, I didn't notice," Doll said as they sat down. "What happened to you, Ellie Byron? Someone hit you, didn't they? I know the bruises of a man's hand when I see them. And your poor mouth. Oh, Lordy, Lordy, a madman has been at you." She glared at Joe.

"Not guilty," he said, more amused than angry. "Ellie was attacked in her bed last night and beaten up. But we'll find the guy."

Doll gave a thin shriek and slapped her hands to her cheeks. She leaned across the table and whispered to Ellie, "Poor darlin'. Did he…you know?"

Ellie said, "He tried and failed," and Joe admired her

cool head. He also thought it unwise to confide in Doll, who would love spreading the bad news.

Missy came to the table carrying a tray. Plates of pastries and mugs were set out—and cream and sugar. She returned with a carafe of coffee and four glasses of orange juice. "You all look as if you need this," she said before going back to the counter to continue filling oil lamps. They had invested in a good generator, but sometimes it was the old-fashioned and familiar that saved the day.

"You need to see Reb," Doll said to Ellie.

"I have. I'm as fit as a fiddle and I'll heal up in no time."

"Wazoo thinks we should have a ceremony to drive bad spirits out of the town," Doll said.

Wally glanced at Ellie. "Father Cyrus says there aren't any bad spirits in Toussaint, we've just had a lot of bad luck."

"I don't normally hold with any of that voodoo nonsense, but what could it hurt," Doll said.

"*Who* could it hurt, you mean," Ellie said. "Cyrus for one. He'd be so disappointed in all of us."

"Joe…" Doll put a hand on top of his. "I've been worryin' myself silly. I heard how Jim Wade left the country, but that doesn't mean he wasn't up to no good here."

"How do you mean?"

"He took photos of Ellie, and he hung around Hungry Eyes all the time. Spyin', if you ask me. Could be that if Wade wasn't the man after her, he was givin' information to the one who is? Seems to me someone should keep followin' up on him. I wish I hadn't been too scared to take the photos and the clippin'."

"Don't you feel bad about a thing," Ellie said. "I understand why you didn't. Joe, I think Doll's right about Jim Wade."

"They are followin' up on him," Joe said.

She frowned at him. "You didn't tell me."

He couldn't argue so he said, "No."

Rather than get mad, Ellie punched him lightly and gave a wry grin. "You've got a long way to go before you get the idea of full disclosure," she said.

Best of all, she leaned against him.

The door opened and Jilly hurried inside. Her eyes were wide and glittery in an ashen face and she walked past everyone without a word.

Doll muttered, "*Well.*"

Joe put an arm around Ellie and said, "Somethin's real wrong."

"If someone hurt Jilly, he'll wish he hadn't." Wally slapped a pastry down on his plate and pushed up the long sleeves on his striped T-shirt. "I'm gonna ask her about it."

"No!" Doll, Joe and Ellie spoke in unison, and Doll closed a hand on her son's wrist.

Very pregnant Deputy Lori came in next with Marc Girard, and Paul stepped in behind them. Wally leaped up and pushed two tables together.

Marc and Lori joined them. Paul behaved as if they weren't there at all and sat as far away as possible.

"Where's Reb?" Doll said. "Is everythin' battened down on Conch Street?"

"On Conch Street and at Clouds End," Marc told her. "Now, if I can just get my wife to stop seeing any patients who aren't emergencies, I could get her back to Clouds End where she belongs."

Conversation fizzled. Marc glanced toward Paul, who sat with his arms on the table and his head hung forward.

The atmosphere turned heavier than it already was,

and not only because the customers at All Tarted Up were strung out and waiting for something major to happen. Humidity fogged the windows behind the shutters and rivulets ran in jerky lines down the glass.

Wally said, "Sh," and cocked his head. "Thunder. It's a long way off."

Joe sighed. "Could be a good sign." He wanted to go to his sister but knew better than to interfere if she didn't let him know she needed him. "Maybe we're in for something less than a big one, after all."

Deputy Lori eased herself down onto a chair. "How you doin', Ellie?" she said. "Vivian called Spike to find out when you were goin' over."

"I'm not going anywhere till I pick Daisy up from Loreauville. Then I'm going home."

"No need," Lori said. "Wazoo's taken her old beater to pick up the dog. She's taking her to Rosebank. Anyway, they're still goin' over your place. Likely they'll be there for hours."

"It's a crime," Doll said.

Joe looked at the ceiling. "You always were a woman of insight, Doll."

Lori said, "Accordin' to Vivian, the storm shutters are up at Rosebank. That place is built like a fort and they're ready for anythin'. Too bad more places around here aren't as solid. The hotel guests out there are leavin' as fast as they can. Mark my words, if there's enough damage to be worth gapin' at, they'll all be back in a few days."

Ellie sighed. "It's good of Wazoo to think about Daisy, but I do want my life back some time soon."

"I think she did it mostly for the dog," Lori said, and grinned. "She's already collected Zipper and they're saying there's a lovefest goin' on between the cat and Vivian's Chihuahua."

Joe had bigger things on his mind than pets—including his sister, who had remained in the kitchen, and Paul Nelson, who occasionally raised his head to watch for her.

Even more immediate, they had an unknown would-be rapist and possibly murderer on the loose, and the law was at square one again.

"Parishioners at St. Cécile got that place bagged up like it was the mint," Doll said. "Gator's gone down there and so has just about every willin' soul who isn't workin' on they own place."

"It's too close to the bayou," Ellie said. "It gets water damage every time."

"Can't hardly move it," Spike said. "Even if they wanted to, where would the money come from?"

"Cyrus would never let the church be moved," Wally said, with a bright spot of color on each cheek. "It's on hallowed ground and it belongs there. Cyrus says it's hallowed ground and that means it's God's. You don't go movin' what belongs to God."

Joe studied the boy and thought how far he'd come from the shy little kid Cyrus had first befriended.

"Cyrus this, Cyrus that," Paul said suddenly and loudly. "Cyrus knows everything. He's got all of you people wrapped around his holy finger, that's for sure. He's got you all talking like you swallowed Bibles, even a kid."

The only sound to follow was the steady beat of rain on the shutters.

"Jilly," Paul shouted. His voice broke and the silence in the shop deepened. "Jilly, I need you. I can't live without you." He rested his forehead on his folded arms on top of the table.

Joe's gut clenched. He pushed up from his chair and went directly into the kitchen, where he found Jilly facing a range with her hands over her ears.

"Jilly? What's happened?"

She shook her head.

"Has he hurt you?"

Silently, she turned toward him and he saw tears coursing down her face. Her throat jerked over and over and he didn't think she could manage to talk if she wanted to.

"Come here." He held out his arms but she didn't move. Joe didn't waste any time before making his own move and holding her against him. "Say the word and I'll make sure he's out of town today. He won't want to stay."

"I was a fool," she said, choking on the words. "He was weak and wrong but I should have figured things out. Please, Joe, stay out of it. This is my problem and I've got to deal with it."

"Should I ask him to leave the shop, though? He's cuttin' up and carryin' on about Cyrus like he's got a grudge against him."

"He spoke to Cyrus—went to reconciliation, maybe— but I don't know why Paul would be angry about that. Don't get in the middle. You'll only make things worse."

"Are you going to talk to him?"

"If he doesn't decide to leave on his own, I'll have to. Go back to Ellie. I saw her face, Joe. There's someone out there with a reason to hate her. He's got to be caught."

Joe stared at his sister. *A reason to hate Ellie?* "Couldn't he be a man with an obsession about her? It happens."

"Do those types usually keep hurting the woman they want for themselves? Darn, what do I know? I'm scared for Ellie is all."

"So am I," Joe said with fervor. "And I'm scared for me."

Jilly looked at him sharply. "You really love her, don't you?"

Why pretend? "I really do. This is a first for me, Jilly, and it has to be the only. I believe we were meant to be together."

She angled her head and gave him a watery smile. "I think so, too. When the right one comes along, hold on to her tight."

From the café, Paul bellowed, "Jilly, don't hide from me." He sounded as if he was in the kitchen with them.

"You've got all this on your hands," Joe said, "but you're still thinking about me. I've always been here for you and I always will. You need space. I'll suggest Paul should take off. Don't worry, I'll keep my cool."

Jilly looked at her hands, then at Joe. "I'll deal with it. This isn't fair to my customers. Go back to Ellie."

Joe followed her from the kitchen. He smiled at Ellie but remained standing when Jilly approached Paul. She said his name quietly and he shot to his feet.

"Jilly," he said, "I said I'm sorry. Nothing like that will ever happen again. I promise you I'm a changed man—because of you. Give me another chance and we'll never look back."

Spike caught Marc's eyes. The other man was embarrassed for Paul Nelson, but he could also be thinking the man should be moved along.

Joe shook his head slightly.

"Let's step outside," Jilly said to Paul.

"It's raining too hard," Paul said. "And you should be with people you trust—with your brother—when you're making up your mind about something important."

"We're upsetting people," Jilly said, and looked at the floor. She showed signs of crying again.

"I want you," Paul said. "I've always wanted you and you said you'd marry me. What I did was wrong. It was so wrong, but it's all over now. And I could have kept it to myself but I wanted to start out with a clean slate."

Ellie got up. She went to Jilly and rubbed her back.

"This is yours," Paul said. He took out a ring box and pushed it across the table toward Jilly. "I was cheated out of what's mine by a woman—that made me promise myself I'd never trust another one—but I'd trust you with my life, Jilly. You're it, the only one I'll ever want."

Lori, her face sad, shook her head slowly.

Doll said, "Ain't nothin' so bad a woman can't get past it for a man who loves her like that."

"You're shamin' yourself—and me," Jilly said.

"Did you hear what Doll said?" Paul asked. He reached for Jilly's hand but she laced her fingers together. "If a man loves you the way I do there's nothing you can't get past."

Cerise opened the door and poked her head inside. She looked around the café, taking note of everyone there. She slipped inside and into the closest chair.

"Coffee, Cerise?" Missy asked.

"Why not?"

Jilly turned toward Cerise, bowed her head and started for the kitchen.

"Don't go." Paul hurried to cut her off. "I'll throw this one on the good people of Toussaint. I've been a fool. I slept with another woman while I was courting Jilly. Today I asked Jilly to marry me and I came clean about my mistake."

Cerise laughed. She rocked back and forth on her

chair. "Didn't work quite the way you had it figured, huh? Jilly didn't fall for your confession? Did you tell her the last time you got out of my bed was this mornin'?"

"Shit," Joe said under his breath. He itched to take Paul Nelson by the throat and drag him outside. Jilly said he'd spoken to Cyrus. No wonder Cyrus had fumed at Joe and called him careless, careless for not watching out for his sister better.

"I'm sorry," Paul said, shaking his head over and over. "I wasn't fair to you, Cerise, but you knew I didn't love you. You said you were okay with that."

"*Stop it.*" Jilly cried. "Enough."

Cerise's smile disappeared and she turned her face away.

Deputy Lori responded to a signal and switched on her lapel mike. "Yeah?"

"Where are you?"

"All Tarted Up."

"Are Ellie and Joe still there?"

"Affirmative."

"Have Joe drive Ellie over here." Spike's voice crackled over the receiver. "And you're going home. Reb just called and said she found out you're still on duty. Whooee, my ears got trimmed. Two officers are coming your way, one to drive you home and one to bring back your car."

"I'm not ready to—"

"I just gave you an order. And I want Joe and Ellie here *now.* We've got the surveillance tapes from Ben's Foods."

35

"Can I get you anything?" Guy asked. He and Spike waited in the interrogation room Ellie detested.

Joe spoke for both of them. "No, thanks." He closed the door and nodded to a young blond officer who stood at ease and ready to show the films. His badge identified him as Turner.

"We all know my current professional status," Guy said.

"For our purposes Guy's an expert with special insight," Spike said promptly.

In other words, Spike liked having Guy around and valued his opinion.

The weakness she'd felt before struck Ellie's legs again. She made herself take deep breaths but couldn't stop the queasiness in her stomach.

"For what they are, they're clear," Spike said. "Come and sit down. Watch carefully and just tell us to stop if you see someone familiar."

She turned blindly into Joe and whispered, "I don't

want to do this." She flattened her hands against his chest, warm through a rain-damp shirt.

"You're not likely to see anyone you know," Joe said. "Other than a clerk or a neighbor." He didn't attempt to smile, but he looked at her with his heart in his eyes. Joe was a caring and a worried man.

Ellie watched his mouth, the way his lips parted a little. "What if I do recognize someone else?" she said.

"Relax." He curled his hands loosely around her shoulders. "If you do, dealing with it won't be your problem."

"We'll take it from there," Guy said. Ellie turned to him and he smiled. He reached out a hand and she took it. "Sit here. You, too, Joe."

"It'll be sharper with the lights out," Officer Turner said. He flipped switches and the room was bathed in shades of gray cast through high windows. The leaden sky squeezed out the day and hurled its burden of rain at the low building with a staccato noise like machine-gun fire pocking a wet street.

A large monitor snapped to life and Spike said, "It really isn't great. Don't feel bad if none of it means a thing to you."

Joe found her wrist and rubbed Ellie's forearm lightly.

The familiar single checkout stand at Ben's Foods wavered a little, but she instantly recognized the checker. Connie sometimes stopped in for coffee at Hungry Eyes. The woman scanned groceries rapidly, sliding them down the counter to a bag boy without glancing in his direction.

The film bore the same date as the one stamped on the grocery receipt.

The picture jumped, faded, then refocused. More customers checked out, many of them well known to Ellie, others with familiar faces and some she'd never seen before. She felt Joe watching her and turned to him.

"Stop the tape," Spike said.

"Sorry." Ellie faced the monitor again and waited for Turner to back up the tape and start it running again.

Connie spent a lull cleaning up around her cash register. She took out a compact and reapplied lipstick, checked her nails, smiled at two girls who giggled while they bought candy.

Ellie sighed. She'd give anything to be in a safe place with Daisy and Zipper—and Joe—and shut the rest of the world outside.

Gator came through the line with a cart filled with toilet rolls. He stroked the hair of a baby in a cart behind him.

"Gator's okay," Spike said.

"Stop it there," Ellie said. "Stop the tape."

"What did you say?" Guy asked.

"I told you," she said. Her blood quit flowing, she knew it. Her body turned cold and still. Even her breath waited.

"Rewind about a minute and stop the tape," Joe said. He scooted his chair until it touched hers and put an arm around her shoulders. "Hang in there. You thought you saw someone you know? Someone who shouldn't be here?"

Voices chattered in her head, rose and fell—and she saw faces.

Turner ran the film again and Ellie said, "Stop."

Guy had come to kneel on the other side of her chair and he snapped out, "Stop it there."

"Now run it," Ellie said.

A well-built man put a basket on the counter. He had

short, light-colored hair and wore a dark, collarless shirt tucked into jeans. He seemed unsure of himself and watched the person ahead of him unload her cart and place a divider across the belt when she had finished. Uncertainly, he kept glancing at the woman while her purchases were bagged and replaced in the cart.

The woman left and the man's face was obscured while he placed his groceries on the belt and carefully used a divider. Then he looked up and Ellie looked into his light eyes. "Stop it there!" She laughed and cried, her salt tears running into her mouth. The sultry atmosphere had already moistened her hair, but it turned cold and clung to her head. She wrenched away from Joe and stood up to walk around and stand behind her chair.

"You know that man?" Spike asked.

The stillness left her and she shook so hard she held the back of her chair for support.

"Leave her," Joe said. "Give her time."

Ellie couldn't look away from the image on the screen. "That's Jason Clark. He's dead."

36

It can't get much closer than that," Charlotte Patin said. Crackling bursts of lightning met the ground neck and neck with a rumbling explosion of thunder.

The earth seemed to rock.

Vivian Devol slapped her hands over her ears and laughed.

"Vivian's like her mother," Homer Devol said, his startlingly blue eyes smiling despite the straight line of his mouth. "I reckon there's nothin' they like better than a good storm. Wild blood in those two, and they've got Wendy just as tickled when the weather gets wicked."

They gathered in the sumptuously eclectic receiving room at Rosebank. Ellie and Joe had decided they should accept the invitation to wait out the storm with the Devols and Charlotte.

Vivian had once explained to Ellie how she and Charlotte had returned the decaying house to its original opulence. They'd inherited the H-shaped mansion from Vivian's father. Originally Vivian's uncle left Rosebank to his brother, who hadn't lived long enough to enjoy it.

Vivian, her mother, Charlotte, and Spike's daughter, Wendy, sat on a couch freshly upholstered in rich gold tapestry. Homer had taken a matching chair. Both pieces had shiny brass elephant feet.

Through high double doors Joe could see the grand entry hall where new chartreuse silk had replaced the shredded version of Vivian's uncle's time. In the receiving room, fringed red velvet drapes topped by swags of palm-tree-print satin were, he understood, also exact replicas of the former window coverings. Supported on legs with bronze pineapples above its wheels, a grand piano dominated the center of the floor.

Ellie continued to feel a fine tremor inside. Jason hadn't died in that basement, but Mrs. Clark had gone along with Ellie's fear that he had. The woman must have been looking for a way to get her out of the house. Jason had been in the woods at Pappy's, telling her he needed her help—and outside Hungry Eyes with his signs. He had injured Daisy.

"You're very tired, Ellie, and you, too, Joe," Vivian said. "Bedrooms are ready for you. The weather won't break before morning. Say the word and I'll show you up for a rest."

Joe didn't think it a good idea to look at Ellie. He doubted he could keep her from seeing the badly timed thoughts he had at the mention of their going upstairs.

"Thanks," Ellie said. "Shouldn't Wazoo be back with Daisy and Zipper by now?"

Charlotte, pretty and petite with close-cropped gray hair, crossed her arms and puffed loudly. "You'd think so, wouldn't you? She gets an idea in her head then she won't listen to reason. Insisted she had to drive straight on into New Orleans for some reason."

"Headstrong," Homer said. "But she's got a good

heart. And it isn't like she's needed to work here when every last guest has scooted for some place where the wind don't blow."

"She shouldn't have taken my pets," Ellie said, listening to the moaning wind that whipped in giant gusts. "I don't want her hurt, either. It's dangerous to be out there."

Joe had turned a battery-run radio on low. He held it to his ear. "Mixed opinions, as usual," he said. He'd been interested in meteorology until he realized that unless he wanted radio or TV work, his options would be narrow. "Right now it's coming right at us, but they think it could make a turn. Either way, we're going to have a big cleanup on our hands."

"Does anyone know where Paul is?" Ellie said, suddenly remembering him. He'd treated Jilly despicably but Ellie could feel a little pity for him. The smartest people could be the biggest fools.

"He's in his rooms," Charlotte said. "Working." From her expression it was clear she knew nothing of what had happened between Paul and Jilly earlier. Ellie felt relieved to know Paul was safe even if she knew he was miserable and thought he deserved to be.

Vivian's cell phone rang and she answered hurriedly. "Hi, cher," she said, then spent a long time listening.

"Tell Daddy to come home," Wendy said, and Vivian patted the little girl's leg.

"I'll tell them," Vivian said. "Wazoo's on the road, even though I told her to come straight back from Ellie's. Yes. She's gone into New Orleans but she wouldn't tell me why."

Vivian winced. "I leave it to you to tell her that. Come home safe…and soon." She hung up.

"What are you going to tell us?" Ellie asked at once.

Beaming, Vivian jumped up, hauling Wendy with her. *"Yes,"* she cried. "The police dropped in on that Mrs. Clark. She said she hadn't seen or heard from her son in several years."

Joe flexed his hands and watched Ellie. The color of her eyes deepened.

"But she lied!" Vivian's delight glowed in her face. "They found Jason Clark hiding in the basement and he's in custody."

Homer cleared his throat and said, very seriously, "Congratulations, Miz Ellie." He gave Joe a sidelong glance. "And you won't want my opinion, young Gable, but if I was you I wouldn't let moss stick my parts together before I did what I had in mind."

Joe thought better than to laugh, which was just as well since Charlotte Patin got up and took Homer by the arm. Muttering words meant only for him, she hustled him out of the room.

"Don't mind Homer," Vivian said. "He's one of the kindest men I've ever known."

Joe smiled and was grateful when Ellie did, too. "Is Jason Clark talking at all?" Joe asked.

"Spike didn't say. But he had more good news. Lucien's turned the corner. He remembers the attack—he says two different men jumped him—and he says he could identify one of them," Vivian said.

"It's good he remembers things, isn't it?" Ellie said, sounding out of breath. "That means his brain is okay. But…two men hit him in my yard? Were they together? Did they know each other?"

Vivian said, "Spike didn't say any of that." She paused and cleared her throat. "When Spike checks in again I'll ask him. Joe, how's Jilly doing?"

"She's trying to be brave," he said. "She's pretty broken up, though."

Ellie didn't like it that Jilly had refused to come to Rosebank with them. She thought Joe should be with his sister but, at the same time, dreaded being without him. Silly when she couldn't expect to have him at her side all the time.

"Cyrus is stopping in at the shop," Joe said. "Jilly can't come here. You can imagine why, but Cyrus thinks he can get her to accept Reb and Marc's invitation to Clouds End. The café will be fine and there's nothing Jilly could do if something happened, anyway."

Vivian's phone rang again. This time she reported it was Wazoo and went back to listening. "No, I bet you don't want to call Spike and it's not because you're afraid of interrupting him. I'll pass your message to him, but you should stay in New Orleans until this storm decides what it's doing and does it." She frowned. "Well, I wish you hadn't left already. Check in regularly. We care about you. Goodbye."

Joe tried not to look too curious, but he would like to know what message Wazoo had for Spike. He felt Ellie studying him and caught her smiling.

"Wendy, honey," Vivian said to the quiet little girl. "You'll find Grandma Charlotte in the round sitting room. She's pretty mad at your grandpa."

"She gets that way when he says funny things," Wendy said very seriously. "I think it's because she doesn't know about jokes."

The three adults grinned and Vivian said, "Go on over there and sweeten her up. You'll be helping Grandpa." She waited until the child ran from the room and leaned forward on the couch. "Okay, this can't mean a thing, but Wazoo went to see someone called Fester at a shop. About a bottle, she told me. She said a lot of things really fast so it was mixed up. I think Spike and Guy told her she wasn't to go near Fester, whoever he is."

"I know about the bottle," Joe told her. "So does Spike."

"I'm not surprised." Vivian squeezed the bridge of her nose.

The grumble of thunder sounded again and for moments the wind died down. White lightning crackled, finding its way through the shutters. Ellie rose from her chair but quickly dropped down again. Thunder boomed and almost at once the gale burst around the house.

"The rose hedges will be ruined," Vivian said. "We may have to start over, but they grow so fast."

Joe cleared his throat. "Was that all Wazoo said?"

"She'll be glad to get back here." Vivian grimaced and pulled her feet beneath her on the seat. "Someone signed for this bottle, but the name didn't mean a thing to me—or to Wazoo."

Joe waited and made sure he looked interested. Ellie held the arms of her chair.

"Do you know anyone called Garvey Jump? That's what it sounded like."

Disappointment wouldn't help a thing but Joe sighed just the same. "Doesn't ring a bell with me."

Ellie shook her head. "I'd remember a name like that." She flopped back in her chair. "Would it really be okay if I rested for a bit? I need to calm down."

Vivian jumped to her feet. "You brought a bag?"

"Just a little one. I can manage. Just tell me how to find the bedroom." To her, quiet time was becoming a memory.

"You'll both be on the third floor of the—"

"What am I thinking of?" Ellie said in a rush. "I must be losing my mind. Garvey Jump's the maniac serial killer in *the* Sonja Elliot books. The heroine is a criminal psychologist. She gets closer to him in each story but you keep thinking he'll kill her next because she's seen too much."

37

"Room 304," Joe said. "This is me." He turned the key in the lock of 304, switched on a light, tossed in his bag and shut the door. He also held the key to 302 and hesitated before telling Ellie, "I'd like to make sure you're settled."

"Okay."

She sounded too meek for Joe's liking.

The rooms were in the central block that joined the north and east wings of the house to the west and south. This was the area Vivian and Charlotte intended to use exclusively for long-stay guests. So far Wazoo and three other employees on the ground floor, and Paul Nelson on the second floor, were the only residents.

Ellie's room was next to Joe's and resembled a Victorian lady's bedchamber, complete with a carved oak four-poster hung with lined chintz that rose to a queen canopy.

Ellie walked in and felt sleepy at the mere sight of the high, soft-looking bed. She glanced at Joe and laughed.

He studied plaster cherubs cavorting around the ceiling, a fireplace where flowers decorated each tile, and the rest of the very feminine room like a man who had mistakenly wandered into a ladies' restroom.

"It's good to hear you laugh again," Joe said, and narrowed his eyes at her. "Are you laughin' at me?"

She shrugged. "Your expression says it all. You're threatened by feminine things—like this room."

"Not at all." He raised his hands as if embracing his surroundings. "I love this room. And you're feminine but you don't scare me, either."

"I don't scare anyone." But she wasn't the total chicken some might think her, or an ostrich with her head in the ground. When the news about Jason's capture came in she had felt giddy with relief—until she learned Lucien had taken blows to the head from two, not one man. Since then Joe had told her that the bottle Wazoo mentioned to Vivian had contained the chloroform used on Daisy. "Whoever bought the chloroform never expected anyone to track down his source or discover he'd used Garvey Jump as a signature. It's the bottle that ties me to two murders—again. He's still out there, whoever he is. He's angry with me, I can feel it." She held the nearest bedpost. "Jason Clark didn't kill Stephanie Gray or Billie Knight."

"No," Joe said. "But you can bet he at least read about Billie Knight, and about you. That's how he found you. You need to let go of it all for a bit. I'll put your bag over here." He looked behind him. "That must be the bathroom." He wondered if he'd ever stop feeling he must check for hidden intruders, ever stop fearing for Ellie's safety.

Chintz paper on the windowless bathroom walls

matched the bed hangings. A huge, claw-footed white tub made him think of drowsing in warm water. Satisfied no one hid under the sink he went back to the bedroom. Ellie stood with her back to him. She had taken off her dress and sandals and was rummaging in her bag.

Each time he was with her he learned a new feeling, a sensation he'd never had before. In her white bra and panties, with fading marks on her back and legs, this woman reached inside him and found what could make a man weak. She seemed small and very vulnerable. And, at the same time, even as he swallowed against tightness in his throat, his body responded to her.

He coughed.

"I know you're there," she said, dragging out a white cotton robe. "You're not seeing anything you haven't seen before."

"Miz Ellie, what I'm seein' is doin' the same things it always does to me. There's no moss growin' on me."

"Men can be so inappropriate," she said, but didn't sound too serious. She draped the robe around her shoulders, and from the gyrations she made inside its cover, he figured she was taking off her bra. Sure enough, it landed on top of her open bag. Ellie wrapped the robe around her and tied the sash. The storm set up a high whining noise and she shivered.

Hoping to correct his cavalier reputation, he went to the bed, took off a heap of cushions at the head and turned down the coverlet. He plumped up the pillows, then noticed a wooden stepping stool intended to make the journey to the top of the mattress less hazardous. He held a hand out to Ellie. "Come on. The steps are on this side. Up you go."

She walked toward him. *Keep your eyes above her neck,*

Gable. Real easy to do, he didn't think. She took his hand and smiled, and moisture clung to her lower lashes.

"Up," he said, and shut his mouth firmly. He had to be careful what he said at a time like this or he'd admit his desire for her.

Two steps, a nimble scramble, and Ellie knelt on top of the bed. She crawled to sit against some pillows and carefully made sure her robe covered her legs. Joe leaned to frame her face with his hands. "You're already healin'," he told her. "It's amazin'." The puncture marks from her teeth were livid on her bottom lip, but the swelling was half as much as it had been. Reddish bruising had faded to green and yellow in spots.

She held still with her eyes downcast and let him examine her.

"May I stay here with you?" he asked. "We haven't had much chance to be alone lately—to talk," he finished in a hurry.

"As long as you don't mind if I fall asleep while you're talking to me."

"That would be fine." It wouldn't, but it was better than nothing. "Excuse me."

In the bathroom he stripped off his shirt and hung it on the back of the door. His shoes and socks came off next and he set them aside. He splashed water over his face and hair, and his upper body, and dried off with a huge, fluffy towel. All he could do with his hair was run his fingers through it and enjoy the cool feel of wet curls on his neck.

"I feel better," he told Ellie when he flopped into an armchair and stretched out his legs. "These old houses were built to deal with muggy weather like this. The tall ceilings and all."

"I won't bite, Joe."

"Huh?"

She patted the mattress beside her. "Stretch out on the sheet. It feels cool. Then you won't do yourself an injury when you fall asleep."

He might do himself an injury if he lay beside her on the bed and tried to pretend he felt more like her brother than her lover. "Thanks, cher, I'll do that."

Ellie sensed his hesitation and decided to be flattered by it. Her challenge of the moment was to look at him without being too obvious. She had to look at him. Naked to the waist, his tanned body gleamed and drops of water from his blue-black hair clung to his shoulders.

He climbed onto the bed, reclined against the pillows and crossed his ankles. Tan linen pants settled over his flat stomach, his muscular thighs and calves. She was a voyeur, Ellie thought, and smiled a little as she shut her eyes.

"The questions you asked earlier," Joe said, looking down at Ellie. She rolled toward him and curled up on her side. "The ones about two men in your yard. Lucien's going to be the one to clear up that mystery. Or he will if he keeps on recoverin' well. Maybe he'll be stronger to-morrow."

"I hope so," Ellie said. "I keep thinking I must have missed something that was right under my nose."

"You do?" He snorted. "That makes two of us."

When she swept the backs of her fingers lightly across his belly, he jumped.

"Sorry," Ellie said. "It's your fault for looking so good."

He expanded his lungs. How was he supposed to react to that?

Ellie propped her head on a hand and turned her face

up to his. "No, no," she said when he smiled at her. "Don't look at me. I'm such a fright."

"You do look pretty bad, but I've got a strong stomach."

Ellie tugged at hairs on his chest and he yelped.

The humidity had turned her hair into tight curls. From his angle he noted how thick and long her lashes were, and how very blue her eyes.

"Could Jason have been back there in the yard?" she asked. "Jason and… No, it doesn't make sense. I can't put Jason together with the other one."

"Neither can I." Carefully, Joe settled a hand on her neck. "Does that hurt?"

She shook her head. "You make me feel better."

"I hope I do. You're makin' me feel better, too. I like your touch—and your feel. Don't hold back. Anythin' I have is yours."

Her lips curved.

The thought of doing more than pet her unnerved Joe. Best hold off trying until she gave him a more definite sign that she wouldn't suddenly become frightened. They had grown so close, but he would never forget the first time they had started to make love.

Shifting closer, Ellie nestled her head in the hollow of Joe's shoulder and used the backs of her fingers again. She covered every inch of his shoulders and chest until she tucked her arm around his waist. "I love being close to you," she told him, and gradually lowered her face to run the tip of her tongue over a nipple. "Anyone who thinks a woman's chest is more erotic than a man's is high on something."

He laughed. "You're killin' me. And as far as which chests are the most erotic, do you think that might be different for different people? A woman versus a man, say?"

She shook her head. "Absolutely not. If you knew how I feel you'd understand I'm right."

"I know what I know," Joe said. He was too hard for comfort, even if the pain he felt was good, too. Hesitantly he cupped her breast through the robe. She moaned and he slipped his hand inside to smooth her ribs, to stroke her breast in wide circles.

This wasn't the time. Joe slid lower and took her in his arms. "See if you can sleep. Later we'll have to deal with Spike and maybe some others we don't even know. This thing has gotten big, cher. I want to know why Clark didn't hunt you down after the first killin'."

"He probably never knew about it. Mostly he didn't take any notice of what went on in the world. And they did a good job of not revealing too much about me then. This time every detail's been in the news."

"You're right," he said. "Forget about it for now."

She was silent. Joe listened to more thunder and the crackling of lightning. It was the kind of storm that started you praying for whatever was going to happen to happen fast.

"Joe," Ellie whispered, "make love to me."

He held his breath and willed his arousal to settle down. "Cher, you aren't up to it yet. I couldn't stand hurting you."

"Please."

He raised her chin. "It isn't easy to stop once I start."

"Do you think I don't know that?" She turned onto her back again and undid her sash. Slowly, she peeled back her robe, bared her body except for her skimpy white panties. "This is only fair."

Only fair? Or taking unfair advantage of a weak man? He kissed her collarbones and tweaked her nipples.

When he pulled on them, she writhed and raised her hips from the bed.

He couldn't get past his fear of reinjuring her healing wounds.

"Joe?"

"Yes," he told her. "Hold on." He undid his pants, lifted his butt and shucked off the rest of his clothes. Then he eased her panties down and over her feet.

Her eyes were wide open.

"Let me do this," he told her. "Just give yourself up to me."

Ellie nodded. The only man she could give herself to without reservation was Joe Gable. Whatever happened, she would never stop loving him.

Straddling her thighs, he made sure she took none of his weight. He smoothed her so softly she whimpered, and when he kissed his way from her belly to her breasts the waiting overwhelmed her.

"Tell me if something's painful," he said. "I want my tongue in your mouth." He slid his forearms beneath her shoulders and held himself so that their bodies barely brushed together. "I'll just have to wait for the kisses. It'll do me good."

Inside, Ellie ached, a deep arching ache. Very slightly, she rocked from side to side, moving her breasts across his chest.

If he didn't take her, he'd explode. Joe parted her legs with a knee and settled his thighs between hers. He used the tip of his penis to excite her and she jackknifed her legs, opened herself up to him. Joe swept smoothly into her but settled a thumb where he could keep on exciting her.

He hadn't guessed that holding back, entering and withdrawing millimeter by millimeter and excruciatingly slowly, could sear him in a way he'd want to be seared many times. Ellie's eyes were closed and tears squeezed from the corners. Her lips pulled back from her teeth, and as if in surrender, she threw her arms over her head on the pillow. Her body jerked with each thrust and her full breasts swayed.

A convulsive contraction squeezed her around him and he poured himself into her, rocking, supporting her head with both of his hands.

Ellie's climax rippled on for seconds, even after Joe had maneuvered himself to her side and taken her into his arms. They didn't speak. She settled her face into his neck and felt a satisfied peace, even as she knew he could arouse her again in a moment if he wanted to.

"I've got an idea," he murmured at last. "How would you like to take a soothin' bath?"

She craned her neck to see his face. "Would that be a bath with you?"

"Would you enjoy it any other way?"

"Mmm, probably not."

Five minutes later Joe lifted her into the deep bathtub, already filling with warm water and some sort of bubbles that smelled wonderful.

"Have you done this before?" he asked.

Ellie shook her head. "Never."

"You'll want to do it again."

She had no chance to protest his arrogance before he got in with her and pulled her legs over his. He drew her close enough to hold him against her. At the same moment he entered her again and she slipped back and forth on the warm enamel bottom of the tub. Joe paused long enough to dump suds on her head and plop a blob on the end of her nose, but went right back to driving her insane. She found her release in that warm, bubbly water, wrapped in the strong arms of a man who couldn't get enough of her, and afterward he held her where she was, joined to him, while he caressed her.

Through drooping eyelids she took in what appeared to be an ocean of sudsy bathwater on the floor—and didn't care.

"Ellie," Joe said. "I love you so much."

She rested her forehead on his and flattened her hands over the sides of his head. "I love you, too."

"Sometimes corny is okay, right?" he asked.

"It's fabulous. It fits just right."

"Like other things around here," he murmured. "Will you be my wife, Ellie Byron?"

Protests rose to her lips. Her mind tumbled with thoughts of the challenges they still faced. *Let the peace in*, she told herself. "Yes, Joe, I will."

38

Joe couldn't believe he'd slept for hours. It was after four in the afternoon and other people would already have arrived at the house. Madge for one needed to get home before darkness, and the danger of flying debris made the trip more hazardous. Apparently her rooms were in the east wing where the family lived.

He slipped from Ellie's bed and pulled on his pants. He'd leave her to sleep. No one would be surprised that she needed rest.

For a moment he watched her. They would be married. This woman had agreed to be his wife. He wanted to shout it out loud.

He collected his socks and shoes and cracked open the door. The hall was deserted and he slipped out, locked Ellie's door and slid the key underneath.

For the first time he got a good look at his own room. He had returned to the land of monkeys, palms and pineapples—and what looked like a harem scene painted on the ceiling. A huge divan heaped with brilliant silks dominated the room.

Joe enjoyed the novelty only long enough to pull on a navy-blue T-shirt and tuck it into his pants. He found a comb and tamed his hair, then set off to join whoever was downstairs.

He reached the second floor and thought of Paul. No doubt he'd still be holed up in his rooms, but it was past time for Joe to talk with him. The idea of setting another man straight didn't thrill him, but this was about his sister and he was all the family she had.

He walked past rooms, a thick Persian runner muffling his footsteps, until he reached a door with small tiles bearing Paul's name beside it. Joe rapped with one knuckle and waited. Not a sound came from inside.

Later would do. He'd already been "careless," as Cyrus called him, for not keeping a closer eye on the type of man Paul was, so a while longer before an unpleasant interview wouldn't make much difference.

Earlier, when Paul had been at All Tarted Up, he'd been despondent. Sure he deserved to be fried for what he'd done to Jilly, but Joe felt disquieted when he considered how Paul might be taking the collapse of all his plans. The guy had shown his temperamental streak before.

Joe knocked again, and when he still failed to get an answer he cautiously turned the handle, not expecting it to open. It did, and a cluttered room, obviously where Paul worked, confronted him. "Paul? Are you here?"

Not a sound.

The dark jacket the man had been wearing when Joe last saw him trailed from the back of a cane-seated chair. On a big Chinese desk, a mug of coffee steamed slightly atop an electric warmer set beside a laptop computer. A red light glowed on the warmer, showing the heating device was on. Paul must have stepped out but intended to return quickly.

Shelves lined the walls and many of them sagged under the weight of books with other volumes set horizontally on top. Books stood in piles on the floor. Several hefty Hungry Eyes bags with handles marched in a row behind the door, each one filled with books. Ellie had mentioned Paul's kindness in ordering books from her. Regardless, Joe wasn't in a mood to feel grateful to Paul for anything.

He sat in a chair facing the desk and prepared to wait. When he craned his neck to see inside the coffee mug he saw a thick skin on top of the drink. It had been there awhile.

The lid of the computer had only been half lowered and the machine whirred softly.

Paul Nelson needed to move on from here and if he didn't like that idea, Joe would see what it took to change his mind. Jilly would heal, but that would take time and running into Paul regularly wouldn't help.

Joe got up and paced. He made a circle around the desk. An open box, also full of books, sat underneath. Other books Paul must be using lay on top—some open and upside down where their spines would be broken.

With one finger, Joe raised the top of the computer. The screen saver was on. He made a move to lower the panel again but it buzzed and came to life. Paul was researching a list of Internet sites.

Joe bent forward and frowned. Why would the man want to know about drowning? Accounts by people who had almost drowned, a theory on the stages experienced by a drowning person, a forensic pathologist's report on the autopsy of a drowning victim.

Quickly, Joe lowered the top of the computer again. His stomach squeezed. He hated Nelson's guts, but he'd be relieved to see him about now.

Would he kill himself because he'd been revealed for the creep he was?

No, there had been too many brushes with unnatural behavior lately and they were coloring Joe's reactions. Paul could be anywhere, he could even have behaved like a total fool and gone out into the storm.

A piece of screwed-up paper had missed the wastebasket. Automatically, Joe picked it up and went to toss it in the right place. He glanced at the door and uncurled the sheet instead. There was just one paragraph at the top of the page, followed by a signature.

The paragraph read: "Hang in there, Paul. In time we hope to continue the project. You know we hold you in high regard and we hate to let you go." "Kathleen" was signed with a flourish.

At the bottom of the page a single line of tasteful gray script identified a New York publishing company: Worth House. The symbol was, appropriately, a small, square house. Paul's trade-size paperbacks with a yellow chevron on each spine were easy to pick out on a shelf near the desk. Beneath each chevron the little gray house was printed.

Joe crumpled the paper again and dropped it into the wastebasket. "Poor bastard," he muttered. Paul had been kicked more than once today.

Rosebank was so large it took Joe almost five minutes to find his way back to the east wing. When he reached the top of the stairs leading to the ground floor he heard a number of voices in earnest conversation coming from the receiving room.

He walked through the door and the talking stopped. Spike, Cyrus and Guy stood around looking anything but relaxed. Madge perched on the arm of a chair. Each one of them showed signs of rain damage.

"Good news and bad news," Spike said. "We've got a big break. Lucien picked out Jason on the Ben's Foods tape."

"Great," Joe said. "Absolutely great."

"We already knew it was Jason," Guy said. His frown turned his brows into a single rucked line. "If Ellie needed backing up this would do it, but Clark is already in custody and apparently talking. Tell him the really rotten news, Spike."

Spike grunted. "Okay. On the night in question, Lucien heard Ellie's window breaking and walked to the end of the square to see what was up. He saw Daisy run into the alley and figured she shouldn't be loose, so he went after her. He found the dog unconscious by the guest house and saw glass glinting on the ground. He was picking up pieces to see what they were when someone jumped him from behind. This guy struggled with him. He held Lucien down and pulled the hand with the glass in it against Lucien's face—forced pieces into his mouth."

Madge put her head in her hands and Cyrus went to her at once. He rested an arm across her shoulders and eased her to lean against him.

Joe saw the other two men looking at them and felt annoyed. Everyone made too much of Cyrus and Madge's strong friendship. That's all it was, a friendship. "So Jason went for Lucien and pushed glass in his mouth. Sick bastard. Does Lucien know what he hit him with?"

Guy and Spike glanced at each other. "No," Guy said. "But it wasn't Jason who hit him the first time—and fed him the glass sandwich. He never saw that man. Jason came along after Lucien listened to the first guy scrabbling around—he was probably stuffing pieces of the chloroform bottle under the siding. Then he ran away. Jason showed up and apparently thought he'd found a dead man. He rolled Lucien over. When he realized he was looking at someone who was still alive, he turned Lucien on his face again and dealt him the blow that nearly killed him."

"So we still don't know who murdered Stephanie Gray and Billie Knight," Madge said. "But we can assume he was sneaking around behind Hungry Eyes with a bottle of chloroform. It makes more sense that the stuff was meant for Ellie, not the dog."

39

Bathing alone ought to be against the law.

Ellie smirked at herself in the bathroom mirror while she did a speedy job of making herself respectable. She glanced at the innocent-looking tub and shivered. Mr. Gable had a lot of style....

She didn't know how long ago Joe had left her but it was after six now and she had a feeling she'd slept a long time.

They were going to be married.

She was grateful to have brought a cotton jacket to go over the blouse she wore with jeans. If she had to guess, she'd say the hurricane was curling its way past the area and its vicious tail was battering them, but although the humidity had to be a hundred per cent, the mugginess had a chilly edge.

The faster she joined Joe, the better, and maybe Wazoo had come back with Daisy and Zipper. Ellie left her room.

There was no need to lock the door. She hurried down the first flight of stairs and collided with Paul when he strolled into her path.

"You okay?" he said, steadying her. "Sorry if I shocked you."

"I'm fine," she told him awkwardly. "I wasn't looking where I was going."

"That's okay, then," he said, looking as if he didn't know what to do or say next.

Ellie put her hands in her pockets. "How are you doing?"

Paul pulled up his shoulders. "Not so good," he said. "Everything that's happened is my own fault and I'd change it if I could. It was too late for that the first time I cheated on Jilly."

There didn't seem to be a right answer. "You love Jilly, don't you?"

"More than anything." Paul looked away. "I'm a fool."

Ellie crossed her arms and waited.

He looked at her again. "Look, would you do something for me? Would you read something I wrote recently and tell me if you think it's any good?"

She almost asked why he thought her opinion would be worth anything. "Of course. Drop it by the shop when things are back to normal."

"No, no." He put a hand on her arm. "It's only a couple of pages—part of a longer piece. I was hoping... What am I thinking of? Forget I mentioned it, Ellie, I'm not myself."

"Nothing of the kind," Ellie told him at once. "I didn't realize what you had in mind. You want me to look at it now?"

"Later will do. You're probably hungry."

She was too excited about Joe to be hungry. "Show me your work now. I'll enjoy it."

He laughed. "Don't say that until you've read it. I would be grateful for your input—my confidence is shot."

Ellie followed him along the second-floor hallway and into his rooms.

"Sorry about the mess," he said. "Take a seat while I find the right bit."

She chose a straight-backed chair with a cane seat and sat down. "This is a great room," she said. "Very Asian and mysterious."

"I like it. Charlotte and Vivian let me pick out what I wanted from all over the house. This place is better than a museum." He hefted a manuscript onto his desk and riffled through the pages. His blond hair looked wet.

"Did you go outside?" she asked, and wished she'd held her tongue.

Paul stared at her. "No, I took a shower."

Her face felt hot. She wondered if there could be a sitting room. The one door she saw stood partially open on a bedroom.

"Here." Paul handed over several sheets. "Look, don't hold back. Say exactly what you think."

Ellie started reading.

"C'mon, c'mon. Don't lose your nerve now, pretty lady. Trust me, it won't take long. That's right, come right on in. Hold my hand and I'll make sure you don't have a thing to worry about."

I wish I could really talk to her like that, but women make me tongue-tied. Anyway, our business isn't personal, not in that way.

She's got a great body. Big breasts turn me on. If I asked, would she take her clothes off? I could put her down right here on the white stone and show her what she's been missing.

This place wasn't my first choice. Maybe it would have been if I'd known about it. I don't have to hurry here because no one will come. Why not enjoy myself first? If she screams I'm the only one who will hear. I'll enjoy hearing her scream.

Forcing a smile, Ellie looked at Paul and said, "This is really something. I didn't know you wrote fiction." She set the papers on her lap and slipped off her jacket. The room felt like a sauna.

"No one knows I write fiction—except you."

Ellie glanced at the closed door to the hall and took deep breaths through her mouth to control waves of nausea. "You're good," she managed to say.

Buy time.

She read on.

"Rub yourself against me, pretty lady. That's right, spread your legs so I don't have to spread them for you. Pull my face to your breasts and warm me there, suckle me there."

This was sick. What kind of man would ask a woman to read his sexual fantasies while he watched her?

"You don't like it when I bite you? But it's payback time. Get up and run—I want to see you run naked, and hear you scream. But I'm so much faster than you are. You won't get away."

Whoops, she tripped. Just like that. Into the water she goes and I shall just have to make sure she stays there.

I'll let her breathe a little longer. Yes, I'll enjoy that. "See, you can trust me just like I told you. Stop coughing, that's the way. Put your arms around my neck. Oh, yeah, that's perfect. Now, wrap your legs around my waist. If you've never fucked in a pool, you've never fucked."

Yes, yes, yes, yes—yes!

It's got to be now. Back she goes. Under she goes. She's strong. She fights hard. Squeeze her neck just so and her eyes pop wide. Down some more. What she sees now is darkness. What she hears is an explosion in her head.

Damn, she kicks. But she's weaker—and weaker. She's going away into the blackness.

Gone. Tow her. Where is the rope? There it is. It's short and the noose slips easily around her neck. The concrete block hits the water and sinks.

Down she goes. Down, down.

I'm free. There's no one left to spoil things.

It was all her fault. I didn't ask her to be where she shouldn't have been, or see what she was never meant to see. As long as she lived I could never feel safe.

40

Where was Ellie?

She'd made the bed. The robe she'd worn was folded on top of her bag. And she'd left without locking the door.

But she hadn't shown up downstairs and it was almost seven o'clock.

Joe's head pounded and sweat stuck his shirt to his back. Walking backward, he left her room. He was a cool man, cool and controlled and too focused to let fear into his life. So why was he falling apart and scared out of his mind?

Find her.

"Joe."

He spun around in time for Daisy to rear up and slap her front paws on his chest. Instead of her favored old cell phone, the battered one Ellie had relinquished to keep her quiet, Daisy carried a fancy red number. Over her head he saw Wazoo hurrying toward him.

Distracted, Joe rubbed the dog's head and pushed her down. "Have you seen Ellie?" he asked Wazoo.

"Not me. I come to bring her Daisy. Oh-la-la, I got so many people mad at me. That Spike, he can have a mean tongue."

Joe hurried forward. "How many ways are there to get out of this wing—other than going down the main stairs to the front door?"

"Just fire escapes up here," Wazoo said.

"You're sure she wasn't downstairs with the others?" How she could be when he would have seen her on the way, he didn't know. Joe broke into a run and passed Wazoo with Daisy at his heels.

"No, sir, she wasn't there." Wazoo caught up. "You afraid. I feel it. How could something happen to Ellie here?"

"I don't know." He stopped running and stood with his fists on his hips, taking sharp breaths. "She's probably exploring the house."

"On her own? Ellie, she don't know this place." Wazoo wrapped thin fingers around his forearm. "Something doesn't feel good," she said. "Something bad happened here."

"Not now." Joe pulled his arm away but couldn't avoid looking into her huge, black eyes. "What is it?" He felt drawn to her by the terror in those eyes. He didn't put any stock in Wazoo's "intuition," but she been right about her premonitions before.

"I go down get Spike and that Guy, me," she said. "Maybe I should bring the God Man, too. What harm can he do?"

Joe watched her sprint toward the stairs with her black lace skirts flying. Daisy followed her. He couldn't even smile about Wazoo's distrust of Cyrus.

He hadn't checked Ellie's shower.

Running again, he slammed into her room and straight into the bathroom. She wasn't there. Back he went, throwing open doors as he went along the corridor and checking inside. Rosebank had to have dozens of ways to the outside, but why would Ellie go out in a storm? And leave her things behind? And go when she knew he was waiting for her—and that Wazoo would be bringing Daisy and Zipper here?

She wouldn't leave, dammit.

On the second floor he went forward, going into room after room, calling Ellie's name, until he reached Paul's door and knocked. "Paul," he called out. One good thing you could say about Nelson was that he was always willing to help out.

Heavy footsteps and a rumble of voices distracted him. Spike and Guy jogged toward him. Cyrus was close behind. Daisy passed all three.

"What was Wazoo babbling about?" Spike asked. "You said Ellie was sleeping."

Joe explained the situation. He held up his palms and said, "Let's slow down. The first step is to see if Vivian or Madge—or Charlotte are showing her the house."

"No," Cyrus said. "They're together waiting to find out what's going on."

"She wouldn't poke around someone else's place without being invited." Joe heard his voice rise with each word. "There's something wrong."

"Hey, hey," Spike said. "Take a breath and simmer down."

Daisy nosed at Paul Nelson's door and it slid open. The dog snuffled her way inside.

"It's time someone taught that one some manners," Joe said, and Guy laughed at him.

"You there, Paul?" Spike called. Daisy had disappeared.

A light shone on the cluttered desk but there was no sign of the resident travel writer.

"I came to try to see him earlier," Joe said, "but he wasn't here. The man's a fool, but I hope he's okay."

The dark jacket was missing from the back of the chair by Paul's desk. Joe took a few steps into the room and saw that the coffee mug had been removed from its heater and the equipment turned off.

"He's been back since I was last here," Joe muttered. "I came in. I had some stupid notion he might have been despondent."

"Maybe he is," Cyrus said.

Joe approached the computer. "This is off. It was on before. Did you ever see so many books in one small place?"

"Nope." Guy inclined his head to look at something on the desk. "Is there anyone in this town who isn't a Sonja Elliot fan now?"

Joe felt irritated. "I'd have thought Paul had better things to do." He felt hot. "We all know he keeps himself pretty busy."

The others had the sense not to laugh.

"I'm calling in the local force," Spike said. Although Rosebank was only minutes from Toussaint, it fell just over the line and into Iberia Parish, and out of Spike's jurisdiction. "We need bodies. The place is too big to cover fast enough. They'll probably curse me out for wasting their time but that's just dandy."

"My God." Joe had gone to stand beside Guy at the desk. "Oh, my God. I didn't notice." He grabbed up an open copy of *Death of a Witness* by Sonja Elliot. "This is coming out early, but not for a week or so if I remember right."

"Looks pretty out to me," Guy said in a monotone.

Joe checked the copyright, which told him nothing except Ms. Elliott had a corporation. The shiny cover showed a body under water, tethered by the neck to a block. The spine gave title, author name, and had a picture of a little gray house. He looked at Paul's travel books and back at the novel. There might not be a yellow chevron on the cover of Elliot's book, but the trademark was the same.

So what, the publisher must put out hundreds of books.

"Don't you feel we're wasting time?" Cyrus asked.

"Yes," Joe said, "but we can't run off in all directions with no plan."

Guy glanced toward the hall where Spike could be heard on the phone. "That would be better than doing nothing."

"Yeah." Joe looked down into the box of books under the desk. More books with the same watery cover were stacked inside. He pulled the box all the way out. "I don't get this," he said, and took an invoice from inside.

"We'd better be careful about interfering with things without a search warrant," Guy said.

"These books," Joe said. "The invoice says they're author's copies. What does that mean?"

"It means just that," Cyrus said, heading for the door. "The publisher sends the author copies of a book that's about to come out."

"But—"

"Wait a minute." Joe had picked the book up again and he cut Guy off. He scanned lines quickly. "Look at this." He put the open volume into Cyrus's hands.

"What is it?" Guy returned and read over Cyrus's shoulder.

"They're on their way," Spike said, stepping back inside. "I suggest we enlist the women. Have them stick together and start a search indoors. We'll go outside. Dog, you're going to get it!" He snatched a piece of clothing from Daisy, who had it between her front paws while she chewed on it.

"This is sick," Guy said.

"Sad," Cyrus added.

Spike snatched away Daisy's prize and a creased sheet of paper fell to the ground.

"That's Ellie's jacket," Joe said, and strode to take it from Spike. "What's it doing...Ellie's been in here." He swept up the paper and only glanced before he said, "Let me see that book.

"The same," he said, and felt his throat closing. "Except for the bit about the white floor. That isn't in the book."

"No," Cyrus agreed, comparing the manuscript page with the book. "In the book this takes place in the afternoon, not the evening, and it's in a creek."

"Shit." Spike dialed his cell again. "Vivian, I want the four of you to start looking through the house for Ellie. The Iberia folks will be along any minute and we're going outside to start looking. I'll try to keep you informed of where we are." He put the phone back on his belt.

Cyrus made a sound and pushed Joe out of the way to get to the door. He dashed along the hall, but in the direction that led away from the stairs.

"Where are you going?" Joe shouted, running after him.

"Side exit," Spike said. He had Daisy beside him.

"There's an outside terrace on this floor. It overlooks the new restaurant in the conservatory building."

"Paul went into Toussaint with you the night Jason Clark broke Ellie's shop window," Cyrus called over his shoulder. "Did he go back with you?" They emerged onto the terrace where broken pots and spilled plants littered the floor. Wind beat at them, made their progress slow. Occasionally they heard thunder far in the distance.

"He didn't come with me—not either way," Spike shouted. "He was there, though."

"I know," Cyrus said, cupping his mouth with his hands. "He's a hard worker. Went too carelessly at it and cut his wrist. He slapped something over it and went right back to workin' on that window."

A wide flight of steps led down to a courtyard.

"I'm not wrong, am I, Spike?" Cyrus said, staggering forward. "Morgan Link's pool house is made of white marble?"

"What pool house?" Guy bellowed.

"Next door at Serenity House," Spike said. "It used to be a private clinic of some kind. There's a white marble pool house behind the main building. The owners aren't here much."

Energy—and wild rage—propelled Joe forward. "Did you see Nelson cut himself on the window?" he asked Cyrus as he passed him. They had cleared the courtyard and the north wing.

"No. We were all busy."

"Couldn't he have cut himself on a bottle in Ellie's backyard then lied about it?"

"I guess so."

"I want him." Guy kept up with Joe. "He's our man."

"He doesn't look like Sonja Elliot to me," Spike said. "D'you think that's all a sham and she's just a front? Maybe he writes the books."

"It doesn't matter," Guy said.

"No." Joe slapped his way through undergrowth and into the grounds of Serenity House. "Now, keep the noise down." Not that they'd be easy to hear over the racket made by thrashing rain and breaking tree limbs.

He saw the pool house and sprinted, smacked obstacles from his path. And he pulled up short. Daisy loped ahead and Joe barely managed to catch and restrain her. Bending, going as fast as he could with one hand on the dog's collar, he approached the marble building.

"Looks like a mausoleum," Guy said in his ear.

Joe grimaced and shook his head. "There's a light on. The doors slide. One's open."

"Don't let Daisy go until we're sure she won't do more harm than good," Spike said.

Cyrus put a hand on Joe's shoulder. "Ellie doesn't have to be in here. She could just as well be with the others by now."

"Yeah." Joe knew better. He motioned for the other men to hold back and had Cyrus restrain Daisy. At least she'd been trained not to bark if given the command.

He got to the door, lay flat in inches of seeping mud and peered inside. The more time he could buy without being seen, the better.

Spike and Guy stood behind the closed door opposite, watching him for any reaction.

He heard Ellie before he saw her and almost cried out to her. His heart rose, but not for long. On the left side, almost at the far end of the too-white interior wall, a shiny steel ladder rose vertically to a catwalk. Ellie huddled up there, pressed to the wall but repeatedly peering down at Paul Nelson.

Nelson held a gun.

The catwalk stretched no more than three feet in either direction from the top of the ladder and gave access to a series of valves.

A wet nose nuzzled Joe's ear and he got a rough licking from Daisy's large tongue. Cyrus crouched beside him. "Are they in there?"

"Yes. Nelson's got a gun and Ellie's trapped on a catwalk. She must have managed to get away and run. Too bad she couldn't get to the door."

"Should we let Daisy go?"

Joe thought about it. "Not yet. Nelson could shoot her and be mad enough to shoot Ellie next. I'm goin' in. Tell Spike and Guy to hold back unless I get into trouble." If Nelson turned around, Joe would be like a huge cockroach on a white tablecloth—the perfect target.

"Talk to Spike and Guy first," Cyrus said. "I'll get 'em."

"No, please don't do that. They'll try to stop me."

"Because it's too dangerous," Cyrus said. "He's got a gun. He'll kill you."

"Better that than have him shoot Ellie. If his attention is on me, those two can take him down."

At the edge of the pool, not far from the ladder, Joe noticed a coil of rope. It rested around a concrete block. Speed was essential, and wanting to rush Nelson brought Joe close to panic.

When Paul started yelling at Ellie, Joe couldn't understand any of it at first. The sound bounced upward and echoed away into the arched ceiling.

"I said I won't hurt you," Nelson shouted. This time

Joe concentrated and made out the words. "Just come on down and we'll work everything out."

Ellie didn't move and Nelson gripped the rails on either side of the ladder. He climbed several steps.

Joe didn't know Spike had moved until he threw himself on the ground beside him. "We're going to pick him off," he said. "I want you and Cyrus back out of the way in case he has time to get a round off."

"I want *you* to listen while I tell you how this is goin' to happen," Joe said. "You and Guy be ready in case I fail but don't shoot unless I *do* fail. All he has to do is squeeze the trigger with the gun pointing upward and Ellie could be history."

"No. I'll be giving the orders."

Joe stared him down in the wash of light from inside the pool house. "This isn't your jurisdiction, remember? So don't try pullin' rank. Once I get inside—I'll stay down flat—I'm goin' to slide into that water and swim to the other side."

"And you don't think he'll hear you, then see you?"

"Not the way I'll be doin' it."

Nelson took another rung, and another. "If you don't want to die up there, you'll do as you're told."

"And die down there?" Ellie said. "Why me? What have I done to you?"

"You saw me in that crowd on Bourbon Street. You shouldn't have, but you did. You looked right at my face."

"No!"

He climbed another rung. "Yes. You've made yourself believe you didn't, but I can't risk having you quit suppressing it and start pointing at me."

"I didn't see anyone. If I did, I couldn't have lived with Charles Penn being convicted."

"He's a criminal. He should be in jail, anyway."

Another rung. "All the evidence pointed to him—you should have left it alone. You've talked about the shape of a face, and impressions. I heard you sometimes think you see a face half blue, half gold."

Ellie craned her neck to check his progress and immediately slammed back against the wall with her hands flattened behind her. "Why don't you just shoot me?" she said.

Joe pounded a fist into the mud. "Because that's not what's supposed to happen," he said. He spared a glance for Cyrus and Spike. "Did I tell you he was researching Internet sites about drowning? There was a list of them on his monitor the first time I went in there. And you saw the book, and his little revised version. He won't shoot her unless he can't get her into the pool."

"Dear Lord," Cyrus muttered.

"That was me. Mardis Gras, right?" Nelson said. "Painted face. Feathers."

"I didn't recognize anyone. All I saw were the bottoms of Stephanie's feet."

Nelson dropped back his head and laughed. "Of course, that was her name. Not that it matters. Neither of them mattered."

Movement made Joe look toward Guy. With his gun drawn, he balanced on his toes, ready to go.

The waiting had to be over. Joe pushed himself inside the door and squirmed rapidly to the right. He stayed close to the wall until he reached several piles of cushions for the lounge chairs that were stacked at the far end of the pool. The cushions weren't directly opposite the ladder, but close enough.

He had two things to pray for—that Nelson didn't see

him too soon, and that neither Guy nor Spike did something risky. He knew he could trust Cyrus to make sure Daisy didn't ruin everything.

"Get away from me." Ellie's voice rang out and she stepped forward, clung to the top of the railings and stamped on one of Nelson's hands as hard as she could.

The man screamed and sent a shot into the ceiling. "Goddamn you, bitch. Come down, or you can start bleeding right where you are."

"If you really wanted to shoot me, you would." Anger overcame fear in Ellie's voice and Joe allowed himself a smile. Nelson wouldn't like that. Her anger would make her more of a challenge and he liked his victims helpless. "You want to do what happens in the book, not spoil your record."

From his hiding place behind the cushions, Joe took quick looks at what went on, and he gauged his distance from the edge of the pool. Then he stripped down to his shorts. Glancing up again, he saw Ellie undoing the chain she always wore around her neck. He remembered the solid cross that hung on that chain.

Nelson moved upward until the top of his head was almost level with the catwalk.

Ellie's sharp breaths filled the building. She whacked Nelson's head with a heel, and when he cried out and looked up at her, Joe saw the glitter of her gold cross as she stabbed it into his face. Again and again she wielded the tiny weapon while Nelson howled and flailed. Finally he reached up with the pistol and struck at her ankles. Ellie cried out.

Joe seized the noisy moment to throw himself forward, reach the edge of the pool and slip quickly and quietly into the water. He had to trust that Guy and

Spike wouldn't risk using their weapons while Ellie was so vulnerable.

The boy who grew up swimming in creeks and rivers, and went on to swim for his university, knew what he was doing when he was in the water. A single breath and he dove smoothly down to within inches of the bottom of the pool. Pushing off the wall with his feet, he propelled himself toward the other side and made it to the surface beneath the rim without a gasp or setting the water slopping.

Nelson made grabs at Ellie's ankles. From his new vantage point Joe could see blood running into her tennis shoes, but he also noted lines of blood on Nelson's neck and was certain the man's face was a mess.

The inevitable moment came; Ellie met Joe's eyes and he held his breath, waited for her to call out to him.

She didn't. She looked away at once, just as Nelson slammed his gun down on the catwalk in an attempt to catch her foot. With no hesitation, and no loss of timing, Ellie stood on the weapon, on Nelson's hand clutching the weapon, and crouched to keep her balance while he tried to yank the hand free.

Joe pulled himself from the water. In one controlled motion he landed a couple of feet from the base of the ladder.

Nelson cursed in a continuous stream. He needed his free hand to hold on to the ladder, and as long as Ellie could keep her feet where they were, he couldn't do much.

"Why did you choose Sonja Elliot's books?" she asked, panting. "And why *those* Elliot books? There are others— earlier ones—in the series."

"Shut up."

"Why not tell me? You intend to kill me, anyway."

"You're a smart mouth. I hate women with smart mouths," he said.

"Why not admit you hate *all* women?"

"I love Jilly. And she'll be mine once all of this is over. I'll never be suspected and people will forget the thing with Cerise. Sonja Elliot made a mistake. She took all the glory and most of the money. Sure, we went fifty-fifty on the advances, but everything else, she took. Movie rights, music tie-ins, all the sales on the fan crap they make a fortune on. And she wouldn't acknowledge I was alive. I was forbidden to approach her."

"You're a ghost," Ellie said, her voice loaded with disbelief. "You write the Elliot books."

"I've written them for twelve years. At first she did the basic plotting, but she soon gave that up. I plot and I write and her name goes on the books. And her face is on the TV. This is all her fault. She did this." He sounded as if he was crying.

"The travel books—"

"I wrote those, too. Still will. I'll probably do the Elliot stuff again once the house gets over being scared by the copycat talk. But next time I'll get my share of everything and it'll be bigger than dear Sonja's."

Joe stood upright at the bottom of the ladder, looking directly up at Ellie. He wished he didn't have to rely on her guessing what he wanted her to do.

She ground her feet into Paul's hand and he shouted.

And Joe lunged up two rungs to grab one of Nelson's feet. He jerked it off the ladder. Nelson screeched. He looked down, trying to push Joe with the loose foot. Joe raised the man's leg and slammed it into the ladder rungs until Nelson sagged, barely hanging on.

Joe opened his mouth to tell Ellie to get the gun when she held it up and cried, "I've got it."

"Give it to me and I'll look after you," Paul Nelson wailed. "I'll make sure you never want for anything. No small-town lawyer can do what I can do for you. Give me the gun and I'll finish him. We can stay in Toussaint if you like. Pulling it off will be easy. We'll blame everything on him."

Keeping one hand on the ladder and rearing back, Joe tugged Nelson's leg far away from the wall, then used it to swing to the floor. He barely got out of the way before Nelson fell.

Daisy, galloping like a small black-and-tan pony with pointed teeth, leaped and landed on Nelson's back. For one moment Joe thought the dog would take out Nelson's throat, but Guy Gautreaux called out a command and Daisy slid to sit beside her victim. But she kept her teeth gripped into his collar.

Cyrus joined the group, looking as if he was ready to punch Nelson out.

"Come on," Joe said to Ellie, and helped her when she turned and started for the floor. "I'm never going to wonder why I want you at my side."

Completely subdued, now the adrenaline had ebbed, she said, "Thank you."

"No, Guy," Spike shouted at the top of his lungs. "Don't do it."

Joe reached the cold white tile again and lifted Ellie the rest of the way. And Guy dragged Nelson to his feet.

"Stop him," Spike said, running toward them.

Guy spun Nelson around and Joe saw his face. Small, deep, three-cornered wounds pocked his forehead and cheeks. Guy landed a fist on the man's nose and followed up with a blistering punch to the gut. Nelson retched and Guy dragged him until his head hung over the pool.

"You like the idea of drownin'?" Guy said. He had the end of the rope in one hand and yanked it with him as he went. "It can be arranged."

A kick to Paul's kidneys finished him and he vomited, all the while flailing and calling for help.

Spike produced handcuffs and secured Paul's hands behind his neck. Guy yanked him to his feet and shoved him toward the door.

"You'll suffer for this," Paul said, sniveling. "They don't take police brutality lightly these days."

Three Iberia officers, their guns drawn, slid around the open doorway. They advanced on the group by the pool.

Joe sent up thanks for Spike being in uniform, and for identifying himself. "This boy is yours for now," he told the new officers. "NOPD will want him for previous crimes, but this one's on your turf."

The three gathered around, smartly changed the handcuffs on Nelson and handed back Spike's. "Thanks," one man said—a sergeant. "We'll need to ask questions. Now would be good, while it's all fresh."

Spike turned to Ellie and gave her a critical once-over. "Look, guys. Miz Byron has been through a rough time. What say we get her some medical attention and let her take the night to rest up. I'll come with you now and get as much done as possible."

Guy opened his mouth, but closed it again and didn't look happy. The man needed his job back.

The Iberia sergeant agreed to Spike's proposal, after he'd told the rest of them not to leave the area and mentioned that the house would be under surveillance.

Spike left with the other officers and Paul Nelson, who had yet to stop arguing his case.

Ignoring Ellie's protests and not giving a damn about what he wore—or didn't—Joe picked up his fiancé and set out for the house with Cyrus and Guy flanking them.

Light flashed in the sky and thunder followed quickly. "I'm thankful we didn't get the hurricane," Cyrus said. "This has been more than enough for me today."

Not fifty yards ahead of them, blinding streaks of lightning shot out of the heavens. At the same time, thunder boomed and the earth shook. "Stand still, everyone," Joe snapped. He felt the vibration rumble through Ellie's body and his own.

A giant oak tree split down its center, parted and fell slowly to the ground in two smoldering, sparking sections.

They didn't speak until Cyrus said, very quietly, "I guess it's not my place to decide when enough is enough."

Homer ran out to meet them, saw the state of Joe, and rushed back to return with an old denim duster. Cyrus took Ellie from him while he put on the coat and buttoned it, but immediately gave her back.

"I can walk," she said firmly.

"Not until we're sure that monster didn't break any bones in your feet or ankles."

Into the house they went, and Homer led the way into the round sitting room with its suspended, striped-canvas ceiling coverings. It reminded Joe of a plush desert tent.

"Ellie!" Charlotte and Vivian spoke together.

Wazoo beamed and jigged up and down. "You done gettin' yourself beat up now?"

Madge said, "How blessed we are," before slipping a hand through Cyrus's arm and saying, "Are you all right?"

He said, "Yes," and smiled into Madge's face as if she were the only person in the room.

"Um, Ellie," Charlotte Patin said. "There's someone here to see you, but I thought we should make sure you're up to surprises first."

Ellie looked blank. "I'm...well, I'm not fine but I'm okay. Who is it?"

Homer left and returned with a grin so large Joe doubted anyone would believe it without seeing it.

Jim Wade entered behind him and Ellie struggled to make Joe put her feet on the ground. He did but she leaned against him. Jim also grinned, but the tall, impressively built man who followed him appeared very serious.

"This is the client I told you about," Jim said. "The one who's thinking of buying property around here."

"Leave this to me, Jim," the man said. He fell silent and walked to stand in front of Ellie. With his head inclined, he smiled at her.

Trembling visibly, she offered him her hand. He ignored it and hugged her instead. The hug lasted too long for Joe's liking, but he suffered in silence, trusting Ellie to explain when she was ready.

"You look great," Ellie said, looking with admiration— or was that adoration—into the man's face. "I watch you often. You're very good at what you do. People love you."

"I wish you had contacted me. You were hard to find."

"Joe," she said, looking at him over her shoulder. "This is my brother, Byron Frazer. Byron, this is my fiancé, Joe Gable."

They shook hands and Joe thought Byron no less impressive than he would have expected a brother of Ellie's to be.

"Everythin's lovely," Wazoo said. "A weddin'. We need another one of them. And you must be so honored, Ellie. Not many people have TV personalities in their families. Dr. Byron Frazer, expert on the family." She showed signs of swooning.

"Pleased to meet you," Byron said, but all of his attention was on Ellie. "Guess I got here in time to give you away."

Ellie blushed and Joe squeezed her arm.

Wazoo sighed. "You'll need a place to stay, Dr. Frazer. I think you'll be comfortable here on the ground floor, don't you, Miz Vivian? In the central wing, naturally."

"That's a good idea," Charlotte said. "But I prefer the third floor. Room 308 is lovely. It'll be even more lovely when the storm shutters come down."

"You're a psychologist," Wazoo said, slipping a hand under Byron Frazer's elbow. "I work with animals. D'you think humans and animals are messed up for the same reasons?"

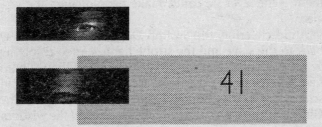

41

Two months later:

"The party's o-o-over. The candles flicker and dim—"

"*Carmine!*" Marc's strong voice didn't make its destination over the din at Pappy's Dancehall. Joe, Spike, Homer, Ozaire Dupre and Wazoo rose up from their chairs together and yelled, "*Turn it off, Carmine!*"

The bouncer, splendid in a brand-new silver-and-white Elvis costume, complete with luxurious black wig and the biggest belt buckle in the South, panicked. Rather than change the song on his prized jukebox, he pulled the plug out of the wall and sparks sizzled in the air.

"You're all mean," Ellie said. "He was trying to be appropriate and got a bit muddled." Smiling, she hurried off, her cream chiffon dress floating and billowing, to have a quiet talk with Carmine. She put an arm through his and led him away to get a glass of champagne.

"That's my girl," Joe said, his chest expanding.

"That's your wife," Cyrus corrected him, and the company laughed as if they had never heard a funnier comment. Whenever he could make people laugh, he was glad.

Amid cheering, the Swamp Doggies made their way back to the stage and the strobe lights started revolving again. Marc and Reb sat at a table with William—who had fallen asleep on Marc's shoulder—and Reb's old school friend, Lea Chesney. Lea had been staying with the Girards about a month while she researched the wisdom of buying out the local, and dying, newspaper.

"This is it," Reb said to Lea. "The metropolis of Toussaint in full, celebratory swing. I'd say about everyone in town has passed through this place since this afternoon and they're decked out like I've never seen 'em before. That Byron Frazer—what a hunk—he invited everyone in town, or so I heard. And it looks that way. He wouldn't listen to arguments from Joe and Ellie about putting on the wedding. Do you think you can make somethin' interestin' out of these people's lives?"

Lea, blond with wise green eyes, shrugged. "We'll see. Let me hold William while you dance."

Once on the floor, Marc held Reb close. They didn't get enough chances to do the things people craved when they were in love. "Do you know how much I love you?" he whispered into her ear. They barely moved. Feeling her back, her waist, and when the lights weren't directly on them, her tight bottom, reminded him why the thrill of making love had never faded. Her sharp mind and imagination didn't hurt.

He leaned away and looked into her face. "You didn't answer my question."

"I didn't think I needed to. Being loved by you is the most important thing in my life—next to loving you back. Is this a good time to ask a question?"

Marc stopped dancing. "That's ominous. Depends on the question, but as much as I like Lea, I don't think she should live with us permanently."

"Neither do I. How do you feel about having another baby?"

"We-ell, maybe it's the wedding today that's got you thinking about babies."

"And maybe I've been thinking about it and waiting for the right time to bring it up."

How had he managed to snare such a woman? "It's crossed my mind, too, so I vote we go for it."

"Don't look now," Reb said, "but Guy's dancing with Jilly."

"I used to like dancing," Guy said, twirling Jilly past the Girards and Doll and Gator Hibbs. "Lost interest somewhere along the way."

"When you didn't have Billie anymore, maybe."

He'd walked right into that. "Yep."

"Grievin's somethin' you can't hurry," she said. "But the people you love and lose don't have to be completely lost. You try to remember the best parts, the happy times and the times when you were on the same wavelength and it felt so good being one of a twosome rather than alone."

"You're right." And she was something. After the treatment she'd gotten from Nelson, her spirit inspired him.

"There was a hearing about your reinstatement," she said, and let the statement hang there.

"I've been reinstated, but I'm on a leave of absence while I decide if I want to go back."

"Give yourself time," Jilly said. "You don't have to rush into anything."

"Because I have no responsibilities?" he said, and

hated himself for sounding mean. "Forget I said that. I'm enjoyin' dancin' again tonight. Thank you. I think our bride and groom look tired, how about you?"

Jilly smiled and looked over her shoulder at Joe and Ellie.

The Doggies struck up a new song. "I want you to myself," Joe whispered into Ellie's ear. She reversed positions and said, "Ditto. But everyone's having such a good time. I don't think we can leave yet."

Joe made a low, growling noise. "Could I show you the inside of my Jeep?"

Under the cover of her voluminous skirts, Ellie squeezed his thigh, squeezed it again, and again, until she reached the part of him that made him suck in a breath. She kissed him at once, smothering any other sound he might be in the mood to make.

"Demon," he said when she allowed him to breathe again.

Ellie smiled sweetly and put her mouth to his ear again. "When I get you alone I'm planning to eat you, bit by bit. Only the best bits, of course."

"I'm going to ignore you," he said, slipping lower in his chair. "But don't blame me if things get out of hand."

She laughed, picked up a glass of champagne and held it while he took a sip. Then she took one of her own and stared at him over the rim of the glass.

"Your brother puts on a great shindig." Joe glanced across at Byron and his beautiful wife, Jade, their teenage son, Ian, and three-year-old Lori. Wazoo also sat with them and they seemed to enjoy her. "They're a great family. It'll be a culture shock to be in Cornwall for our honeymoon."

"We'll love being in England," Ellie said. "Spike and

Vivian insist they can manage Daisy and Zipper at Rose-bank—with Wazoo's help."

"You know Vivian's pregnant?" Joe asked.

"I had noticed," Ellie said. "She looks lovely."

At the far end of the head table, Spike and Vivian sat with Charlotte, Homer and Wendy. They had pulled their chairs into a semicircle and watched Daisy tease Reb's Gaston and Vivian's Boa. Wally brought another chair and joined them.

Jade Frazer leaned on her husband. Lori stayed close to her brother and asked him a stream of questions. "It's all so different here," Jade said. "Different from San Francisco or New York, but most of all from Cornwall."

"Do you like it?"

Jade looked into his eyes and then at his mouth. "I do. And I really like your sister, and Joe. I'm glad they want to be involved with us."

"I look forward to seeing them in Cornwall. Your dad will give them the once-over, and your mom."

"They're up to it." Jade rubbed her husband's arm. When she thought of it, she still felt surprised that this big, impressive, sought-after man had come into her life. "Look at those dogs, Ian. They're so funny."

Homer tried to put the toe of a boot on Daisy's red cell phone. She was too fast for him. "That's what I call a dog," Homer said, giving Boa and Gaston a significant look. "It's about time you got a fine fella like Daisy and gave the Chihuahua to a needy little old lady."

"Daisy's a female," Spike told his father, mildly enough. "And Boa's a spirited dog. I won't say much about Gaston except you'd better not pick on him."

Daisy pushed her phone toward Gaston, but snatched it back when the poodle showed interest. Next Daisy placed the phone in Boa's reach. Boa sniffed it, stood up and rotated, and flopped down with her back to Daisy.

"In other words," Vivian said, "you know what you can do with your silly red phone." She took hold of the hand Spike offered and they left to dance.

"Homer," Charlotte said, leaning toward him. "Cerise just came in."

"Fool woman." He turned around to look at her. "Doesn't have any shame."

Guy had joined Jilly at her table and they sat there saying very little. Doll and Gator Hibbs, Jilly's table companions, had left to dance and she noticed they didn't return when the music stopped.

"Cerise," Jilly said suddenly, sounding out of breath. "She's coming this way."

Guy didn't say anything, but neither did he acknowledge that Cerise had arrived.

"I've come to apologize, Jilly, and to try to explain something. I don't mean I want to say there was a good reason for what happened, just that I know about one thing."

"Sit down," Guy said, without getting up. "Make it fast."

Jilly couldn't look at the other woman, not so close up.

"I'm very sorry for causing you pain. Things started out differently between Paul and me, then they went sour. I want you to know that I'm staying in Toussaint. I want a chance to prove I'm not as bad as the town thinks. And I'll be testifying against Paul when he goes to trial."

"Thanks for telling me," Jilly said.

"There's something else," Cerise said. "I'm sure Paul didn't set out to hurt Ellie's dog. The opportunity must have come up so he did it because he thought Daisy would get in his way later...later when he...well, when he went after Ellie."

"He had chloroform with him," Jilly pointed out.

Cerise blushed and cleared her throat. She crossed her legs and jiggled a foot. "I know," she said. "But he didn't get it for the dog. He was bringing it to my place."

"Why?" Jilly said, puzzled.

"You know," Cerise said. "Sex needs a lift sometimes, something different. That stuff makes you kind of—"

"I'll explain later," Guy said hurriedly. "I appreciate the information, Cerise. I'll see you to the door."

He didn't need to, she all but ran from Pappy's.

Cyrus and Madge watched the small drama Cerise brought into Pappy's with her. By the time she went on her way, they were stepping outside into a clear, cool night.

"I never saw more people turn out for a wedding," Madge said.

Cyrus laughed. "And I never saw so many people in church at one time. I thought the wedding was beautiful. Those two are committed."

"They're completely in love," Madge said softly.

"Indeed." He thought about the past weeks and the comfort and laughter he and Madge had shared. They couldn't have what Joe and Ellie had, but he believed their closeness was very special.

"We shouldn't be out here long," Madge said. She thought carefully about her next move before she held Cyrus's hand and pulled him uphill a little way, to the place where a railing cut off a small but swiftly flowing river. "Listen to it here," she told him.

"I'm listening. It's alive out here. I like it." He laced

their fingers together and held her hand tightly. "You and I have a lot in common, Madge. We both appreciate simple things."

A too-familiar pain gripped Madge's throat. He was right, but she wished fate hadn't made Cyrus a priest, especially when the same fate assured that she would love him regardless.

She felt him looking at her in the darkness and turned her face up to his. "We do like simple things," she said, and smiled.

He sighed. "This is so unfair on you, but I don't know what else I could do about it."

She had already figured out that she would take whatever she could have of him, and decided she must never push him for more. "It's fair," she said. "We understand what's expected of us and we live within those boundaries. I'm happy, truly I am."

Cyrus put his arms around her and spread the fingers of one hand on her cheek. They rocked together. Madge felt him tremble.

Quickly, she bobbed to her toes and kissed his cheek, then she laughed as she ran ahead of him toward Pappy's.

The Swamp Doggies had found their second—or third—wind and played with huge energy.

Ellie saw Cyrus and Madge come into the building but didn't mention it to Joe. In fact, each time she looked at Joe her excitement rose. She wanted them to be alone. As soon as they could leave with some grace, they would drive in Joe's Jeep to spend their wedding night in New Orleans—in a fabulous suite on a riverboat owned by Cyrus's sister and her husband. Surely the clocks had stopped. It had to be later than nine-fifteen.

"Excuse me while I walk around a bit," she said.

"We already greeted every guest," Joe reminded her.

"I won't be talking to guests." She got up and sauntered away, swinging her hips and spreading her floaty skirts.

She went into the ladies' room for a few minutes, hoping that guests would be too busy to see her leave again. Then she slipped out and instead of going back, she wandered down an empty passageway until she reached what she knew was a storage room. Joe caught up with her and she pulled him inside with her.

"I knew you'd follow me," she said, putting her arms around his neck. "I want to kiss you, really kiss you, and we can't do it out there."

"Really?" Joe pulled a hanging string to turn on a tiny overhead bulb. "I wouldn't have had any problem with it."

Ellie pretended to scowl. "I don't like public displays."

"You're right, of course." He took off his tuxedo jacket, stiff collar and bow tie and slid them on top of canned goods stacked on a shelf. His shirt followed.

"*Joe*," she whispered fiercely. "Put those back on right now."

Instead he kissed her mouth. Running his thumbs back and forth over her ears, he gave her a long, tender kiss, but only until she heard him groan and he put his tongue in her mouth. Their faces rocked together, finding every angle they could to deepen the kiss. Ellie leaned against him, caressed his body and blessed him for getting naked to the waist.

Without warning he pulled his mouth away and bent to lick and kiss the swell of her breasts above the low, tight bodice of her wedding gown.

"Thank you for wearing this dress," he said, dipping his

fingers inside to pinch her nipples. When they were hard, he eased them from the neckline of the gown and ran his tongue around each one, until she pulled his head hard against her and he drew the tip of her breast into his mouth.

"Joe," she whispered. "Please let's go. You probably think I'm a wild woman but I want you—all of you."

He dropped to his knees, lifted her skirts and put his head beneath.

Ellie batted at him but to no avail. She wore a garter belt and cream silk stockings with a tiny pale pink thong underneath, and she felt him work the thong free of the belt in front, pull it down and shoot his tongue into her most vulnerable place.

She tried to pluck at him, slap him, reach under her skirts and grab him—but only until her knees weakened, her legs buckled and she slid until he supported her weight while he sent her into a wonderful abyss.

"Okay?" His voice came to her, muffled, from beneath her skirts.

"Wonderful," she said in a wobbly voice. "Absolutely wonderful. But we can't risk being found in here."

"We won't be." In the dim light, Joe's skin appeared gold. His mussed black hair and dark blue eyes gave him a piratical look and Ellie almost laughed.

She didn't laugh long. One after the other, her garters pinged undone and Joe lifted the belt around her waist. He stood up, took off the rest of his clothes and threw the dress over her head.

"Joe!" she cried through many layers of chiffon.

He wasn't listening. Gripping Ellie by the waist, he lifted her. "Put your legs around my waist," he told her. "And hang on."

One thrust and Ellie tottered back against the shelves. Joe went with her, hauling up the back of her dress to make a cushion behind her back.

They bucked and grasped each other—and ricocheted around the cupboard. Finally Joe lost any control and let his body take them both over the top.

Cans shot from shelves and the two of them stumbled around, trying to keep their balance.

Then Joe stopped, took Ellie in his arms and kissed her with the kind of finesse he seemed to have forgotten only moments earlier. He rested his forehead on hers and said, "I don't want to bore you, but I love you, Ellie Gable."

Tears filled her eyes. "I love you, too, Joe. Get dressed while I fix my stockings. Let's say we're tired and leave."

"You've got it."

Abruptly, fists hammered on the door and whoops went up from the outside. "We know you're in there takin' a *nap*. Our fiddler, Vince Fox, is going to lead us in a set of polkas. And the two of you get paid for dancin' with anyone who'll pay."

Epilogue

Spike reached the rectory and stamped his feet on the mat outside the front door. They were in for an unusually cold winter and he could already feel it coming.

He rang the bell but walked in without waiting and waved at Madge whom he could see through the open door to her office.

"He's in there," Madge said, pointing toward Cyrus's study.

"And he hears every word," Cyrus shouted. He rarely closed himself away. "Get in here, whoever you are."

Unbuttoning his duster, Spike took off his hat and grimaced when water ran from the brim onto the carpet, but he followed Cyrus's instructions.

"Hey there," Cyrus said, grinning when he saw Spike approach the study desk. "What brings you around so early?"

"Mornin'." Spike reached into a pocket and drew out a single sheet of paper. This he flattened out and slid toward Cyrus. "Thought you might like to see this. It's just a summary. Early days yet."

Cyrus grunted. "Heard from the lovebirds?"

"A card," Spike said, and chuckled. "They don't have time for a lot of writing. I'd say they're pretty taken with Cornwall, though."

"Who wouldn't be?" Cyrus frowned down at the paper, which he scanned rapidly. "I'm not a vengeful man but this sounds fair to me," he said.

> Paul Nelson is charged with two counts of murder and one count of attempted murder. He is being held without bail pending trial. The district attorney will seek the death penalty.

> Jason Clark is charged with rape, attempted murder, attempted rape, sexual assault, battery and unlawful imprisonment. He is being held without bail pending trial.

> Alice Clark is charged with unlawful imprisonment, and being an accessory to rape, sexual assault and battery.

> Charles Penn is being held in Canada pending extradition to the United States.

"Fair," Spike agreed.

* * * * *

Turn the page for an excerpt from Stella Cameron's
next romantic suspense novel

A GRAVE MISTAKE

Available Fall 2005 only from MIRA Books

Toussaint, Louisiana.

Jilly Gable had a man to confront.

Jilly pulled her aging VW Beetle into the forecourt at Homer Devol's gas station and looked around. Nothing on two legs moved. With her head out of the window, she called, "Guy!" then screwed up her eyes and listened. No response. She looked quickly toward the road. All day she'd had a sick sensation that she was being followed, watched. Last night she'd had a warning, even if it wasn't direct, that someone was watching her movements. Who better to advise her than Guy, a New Orleans Police Department homicide detective on extended leave?

She got out of the lime-green Beetle and went through the useless exercise of trying to take in a breath. Hot didn't cover it. Heat eddies wavered above the burned-out grass and did their shaky dance on tops of the roofs. From where she was she could see cypress trees crouching, totally still, over Bayou Teche. Beards of Spanish moss hung from branches as if they were painted there, and the pea-green surface of the bayou might have been setup Jell-O. Even the gators would be sleeping now.

Guy's beat-up gray Pontiac hugged a slice of shade beside the store, but she saw no sign of the man, either in the gas station or the store.

A walk toward the bayou ended her search. He stood on the dock, a cell phone clamped to his ear, his arms crossed, and his face turned away from her.

Jilly hurried downhill.

Guy was leaning over, pushing off one of the rental boats. A couple of guys with fishing gear started the outboard and phut-phutted into the middle of the channel. With the phone still clamped to his ear, Guy stood up and saw Jilly. He gave her a brief wave and started meandering back along the dock. They'd met the previous year when an investigation brought him to Toussaint, and he'd become her friend. He had never attempted to turn their relationship into something deeper, but Jilly had seen the hot looks he quickly hid—she wasn't the only one frustrated by the sexless hours they spent together.

"Take your sweet time," Jilly muttered. How could a man walk that slowly? "Just let me squirm as long as possible." *Do I admit I'm scared and I need to tell you about it?* If she did, he'd probably jump all over her, say she was putting herself in danger. Get out of the situation. End of discussion.

Guy stuck the phone back on his belt and speeded up. A tall, rangy man, in faded-out jeans and a navy T-shirt with holes in it, he could cover the ground quickly when it suited him. He met Jilly before she could put a foot on the dock.

She looked up at him, at his unreadable, almost black eyes, and almost wished she hadn't come.

"Guy, can I ask your honest opinion about something?"

He swallowed and rubbed the flat of his right hand back and forth on his chest. *Jilly, you can ask me anything. If I was any kind of a man, I'd get over what I can't change and find a way to be what you need, what you want me to be.* "Ask. Maybe I can be useful—maybe not."

"Okay," she said, then paused. "No, it isn't okay. It's going to sound stupid. Forget it."

He leaned down and put his mouth by her ear. "Listen to me carefully. You and I will stand right here until you come clean."

She took a deep breath.

"I think I was followed back to my place last night. It was getting dark but when I got out of my car in the driveway, a car drove by slowly."

If he showed any sign of the sudden panic he felt, she would be terrified. "That doesn't mean it had anything to do with you."

"When I was inside, I went upstairs and looked out of a window. A man was standing close to a tree at the corner, watching my house. I would have missed him if he hadn't drawn on a cigarette."

Guy set his back teeth. "He didn't have to be looking at your house—and he didn't have to have come from the car you saw being driven past."

"No. Except I just knew he was looking at my place, and I could see the back of the car around the corner."

Guy put his hands on his hips and expanded his lungs. He felt an artificial calm in the air, as if the world was about to split wide open.

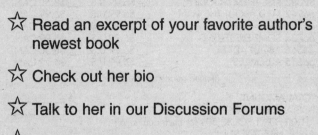

STELLA CAMERON

32148	TESTING MISS TOOGOOD	___ $7.50 U.S.	___ $8.99 CAN.
32083	KISS THEM GOODBYE	___ $6.99 U.S.	___ $8.50 CAN.
66942	MAD ABOUT THE MAN	___ $5.99 U.S.	___ $6.99 CAN.
66795	7B	___ $6.99 U.S.	___ $8.50 CAN.
66734	SOME DIE TELLING	___ $5.99 U.S.	___ $6.99 CAN.
66666	ABOUT ADAM	___ $6.99 U.S.	___ $8.50 CAN.
66615	ALL SMILES	___ $5.99 U.S.	___ $6.99 CAN.

(limited quantities available)

TOTAL AMOUNT	$ _____
POSTAGE & HANDLING	$ _____
($1.00 FOR 1 BOOK, 50¢ for each additional)	
APPLICABLE TAXES*	$ _____
TOTAL PAYABLE	$ _____

(check or money order—please do not send cash)

To order, complete this form and send it, along with a check or money order for the total above, payable to MIRA Books, to: **In the U.S.:** 3010 Walden Avenue, P.O. Box 9077, Buffalo, NY 14269-9077; **In Canada:** P.O. Box 636, Fort Erie, Ontario, L2A 5X3.

Name: _____
Address: _____ City: _____
State/Prov.: _____ Zip/Postal Code: _____
Account Number (if applicable): _____

075 CSAS

*New York residents remit applicable sales taxes.
*Canadian residents remit applicable GST and provincial taxes.

MIRA®

www.MIRABooks.com   MSC1005BL